A time for
A time for bells,
A time to find

A CHRISTMAS
TO TREASURE

Renowned authors Mary Anne Wilson
and Judy Christenberry introduce
two strong, sexy, stubborn bachelors
who don't believe in the season of
joy—then they discover their own
little miracles!

MARY ANNE WILSON

is a Canadian transplanted to Southern California, where she lives with her husband, three children and an assortment of animals. She knew she wanted to write romances when she found herself 're-writing' the great stories in literature to give them 'happy endings'. Over a ten-year career, she's published thirty romances, had her books on bestseller lists, been nominated for Reviewer's Choice Awards and received a Career Achievement Award in Romantic Suspense. She's looking forward to her next thirty books.

JUDY CHRISTENBERRY

has been writing romances for fifteen years because she loves happy endings as much as her readers do. A former French teacher, Judy now devotes herself to writing full-time. She hopes readers have as much fun reading her stories as she does writing them. She spends her spare time reading, watching her favourite sports teams and keeping track of her two daughters. Judy is a native Texan.

A Christmas to Treasure

MARY ANNE WILSON
JUDY CHRISTENBERRY

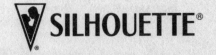 SILHOUETTE®

*All the characters in this book have no existence outside the imagination
of the author, and have no relation whatsoever to anyone bearing the
same name or names. They are not even distantly inspired by any
individual known or unknown to the author, and all the incidents are
pure invention.*

*First published in Great Britain 2003
Silhouette Books, Eton House, 18-24 Paradise Road,
Richmond, Surrey TW9 1SR*

A CHRISTMAS TO TREASURE © Harlequin Books S.A. 2003

The publisher acknowledges the copyright holders of the
individual works as follows:

Millionaire's Christmas Miracle © Mary Anne Wilson 2001
Cowboy Santa © Judy Christenberry 1998

ISBN 0 373 60151 4

102-1003

*Printed and bound in Spain
by Litografia Rosés S.A., Barcelona*

MILLIONAIRE'S
CHRISTMAS MIRACLE
Mary Anne Wilson

To Taylor Anne Levin
The real miracle in my life…
XOXOXO

Prologue

Houston, Texas, December 23

"Come on, Dad, you're single, rich, a great catch. You need to find someone and—"

"Okay, Mike, that's enough." In the back of the limousine, Quint Gallagher cut off his son's words coming over the cell phone. "I'm here to work tonight. It's a reception, a business function, not a singles' party. Everyone, including me, will have an agenda with them and they're all business."

"Bummer," Mike murmured.

Quint could almost see his twenty-two-year-old son sitting in his apartment in Los Angeles, probably with clutter all around from his move last month. "Yeah, bummer," he echoed. "But it's part of the package with LynTech and something you'll learn at your job."

"I'm never going to be like that," Mike said. "My work isn't my life. It's so I can live life."

"So you've told me many times," Quint said as he stretched his legs out and slipped lower on the leather seat, enjoying the roominess of the limousine as he tried to ease muscles still tight from the long flight in from New York.

"I mean it. You did your thing the way you wanted to, but I'm not doing it that way. I wish you weren't anymore. You've got all the money you'll ever need, and you could just cut loose and have some fun. Why don't you start by ditching the reception and going somewhere else?"

"That's not going to happen."

"Dad, I hate to say this, but you need to get a love life, to—"

Quint cut that off right away. "What did you call for, besides checking on my love life?"

"So, you do have a love life, huh?" Mike murmured.

"That's none of your business." He and Mike had always talked about anything, but right now, Quint was setting the limits. He wasn't about to go into this with his son. There had been women over the years; they'd come and gone, but he'd kept them separate from his real life as a single father to his only child Mike, and from his work. He'd never introduced those women to Mike, because he hadn't wanted to have another woman do what Mike's mother had done—walk out. It had been a conscious decision on his part to stay free of that possibility ever becoming reality again, and now it was a habit that fit him well, just not to get involved. "Now, are you going to tell me why you called?"

"Okay, okay. Since you aren't going to come out here for Christmas and Grandma and Granddad are going to Florida for the holidays, I was going to head up to Tahoe for some skiing. I just wondered if you had Joe Kline's number so I could see if we could use his condo? I can't find it anywhere.''

Quint passed the cell phone to his other ear and looked past his reflection in the tinted window to the night streets of Houston glittering with Christmas decorations. ''I don't have it with me, but you can get it from his son, Dane. He's listed.''

''Great, thanks.''

''Who's the 'we' in 'we could use his condo?' ''

''A friend.''

''Okay, fair enough,'' he murmured. ''Just be careful, have fun and leave—''

''—it the way we found it,'' Mike said, completing the sentence for him.

''You read my mind.''

''Now, that's an easy job. Just think work and responsibility.'' Before Quint could counter that, Mike asked, ''So, are you going to be out at the ranch or what?''

''I'm staying at the Towers Hotel in the city. It's just easier than being all the way out at the ranch.''

''How'd you convince Grandma that you weren't staying with them now that you're back in Houston?''

''Unlike you, your grandmother understands what work is and how important it is to be close to that work.''

''Obviously you haven't talked to her since you landed.''

''I called and left a message. What's going on?''

''I talked to Grandma yesterday and she's worried

about you. She thinks you should take advantage of being on your own again, that you should find some nice girl and settle down.''

Quint narrowed his hazel eyes at his own reflection in the tinted windows, a man with gray-streaked dark hair brushed back from a face that was all planes and angles, dominated by a full mustache. Hardly a "kid" a mother had to worry about. "She's wasting her time on that line of thought." He'd settled down once and lived to regret it. He'd never regret having Mike, and if he'd been able to have the same child without ever having had Gwen in their lives, he wouldn't have hesitated for a minute. But it didn't work that way. "I'm too old to buy into that scenario anymore."

"Why don't you rewrite the scenario and forget the 'settling down' part? Just find some sexy woman and go with the flow? Let it happen. Relax. Chill out."

"God, you sound like some hedonistic hippy," he said. "And any lady my age isn't into the party scene. She's sitting at home with her grandchildren."

Mike laughed at that. "Dad, you're not old. You're only 49. Besides, who says you need someone your age? You know what they say—if you're in this world at the same time, age doesn't matter. So go with that."

"If you say, 'let it all hang out' I'm hanging up on you," Quint said.

Mike laughed again. "Okay, okay, I won't, but can't you ditch that reception and go party?"

"You go to Tahoe and have a great time, and I'm going to work at a job that's going to be a killer."

"I'll bet you're even thinking of working on Christmas."

Without Mike around and with his parents away, Quint would be alone. "It's just another day."

"What about on your birthday?"

Quint seldom thought about birthdays, and this one was no exception. "It's just another day," he repeated.

"It's New Year's and it's your birthday."

"Why waste a perfectly good day?"

"I don't think you remember how to have fun," Mike said, then chuckled ruefully. "I guess, with it being Christmas and all, I was hoping for a miracle."

"I don't need a miracle. I'm fine."

"I hope so," Mike murmured, then said, "Merry Christmas, Dad."

"Merry Christmas, son," Quint said, then turned off the phone and slipped it into one of the inside pockets of his tuxedo.

Mike would learn soon enough that there were no miracles in this life. Quint had learned that the hard way.

Chapter One

Four hours later

Quint left the gold and silver shimmer of the huge room on the corporate level at LynTech behind him. He closed the doors on the Christmas music and chatter blending in a strange rhythm and went out into the broad corridor. If he hadn't quit smoking years ago, he would have lit up and let the acrid smoke fill his lungs, perhaps dispersing the frustration and sense of wasted time that dogged him at these events. And with jet lag mixed in, he was ready to make his escape.

He'd needed to make contact, to get a sense of the place, a sense of the people, but it was time to leave. He nodded to a couple going in, got a blast of the noise as the doors opened, then there was just the quiet of conversation farther down the hallway as the doors closed. He looked in that direction and saw three or four people waiting by the elevators. Robert Lewis, the founder of LynTech, and a dapper man with white hair, was deep in conversation with his daughter, Brittany, a stunning woman with flame hair and exquisite green eyes. To her right stood Matt Terrel, one half of the CEO position at LynTech, a sandy-haired man the size of a linebacker. Wedged between Brittany and Terrel and hugging both of them, was the nine-year-old boy who had been hanging around all evening, Anthony, in a miniature tux.

The four people looked happy enough, very close, but he wasn't about to get near them. He'd talked to Robert earlier that evening to discuss his original vision for LynTech, but had ended up hearing all about his problems with Brittany. Right then the elevator arrived and the doors slid open.

Anthony grabbed Brittany and Matt by their hands, tugging them into the elevator, followed by Robert who turned as the doors started to close. Quint caught the older man's eye long enough to see Robert smile at him, then the barrier shut and Quint was alone in the corridor.

He headed down past the bank of elevators and went directly to the exit door for the stairs. He pushed it back, and his dress shoes tapped on the metal stairs as he headed down to the bottom floor. He was a bit amazed at the congeniality he'd just witnessed, considering the mood Robert had been in an hour ago. Back then, he'd been very upset over Brittany's attitude and actions.

"My Brittany just can't focus, she can't seem to settle," the man had said. "She runs here and there. She's started so many university courses, so many majors that it's ludicrous, then she just walks away. I'd hoped that getting her to come to work here would help, and I thought it had, but now…'' He'd shaken his head as if he'd lost all hope. "I've tried, but I admit that I'm at a loss.''

Quint had never been the sort that people opened up to and confided in, partly because he wouldn't have done that with someone else. He'd learned to keep his distance to make working with people easier, and he really had no answers for anyone's personal life. With the exception of Mike, he'd made a mess out of his personal life.

His hand skimmed over the coldness of the metal handrail as he rounded the corner on the stairs. He'd told Robert to do what any parent did—his best. That was when the conversation had gone beyond what he wanted to discuss. "I've tried, but how I wish her mother was still alive." Robert had exhaled, a sound that was more of a sigh tinged with a shadow of sorrow. "I think I missed having her mother there more than Brittany did." Yes, sorrow. "I heard you'd raised your boy alone, so you understand."

Quint kept going down, level by level. Robert's comment had struck an unexpectedly still-raw nerve in Quint. Whatever mistakes he had made with Mike wouldn't have been righted if Gwen had stuck around. But Robert had obviously loved his dead wife. Quint couldn't relate to that and had been unnerved that the old bitterness about what had happened so many years ago had reared its ugly head.

He went down more quickly, the movement doing nothing to stop the thoughts that came to him in a rush. Plunging into a hurried marriage with Gwen when she'd informed him she was pregnant had begun the nightmare. Then there had been that long year when Michael had been born and Gwen had realized that not only did she not like being a wife or mother, but she wasn't even going to go through the motions. She'd left with little more than a glance back and a thin explanation about being worried she'd end up hating both him and Michael if she stayed.

Before Robert had been able to say the usual when Quint had told him he was divorced—how sorry he was to hear about Gwen leaving, and how sorry he was that Quint had had to raise Michael alone—Quint had pleaded jet lag and gone to get another drink, which hadn't helped at all. And neither had the next drink. That's when he'd known he'd had to get out of there. He was ditching the party, just as Mike had suggested, but he wasn't going to "find some sexy woman and go with the flow."

He slowed slightly. Instead of celebrating Christmas, he was going to work on the company prospectus and start his planning. Being brought in as a growth consultant meant a lot of research. Instead of getting crazy for the New Year, he'd probably have an early dinner, get his files in order and ring the New Year in studying financial profiles. He wouldn't be looking for any miracle beyond the miracle of helping a faltering, previously family-owned business become a viable, thriving corporation.

He reached the lobby level, and stopped, took a deep breath, once, twice, then pulled back the door and stepped out into a side area off the main reception space. He glanced past the elevators, past the glitter of Christmas that seemed to be everywhere in gold and silver, and saw clusters of people waiting for their cars to be brought around to the front. Limos lined the curb out in front and a bar had been set up near a stunning Christmas tree.

He spotted several people he'd been introduced to during the evening in the crowd, but he had no desire to renew any conversation with them. So, turning his back to the crowds, he discovered a hallway that seemed to lead to the rear of the building and probably a secondary exit. He'd head out that way, forego the company-provided limousine and grab the first taxi he spotted to get back to the hotel.

"If you do that, you'll be sorry, Charlie. I swear, you'll pay and you'll pay big-time. And that's a promise!"

The voice seemed to come out of nowhere, and even though it wasn't terribly loud, it came to him over the drone of voices behind him. Maybe it was the passionate intensity in every word, he didn't know, but it made him stop and turn to see where it was coming from.

There were double doors across from the elevators, one true blue, one bright red, and both shared a rainbow logo splashed across them—Just for Kids. It had to be the new location for the company child-care center, a place he'd avoided earlier when tours were being formed to see the facility.

"Charlie, you're vermin!" the voice said and he could tell it was coming from beyond the red door, which was slightly ajar. He couldn't hear whether or not Charlie was defending himself, but he could definitely hear the woman. "If I let you live, and at this point in time, that's a big if, you're going to pay for this.''

He went closer to the door. The voice, touched with a slight huskiness even through the frustration and anger, was starting to intrigue him...really intrigue him. There was the promise of murder and mayhem in the words, but the voice could have been sexy if the words had been different. That thought was shattered when he eased back the red door and glanced inside the facility as the woman ground out, ''You rat! You miserable rat!'' Not sexy at all at that moment.

He looked down a short, wide hallway to the center of the facility where twinkling lights seemed to be everywhere, and the scent of baking gingerbread drifted on the air. He couldn't see anyone, but the voice was still there, somewhere ahead of where he stood.

''If you move, if you so much as turn, it's going to be your last move.'' The words were lower now, a bit muffled. ''My panty hose are history, just ruined.'' There was a tearing sound, and the woman gasped, ''My dress! Oh, great! Now it's ruined, too, and it's not even mine! Jenn is going to be as mad as I am. You'll have her to deal with after I'm through with you.''

This was none of his business, nothing to him if employees or guests got drunk and made out in the day-care center, then had a horrendous fight. Torn dresses, ruined panty hose and threats of murder— none of that stopped him going farther into the center until he could see that the twinkling lights were draped all over a climbing-frame tree that stood dead in the middle of the huge main room. Massive branches that probably masked climbing trails spread to four corners and into what looked like four separate tree houses suspended under a domed ceiling over the carpeted floor.

He was beginning to feel suspiciously like a voyeur and would have left right then if he hadn't seen movement high in the center of the tree. It was a quick movement, little more than a flashing image of a woman with dark hair and her back to him. Then she was gone, but the voice was still there, echoing in the gingerbread-tinged air.

"What a waste, the dress, the panty hose, the stupid gingerbread family! I thought it would work. Well, color me wrong, very wrong."

He smiled as he moved a bit closer, the voice drawing him as surely as the words she uttered. Then there was more movement at the bottom of the tree, and he could have sworn he saw a bare foot coming out of an arched hole in the trunk. It *was* a foot, then another, coming out soles-first, followed by an expanse of legs tangled in some material that could have been ice blue, but the lights were too low to let him see if he was right or not.

What he did know was that a woman was backing out of an arched hole in the tree trunk on her hands and knees. She was slowly inching out, showing a swell of slender hips, and all the time muttering. "Well, never again. Once burned, that's it with me. You've run out of chances, Charlie."

A narrow waist, then she was out with her back to

him. But he could see that she was tiny, slender, and when she shook her head, hair the color of night tumbled around her bare shoulders and partway down her back. He remembered hearing somewhere that long hair was sexy on a woman, but he hadn't realized the truth of it until that moment. Sexy. Damn sexy. As sexy as the way the fine material of her dress defined a tiny waist, clung to her hips and the ripped hem tangled with her slender legs.

Lucky Charlie, he thought, as something stirred in him, something so basic and sexual, that it startled him. He hadn't felt anything like this for a woman for what seemed ages, if ever. No matter what his son thought, he'd had a personal life, but right then he knew that he'd never let himself really go.

Just find some sexy woman and go with the flow? Let it happen. Relax. Chill out.

Looking at the woman, he thought that maybe it was time to just go with the flow, to let whatever happened happen and not look back. He was on his own. He wasn't protecting anyone anymore. He wasn't looking for a miracle. He was looking at a woman who stirred him, and he hadn't even seen her face.

He would have spoken then, said something to get her to turn so he could see her face. As if on cue, she started to turn, one arm tucked out of sight in front of her. Quint literally felt his breath catch in his chest with anticipation as he took in her profile, the elegant sweep of her throat, a small chin, softly parted lips, a tiny nose, improbably long lashes.

Then she faced him, her features filled with delicate

beauty that he knew could haunt a man's dreams. When she saw him, dark eyes widened with shock, and in the next second, she screamed, her hands flew up, and something came flying through the air toward Quint.

Amy Blake hadn't known there was anyone else in the day-care center until she'd turned and found a tall, lean stranger, all in black, no more than two feet from where she stood by the tree. The world suddenly moved in slow motion as her first thought was to protect herself. And that meant instinctively thrusting out her hands to ward the man off. That's when Charlie, the fat black-and-white pet rat, flew out of her hands and sailed through the air, headed right for the stranger.

Her second thought was that no matter what misery the animal had caused her by getting loose right before she began to close up and leave, she was sending him to his death. His little legs were flailing as he flew through the air, right at the stranger's chest.

She lunged in an effort to save the poor animal from meeting a horrible end, and realized the stranger was moving, too, right at her. In a heartbeat he had the rat in both hands, but she couldn't stop her own momentum any more than he could stop his. She was as out of control as Charlie had been a split second ago, but she wasn't being caught and rescued. Instead, she hit the stranger, tangling with him, feeling a stinging blow at her forehead, inhaling a jumble of scents, from gingerbread to aftershave, all layered with body heat.

The momentum kept up, the uncontrolled tumbling

with the man until she hit the ground, felt the back of her head make contact with the floor, gasping as the man seemed to be everywhere. In the next heart-beat she twisted and the world stopped. All motion ceased. She'd gone from flying wildly into a stranger, to lying on top of the stranger on the floor with her eyes tightly closed.

She could literally feel his heart beating, and it took her a second to define the fact that her breasts were pressed to his chest, that his body was under hers, a hard, lean body, filled with heat and strength. A horrid thought—she hadn't been this close to a man since Rob had died—was there before she could stop it. All she had to do was open her eyes and see the man, but she couldn't. She wouldn't.

She pushed back then opened her eyes and was thankful that the man was little more than a blur of darkness to her. His hand was on her arm, his fingers all but burning her skin, and she tried to jerk free. But he wasn't imprisoning her, just holding her, and the motion of pulling hard sent her to her right, and she fell sideways onto the carpet.

She closed her eyes again, so tightly that colors exploded behind her eyes. She gasped for air, while her mind raced. Just explain that she was tired, that Charlie was important to Taylor and the other kids at the center, and that she was ready to leave. That was all true. Very true. Weariness ate at her, weariness that sleep didn't dispel, when she could sleep.

''Whoa, lady,'' the man uttered in a deep, rough voice touched by a faint Texas twang.

She kept her eyes closed for a long moment, then

scrambled to her feet, her chest tightening as she finally opened her eyes to look at the man. He was flat on his back on the floor, and his image was painfully clear to her, from the thick dark hair streaked with gray brushed back from a face with sharp features, a full, graying mustache and a strong jaw. But it was the eyes that caught her attention and held it. They were dark eyes, partially shadowed, narrowed as they looked up at her, yet capable of making her heart lurch in her chest. It didn't help that they were crinkled at the corners from humor, the same humor that made the mustache twitch above a mouth with a decidedly sensuous bottom lip.

She looked away quickly, not prepared to be so instantly uneasy with a man, especially with a man who was smiling at her. No, it wasn't exactly uneasiness she felt. As her eyes ran down his lean frame, over the perfectly cut tuxedo, she knew that she was disturbed. Very disturbed, and she was embarrassed by it while he lay on the floor laughing. She was also embarrassed by her own clumsy stupidity. She felt heat rising to her face.

"I am so sorry, I mean, really sorry," she said in a rush, crouching down by him as she held out her hand to help him up. "You scared me and I didn't think. Poor Charlie, I sure didn't mean to throw him at you like that."

"Poor Charlie is right," he murmured in a low rumble.

"Poor Charlie is—" Horror shot through her. "Charlie!" Instead of taking his hand, she grabbed at the shoulder of his tuxedo, tugging with all her strength to move him quickly. But it was like trying to move the Rock of Gibraltar. "Oh, God," she gasped. "Charlie—you're killing him. Move, get off of him!"

He moved then, scrambling away from her and the rip of material was jumbled with frantic movement, then her own sigh of relief when she saw the carpet under where the stranger had lain. The only thing there was the vague imprint of his body on the new carpeting.

Relief almost left her giddy, and she exhaled in a rush as she sank back to sit on her heels. "Oh, thank goodness," she said on a relieved sigh. "You didn't kill him."

"Kill him?" he asked from right beside her. "You're the one who threw him at me."

"I know, I know, but I thought you were lying on him. Crushing him." She shuddered. "I was sure he was a goner."

"All of this concern seems odd coming from someone who was threatening him with murder a few minutes ago."

"Well, sure, but I didn't want him dead."

That brought unexpected laughter from the man as he crouched right in front of her. She looked into those eyes and saw they were a rich hazel filled with flashing humor. "I'll take your word for that, but either way, neither one of us committed raticide."

"Raticide?"

"The murder of a rat? I thought that was going to happen when you threw the thing at me, right before you attacked me."

"Attacked you?" She scrambled backward, grabbing at the tree trunk to get to her feet. But as she stood, he was on his feet, too, right in front of her. "No way. You're the one who scared the bewaddle out of me by sneaking up on me like that."

A grin came with her words, a grin that stunned her when she realized how seductive an expression it was. She was more tired than she'd ever dreamed. "Bewaddle?" he asked. "Lady, you're definitely going to have to define *bewaddle* for me."

She brushed at her hair as it tangled around her face, regretting taking it out of the clips when she'd thought she was leaving. "Bewaddle is...well," she began with a shrug. "It means you really scared me so badly that I...I wasn't responsible for what I did, and I wasn't attacking you, I was trying to save poor Charlie."

"So, bewaddle made you throw a rat at me?" he asked with mock seriousness. "And saving him meant you attacked me?"

"Oh, for Pete's sake, I never—" She remembered what she was doing to begin with, before this man ripped into her world and turned it and her on their collective ears. "If you weren't lying on Charlie, then where is he?" She turned from the grin and scanned the center.

"If he's not dead, he's loose," the man said.

She glanced back at him, at that smile that seemed a permanent fixture, and immediately regretted her next words. "And it's all your fault."

She turned from him, embarrassed to be so petty at the moment, and she wasn't prepared for him to touch her. His fingers pressed heat to her arm, and she jerked back and around to face him again. "Lady, we should all be thankful you aren't sitting on any jury trying me," he drawled. "Hell, you'd give me the death penalty for jaywalking."

She barely knew him, but she knew for sure that she'd never vote to stop whatever time he had left on earth. "I'm sorry," she said. "This has just been the most awful evening. There was so much work and so many people crawling out of the woodwork asking the dumbest questions. I tried, I even made a gingerbread family thing, and that drove Charlie crazy. He loves gingerbread. And my dress..." She brushed the tear in the skirt. "It's not even mine, I mean, my—" She bit her lip, not about to explain anything else to this man. A stranger. She didn't even know his name. "Listen Mr....?"

"Gallagher, Quint Gallagher."

She stared at him. Quint Gallagher? Oh, no! Gallagher, the planner, the man brought in from New York by Matt Terrel to map LynTech's future. The man who, so she'd heard, had refused to go on one of the tours of the center they'd arranged for this reception. And she'd thrown a rat at him, knocked him over and accused him of killing that same rat. "Oh, Mr. Gallagher, I didn't know."

"Stop. Let's just start all over again." He held out his hand. "I'm Quint Gallagher."

She would gladly start all over again, but when she slipped her hand into his, she knew that whatever was spooking her tonight was just getting worse. She had to try twice to say her own name. "Blake...Amy."

"What goes first?" he asked, his gaze flicking over her as he kept his hold on her hand.

She drew back on the pretext of smoothing the dress she'd borrowed from her sister-in-law. "Amy… that's first."

"Amy Blake. And you're here because…?"

"I was giving tours of the center to the people invited for the reception."

He eyed her again. "A professional tour guide?"

"No, I work here in the center, and right now, I need to find the rat."

"No, he found you," Quint said and pointed down at her feet. Sitting on the carpet, right between the two of them, was Charlie methodically licking his paws then cleaning first one ear and then the other. "And if you don't move, I think your worries are over," he murmured in a half whisper.

Slowly, he sank down to his haunches and Amy watched with fascination as he reached out strong, tanned hands, easing them cautiously toward the rat. He cupped his hands around and behind the rat, then closed them around the animal. Charlie squealed once, then Quint stood with the rat at his chest, just the head peeking out and the nose twitching in the air. "Okay, Amy, show me the cage."

"I'll get it," she said and hurried around the tree and back to her office, trying to ignore the way the ruined skirt of her dress was riding up on her thighs with each step she took. She flipped on the overhead light and crossed to her cluttered desk where she'd left the metal cage. Grabbing the wire handle, she turned and ran right into Quint behind her. Heat, muscle, fine material, that aftershave, all mingled, and she gasped. "Good heavens," she said as she moved back, her hips pressing against the edge of the desk to help her keep her balance. Amazingly, she didn't drop the cage, but the handle began to bite into her hand as she saw that smile again, that slow, seductive curve to his lips. "That is a horrible habit you've got there," she muttered, not daring to move because she didn't want to touch him again.

"Well, catching rats isn't my idea of a habit," he drawled while Charlie cuddled in his hands against his chest. Even the rat liked the guy. Damn that amusement deepening in his eyes.

"No, you sneak up on people." She turned from him, plunking the cage back on the desk, then she turned to take Charlie out of the man's hands. "I'll take him," she said, and reached for Charlie, being very careful to make as little contact with Quint as possible.

She didn't reckon on the man's heat being in the rat's fur as she cupped Charlie and eased him through the door of the cage. She set him down, then snapped the clip to secure the door. She stared at the rat instead of turning back to Quint as he spoke.

"I wasn't sneaking anywhere the first time. I heard you talking to Charlie, and I thought…" The sudden chuckle was rich and deep and disturbing. "Lady, why don't you just forget what I thought. Everything's turned out just fine."

Well, it wasn't just fine. She was harried and tired, and feeling just a bit sick about being near a man who so disturbed her. She seldom noticed men. Even before Rob, she'd walked past most men in this life. Then Rob had shown up in her world. He'd been the other part of her soul, and she knew that the wait had been worth it.

This wasn't happening to her. She wouldn't let it. She didn't want it. "Never mind. It's late," she said softly, then turned as he moved back half a step.

"Would you do me a favor?"

"I don't know what favor I could do for you." She edged around him as she spoke, making it past without touching, and headed for the door to go out into the main area. He was there, she felt him behind her, and she kept going toward the tree.

"Amy?" he said right behind her as she stopped by the tree.

She touched the painted bark with one hand, the hand with her wedding ring on it. The gold band glinted in the twinkle of lights, and it centered her. Grounded her. As she turned to Quint, she felt a control that she hadn't felt since he'd walked in on her. "I'm sorry, what was that favor?"

"I missed a tour of this place earlier, and I thought since you're here and I'm here, I wouldn't mind looking around."

She clasped her hands behind her back and relished the feel of her ring, smooth and warm and comforting. "Well, if you really want to. Where did you want to start?"

He shrugged, the action testing the fine material of his tux jacket. "Surprise me," he said in a low voice that ran riot over her nerves.

She turned to avoid looking at him and to concentrate on the center, but as she turned, she realized that the fragrance of baking gingerbread coming from the new oven in the redone kitchen had become a pungent odor. And smoke was seeping out through the swinging door of the kitchen.

Chapter Two

Quint didn't realize what was going on until Amy turned and sprinted barefoot across the room, then he saw the smoke. She burst through swinging doors and disappeared as smoke spilled out into the room. He ran after her, heading for the smoke, and suddenly a sound split the air—a smoke alarm.

He cursed himself for being so distracted by the woman and the rat that he hadn't noticed anything else. Instead of paying attention, he'd been trying to figure out if Mike's advice was worth taking. The damn building could be burning down around him, and he was trying to figure out if he should go for it and ask Amy out for a drink, stalling for time by asking her to give him a tour of the place. He shoved back the door and stepped into a room filled with smoke.

"Amy!" he called above the alarm, coughing when he took a breath.

Quint heard a scream, a crash, and he dove into the smoke as someone behind him called out, "What's going on?"

Through coughing, Amy's disembodied voice came from inside the room, "Gingerbread."

There was movement behind him, then a motor started up and the smoke began to thin dramatically. Quint spotted Amy crouching on the far side of the room by an open oven surrounded by shattered glass from what looked to have once been a dish and a number of blackened, smoking lumps. He went to her, dropped to his haunches and made himself not touch her. That scream had shocked him, followed by his reaction that something had happened to her.

"Are you okay?" he asked.

She stared at the mess in front of her, coughing again before she answered him. "Yes, I'm fine."

Someone else was there, rushing around doing something to controls on the wall. But all he could focus on was Amy and the charred mess between them. "The gingerbread family, I take it?"

"Exactly." Amy waved at the air in front of her as if she could disperse the last of the smoke. "I was baking them to show off the oven and to make this place smell nice. You know, the trick Realtors use to make houses more inviting? Bake cookies or something that smells great? Well, I had some dough left, so I put them in to take home with me when I went, and I forgot all about them."

"The family's toast," he murmured.

She looked at him, grimacing. "That's terrible."

"Sorry."

"So am I," she muttered as she frowned at the broken glass all around them. "I'd hoped the smell of it baking would cover the paint and new carpet smells and people would think the place was homey and nice.'' The alarm stopped as she added, ''What a mess.''

He watched her in profile, and didn't miss the slight unsteadiness in her chin. ''For what it's worth, it worked. That's the first thing I smelled when I came in.''

She looked up at him. ''Then the smoke, huh? I can't believe I got so distracted.'' She bit her lip, then finished. ''Charlie has one more thing to answer for.''

She stood, then turned to the guard who was coming toward them through the haze of smoke lingering in the room. ''Sorry, Walt, the gingerbread is a bit overdone. I hope this didn't mess up things too badly for you.''

''No, I got to the sprinkler control before they came on and I got a couple of fans going. The smoke's almost gone.'' He went over to a central range with a huge hood over it and flipped a switch. Another fan roared to life. ''I'll leave them on for an hour or so, then check back here.'' He turned to Amy and Quint. ''Meanwhile, I'll get maintenance in here to clean this up.''

''No, please don't,'' Amy said as she stood. ''I did it. I'll clean it up.''

''Whatever you say, ma'am,'' Walt said. ''You two okay?''

''We're fine,'' Quint said and then heard glass crunch under the man's shoes as he turned and left. ''Where are the brooms kept?'' he asked Amy.

''I'll get them,'' she said, and she would have if

he hadn't stopped her by capturing her upper arm and stopping her before she could take a step.

"Don't move," he said, trying to block out the pleasure of her soft skin under his hand.

He drew back as she turned to him. "What are you doing?"

"Stopping you from getting cut." He pointed to her bare feet. "There's glass all over this place. I've got shoes on. You stay put and tell me where the supplies are."

She glanced down, then back up at him, her lashes partially shadowing her deep-brown eyes. "I never thought…" She bit her lip. "The broom is in the closet to the right of the door over there." She pointed behind her. "There's a dustpan, too, and a bucket of some sort to put the pieces in."

As Quint crossed to the cupboard, he heard glass crunch under his shoes, too. He got the broom, pan and bucket, then went back to where Amy stood very still. He handed her the pan. "Just hold this and don't move your feet."

"I never thought of that," she said as she crouched down and he started to sweep the pieces into the dustpan. "Thanks."

"No problem," he said, sweeping the shards into the pan. By the time the floor was clear, the smoke was gone, but the odor still lingered. "You stay here," Quint told her as he went to put back the equipment, and when he turned she was where he'd left her, her hair mussed, her feet bare, her dress torn and little or no makeup on her face. Not only was she beautiful at that moment, but she made his decision for him. Mike had been right after all. He needed this, a diversion, some time off to "go with the flow."

He went back to her, and she coughed softly. "Thank goodness everyone had pretty much left before that happened." She looked up at him and said, "If anything had happened to this center, after everything everyone's gone through..." She sighed heavily. "I don't know what I would have done."

Not willing to think back to that moment of sheer horror when she'd disappeared into the smoke, he tried to make a joke. "If anyone asks about it, do what you said you were going to do, blame it on the rat."

She looked at him, and for the first time since he'd glimpsed her, she was smiling. Not hugely, but a soft lifting of her pale lips, and there was a sparkle deep in her dark eyes that accompanied that touch of humor in her. It made him wish he could see her smile fully realized. "Poor Charlie, how do you suppose I convince everyone that the rat burned the gingerbread family?" she asked.

He shrugged. "Well, lady, my theory is, if a mouse can own one of the biggest theme parks in the world, a rat could have done this."

His wish came true and she smiled at him, really smiled, and the sight of it literally made his breath catch in his chest. Beautiful? Was that what he thought? This woman was beyond beautiful. "I guess that's why they pay you the big bucks, huh?" she asked.

"What?" he asked, his thinking not exactly clear at that moment.

"Coming up with ideas to fix what's going on in this place. I think they called you a 'visionary,' and I know that visionaries don't come cheaply, at least not in this world. So, solutions equal big bucks."

"I just do a job," he said, noticing the faint touch of a dimple to the left of her mouth. Just the suggestion of a dimple. "That's all."

She exhaled, and the smile started to fade a bit, something he regretted greatly. "It's time to leave, before I really burn this place down," she said and looked down at the floor. "I hope all the glass is gone, because with my luck today, I'll find the last piece, cut myself and really make a mess."

"Amy, you're brilliant. As a visionary, I can see you're absolutely right. You'll do that very thing." She frowned slightly, as if trying to figure out where he was going with this. "And since I'm being paid big bucks to keep this company on the right path, I figure that keeping an employee from hurting herself is all part of the job description, and one of the reasons I make all those big bucks."

He went closer to her as he spoke, so close he could see that there was a deep amber burst around the pupils of her eyes.

"Mr. Gallagher—" she started, but he stopped her.

"It's Quint, and let me earn my money." Before she could evade him, he picked her up. She was as light as a feather, but a feather wouldn't have twisted the minute he held it, or gasped with shock as he caught it high in his arms.

"Put me down," she was saying, but he was busy trying to absorb the way the fascination he'd had with her from the start was transforming into a basic need to keep this contact.

"Not in here," he said.

She felt soft and warm and smelled like burnt gingerbread and flowers. Her hair tickled his face as she wiggled around, pressed one hand to his chest and looked him right in the eyes, her face inches from his own. "You do not have to do this."

He did, but he couldn't explain to her why he did. He couldn't explain it to himself. "Oh yes I do," he said, carrying her across the room to the door. "It's for the good of LynTech."

"Oh, come on," she muttered, finally stilling in his arms.

"Oh, yes, if you cut your foot, you'll go on disability and lose time, and the company will lose your work time, and you can see that we'll all be headed down the road to ruin."

She stared at him as they went out into the main room, then suddenly that smile came back. "You're ridiculous, you know?"

"I've been called worse than that," he said. There was carpet underfoot now, but he kept going with her, taking her over to the tree before he even considered letting her go. And when he let her down, he had to quite literally keep himself from reaching out to brush at the hair clinging to her cheeks as she stood to face him.

"You've earned your big bucks," she said, her face slightly flushed, probably from all the excitement.

He was going to ask her out for drinks or coffee

or something. Anything to prolong this evening. "We've got our stories straight, right?"

"What?"

"You're pulling a Watergate. You need to blame someone else for all of this, and Charlie is an excellent scapegoat."

Her eyes widened. "Oh, Watergate? Sure, of course. Boy, that's pretty ancient history, isn't it?"

Ancient history? It had happened during his college years. He looked at her then, really looked at her, beyond that incredible sensuality that rocked him, beyond the voice and the eyes. She was young. It hadn't even hit him before. He'd been too busy "going with the flow" and with everything else. "Very ancient," he murmured, then found himself saying, "How old are you?"

He hadn't meant to ask that bluntly, but it was out there and he waited. "How old are *you?*" she countered without batting an eye.

"Let's put it this way, I was there when ancient history was made." He tried to joke, but it seemed flat in his own ears.

She smiled again. "Well, if you were there for the Civil War, I want to know if Scarlett and Rhett ever got back together?"

Her smile was melting his reason—big-time. "I never met the lady, but rumor has it that she kept Tara and lost that Butler fellow."

"Too bad. I heard he was pretty cool."

If you're in this world at the same time, age doesn't matter, Mike had said, and looking at Amy right then just solidified that for him. Besides, he wasn't looking to "settle down" or anything like that. Drinks, talk, a bit of fun, a diversion. Time out of time. If Mike were here, he'd call this decision a miracle. Quint just called it a good idea. "And I bet he got paid big bucks, too."

She laughed then, really laughed, and the sound floated around him and seemed to seep into his being. God, it felt wonderful. He wanted to ask her out right then, but he felt almost as uncertain as a teenager as to how to go about it. He was out of practice with this dating thing. But she seemed like such a perfect person to start practicing with.

"I bet he did," Amy said, then sighed. "Thanks for everything, including the lesson in excuses. Now, I need to get going."

It was now or never. "It's getting late, but I wanted to ask you something," he said quickly, before she could just take off.

Amy had barely recovered from him carrying her, from that sense of being supported and surrounded. She hadn't realized until the moment Quint picked her up that she sorely missed that sort of contact. The strength of a man, the scent of a man. She pushed the thought away. That was a foolish path to take. That was part of the past, not here and now. "What?"

"Would you like to go somewhere and recover?" he asked in his low, rough drawl. "We can have drinks or food, or both, and work on your defense some more."

He couldn't be asking her out. No, he wasn't. She probably looked like she needed a stiff drink. She knew she felt as if she could use one. "I don't think so."

"Listen, I'll be honest with you. I'm no good at small talk or playing games. I never have been." His hazel eyes narrowed on her. "I'll just say this right out. I'm attracted to you, and I'd like to get to know you better."

She stared at him, her heart starting to beat faster, and she pressed her hand to it, a futile action that made no difference to her heartbeat. She touched her tongue to her cold lips. "No, thanks. I'm sorry."

He glanced down to her hand pressed to her chest, and everything changed when he shook his head. "I'm the one who's sorry. I had no idea that you were married. I'm more out of practice than I thought."

Married. Oh, God. She could feel her stomach tense, and sickness rise in the back of her throat. He was looking at her wedding band, the simple gold ring that Rob had given her three years ago. The ring she'd never taken off since he'd put it there. She lowered her hand, pushing it behind her back and clenching her hand so tightly that the ring pressed into her fingers.

Quint was watching her, waiting, and she didn't have a clue what to say or do. She could let him just believe she was married and he'd leave. It seemed like such a simple solution to stop whatever was going on. But she couldn't lie.

She took a partial step back. The words were there, but she found them as hard to say now as she had right after Rob had died. Touching her tongue to her

lips, she swallowed hard and made herself say them.
"I'm...I'm a widow."

The look that came to everyone's eyes when they
found out about Rob's death was there in his. Pity,
sympathy. She hated it, but she could deal with it.
What she couldn't deal with was Quint being so close,
so close that when he spoke again, she could have
sworn that she felt his breath brush her cold cheeks.

"Boy, I'm so sorry. I had no idea."

"Of course you didn't," she said, her voice
vaguely tight now. "It's getting late." As she spoke,
she turned to get more space between them, but that
simple act backfired when her foot tangled with the
silver slingback heels she'd left by the tree when
she'd had to crawl inside to get Charlie.

Quint had her by her upper arm, gently easing her
back, and she was facing him, inches separating them,
and there was no way she could ignore him. Trying
to ignore him at that moment would be about as easy
as walking on water for her. So she stood very still,
tried not to inhale too deeply and tried very hard to
think realistically to explain her scattered emotions
right then.

She was lonely. She'd been lonely for what seemed
forever—or at least since the car accident that had
taken Rob's life. And she wasn't having a good evening. Quint just happened to be here, and he was a
man. A man who happened to make her remember
more of what she'd lost than she'd remembered until
now.

"Are you okay?" he was asking.

She wanted to pull back and free herself from his

touch, hoping that would help her think more clearly. But she was embarrassed enough by all of this and not about to make any more of a scene than she already had. "I promise you that I'm not self-destructive, and I don't usually need help staying on my feet."

"That's good to know." He exhaled and she felt the vibration through his hand and into her arm. "Amy, let me be totally honest about this," he said in a low voice. "I told you I'm not good at this. I'm way out of practice." That suggestion of a smile was there, but now it was tinged with what could have been uncertainty. "I'd like to sit and talk with you, just get to know you."

He drew back from her, his hand letting her go, but without physical contact he was still affecting her on some level that she didn't want to admit. She didn't want to feel heat and she didn't want to feel an aching loneliness. She was being pulled into something that terrified her, and all she wanted was to be out of there and away from Quint. "I'm not dating now," she blurted out.

He was just inches from her, his eyes narrowing on her. "That's a shame," he murmured as his gaze flicked over her and her stomach clenched. "But I understand. It's too soon?"

Honestly, she'd never thought of ever dating again. That wasn't in her plans. She'd had love once, real love, and she knew that only came to a person once in a lifetime. "I just don't date." She felt her wedding ring almost biting into her from clenching her hands at her sides. She had Taylor, worked ten-hour days and didn't think too much about what she didn't have. She didn't want to start now. "I'm really too busy."

"I understand about work," he said, but he didn't make any move to leave.

"Work and other things," she murmured as she scooped up her shoes and looped the straps over her fingers. "And on top of everything, I haven't gotten all my Christmas shopping done."

"That's a big chore?"

She fingered her shoes nervously, shrugging. "With a two-year-old, everything is a big chore."

"A niece, a nephew, brother, sister?"

"A daughter, Taylor."

Words that made her smile did the opposite to Quint. They brought a slight frown, killing that shadow of a smile that she'd thought was semi-permanent with the man. He glanced at his watch, then back at her, and it was as if a curtain had dropped between them. "You're right, it's time to go," he said. "It's late, and I'm keeping you from your shopping."

It was what she'd wanted, him leaving, but she didn't count on it being so disconcerting for her. Then she realized what was happening, something she should be very grateful for, but something that almost made her angry. "That's why you didn't take the tour earlier, isn't it?"

"I didn't have the time to take any tours."

That didn't wash with her. He was here now, killing time, and obviously in no hurry until he'd found out she had a child. "You don't like kids, do you?"

"Oh, lady," he said with a chuckle, but it had little humor in it. "You're way off the mark with that."

"You didn't do the tour, and now that you know that I have a child, all bets are off?" That sounded ridiculous to her, but it made sense. "So you're going to say good-night, and goodbye and walk out."

"You said you didn't date, so I guessed you didn't want to go and have a drink."

"But you—" She bit her lip to cut off the words, stunned that she was arguing with him, when he was set to do what she wanted him to do—leave. "You're right. I don't."

He hesitated, then said, "Let's leave it at that. I'm right and you don't."

She hated it, but wasn't going to argue anymore. She just wanted him to go. "Okay. Thanks again for your help."

"Sure, and merry Christmas. Good luck with this place."

"Merry Christmas and good luck with your new job."

He looked at her, hesitated, then said, "Can I ask you one more thing?"

She braced herself, but asked, "What now?"

"How are you with plant identification?"

"Excuse me?"

"Plants." He nodded above them, and she looked up to see the sprig of mistletoe that Anthony, the boy who had latched onto Matt and B.J. had put up earlier. He'd said he wanted to get Matt and B.J. in here to stand under it. Now Quint was pointing at it above them. "Is that mistletoe?"

"Yes, but…"

Her words died on her lips when he took a step closer to her, so very close, then one finger touched her chin, a single contact point, yet it robbed her of all her strength to move away from it. The world slowed for the second time that night, but her mind raced. This couldn't be happening. It couldn't be. Not to her. Not here, not now, not with this stranger.

But it *was* happening, his head lowering toward hers, then his lips found her lips and a kiss brought her world to a complete stop.

Chapter Three

Pulling back from the impulsive kiss under the mistletoe, then turning away from Amy and leaving, was one of the hardest things Quint had ever done.

But it was the right thing to do. The situation with her wasn't what he'd thought, certainly it wouldn't be possible to do what Mike had said and "go with the flow," not when a child was in the picture. He sure as hell wasn't looking for anything long-term, and anything less than that would definitely affect a small child. He couldn't be part of any passing fling. A two-year-old. God, he remembered Mike at two. A child was to be protected, so a "good time" wasn't an option, at least not for him.

He felt the doors to the center whoosh shut behind him, and he kept walking before anything beyond the need to leave could settle into him. His hesitation before had brought on the kiss, and he knew how thin the ice was that he stood on when he was around Amy.

He entered the lobby where crews were starting to dismantle the temporary bar and take down the banners and reception desks. The guard standing by the front doors was the same man who had burst into the kitchen when the smoke alarm went off.

"Everything okay in there?" the man asked as Quint got close enough to him to read the name Walt on his badge.

Nothing was okay, Quint admitted to himself, but to the man he said a simple truth that became a fact when he walked away. "Everything's under control. Thanks for your help."

"I'll check it out later, just to make sure."

"Good idea." He stopped by the glass doors. "I don't know if my car's still waiting for me, or if I'll need a cab."

"I'll check it out for you. What's your name?"

"Gallagher, Quint Gallagher."

"Quint Gallagher?"

Quint turned when someone repeated his name, and saw a middle-aged man wearing a tuxedo with what looked like a tie-dyed bow tie at his throat, striding toward him. What was even odder was the ponytail of long graying hair, a number of studs in one ear and the total lack of the "corporate smile" on the man's face.

The man stopped in front of him. "So, you're Quint Gallagher?"

"That's me. And you are?" he asked as the guard went outside to find his ride.

"I've been looking all over for you," the man said, but didn't hold out his hand. "I'm George Armstrong, shareholder, and I've got questions for you."

"Well, Mr. Armstrong, I'm just leaving and it's late," Quint said, turning to look out the door and definitely relieved to see the guard motioning a limo to the curb. More corporate talk wasn't what he wanted right now.

"Your limo?" George asked, glancing past him.

"I think so. Maybe you could call and make an appointment? I'll be in the executive suites on the top floor, I believe, and you can contact Ms. Donovan. She's an executive assistant, and she can—"

"I'm leaving now and I could use a ride," George said, cutting off Quint's offer. "And since I'm what they call a 'major stockholder' in LynTech, I believe, technically, that that limo is partly mine, too." Quint wasn't given a chance to challenge that flawed reasoning, because as the man spoke he pushed back the entry door and glanced at Quint with a lifted eyebrow. "So, would you like to join me?"

If it hadn't been so late, Quint would have told the man to take the limo and have it drive him anywhere he wanted to go, and he'd take a taxi. But if he did that, he'd be stuck here for a while, and Amy was still in the center. And he wanted distance. "I think I will," he said, and followed George out onto the street.

George spoke all the way to the limo, a blur of words that ran on until they were both in the back seat, then George gave the driver an address. Quint recognized it as an industrial area. "Drop me at the hotel on the way," he told the driver.

As the limo pulled away from the curb, George started up the talk again. "I spent a great deal of time fighting what we called 'the establishment' years ago, until I figured out that joining them beat the heck out of fighting them from the outside. So, I found a company founded on principles and got on board.''

''And your point is?'' Quint asked, trying to keep the man focused.

''The point is, you've got a track record for being corporate-oriented, and, from your financial statements filed at LynTech, you've made, and continue to make, obscene amounts of money at what you do. But you need to know that LynTech is a special corporation, a corporation formed with vision, not avarice. Mr. Lewis was a throwback to a time when people cared.''

''Mr. Armstrong, I don't know what you think I'm doing here, but believe me, I'm here to look after the good of the company, not to destroy it.''

''My point exactly,'' George said. ''And I've got some ideas to throw out for you to consider. A few smart things to do.''

Quint knew he'd been smart to leave when he had, and if he hadn't taken a detour into ''never-never land'' with Amy, he would have been safely back at the hotel by now. Instead, he was listening to a man with a ponytail tell him what was best for the company. And all the while, all he could think of was how to forget about a stunning woman with a tiny child. That was the real ''smart thing to do,'' but it was damn hard to accomplish when he was almost certain he could still taste her lips on his.

AMY SANK slowly down to the floor as Quint walked away, her back against the fake tree. Then the doors closed and Quint was gone, leaving her stunned. That she'd let him kiss her was beyond reason, and that he was the one who had drawn back first was humiliating. She scrubbed her hand over her mouth, trying to rid herself of that feeling of his lips against hers. She didn't want it.

She reached for her shoes that had fallen to the floor and started to put them on, cursing the fact that her hands were so unsteady that she had trouble redoing the buckle on the strap. She was lonely, and she hated Quint Gallagher for showing it to her so clearly with a careless kiss. That sense of loneliness that she'd avoided like the plague was almost unbearable at that moment.

She hurried with her shoes, trying to kill an anger in her that made no sense. Anger at a stranger. Anger at herself, and anger at Rob for dying. Stupid, stupid, foolish things to have anger over, and she fought against it.

It was as irrational as letting that stranger kiss her. It was as irrational as the fact that she hadn't slapped the man. And as irrational as the tears that burned behind her eyes. A night that had started with such promise had spiraled out of control completely, topped by Quint's appearance in the center.

"Damn you," she muttered, not sure who she was damning at that point in time.

She pulled herself to her feet, swiped at her tangled hair, then pulled out the remaining pins. She took several deep breaths, the need to see her daughter almost choking her. She wanted to hold on to Taylor and make all of this confusion go away. As she turned, she felt her shoe strike something and saw a man's wallet skittering across the carpeting.

She crouched by the wallet and picked up the soft black leather folder. She stood as she flipped it open and saw a New York State driver's license. Quintin Luther Gallagher, six foot tall, a hundred and seventy-five pounds, and a birthday on January first. His next birthday would make him fifty. She looked at the picture, and saw a man with raw attractiveness, a bit less gray in his hair and mustache—and those eyes. Even in the picture, the eyes seemed able to see right through anything and anyone.

She looked away from it, at a side slot with credit cards, then she opened the back to find money. One-hundred-dollar bills, about a thousand dollars. She closed it, then looked at the door and hesitated. Go after him, she told herself, just take it to him. But something held her in place. An uneasiness at seeing him right then, of meeting his gaze again.

''You fool,'' she muttered and knew exactly who she was berating. It wasn't Quint's fault that he took her off balance and kept her there, or made her feel uneasy with the feelings that his look could suggest.

She clutched the wallet and headed toward the doors and in a few seconds, she was out in the lobby where the festivities were almost a memory. Just the beautiful tree still stood there. The rest had been cleared away. The only person she saw was the guard, Walt. He spotted her, smiled and called out, ''The building isn't going to burn down, is it?''

She tried to smile and found the expression was easy enough to produce for this man. He certainly didn't bother her, or set her on edge. She crossed to him. "No, thank goodness."

He looked at the wallet in her hands, then up at her. "What's going on?"

"I was looking for Mr. Gallagher, tall, gray hair...?"

"I know him. He went out two or three minutes ago with another man."

She looked out the windows at the street with its garlands on the light posts and potted plants by the doors strung with multi-colored lights. "He's out—"

"He's gone. He left in a limo."

She looked back at Walt. "The company limo?"

"No, ma'am, one of those rentals."

"I need to contact him. Is there any way to get a phone number for the limousine or find out where it took him?"

"I guess so, from the rental company, but I wouldn't know which one he used or where he'd be going. What do you need?"

She looked at the wallet. "This fell out of his pocket, and he probably doesn't even know." She looked at Walt. "Can you get into the safe?"

"Oh, no, I can't. I can put it in a desk drawer back there, and that locks, but it's hardly secure."

She couldn't take that chance with the credit cards and a thousand dollars. "I'll keep it, and if Mr. Gallagher calls or comes back, tell him I have it and...tomorrow, I'll put it in the company safe. He can pick it up there."

"Okay, no problem." He glanced at his wristwatch. "It's getting late. Aren't you ready to leave yet?"

"I'm on my way out," she said.

"I'm heading off for my rounds, so why don't I walk you out? That parking garage is pretty empty this time of night."

"Thanks," she said and headed back to the center with Walt following her. Stopping at the climbing-frame tree, she looked up at the mistletoe, then at Walt. "Can you reach that and take it down?" she asked, pointing to the plant.

"No problem." The man reached, jumped slightly and grabbed the mistletoe, tugging it free. He held it out to her.

She took the mistletoe gingerly, holding it between her thumb and forefinger. "Thanks," she muttered as she turned and went back to her office. She dropped the plant in the trash, grabbed her purse and pushed the wallet into it, then turned to get on with her life.

QUINT STOPPED listening to George somewhere between his tirade against the lumbering industry and his involvement in some demonstration in Washington, D.C. Quint's mind wandered but always came back to that moment under the mistletoe when he'd thought, "What the hell," and done what he'd thought about from the first glimpse of Amy's lips. The kiss.

"Well, that went quickly," George was saying as he touched Quint on the arm.

The limo was stopping, and Quint looked out the tinted windows at the hotel, a towering, glittering glass structure in the Houston night. The driver was at his door, opening it.

"We'll talk more," George was saying. "I'll drop by your office, and we can hash out the resource problem."

Quint didn't know what the man was talking about, but got out and turned to look back in the limo. "You do that and we will," he murmured, taking the hand George was offering. The man's handshake was strong and sure, then Quint stepped back.

"Merry Christmas, Quint," George said with a smile and a familiarity that Quint had no idea had formed between them.

"Merry Christmas," he echoed and swung the door shut.

He didn't wait for the limo to leave before he turned and went past the valets into the lobby of the hotel, a vast space with not one, but three Christmas trees, two on either side of the reception desk and one huge tree dead in the middle of the marble floor. Quint strode past the middle tree toward the elevators, but at the last minute he saw the bar and veered off toward it.

Going to his room to work had been his plan ever since he'd left the reception, but now that didn't sound very good to him. He needed a drink. He needed to refocus. He slipped onto a high-backed stool in the pub-like bar and ordered a Scotch straight up. A sip of the fiery liquid got his attention, and he exhaled harshly. It was time to head up to the room.

He reached for his wallet, slipping his hand inside the tux jacket. His cell phone was there. The wallet wasn't. He patted the jacket front and didn't feel it. He'd had it earlier. He remembered making the decision to carry it and the cell phone. He'd had it when he'd left the executive suites, because he could remember patting his pocket and feeling it there. And he'd probably had it until the day-care center and all of the calamities there, from the rat fiasco to the smoke in the kitchen.

He looked at the bartender and motioned him over. "I need a phone for a local call."

"Yes, sir," the man said and reached below the bar to produce a corded phone that he placed on the bar in front of Quint. "Just dial nine, then your number."

Quint dialed information and got a general number for security at LynTech. He punched in the number, heard it ring five times, do a quick double ring, then it was answered. "Olson, maintenance."

"Maintenance? I was trying to reach security."

"Sorry. Security isn't available. They reroute to me at this time of night. Can I help you with something?"

"This is Quint Gallagher. I'm just start—"

"Yes, sir. I've heard about you."

"Okay, I misplaced my wallet tonight, and it's either there, at LynTech, or in the limo that brought me back to my hotel. I don't suppose you know the number for the limo service?"

"No sir. But if you tell me where you were tonight, I could take a look around here for it."

"I'd appreciate it." He gave Olson a general rundown of his movements. "I remember having it on the twentieth floor, in the hallway by the elevators, and that's it."

"I'll let security know, and if you give me a number where I can reach you, I'll take a look and get back to you.''

He started to tell Olson to call the hotel, but he was stopped by the man saying, ''Sir, could you hold for a minute?''

''Sure,'' Quint murmured, and he heard a muffled conversation for a moment, then the man was back on the line.

''Good news. Mrs. Blake in the day-care center has your wallet.''

Relief was there, but so was a certain tightness in his chest. ''What?''

''She told Walt, the security guard, that she'd found it, and if you called, to tell you that she'll bring it in tomorrow and put it in the security safe. You can get it from there.''

There wasn't anything he couldn't live without until tomorrow, but he should probably call her anyway. ''Do you have a phone number for Mrs. Blake?''

''Oh, no sir. That'd be in personnel and I don't have any access to that. But she'll bring it in, and they'll put it in the safe. Just ask at the front desk and they'll tell you where to go.''

He wouldn't have to see her again. He should be relieved by that, but instead he found himself muttering, ''Thanks, that's great,'' hanging up and motioning to the bartender to refill his drink. He didn't have a clue why he felt vaguely let down and restless. He'd put another drink on his tab, then he'd go up and work.

''MAMA,'' the child's voice, edged with a whine, said, getting Amy's attention immediately. She was

on her feet, hurrying into the bedroom where she
found Taylor in her crib, standing, arms out to be
picked up.

Amy scooped up the child and cuddled her to her
chest as she walked back out into the living room of
the tiny apartment. She avoided the only mirror in the
room, a small square over the desk by the door. She
didn't need to see herself to know she looked like
death warmed over. No makeup, her hair in a ponytail
and dark circles under her eyes from being up half
the night with a sick child. That night after her fiasco
with Quint had been followed by a day of waiting in
the pediatrician's office, picking up medicine and trying to comfort Taylor.

"She's fine, Mrs. Blake, just teething and a bit of
a cold, but nothing serious," the doctor had told her,
a doctor who had been through this before with the
two of them.

When Taylor got sick, Amy overreacted and she
knew it. She sank down in the old rocking chair, felt
Taylor snuggle in with her, and she rested her head
on the back of the chair. As she closed her eyes, she
caught a red flash out of the corner of her eye and
turned to see the message light blinking on the answering machine.

She hadn't even thought to check messages today.
She maneuvered Taylor to her other arm and reached
to press the Play button.

"Amy, it's Jenn." Jenn, Rob's sister, was the only
relative she or Taylor had, and Jenn worried about the
two of them. "Thanks for letting me know what the
doctor said. If you two aren't up for Christmas to-

morrow, we can postpone. Tay-bug won't know the difference if we put it off for a day or two until she feels better. I'll call or drop by later to check on you two. Love you both.'' There was a beep, then a date/time stamp that showed the message had been left almost four hours ago. Another message started.

''This is Quint Gallagher.'' She must have started at the sound of that deep drawling voice, because Taylor whimpered slightly, then resettled in her arms.

''I was told you had my wallet and would be bringing it back to LynTech today, but I haven't been able to track you down or find my wallet. Could you call and let me know what's going on?'' He left a number and an extension that she knew was on the top floor in the executive suites. ''I've got a dinner appointment, and I'd appreciate a call before five. If not, call this number.'' He gave another number, then there was a hesitation before he ended with, ''I'll be waiting for your call.''

The beep came, then a date/time stamp and she looked at the wall clock by the tiny kitchen alcove. Six o'clock now and he'd called about two hours ago. She should have checked the messages, but she seldom got any that were important. And she hadn't called LynTech because this was normally vacation and anyone she might have talked to, was gone. The wallet was in the bottom of her purse and she hadn't even thought about it.

She kept rocking, then knew that she had to try and contact Quint. She eased Taylor more onto her right arm, grabbed the phone with her left hand and caught the receiver between her ear and shoulder. Awkwardly, she dialed the company number, then the extension, but it clicked over, said that the person hadn't set up a voice mail system yet, then it clicked off. She hung up, dialed the second number and it rang at the same time as her doorbell sounded.

"Great," she muttered, trying to get to her feet, balance a now-sleeping Taylor on one arm and the phone with the other hand. "Just a minute," she called out, wishing that Jenn would just use her key. "I'll be right there," she called again, as she crossed to the couch and gently put Taylor on it. The baby rolled onto her side and pulled her knees up to her tummy, then Amy reached for a juice bottle she'd put there earlier and gave it to her. Taylor held it, but didn't drink it as she settled back into sleep.

The phone at her ear rang one more time, then was answered. "Gallagher."

She hesitated with her hand on the coldness of the doorknob and had to swallow once to find her voice. "This is Amy Blake," she began and tugged back the door.

"So it is," Quint said, over the phone, but he was right in front of her in her doorway. Dressed in a dark blue business suit that set off his tanned skin and graying hair, he had a cell phone pressed to his ear and that shadow of a smile playing around his lips.

Startled, she lost her grip on her phone and it fell to the floor between them.

Chapter Four

Quint knew he was staring, that Amy was flustered as she scrambled to get the phone she had dropped. Then she was standing with it in her hand, and he didn't move. He just took in the scene in front of him.

Amy looked for all the world like a teenager in an oversize gray sweatshirt with long sleeves that almost covered her hands. Her jeans were worn, her hair pulled back from her face in a ponytail, exposing freckles that he'd never even noticed the night before. She wasn't wearing a hint of makeup, her dark eyes were shadowed, as if she was very tired, but that only emphasized the translucence of her skin and a type of beauty that didn't owe a thing to artifice.

He lifted his phone slightly as he closed the front on it. "I guess I don't need this anymore."

"What are you doing here?" she asked, her voice breathless and low.

He slipped his phone in his jacket pocket, not about to tell her he didn't have a clue why he'd finally driven here instead of sending a messenger or letting it go until she phoned him back. Wrong thing to do, he could admit now. If she'd been provocative the night before in her ruined dress and with the mistletoe overhead, she was downright disturbing right now. "My wallet?" he finally said.

The color in her face deepened, making the freckles stand out even more. Her tongue touched her lips quickly. "Oh, yeah, sure," she muttered. "Shoot, I forgot. Let me get it for you."

She turned and went back into the apartment, and he hesitated, then followed her. As Amy crossed the room, grabbing at toys and discarded clothes, gathering them in her arms on the way, he glanced around.

The inside was a lot more "homey" than the outside of the building. He'd circled the block twice before parking in front of a series of apartment buildings in a low-rent section of the city, buildings from the sixties, three stories, with flat roofs and not much landscaping except for a few shrubs here and there and narrow strips of what should have been green grass, but was just brown. The whole place had seemed depressing, old, poorly kept and reeking of disinterest, with just a few Christmas touches in sight.

But in here, despite the clutter, the tiny size and obvious lack of luxury, it seemed invitingly warm. Odd, unmatched furniture crowded the space, along with a stack of laundry on a side chair, a TV on top of a low bookshelf, and a small Christmas tree decorated with popcorn garlands and colored paper chains sitting in front of a window covered by shades. It had an angel at the top.

"Excuse the mess," she was muttering as she dropped the things in her arms in a pile on the floor by the Christmas tree, then went into what looked like a kitchen alcove ahead and on the left. "I meant to bring the wallet to work today, but I didn't go, and I just totally forgot about it," she said disappearing from sight.

It was then that he noticed the child curled up in a ball on the sofa to the left. She was a tiny thing for a two-year-old, in pink sleepers lying with her back to him. Wisps of feathery dark hair were damp and clinging to her flushed skin. "She's sick?" he asked.

"Teething and a bit of a cold," Amy called from the kitchen. She appeared with a purse in her hands, setting it on a half wall between the kitchen and living area. She waved a hand at him as she opened the purse and started to rummage inside. "Sit down if you'd like," she said as she went through her purse.

He looked at an overstuffed chair that faced the couch, alongside a wooden rocking chair. The upholstered chair was filled with what looked like clean laundry, so he crossed to the rocking chair, sat down and looked back at Amy, who was literally turning her purse upside down to let the contents fall on the divider. "It's here," she muttered. "I remember seeing it."

He glanced from her to the child. "Is she why you didn't come into work today?"

"Pretty much," she muttered, then turned with his wallet in her hand. "Success," she said and crossed to hand it to him.

"Thanks for finding it," he said as he took it.

She stood over him, tucking a strand of hair that had worked its way out of her ponytail behind her ear. "Sure, no problem." She glanced at the child, then back at him. "Go ahead," she said, motioning to his wallet. "Look in it. Everything's there, including the money."

He wasn't even thinking about the wallet. "I trust you."

"Okay, can I offer you something? Coffee or tea? I mean, you had to come all this way and everything."

"No, thanks." He was going to say she must have plans for Christmas Eve, but that sounded ludicrous. A sick child. That was her plan.

"Good, good," she said, hesitated, then turned and scooped the laundry out of the overstuffed chair, and moved it to the coffee table that was partially filled with wooden blocks and some small plastic animals. She plunked down in the chair, twisted to face him and tugged her feet up to cross her legs. "So, you're doing okay at LynTech?"

"Fine. Settling in at work."

"And..." She waved a hand vaguely. "Houston? You like it? I heard you were from New York."

"I was born here." He slipped his wallet in the inside pocket of his suit coat. He should be going, he should be saying goodbye and getting out of her way, but he wasn't anxious to leave just yet. Since he'd walked away from her the night before, he'd had a strange sense of being alone. Singular. He'd even tried to call Mike to connect with him, but had missed him. He'd worked until the small hours of the morning.

The feeling had persisted all day, and it hadn't faded at all until Amy had opened the door. He could just talk for a few minutes, then go to dinner. Just a few minutes.

"So, that explains the accent," she said.

"Accent?"

"Okay, *twang* would be a better word, definitely Texan, though."

It was her voice that had lingered with him, but not because of any accent. There was something in it. He didn't know what, but it touched something in him. "Lady, I just talk," he said with a shrug, "but you, on the other hand, have no discernable accent at all."

That made her smile, and the simple action had the same effect on him as the sun coming out after a long, gray, cold rain. Brilliant, warm and so welcome. "That's because I'm homogenized," she said. "I've lived all over and sort of mixed any local accents up together, so they come out as nothing, sort of like colors."

"What?"

"You know, you mix up all the colors and you get black. And most people don't think of black as a color, but it's the combination of every color in the spectrum. An absolute of colors, a…" She bit her lip. "Sorry, I'm so used to talking to kids, explaining everything, that I forget when I'm around adults."

He had to go, because all he could think about when she was talking was her hair, black hair, but with glints of colors, rich, deep colors. He stopped that thought, and said the first neutral thing he could think of. "Charlie's fine."

She looked puzzled, then her eyes widened. "Oh, Charlie. How would you know how he is?"

This was definitely safe territory. "I went down looking for you earlier and he was in the cage sleeping. Safe and sound." He wouldn't mention the half hour he wasted in personnel getting the secretary to let him get a look at her files. That had only been accomplished by a call to Matt Terrel, one of Lyn-Tech's CEOs. "But you were nowhere in sight and no one seemed to know what was going on."

"I never went in at all today," she said with a shrug, that smile completely gone, and something else hit him dead center. He hadn't realized how much he missed a woman who could smile...really smile. "With Taylor sick and one thing and another, the day just went." She pressed her hands to thighs covered by the faded denim of her jeans. "Didn't you say in your message that you had a date or something tonight?"

The word *date* threw him for a second, then he shook his head. "A dinner appointment. Not a date. I'm too busy with work for that, and even if I wasn't, I told you last night, I'm way out of practice playing that sort of game."

She narrowed her eyes on him, an intensity suddenly there. "You think that having a relationship is a game?"

He'd said the words offhandedly, for something to say that wouldn't make things complicated, but he sensed a complication coming on. "What would you call it?"

She shrugged. "If it's just for the moment, I guess it is a game, but not if it's forever."

"What is it if it's forever?" he asked.

"It sure isn't a game," she said and was on her feet, heading toward the kitchen. "I need some tea," she was saying over her shoulder. "How about some tea?"

He heard some clinking of dishes, then water running. The next thing he knew she was back looking at him over the half wall. "I put on some water for tea or coffee. Both are instant, and the coffee's decaffeinated. Changed your mind?"

"No, I haven't. I need to get going," he said, finally standing and making a move he should have made a lot sooner.

She took a deep breath, and he wished that she'd smile again. He hated that look on her face now, almost a pained look. "Sure, of course, business and things," she said.

"You probably have things to do...for Christmas Eve," he said.

She glanced at her daughter sleeping on the couch, then back at him. "Yes, I do have things to do," she said softly.

"It's hard doing it alone, isn't it?" he asked before he measured his words, and whatever pain he thought he'd inflicted on her before with his glib talk about dating and games, was nothing compared to the literal flinch he caused this time.

He was floored, absolutely undone by her pained expression, but didn't know what to do about it. "Well, it isn't what I planned," she said in a low voice, then forced the suggestion of a smile. But there was no light in her eyes this time. No reality to the expression.

He knew something about Amy Blake at that moment, even though he'd only known her a day. She'd loved her husband completely, and for her being alone wasn't a relief, but something to endure, to survive. Just the opposite of what it had been for him with Mike, because he had never known the kind of love that could cause that kind of sorrow. He truly doubted that it came to more than a handful of people in this world, but she'd had it.

"Thanks for finding my wallet." Mundane words that sounded awkward in his own ears.

"Thanks for checking on Charlie," she said.

"No problem. That rat and I…well, I think we bonded." Thank goodness that brought a slight smile that seemed real, as if he had finally done something to ease her tension. "We understand each other."

"Good, that makes up for me wishing awful things on him last night, I guess."

A sharp whistling cut through the apartment, and Amy hurried back into the kitchen again. As she disappeared, Quint caught movement out of the corner of his eye, turned and saw the little girl stirring. She stretched a hand over her head, and the next thing he knew, she was twisting around, toward the edge of the couch, and he knew that she was going to fall off. He moved quickly, getting to her right when she started to tumble over the edge. He made a grab for her, literally catching her in midair when she started the fall, then he straightened with her in his arms.

He shifted her until she was upright in his arms, and she was stunned for a moment. She twisted around, with a juice bottle safely in one hand, looking at him with eyes as dark as her mother's, and bleary from sleep. Gradually they widened, and he could almost see her realizing that a strange man was holding her. As that thought materialized, she stiffened, and with her free hand, she touched his chest, then straight-armed him, trying to get back as far as she could from him.

Her flushed face puckered up, and the crying began. She was overly warm, miserable from being sick and being scared awake. And the cries built to screams. Quint might have been years away from dealing with a toddler, but the old habits kicked in. He knew better than to try and pull her against him, but instead rubbed his hand up and down on her back, jiggling her slightly and speaking in a low, soft voice that was almost obliterated by her cries.

"Okay, okay, it's okay. Shhhh, it's okay. You didn't go boom. You're just fine. It's okay."

He heard Amy behind him and caught a glimpse of her, almost touching his left arm. "What happened?"

The baby's cries were faltering, and he could feel her relaxing just a bit. A hiccup shook her little body, then a sniffle and a shudder and she was quiet, but still braced with her hand pressed against his chest.

"She's just like her mother," he said, and realized how true it was, from the eyes to the way she had of frowning slightly as she stared at him to ending up in his arms.

"What did she do, throw a rat at you?" Amy asked.

"No, she's got a problem with falling. She almost rolled off the couch."

"Nice catch," Amy murmured. "For hating kids, you're awfully good with them."

Quint looked at the tiny human being in his arms. "I don't hate kids," he said. "I'm just past that. Way past it."

"Been there, done that?"

He looked at Amy. "Years ago," he murmured to remind himself that this scene wasn't his, and it wasn't something he wanted. No matter how appealing the woman was, she had a hell of a lot of baggage that came right along with her.

He started to turn to give the child to her mother so he could get out of there, but when he tried to do that simple thing, it backfired. The minute he moved, the child let out a squeal, stiffened again, and there was a flash of movement, something struck him in the chin, then cold wetness was everywhere.

That's when he saw the bottle again, but now it was almost empty, the top was gone, and what looked like orange juice was all over him. He could feel it trickling down his cheek and onto his chest through his shirt. Amy took the child, talking quickly. "Oh, heavens, Taylor, look what you did," she was saying as she reached with a free hand for a towel in the laundry on the coffee table. She dabbed at her daughter who had the liquid in her hair, on her face, and staining her pink sleepers.

Perversely, Taylor was smiling now, enjoying the mayhem she'd loosed on him, and she was threatening to upend the rest of the bottle onto the floor. But

Amy was too fast for her. She grabbed the bottle, then set the little girl down on the floor by the couch. "No, no, no. No more mess," she said sternly, took one last swipe at the little girl's face with the towel, ruffled her hair, then straightened up and turned to Quint.

There was a flash of something that looked suspiciously like a smile in her eyes, then it died and she was doing for him what she'd done for the child, blotting his chest, the shirt and suit coat, then his face. She stopped short of ruffling his hair before she drew back. "I am so, so sorry," she said. "I've had trouble with those bottles. The lids…" She shrugged. "She must have squeezed it too hard and…" She narrowed her eyes, as if studying him. "You've got orange juice in your hair, and on your shirt and your jacket and…" She reached toward his face, but stopped short of touching him before drawing back and vaguely wiped at her ear with her fingers. "And your ear, it's got some on it, too."

He took the towel from her, rubbing the rough terry cloth over his hair and face, then looked at her. "Gone?"

"Well, yes, but that bit on your ear?"

He dabbed at his ear. "Now?"

"Yes, it's gone," she said, then looked at his clothes. "Your jacket and shirt." She grimaced. "Oh, boy, your tie's a mess. Give them to me and I'll sponge them off with cold water," she said, literally reaching out and undoing the buttons on his jacket. "You can't let it set up."

He looked down at his one-of-a-kind suit jacket, but didn't really see it. What he saw were her long, slender fingers, furiously tugging at the buttons and the material, slipping it off his shoulders. The next thing he knew, she had his jacket, holding it by the collar. She was staring at his shirt. "You...you take off your shirt and tie, okay? And I'll get working on this."

After a quick look at Taylor, who was busy taking the laundry off the table, one piece at a time, Amy hurried out of the room through a door to one side of the kitchen. She kept talking until she was a disembodied voice, just as she'd been at the center last night when she was backing out of the tree. "Just take those things off and bring them in here, the sooner the better."

He did as he was told. He undid the tie, tugged it off, then unbuttoned his shirt and slipped it off before following her. He found her in a tiny bathroom off a short hallway, furiously sponging at his jacket with a facecloth she dampened from the faucet in a small sink. "Don't do that," he said, seeing the water seeping into the fine material of his suit coat. "Please."

Amy stopped swiping at the stain and turned, ready to tell Quint that she wouldn't stop until she had his suit jacket back to good-as-new condition. But the words caught in her throat when she saw him in the doorway, stripped to the waist, holding his shirt and tie in one hand.

All she could see was the expanse of bare chest, the slight tan to the taut skin, the light sprinkling of dark hair forming a T that disappeared into his waistband. Her mouth went dry and she jerked her eyes up, praying that he wouldn't have a clue where her thoughts had been going. She felt sick from it, and she literally had to swallow twice before she could speak to him. "I'm taking care of it."

"Amy, it's ruined," he said in that low grumble of a voice that only added to her discomfort at his closeness.

She turned away from him, gathering her thoughts, and stared at the jacket. The stain was still there, now darkened by water. "No, I can fix it."

"Forget it. It's finished."

She still thought she could make it okay, but if he didn't, she wasn't going to fight him. "Okay, how much did it cost?"

"You don't have to do that. It was an accident, but I have to say that you and your daughter are quite a pair, wreaking havoc on everyone and everything around you."

She looked up, catching herself in the mirror of the medicine cabinet, Quint's reflection right behind her, Quint and that half smile he had playing at the corners of his mouth. "How much?" she repeated. "I need to pay for it if I can't fix it."

He watched her for a long moment, then shrugged, "Lady, it's off the rack and cost about two hundred dollars, but it's old and it was time to get rid of it. You saved me a trip to the secondhand store." He leaned one shoulder against the door frame and studied her with those hazel eyes. "You've got better things to do with your money than buy a jacket for me. Just do me a favor and throw it out." He held out his shirt and tie to her. "And these, just throw them out, too."

She took the ruined shirt and tie out of his hand, laid them over the jacket on the sink's edge, then looked at him again. He had his arms crossed over his naked chest, showing surprising muscles, and she forced herself to look him right in the eye. "This is the deal. I'll do what I can for all of the clothes, and if I can't clean them, I'll throw them out and pay you for them." When he would have objected, she stopped him. "That's the deal, period. No negotiating about it."

He stood straight, hands lifted, palms out toward her. "Okay. You win. Deal." Then he looked down at his lack of clothing before he met her gaze again. "Can I ask a favor?"

Taylor came up behind Quint right then, and Amy barely had time to get to her before she tossed the bottle at Quint again. She thought she'd put it up high enough, but obviously she hadn't. She grabbed the bottle, hitting Quint in the shoulder in the process, but keeping his slacks safe from the remainder of the juice. Taylor plunked down on her bottom in the hall behind Quint.

"Thank goodness," Amy breathed, straightening with the topless bottle, relieved to have averted another catastrophe, at least until she turned and found herself with no more than two inches between herself and Quint's bare chest. When she looked up, his face seemed so close that it was slightly blurred.

"Lady, you're good."

She sidled to the right, into the hallway, to get distance, and scooped up Taylor, setting her on one hip. "I'll find you something to wear," she said quickly, carrying Taylor and the bottle back into the main room, then through to the kitchen. Tossing the bottle in the sink, she turned and saw Quint across the half wall, in the living area, watching her, his expression unreadable.

"I refuse to wear a blouse," he said.

Damn it, was he joking as if this was all fun, when it was stressing her so much she had to remind herself to breathe? She went back into the living area, put Taylor down by the window near her open toy box and crossed to the coffee table. "There has to be something in here you can wear," she muttered, sorting through clothes that she knew darn well wouldn't fit him. But she had some oversize T-shirts, a couple of sweatshirts that might work.

"How about this?" Quint said and she looked up to see that he'd found a T-shirt that she'd had forever. But he wasn't going to wear that shirt. It had been Rob's. It was one she'd kept, and one she wore to sleep in sometimes.

Before she could snatch it back to safety, Quint was shaking it out. "Super Dude?" he asked, looking at the logo that had faded so much from time and use.

She wanted to reach for it, but made herself speak calmly. "Not that one."

"Why not? It looks like it'll fit," he murmured.

"It's old and you have that dinner appointment, and..." She put her hands behind her back to keep herself from diving at him to get it back. "It wouldn't be cool to go in as Super Dude."

His crooked grin was accompanied by him turning the T-shirt around and holding it up in front of his bare chest. "Oh, I don't know. Super Dude sounds about right for what I have to do." He looked down at it. "What do you think?"

She stared at him, and what she'd dreaded happening didn't happen. Something worse happened. She didn't look at Quint holding up the shirt and see Rob in that shirt making silly comments about "being super." Instead, in a truly frightening moment for her, she couldn't see Rob at all. She couldn't remember what he'd looked like in the shirt, and that shook her. "That's stupid," she mumbled and clutched her hands behind her so tightly that her nails were digging into her palms. But even that didn't help.

"Hey, lady," he said, his smile fading. "That's a joke." He was coming closer and she closed her eyes tightly, willing the image of Rob to come to her. It was there, a solid man with gray eyes, sandy-blond hair and... She willed the image to be clearer, but instead it started to fade. She opened her eyes quickly, and was shocked to find Quint not more than a foot from her. His image was so clear it was literally painful for her.

His hazel eyes were narrowed on her, but that didn't lessen the pain that was all around her. She swallowed hard, fighting the burn of tears. She sensed Taylor happily playing in the clothes while she stared at the man in front of her and was terrified that she would start to cry. She'd frighten Taylor, and she'd embarrass herself with Quint over an old T-shirt. But Taylor kept playing, and Quint didn't say anything.

He did something far worse.

He touched her, lightly brushing the tips of his fingers along her jawline before he cupped her chin. The contact was as insubstantial as the touch of a feather, but it became the center of her existence at that moment. All she could do was stand there, staring at him, silently cursing him for being there, for being so alive and for making the past seem so remote and so faded.

"I'm sorry," he murmured. She didn't have a clue what he had to be sorry for. Then he gave her an out. A rational explanation for something that had no explanation. "It's rough with a sick child, and it's rough having to deal with it."

He thought she was upset over Taylor being sick, and she grabbed at that as an explanation for herself, too. That made sense. It explained why she felt so fragmented and why him holding an old T-shirt was making her crazy. And why she wished with all her heart that he had his clothes on and was at his damned dinner appointment and not here…so close…and so gentle, and why she was hearing…bells, jingle bells?

Then the bells were overlaid by a jarringly cheerful voice calling out, "Hello, hello, hello and a very merry Christmas to one and all!"

Quint slowly withdrew his touch from her chin, then she took a breath and turned away from him. Jenn was coming in the door, actually backing in with her arms full of presents. Amy hadn't heard any knock on the door, or the key being used. But when she saw Jenn, she felt as if she'd been thrown a lifeline, and she knew what she had to do. Get rid of Quint. Get him out of there and get the T-shirt back.

Chapter Five

Jingle Bells? Merry Christmas?

Quint had to literally make himself draw back from Amy, to break the contact, so he could make sense out of what was going on. For a man who usually understood everything happening around him, he understood very little of what had happened in the apartment since he'd knocked on the door. And for a man who understood his limitations and knew when to cut his losses and run, he was hanging around like some moonstruck teenager, standing half-dressed in front of someone who looked deeply relieved to have an interruption in whatever was happening between them.

He curled his hand around the T-shirt and watched Amy smile as a woman entered the apartment and set a pile of brightly wrapped presents on the floor. Amy hurried over to the woman, but Taylor beat her mother there, and was scooped up into a huge hug.

The newcomer was all in red and trimmed in jingle bells, from the two tied at the top of each red boot, to those sewn on dancing reindeers embroidered on an oversize sweatshirt and those fringing a Santa hat worn over pale-blond hair. She was laughing, hugging

Taylor, calling her, "My munchkin," then leaning over to kiss Amy on the cheek, before she looked up finally and saw him there.

She had to be in her late twenties, pretty in a "cute" way, and obviously a woman with control, because she didn't say a thing about him being half-naked. And she was a woman who didn't mind a little girl tugging a Santa hat right off her head to throw it in the air. Instead, her eyes flicked over his bare chest, then she met his gaze. "I left a message I'd call or come by later," she said without looking away from Quint.

"Yes, Jenn, I got it," Amy said as Quint shook out the T-shirt, fully intending to put it on to try and make the situation less awkward. But before he could, Amy hurried back to him, saying. "And I was hoping you'd stop by. I'm very glad that you did." Then she startled him by reaching for the T-shirt, tugging it out of his hands.

Without missing a step, she kept going, through the mess of laundry Taylor had scattered from the table to the floor, and across to the bookshelf the television sat on. She was still talking. "Just come on in, and we'll open presents and have a good time, as soon as I take care of this." She bent down and opened a drawer in the chest, then stood and turned with something navy in her hands. "This is better, warmer and more..." She shrugged, an action that seemed tinged with a degree of vulnerability to Quint. He barely had time to absorb that before she finished with, "Suitable."

That's what this whole experience wasn't—suitable. He was older and wiser, and wasn't looking for any of this. This definitely wasn't going with the flow or chilling. It was stupid. Then Amy was there holding out a navy sweatshirt to him.

"Yes, that's suitable," he said, taking it from her.

Even as he spoke, she was moving again, going over to Jenn, who was still holding Taylor.

He shook out the sweatshirt, put it on, tugged it down, then raked his fingers through his hair. "It fits," he said.

"I'm Jenn Blake," the visitor said out of the blue. Quint looked at her and met a smile. "And you are…?"

"He's late. He's got an appointment," Amy said before Quint could say anything, and started to pick up the presents Jenn had put on the floor. "Wow, you outdid yourself with all of this, Jenn."

Jenn was still looking at Quint. "Whoever you are, won't you stay for some hot cider, or carol-singing or some holiday spirit, or just plain old spirits, as the case may be?"

He liked her. She had the ability to go with the flow, just adjust to whatever she found, even a half-naked man. He just wished he had that ability at the moment. "I really have to be going. I've got an appointment, business."

"Oh, not on Christmas Eve, surely," Jenn said, as Taylor squirmed out of her arms to get to the presents on the floor.

Amy crouched by Taylor, offering her one of the smaller gifts, but looked at Quint over her daughter's head. "I'll get back with you about your clothes," she said, while Taylor ripped the silver paper off the package.

It was obvious she wanted him out of there, and he should have wanted out of there, too. "Don't worry about it," he said as he crossed the room, picking his way past the laundry to get to the two women and the child.

He looked at Jenn. "By the way, my name isn't 'he's late.' It's Quint Gallagher. And it was nice to meet you."

He glanced at Amy, and found her face slightly flushed and her eyes narrowed. Oh, yes, she wanted him long gone. What galled him was, just looking at her made him think things he didn't need to think. Feel things he didn't need to feel. The safest of all the feelings was the urge to brush at a single strand of hair that had fallen loose from the ponytail and lay against her throat. That was foolish. And the thought of kissing her again was definitely insane.

So he said, "Merry Christmas," and turned away before he acted on impulse. He wasn't an impulsive man, never had been, but this woman brought out the worst in him.

He went out into the hall, swung the door shut behind him, and walked away, the way he had the night before. But this time it was even harder to keep going.

AMY SANK DOWN on the floor with Taylor, sitting cross-legged while she watched her daughter stack the colored blocks that had been in the wrapped box. She braced herself for the questions that would be coming, but Jenn surprised her by kneeling by the two of them and reaching to stroke Taylor's silky hair. "Such a relief to see her feeling better," she said.

"She's a lot better, thank goodness." Amy looked at her sister-in-law. "And I owe you an explanation."

"Me? No, no way. But, if you feel compelled to tell me why you had a drop-dead-gorgeous half-naked man in your apartment, I'm as open to an explanation as the next shocked-out-of-her-socks aunt." Jenn grinned at her. "Okay, who is he?"

Amy envied Jenn's ability never to take life too seriously. *Really* envied her sometimes. "He works for LynTech, just came on board, and he left his wallet at the center last night."

"That's all fascinating, but that doesn't explain how he ended up here on Christmas Eve, half-naked." Her smile faded a bit. "Listen, Amy, you don't have to explain any of this. It's been two years since Rob died, and that's a long two years."

Her stomach twisted. "It isn't like that. No. Never."

The smile was completely gone now. "Honey, don't ever say never. You're young and if—"

"Jenn, please, don't start."

"I'm not. I won't. I just want you to know that if, and I'm saying 'if' you ever want to get on with your life—"

"You make it sound as if I stopped my life, and have to restart it some way."

"Don't you?" she asked softly. "Sweetie, do you think it's normal to be still sleeping in that damn T-shirt after two years, just because Rob wore it so much?"

She stood quickly, sick that Jenn had seen through her about the T-shirt. "He came here to get his wallet back, and Taylor spilled juice on his clothes. I offered to clean them for him. And in order for me to do that, he had to take them off."

She went back into the bathroom, picked up the jacket and returned to show the coat to Jenn. "See? He said it's old and not worth much, but I need to clean it anyway." She shook it out and something flipped into the air, landing with a faint plopping sound on top of one of the gold-wrapped presents. Her heart sank. His wallet.

Jenn picked it up, then held it up to Amy. "Is this the wallet that's given to wandering off on its own?"

"Shoot," she said, taking the wallet. "Stay here with Taylor. Maybe I can catch him before he takes off without it again."

"A bad habit," she heard Jenn say as she ran out the door. She hurried down into the lobby and through the security door that hadn't locked since she'd moved in, into the cold night, but she couldn't see a limousine anywhere.

The street was almost empty, with just a few cars passing by. No Quint. She looked down at the wallet, then turned and went back inside. "Shoot, shoot and double shoot," she muttered as she trudged back up the two flights of stairs to the apartment.

When she went in, she found Jenn and Taylor huddled over a new doll. Jenn looked up. "Sorry, we opened another one," she said, motioning toward the doll. "I have a heck of a time saying no to this little thing.'' Jenn glanced at the wallet in Amy's hands. ''I take it you didn't catch him?''

''No, not even close.''

''He'll be back,'' Jenn said. ''As soon as he figures out that he left the damn thing again.''

That was what she was worried about. She sank down on the floor with the wallet still in her hands. ''He knows where I live,'' she muttered.

''Oh, by the way?'' Jenn said as Taylor took the bonnet off the baby doll. ''The suit coat?''

She looked up at Jenn who was reaching to snatch the jacket off the chair where she'd dropped it before going outside. ''What about it?''

''It's not going to get clean. It's ruined.''

''Are you sure?''

''Very sure,'' she said, touching the damp spots on the front. ''The juice is so acidy…'' She shrugged. ''That just ruins that kind of material.''

''Great. Now, I'll have to get him another one.''

''Sweetie, that sounds good, but do you have any idea what that jacket probably cost?''

She shrugged. ''He said it cost maybe two hundred dollars, and I'm thinking that means the pants and the jacket, and the pants were just fine, actually.''

Jenn actually snorted at that. ''Boy, either I'm losing my touch with fabric, or he's delusional.''

''What are you talking about?''

''The jacket isn't just a jacket, it's a creation. It's a Marno. Italian. Custom-made.''

Her heart was starting to drop. ''You're kidding, aren't you?''

''I wish I was. Even the label isn't a label, it's a

hand-embroidered statement on the lining over the heart,'' she said as she reached for the jacket and opened it to show the lining in the front. She pointed at something that looked like an irregularity in the silky fabric, until she looked closer. It was a flourish in embroidery that looked as if it could have said, Marno, with numbers under it. She swallowed hard. ''How much is it worth?''

Jenn studied the jacket, felt the material, then touched the label before she looked back to Amy. ''Honestly?''

''Please, don't lie to me, okay?''

''Marno creations start at five thousand, and take six months' worth of labor.''

''Holy kamoley,'' Amy breathed, as she sank back on her heels.

''Listen, it obviously doesn't mean very much to him. These things are all relative. And if he didn't tell you how much it really costs, he doesn't want your money.''

''Of course, he felt sorry for me.'' She hadn't wanted his sympathy when she'd told him about being a widow, and she sure as heck didn't want his pity.

''You can't afford to have another one made for him, and even if you could, you'd have to find the tailor with Marno who does his work and do it through him.'' She touched Amy, covering her hands with hers. ''Sweetie, don't kill the wallet.''

Amy looked down at the wallet she had been unconsciously twisting in her hands. She dropped it on the floor, and stared at it. There had to be a thousand dollars in it, and he hadn't even remembered to take it again. Jenn was right. Money didn't mean a lot to him. Taylor crawled into her lap and cuddled into her mommy, holding the doll to her. "I'll worry about this later when I can think straight," she said, kissing Taylor on the top of her head. She could feel the fever creeping back. "Right now, I need to give her some more medicine."

"I'll get it. Just tell me where," Jenn said, getting to her feet, the jingle bells ringing.

"In the fridge, pink, in a bottle, and there's a measuring cap on it."

Jenn crossed to the kitchen, jingling all the way. "How about you, do you need a drink?"

She thought a whole bottle of something very strong wouldn't be all bad, but she called after her sister-in-law, "Maybe later."

"I've got an idea," Jenn said from the kitchen. "Why don't you two come to my place and spend the night?" She peeked around the corner and into the room. "We could do the whole S–A–N–T–A thing." She ducked back into the kitchen. "We could do stockings and everything."

Amy felt Taylor sigh as she relaxed, and she looked around the tiny apartment. "That might be a good idea."

"Great. Are you sure you don't want anything right now?"

"Five thousand dollars," she muttered.

"What did you say?"

"A miracle for Christmas," she said, and was startled by the phone ringing. "Can you get that?" she called to Jenn, not wanting to get up and disturb Taylor.

"Sure." Jenn came back into the room holding the bottle of medicine and the dose cup, grabbed the phone on her way, and as she said, "Hello," into the phone, she handed the medicine and dose cup to Amy.

She frowned slightly as she listened, then smiled. "Oh, yes, of course. We found it right after you left." Quint. Amy watched Jenn. "Of course, of course. Just a minute." Jenn pulled the receiver down to press it into her chest and spoke to Amy in a low voice. "It's him, and he asked me to ask you when you'd be back at LynTech working so he can get his wallet?"

She felt very relieved he wouldn't show up on her doorstep again. "I don't know. Maybe the day after Christmas, maybe not until a few days after Christmas. It all depends on Taylor and how she's doing."

Jenn put the phone back up to her ear. "She doesn't know," she said, editing the whole statement down to a three-word sentence. "Do you want to come back and get it now?"

"No, no," Amy protested, waving the hand that held the medicine in the air to get her sister-in-law's attention.

But Jenn ignored her and said, "I don't see why not."

"Jenn, don't let him come back," she whispered tensely. "Tell him we're going away, anything."

"If you're sure?" Jenn turned her back slightly to Amy, obviously shutting out her gesticulating and hissing whispers. "Okay, sure, no problem." She hung up the phone, then turned to Amy. "Well, that's settled."

"I told you not to let him come back here," she said, annoyed with Jenn for what could have been the first time since they'd met. "I don't want him here."

Jenn dropped down by them again, jingling as she settled. "Don't look so scared. He's not coming back tonight."

"I'm not scared," she said, but knew that was a lie. "So, what were you agreeing to?"

"He wanted to know if you could drop it off with the concierge at the hotel tomorrow sometime? I told him okay."

"Oh, Jenn, it's Christmas."

"So, between the turkey that I'm going to make, and the pumpkin pie that I've bought from that little bakery down the street, either you or I can run it over to the hotel and leave it. Makes sense, doesn't it?"

She shifted Taylor, trying to get the lid off the medicine and pour a dose in the little cup. "It would make more sense if I knew what hotel he was staying at."

Jenn took the bottle from her, undid the lid and asked, "How much?"

"The second line," she said, holding up the little cup for Jenn to pour the medication into it. "That's it," she said, then spoke to Taylor. "Come on, baby, a little nummies to make you feel better."

Taylor turned her head away, burying her face in her mommy's chest. "No want," she mumbled.

"Tay-bug, please, take the meddies, it'll help you feel a whole lot better."

"Tay?" Jenn said, getting close and speaking

softly. "If you take your meddies, Santa will bring you something extra-special wonderful in the morning."

Taylor twisted, looked at Jenn. "Santa? Get Bonkies?"

Jenn looked at Amy. "Bonkies?"

"It's this little dog that jumps and barks by itself."

Jenn brushed at Taylor's fine hair. "Sure, Santa will get Bonkies for you."

"Jenn, they cost eighty dollars."

Jenn shrugged. "She's worth it. Tay-bug gets Bonkies."

That did the trick and Taylor took the medicine, then twisted to bury her face in Amy's chest again. "Thanks," Amy whispered to Jenn as the other woman took the medicine dispenser. "Now, how in the heck are we supposed to get that wallet to a hotel in the city when we don't know what hotel to take it to?"

"No problem. He said he's staying at the Towers, downtown, near that restaurant-row thing. Do you know it?"

The Towers. Hundreds of dollars a night for a room, and the suite went for a lot more, but it seemed like the place for a man to wear a five-thousand-dollar suit. "I know it, but what if Taylor's still sick tomorrow?"

"I'll stay with her while you go. I've got that turkey to do, but heaven knows, it's a little off-putting to read the recipe and see the phrase 'insert your hand in the body cavity of the bird.'" She gave a mock shudder. "Maybe I'll let you invade the bird and I'll see the concierge. Whatever works out.'' She sat back. "Now, let's get going. I've got to find a B–O–N–K–I–E somewhere and do the S–T–O–C–K–I–N–G–S.'' Jenn reached for Taylor. "I'll hold her, and you get what you need for tonight.''

Amy transferred Taylor to Jenn, then stood and went to put a bag together for the two of them. When she came back into the room, Jenn was in the rocking chair with Taylor sleeping in her arms. "Got everything?'' Jenn asked in a whisper.

"Almost.'' She crossed to the TV and reached for Rob's T-shirt, stuffing it in the bag before Jenn could see her doing it. Then she went back and touched Jenn on the arm. "I'll take the things out to your car, then come back and get you and Taylor. Okay?''

"Perfect.'' Jenn glanced over at the floor where they'd been sitting. "You might want to pick that wallet up on the way.''

Amy spotted the wallet and stooped to get it. "I'll be up in a minute,'' she said, carrying the overnight bag out with her. As she went down the hallway, she opened the top zipper of the bag and pushed the wallet inside.

Three days after Christmas

SHADOWS were gathering in the corners of the office on the twentieth floor when Quint sat back in his chair and stretched his arms over his head in an effort to ease the tension in his shoulders and neck. There was a lot more work to be done at LynTech than he'd thought, but he had been warned. When Matt Terrel had talked to him the night before he'd flown back to Houston, he'd admitted that this wasn't going to be easy. Robert Lewis had run the company for years with an open heart and an open wallet.

Quint knew that was true. The figures and prospectus were in trouble. Nothing fatal, but it was going to take a lot of figuring to pull this out. He wanted to talk directly to Zane Holden, because they'd only talked on the phone before. But the man was off on a honeymoon in Aspen. Now Matt Terrel was talking about leaving for a week after his own marriage, a private affair on New Year's Eve. "Talk about rats deserting a sinking ship," he muttered as he stood.

He turned to the windows, to the city below with Christmas decorations still up, but there was something almost forlorn about them, as if they were a bit out of place. The way he'd felt many times before. Maybe that was why he was a bit annoyed at the two top men of LynTech taking off at the worst of times for the company. Maybe the company was in more trouble than even he could see if the executive level put so much ahead of the welfare of the corporation.

He rolled down the sleeves of the dove-gray shirt he was wearing, then reached for the dark, double-breasted business jacket. As he shrugged it on, he automatically felt for his wallet in the inside breast pocket. It was a habit he'd developed since Amy had dropped the wallet off with the concierge on Christmas Day. That habit had been born after meeting Amy, and so had the habit of checking the sign-in book at the front desk when he came to work each day.

With the company basically shut down between Christmas and New Year, anyone coming into the building to work had to sign in. Quint checked every morning for the names above his own signature, and every morning he saw A. Blake. She was there, but he didn't go and check for himself. The only thing he gave in to was to call down to the new center yesterday and ask how Taylor was doing.

No one had answered the phone.

He reached for his briefcase and crossed the room, his mind filled with thoughts of Amy and Taylor. The daughter splashed juice all over and the mother threw rats. He flipped off the lights and left the office, heading for the elevators. Quite a pair. He took the car down, stepped out and found himself facing the same doors he'd faced every day since he'd been here—the doors to Just for Kids, bright colors and the logo imprinted in his mind.

He'd done what he'd done every day since Christmas, called down to let security know he was leaving, then gone directly to the back and into the security parking area without seeing Amy.

He headed toward the car he'd leased, a midnight-blue Mercedes SUV. A flash of movement caught his eye and he turned to see Walt, the security guard, coming out the back door. "Sir?" he called when he spotted Quint. "There you are. Just a minute."

The guard crossed to him and held out an envelope. "I forgot when you called down, but Mrs. Blake asked me to give you this when you left."

He took the envelope bearing the company logo on the top left corner. "Thanks," he murmured, and as the guard turned with a, "Have a good evening," Quint opened the envelope and took out a piece of folded paper. When he opened it, more paper fell out of it and fluttered to the concrete floor.

He stooped and picked it up, a check made out to him by Amy Blake for fifty dollars. He looked at the paper that had come with it:

I appreciate the truth. Your jacket is ruined. I'll pay you each week until it's paid for.

A.

That was it.

He looked up, but the guard was gone and the door was closed. Fifty dollars? Damn it, he'd told her not to worry about it. She couldn't afford fifty dollars. He knew that. He went back inside and spotted Walt near the front lobby.

"Walt?"

The guard stopped and turned. "Yes, sir? A problem?"

"When did Mrs. Blake give you this for me?"

"Oh, around noon, I guess. She just said to give it to you when you left."

"Has she left?"

"I don't think so. At least, she hasn't signed out."

"Okay, thanks," he said.

"Yes, sir. Have a good evening." The guard touched the peak of his cap before turning and going back toward his station in the lobby.

Quint stood there, the check in one hand, his briefcase in the other. He wasn't going to let her do this.

He turned to the doors for the center, hesitated for just a moment, then crossed and pushed them back to go and find Amy.

Instead of the scent of gingerbread greeting Quint this time, the odor of paint hung in the air and music was playing softly, lullabies of some sort. As he let the door close after him, he saw that the twinkle lights were still highlighting the tree, but there was no woman climbing out of the opening. Instead, Taylor was there, lying on a blanket on the floor, sleeping, cuddled up with a teddy bear and a doll with hair as blond as the child's was dark.

He moved closer and saw Amy off to the right, dressed in jeans and a loose blue sweater. She was on her hands and knees, the way she'd been the first time he'd found her here. But this time there was no rat, only what looked like a white stain on the carpet. She was using a brush, scrubbing at the stain.

He braced himself as he went closer. Her hair was tied back in a low ponytail and her feet were bare. She rubbed the brush over the stain, and he could vaguely hear her humming to the music. She looked so tiny, so… He stopped. He had a reason to be here and it wasn't to admire her.

He didn't want to talk too loudly and wake Taylor, so he stopped by Amy and said in a half whisper, ''Excuse me?''

Chapter Six

Amy had thought Quint might stop by, but she'd hoped she'd be wrong about it. She wasn't. She heard his voice at the same time she saw his polished wing-tipped black shoes by her right side. Closing her eyes for a brief moment, she stopped scrubbing and twisted to look up at Quint.

She hated the way he towered over her, but she couldn't do a thing about it, no more than she could control the way he looked in a dark-gray suit that defined strong shoulders and muscular thighs. It had probably cost him over five thousand dollars. She looked back down at the white paint that Taylor had spilled on the carpet and started scrubbing at it again. "You got the check I take it?" she asked, not about to play games about this.

"I got it," he said, and she could see him come a bit closer as he spoke. "I don't want it."

She stopped scrubbing, but she didn't look up. "Then give it to charity. I don't care. But you'll get one every week until I pay off that jacket."

"I don't want it," he repeated in a low voice as

he dropped to his haunches beside her. "Here. Take it," he said as he handed her the check.

She kept scrubbing, ignoring the check as anger surged in her, and the carpet was taking the brunt of that anger. Then he dropped the check, right on the stain, forcing her to stop. Before she could do anything, he stood and walked away.

That did it. She scrambled to her feet, grabbing the check and hurrying after him. She got between him and the door before he could get out of the center. Damn it, she hated being so short. She hated having to tip her head up to look him in the face, and she hated the way her heart was racing. "Don't you dare," she barked, tossing the scrub brush across to where she'd been, then held the check out to him.

"Don't I dare what?" he asked, matching her tone of voice.

"Don't you patronize me. Take this."

"No."

She hated the unsteadiness of her hand, but she kept the check held out to him. "Just take it." Her voice rose slightly, and she heard Taylor stir. She looked at her daughter, watched her as she settled back to sleep, then she turned back to Quint. "Take it," she repeated, dropping her voice to a tense whisper again.

"I'll just tear it up," he said.

"Then I'll send cash up to your office, and you can tear it up, or you can light a hundred-dollar cigar with it, for all I care."

He stared at her, his gaze intent. "I don't get this," he whispered. "I told you not to bother with the jacket, and now you look as mad as..." He shrugged. "I don't get it."

"You lied to me." She drew the check back, folding it in half and closing her hand over it in the hopes of stopping the trembling.

"I'm not a liar," he muttered.

"Oh, that was a two-hundred-dollar suit Taylor tossed juice on?" she whispered.

He had the decency to look taken aback, at least a bit. "I don't know exactly what it's worth."

"Try five thousand dollars."

He exhaled with a shake of his head. "Lady, who cares?"

"It's a Marno, isn't it?"

"I don't know. I don't check labels before I put my clothes on."

"Of course you don't. What's five thousand dollars to you?"

He looked past her at Taylor, then leaned toward her, erasing the illusion she had of any distance between herself and Quint. "Can we go someplace so we can talk in a normal voice?" he whispered.

Without saying a thing, she moved back, crossed to the entry area and locked the doors. Then she motioned him to follow her. She led the way to the hall in the rear without looking back, turned right and took a quick turn into her office. She knew he was there, just as she had the first night. She literally felt his presence and was thankful when she got into the office, turned and found out he'd stopped just inside the door.

"Okay, normal voice." She opened her hand, saw

the ruined check and tossed it on the desk. "I'll send the cash up to you tomorrow. I'll have Walt run it up."

He stared at her hard, then came closer. "Let me explain that I don't want your money. I'll send Walt back down with it." That wry smile was almost there, and it made her ache slightly in her middle. "The guy might need the exercise, but why put him through that?"

She didn't want humor. She wanted this settled. She wanted him to leave and let her keep going with her own life. "Then don't send him back down."

He exhaled in a sigh. "Lady, listen to me. I know where you are. I've been there. I was a single father with a little boy and with more ability than money. Every penny counted."

Oh, no, she didn't want this, not his empathy. Sympathy, pity, empathy. She didn't want any of that with this man. "You don't know anything about me, but I do know that my daughter ruined your expensive suit. And it's up to me to make good on that."

"I'm not a liar. I just thought..." He shrugged. "Oh, sue me, I honestly didn't care much for that suit and I probably would have tossed it sooner or later, so why would I want you to buy me another one?"

"You're that rich?"

"What?"

"A five-thousand-dollar suit and you probably would have tossed it sooner or later without batting an eye?"

"I'm not rich, I'm..." He shrugged again. "My net worth has nothing to do with this."

"What are you worth? One...two million?"

"I don't know, exactly."

"You're a millionaire?"

His exasperation was evident by the rush of released air before he said, "Technically."

She laughed, but there wasn't humor in the sound. "Oh, *technically?* As in, you have millions, but you only keep about a thousand of it in your wallet at one time?"

He cocked his head to one side and narrowed his eyes on her, and that teasing was there, even without the smile. "So, you peeked, huh?"

"Excuse me?"

"My wallet. You peeked?"

She turned from him before the smile could come, and looked down at Charlie in his cage. The lucky rat only had to nibble on the seeds in his dish. He didn't have to deal with a thoroughly infuriating man. "If you didn't keep losing it, I never would have had to look in it to try and find you to get it back to you, would I?"

"You've got a point, now tell me one thing. How did you know what that suit cost?"

She stared at the rat, methodically nibbling on a compact pellet of food. "Jenn. She's a buyer for one of the top specialty stores in the state. She knows fabric and she knows tailoring. And she said that it's a Marno, and she showed me the thingy on the lining." She took a breath. "And she said that they took six months to make and that they cost anywhere from five thousand dollars up."

"They start around two and go up. And that suit,

if you have to know, was probably around three or so. It's a business suit, not an evening suit.''

She turned and he was there, so close. She stayed very still as she met his hazel gaze. ''Were you really going to throw away that suit?''

He was silent for what seemed a long time, then he said bluntly, ''No.''

She sagged back, sitting on the edge of the desk. ''Why couldn't you just say that at the first? Why couldn't you have just said, 'That's a very expensive suit that I'm not about to throw away,' instead of, 'oh, it's off the rack and cost about two hundred dollars'?''

''Do you want the truth?'' he asked in a low voice.

''I thought that was the point of all of this discussion?''

''Okay, what I said before was the truth. I've been there, juggling a job, a kid, worrying about money. We were never poor, but we weren't flush, either. I figured that telling the truth at that point in time would be counterproductive, and I was right.''

''That's your opinion,'' she muttered.

''Lady, you'd try the patience of a saint!''

''Oh, and you're a saint?'' she asked without thinking.

There was dead silence, as if she'd hit a nerve, then a soft, almost rueful chuckle. ''Not even close,'' he murmured.

''So, you'll take the money for the suit?''

''I don't want your damned money. Don't you understand that?''

''And I don't care what you want,'' she countered

in a voice that sounded tight in her own ears. She touched her tongue to her lips and turned away from him, back to the rat on the desk as she asked, "Don't you understand *that?*"

She was startled when he touched her, catching her by her upper arm and literally spinning her around to face him. She felt as if the world centered on the place he touched her, that and the fact that she could feel each breath he exhaled, brushing her face with heat.

His hold on her tightened slightly, hovering just this side of real pressure. But she didn't move. She didn't dare move. "*This* is what I want," he murmured in a low, rough voice, and before she could think or move, he was kissing her.

She felt the brush of his mustache, then his lips found hers and any thoughts she might have had of pushing him away scattered and were lost to her. All she knew was the feel of his mouth on hers, the touch of his tongue, the way her lips opened as if of their own volition, and surrender was there without any warning.

She tried not to move, not to put her arms around his neck, not to arch her body toward his, not to absorb that heat that seemed to be seeping into her soul. But there was a raw hunger in her for his taste, for his touch, for closeness, for a sense of not being alone. She ached to stop feeling singular, to stop feeling as if she was drifting, and Quint was making that all change. Just being there, touching her, kissing her.

"Mama?"

Taylor's voice came down the hallway, jerking Amy back to her senses and to the realization that she was desperate. Painfully desperate at that moment. She pushed away from Quint, breaking the contact that was threatening to drown her. Twisting to one side, she gripped the edge of the desk, then pushed around him and hurried out of the office.

Quint stood very still, letting his body settle and his mind start to function again. Impulsively kissing Amy under the mistletoe had been one thing. But this kiss was impulsiveness risen to a new height. She'd been so close, the scent of her filling his being, that all logic had disappeared. It was a shame that logic had come back, he thought ruefully. But it was there, cold and glaring. And he couldn't avoid it.

He ignored the ache in his body and the lingering scent she wore that hung in the air around him. He'd forgotten about the way it felt to have a woman so close when he felt her start to melt against him. Now, he turned and went after her. In the main room, he saw her right away, hugging Taylor to herself, rocking back and forth, whispering softly to her child.

It hit him in the gut right then how much Mike had missed growing up without a mother, and how much he had missed, spending the past twenty years without a wife. Amy was everything those roles embodied— and he was twenty years too late to do a thing about it.

She turned, as if she knew he was there, and she looked directly at him. At the same time, Taylor turned, saw him and wiggled to get free of her mother's hold. Amy put her down, and the little girl in pink overalls and a yellow T-shirt, hesitated, then slowly came toward him.

"I'll write you a new check," Amy said as Taylor came to stand in front of Quint.

He stopped himself before he said, don't bother, and instead said, "Whatever you want to do."

Without a word she passed both him and Taylor, going back toward her office. He didn't turn to watch her go. He watched her little girl instead. A two-year-old. He remembered Mike at two, and wished he hadn't had to work, that he could have been there for every event, every advance that he'd made. Working mostly from home and occasionally using a nanny had kept him close physically, but that didn't mean he'd had the time to really enjoy things, to relish them. That was another way both he and Mike had been shortchanged by his stupidity in marrying the wrong woman.

Taylor was right in front of him, and he automatically dropped to his haunches in front of her. "So, how're you doing?"

She cocked her head to one side, and long, silky lashes fluttered slightly. "Got baby," she said, and he realized she had a doll in one hand. "Yike it?" she asked, holding it up to him.

He took the doll and fingered its slightly damp dress. "Yeah, I like it," he said, "but she's not as pretty as you are."

Taylor studied him with huge brown eyes, then grabbed the doll back from him, hugging it to her. "Tay's baby."

"Yep, it's yours."

He didn't hear Amy come back, but he felt her by him and he slowly stood. She was within a few feet of him, holding out another check. "Here you go. I'll try to get one to you every week or so."

He hated this. He didn't want her money. He wanted her. That stopped him dead. He took the check, folded it in half and pushed it into his pocket, but he never looked away from Amy as she crouched by Taylor, brushing at her hair.

"Sweetie, go and get your coat and we'll go home, okay?"

"Huh," Taylor said with an emphatic nod, then toddled off toward Amy's office.

Amy stood and faced him. "It's late," she said.

"Yes, it is." He exhaled. "You know when I told you before that I don't play games?"

She shook her head. "It's late. I'm leaving. And you've probably got a...an appointment."

"As a matter of fact, I don't. But I do have to say something."

He could quite literally see her bracing herself, stiffening slightly, one hand reaching out to touch the wall close to her right side. "I don't suppose I can get you not to say anything, can I?"

"No."

"Then I'll say it for you. That was a horrible mistake in there, and it won't happen again."

He watched her closely. "Lady, what are you, a mind reader?"

She shrugged, but it ended with a slight shudder. "No, just telling the truth."

He'd meant to say he was too old, and she was too young, and she had a little child, and he was past that.

But instead he found himself saying, "It wasn't horrible."

She waved her hands as if to ward off his words. "Okay, but it was wrong."

"Absolutely. It was wrong. I don't date, you don't date. I'm way past being around kids. You're just starting out with them."

"This isn't a joke," she muttered.

He wished it was, but she was right, it wasn't funny. "Damn straight it's not a joke. And just because I'm single and you're single, doesn't mean we're on the same page." He touched her chin with the tip of his forefinger and felt her tense. "And that's the real shame here." He looked at her lips, softly parted and murmured, "A damn shame."

He felt something hit his leg and looked down at Taylor hitting him with a rubber hammer on the thigh. "Bang, bang, bang!"

Amy turned away from their contact, and Quint knew that whatever had barely started tonight was well over and rightfully so. "Okay, I'm leaving," he said to the little girl and was rewarded by a bright smile. His leaving made her happy. He just wished it made him happy.

He looked back at Amy and knew he couldn't just leave with bad feelings between them. "Listen, can we start over? No rats? No dead gingerbread family…and none of this? Can we just be friends?" That appealed to him on so many levels, just to talk to her, to look at her, to hear her voice. "Can we do that?"

She hesitated and oddly, he felt as if he couldn't breathe until she finally nodded. "Okay."

He held out his hand to her. "I'm Quint Gallagher. I work here."

That brought a hint of a smile, and he loved it. "Amy Blake."

The minute she put her hand in his, the minute he felt the fine bones and the heat in her, he knew he was a total liar and a sham. Damn it, he wanted to be friends, but there was more, so much more. "Good to meet you," he murmured.

"Yes," she breathed, then the contact was gone.

He forced a smile of his own. "Okay, I'm leaving. Maybe we'll run into each other and...be friendly?"

Her smile was bigger now, but he hated that bit of relief he saw behind it. "Yes, of course. You're welcome down here anytime."

"Thank you." He ruffled Taylor's silky hair, bent down and said, "Remind me to never get you a real hammer. Bye bye."

She looked up at him and frowned. "Bye bye."

He glanced at Amy. "Good night," he murmured and headed toward the door. It seemed to him that he was always walking away from her. A man not used to walking away from anything, was making a habit out of it with this woman.

AMY WATCHED Quint go and finally gave in to the need to hug herself tightly, as if that could stop this sense of fragmentation that had happened the minute the kiss had stopped.

Then Taylor toddled after him, and it was all she could do not to yell at her to stop. Quint must have heard her coming after him because he turned around.

She watched the tiny child and the tall, lean man facing each other. Amy had a flash of what never had been for either of them. Rob and Taylor. It never had been. And in that moment, the sorrow over what could have been and never would be, hit her hard. She watched her daughter, so small and vulnerable, then Quint hunkered down to her level.

"You go back to mommy, Taylor, okay?" He looked at Amy over Taylor's head, but was still talking to the child. "I have to leave."

Amy couldn't move. She felt immobilized by something beyond the grief, something she couldn't understand. Then Quint urged Taylor toward Amy. Oddly, Taylor resisted for a minute, then Quint said, "Go and find baby."

With that, Taylor took off, running back toward Amy while Quint straightened up. He looked at her from across the room, then turned and was gone.

Taylor found her baby and plunked down on her bottom, sidetracked with taking the doll's clothes off. And Amy leaned back against the wall. Slowly, she sank down to sit on the carpeting, using the wall behind her for support, unnerved to be trembling. She closed her eyes tightly to stop the burning, then took a breath to try and ease the pain that came from nowhere to engulf her. Damn it, she'd grieved, really grieved, and she'd accepted being alone with Taylor. And she hated Quint for being there, for reminding her of that pain.

She had a life, a good life with Taylor. Not what she'd planned, but it was more than just existing or marking time, the way Jenn had suggested. She tried to breathe and calm her heart. She tried to let the pain go. And she tried not to remember what she'd lost. It was okay. It was part of grieving, to feel okay, then have the pain hit. She knew that. It had happened so much before, but it had been lessening. Until now.

She willed up the image of Rob, solid and blond, tanned in the summer, with the grayest eyes. An image she'd called up so many times to help her remember. But it only made things worse this time. She couldn't quite see his face. She couldn't quite make him out. She couldn't claim that comfort the way she always had in the past.

She felt a real fear in her. A fear of forgetting. She scrambled to her feet and hurried back to the office. She went inside, crossed to the desk and found what she needed. A photo of Rob she kept on the desk, but it had been hidden behind stacks of papers and a box of labels. She pulled it out and stared at it, at his smile that crinkled his eyes as they narrowed in the brightness of the sun. Hair that refused to be tamed, worn a bit longer than fashion dictated, and the shirt, the Super Dude T-shirt. A moment frozen in time, a year before he was gone forever.

She hugged the picture to her, fighting the tears, and forced herself to put the picture back on the desk. She made herself pick up her purse, took a swipe at her eyes, then left the room. She could be friends with Quint. She could do that. Taylor spotted her and ran for her, falling into her open arms. "Time to go home, baby, just you and me."

"Get candy?"

"Sure, we'll get something on the way home," she said.

Taylor bounced in her arms as she locked up and headed toward the back exit for the parking garage. She stepped out into the cavernous area, where there were only a few cars due to the holidays. Matt's car was still there, a service truck off to one side, a midnight-blue SUV that was still so new it had dealer plates on it, and close to the door, her car, an old blue compact.

She turned, locked the security door, then headed for her car. She stopped, thinking she saw something moving near one of the thick pillars, but there was no one there. "Hello?" she called, her voice echoing in the garage. But there was no response.

She headed for her car, got Taylor in her car seat in the back, then slipped in behind the wheel. A friend. Yes, that would be good. She'd be running into Quint at LynTech from time to time, and better to be friends than to dread spotting him. Friends.

Chapter Seven

December 30

Quint turned from the rain that had been drenching the city all day and flipped off the lights in his office. He strode through the dimness of the reception area into the hallway. He wasn't going down to the lobby tonight. He'd called down to Walt moments ago to let him know he was on his way out, but he'd take the executive elevator instead of the main elevators. He didn't want to see Amy.

He went past the elevators and headed through Zane Holden's private offices to the executive elevator. He'd come in at seven, but Amy had been here before him, her name written in precise script just above his in the check-in book.

It was then that he'd looked up and seen her, carrying Taylor. As if she'd known he was there, she'd turned, nodded slightly to him, and Taylor had spotted him. The little girl had smiled hugely and waved, bouncing in her mother's arms, reminding him so much of Mike that it had almost hurt. A trusting child, sweet, happy. But Amy hadn't turned again, just gone into the center with her daughter and closed the door.

What a fool he'd been to think they could be friends, that he wouldn't have any reaction to seeing her, or that that reaction wouldn't intensify with each encounter. He was old enough and smart enough to know that the best way to counteract that very thing was to avoid her. So he went down the back way, took the elevator directly to the parking garage and stepped out into the almost empty cement structure.

He headed for his car, pressed the security button on his key, heard the click of the locks, saw the interior lights come on, and was reaching for the door when he was stopped dead in his tracks. There was a cry, sudden and piercing, echoing in the cavernous space around him. It took him a moment even to figure out where it was coming from, and in the next second he recognized it as a baby's cry.

He scanned the area by the day-care center security entrance, the source of the sound. There was no baby, but oddly, there was a rock on the single step going to the security door, a rock with something white under it. Then he saw the box, a plain cardboard container with no top on the far side of the step. The box was moving as the cries increased.

He tossed his briefcase in the car, then hurried over to the box. He crouched down, shocked to see a baby, little more than a newborn, swaddled in a blue blanket, in the box. With just the palest of fuzz on its head, its face contorted with misery, eyes scrunched tightly shut, and skin brightly flushed, the baby cried at the top of its lungs. A pacifier was on its chest, partly tangled in the blanket.

Quint acted out of twenty-year-old instincts, reaching for the baby and getting the pacifier, too. As he stood up, he cradled the child in his arm, offered the pacifier and was relieved to feel a tug on the soother immediately. The cries stopped and Quint looked down into eyes that might turn out to be blue, with long lashes spiked by tears, and he felt the baby shudder as it cuddled into his hold.

He looked around the garage, but there was no one there. And the idea that anyone in the center put the child out here was ludicrous. He turned, tried the door to the center, but it was locked. Making a fist, he hammered on the door, and within a few minutes, the door opened and Amy was there. Amy, in jeans and a loose white shirt with her feet bare. Her hair, in two braids, was skimmed back from her makeup-free face.

"What are you—" Her words were cut off as her eyes widened on the baby in his arms. "That's a baby," she said.

"It looks that way," he muttered, moving to go past her into the center. She stood back, letting him pass, then she was on his heels as he went down the hallway and into the main room.

"Quint?" she said, stopping by him, staring at the baby who was remarkably quiet now. "Who…where did you get a baby?"

He stopped by the tree. "Outside your door."

"What?" she whispered, ignoring Taylor who had appeared to hug her mom's leg.

"In a box outside your door. I was leaving and

heard it crying.'' He looked at Amy, but she was intent on the baby, reaching to brush its silky blond hair, what there was of it, and the pacifier bobbed up and down in its mouth. ''It was in a cardboard box screaming its head off.''

''Let me,'' she said, easing the baby out of his arms, then cuddling it to her. ''Before he spits up on your suit.''

He frowned at her. ''I wasn't worried about the suit,'' he said.

She ignored that as she cradled the baby to her. ''I don't understand,'' she whispered, brushing the tip of her finger on the baby's tiny hand.

''That makes two of us.'' God, she was meant to be a mother. The gentleness in her, the caring, was almost tangible at that moment. She was perfect with children around her, holding them, cradling them, loving them. ''Stay here with it and I'll go and look around.''

''Sure,'' she said, crouching to let Taylor see the baby in her arms. ''It's a baby, sweetie. And maybe he's a boy, with a blue blanket. That's his bow.'' She touched the pacifier as she spoke softly to her daughter. ''That's what you used to have, but now Taylor's a big girl and you don't need a bow.''

He left the three of them and headed back out into the garage. The box was there and the rock, but no human being. He glanced down at the rock, saw that there was a piece of paper under it and picked it up, then reached for the box. He brought the paper and box back into the center where he found Amy sitting on the floor now, cuddling the baby and smiling at Taylor.

He put the box down by Amy who had Taylor halfway on her lap and the baby on her shoulder, patting its back. "Did you find anyone?"

"No. Just the box and this paper." She looked up at him, then at the paper as he spoke. "It was under a rock by the door, sort of guaranteed that you'd trip over it, or at least see it, and stop, then find the baby."

He hunkered down by the three of them as he unfolded the paper and found words, not in writing, but in a childish rounded printing, with childish misspellings for common words.

His name is Travis. I can not keep him. Pleez take care of him and make sure he is happy and safe. He is not sick and he sleeps good and he likes muzik and his binky. His birthday is December 1 and there is food in the box. Thanx.

Quint sank down beside Amy with his back against the wall and held the note so she could read it for herself. "A teenager who thought a baby would be like having a doll?"

She read and reread the note, then leaned back with a sigh. "Looks that way."

"So, he's no doll and she dumps him?"

"She didn't just dump him," she said, smoothing her hand on his tiny back as Taylor hovered at her shoulder, staring at the tiny face.

"Amy, he was in a box, like some puppy being given away, and left all alone in a garage that was pretty much deserted. That's being dumped to my way of thinking.''

She met his gaze. ''I know it looks bad, but whoever left him there loved him in their own way. They wanted him to be happy and safe and even told us what he liked and when his birthday is.'' She closed her eyes for a fleeting moment. ''Maybe a teenager did this, but whoever it was was overwhelmed and probably didn't see anything else they could do. They love him, no matter what.''

''They love him? That doesn't compute.''

Her eyes opened and met his again, her expression tight and tense. ''They didn't leave him in a garbage can, or under a bush in the cold and rain, and they didn't abuse him. He looks healthy and well fed and cared for. They didn't do the right thing, and that might not be your idea of caring, but the world can be overwhelming with a child. And it sure could be overwhelming if you're just a child yourself.'' She barely intercepted Taylor's attempt to take the baby's pacifier. ''No, Tay-Tay, that's not yours.'' She shifted the baby, drawing her knees up and lying him back against her legs. ''Isn't he just about the sweetest thing you ever saw?''

He glanced at the face, a cherubic face at ease now, with eyes closed and the pacifier bouncing up and down. ''He didn't deserve to be dumped like that.''

''No, he didn't,'' she said, ''but he's safe. He'll be okay.''

''Thank God he was found. I'll call the police,'' he said, reaching into his inside jacket pocket for his cell phone, but Amy caught him by his arm, stopping him.

"No, don't."

He looked down at her hand on his arm, then at her, "We need to contact someone in authority to take care of this."

"No, no we don't," she said, slowly letting go, but the intensity in her expression didn't ease. "What's in his box?" she asked, looking past him at the cardboard box. "He's damp. Maybe there's diapers in it."

He hesitated, then figuring that another few minutes wouldn't matter, he reached for the box and looked inside it. There was a package at one end wrapped in another blue receiving blanket. He took it out, laid it on the floor and unwrapped it. "Some diapers, a bottle, a couple of cans of formula, an extra pacifier." He itemized the meager bundle for her. "A nightgown, a cassette tape." He lifted the tape and read, "Baby songs, everything from 'Rock-a-bye Baby' to 'Itsy-Bitsy Spider.'" He put the tape back with the rest of the supplies. "That's it. Now, let's get the authorities to come out and—"

"We can't do that."

"Why not?" He glanced at his watch and was surprised to see that it was almost eight o'clock. "It's getting late and he's been abandoned."

"She'll be back for him," she murmured as she gathered him close to her again.

"I doubt it," he said, wrapping up the supplies and putting them back in the box.

"She will be. I know it, and if we call the police, they'll call in Child Protective Services, and it's out of our hands...and out of the mother's hands."

"Then she can talk to the police or Child Protective Services, or whatever."

She shook her head. "No, if we call in the police or get the social service system involved, it will only make things worse. And it's the holidays, and he'll be lost in the system until well after New Year's. And God knows where he'll be kept until they figure out what to do." She shook her head again. "I can't do that."

"You have to."

"No, I don't have to," she said, casting him a narrowed look. "I won't."

"What's your option, sitting here and waiting for her to come back, then you're going to hand a baby back over to a parent who dumped him like that?"

"No, I'll try to help, to get her help. There's all sorts of agencies that can help."

"Like Child Protection Services?"

"No, no," she muttered as the baby began to squirm in her arms. "He's hungry and he's probably wet. While we're debating this, could you make up some formula in the kitchen, and I'll change him? Or you can change him, and I'll mix the formula?"

She wasn't going to give in easily, he knew that. "I'll take the formula. I've done that often enough. I'll leave the diapers for you. Then once he's fed and dry, we'll get help. Agreed?"

"Give me the extra blanket, please."

He held it out to her.

"Put it on the floor," she said.

He laid out the blanket, then she put the baby on

it and started to change his diaper. "We'll get help, right?" he asked again.

She hesitated, then tugged at the tapes on the baby's disposable diaper. "We'll talk," she murmured.

"No, we'll—"

The baby suddenly let out a cry, and Amy caught the pacifier when it shot out of his mouth before Taylor could make a grab for it. She gave it back to the baby, then looked at Quint. "Give me a clean diaper?"

He grabbed one, handed it to her, and felt as if they were speaking two different languages. She understood, but she wasn't giving the answers she should have been giving. "Amy, there isn't anything to discuss on this."

She already had the baby's diaper off, a diaper that was only wet, and was putting on the clean diaper. "Are you going to get that formula for him?"

He exhaled, then got to his feet, grabbed the can of formula and a bottle and started for the kitchen. Unexpectedly, Taylor toddled along with him. "There's cookies in there, and she can have one, but that's it, just one, or she'll never sleep tonight," Amy called after them.

"Sure, sure," he called over his shoulder, then looked down at the little girl half running to keep up with him. "You can have as many as you want," he said in a low voice as he reached the kitchen door.

Amy looked up as Taylor and Quint disappeared into the kitchen, the door swinging shut behind them. She'd been shocked to see Quint at the back door with the baby cradled in his arms. He'd looked so natural with the blue blanket against the expensive charcoal-gray business suit and a perplexed look on his face. If she hadn't been so shocked herself, she would have laughed. Another expensive suit in jeopardy? But any humor died when she remembered the situation.

She picked the baby back up and cuddled him to her. He was the sort of baby that seemed to melt into you, the way Taylor had when she was tiny. She knew he was used to being loved. And he'd be so easy to love.

The baby stirred in her arms, then snuggled so trustingly into her neck. With a sigh, he settled against her and she knew right then that she wasn't going to let him be hurt, not if she had any say in it at all. And calling the police was the one thing she wouldn't let Quint do, no matter what.

"Mama," Taylor called, coming out of the kitchen before Quint. She ran for her mother, a cookie in her hand, and Amy barely stopped her from throwing herself into her arms and against the baby.

"Whoa, there, honey," Amy said, circling Taylor with her free arm and drawing her onto her lap. Looking over her daughter's head, she saw Quint standing over them with the bottle in his hand.

"He's asleep?" he asked.

"Seems so. I guess the wetness was enough to make him fuss."

"Give baba," Taylor said, reaching up for the baby's bottle.

Quint dropped to his haunches. "No way. This bottle is a very special bottle." Taylor looked at the man with huge eyes, apparently fascinated by his low, slightly rough voice. "It's a boy's bottle. See, the top is blue. And your bottle is a girl's bottle. Pink. Girls' things are always pink."

Taylor frowned at the man, then went closer to him. "Baba, blue boy?" she said with all seriousness.

"You got it," he said with a smile for her. "Very smart. Very good girl."

"I was wrong. You don't hate kids. You're good with them," she said.

He reached for the doll Taylor had discarded earlier and gave it to her. "Here's your baby. She wants her bottle, I bet."

"Huh," Taylor said with a shake of her head. "Baby's baba." With that she took off toward Amy's office.

Then Quint was looking at her. "It won't work."

"What?"

"Buttering me up, saying how good I am with kids. We have to call the police."

"But you *are* good with kids," Amy said, embarrassed that he'd seen through her so easily.

"Just old habits, twenty-year-old habits." He came closer and sank down on the floor in front of her. "Now, quit trying to sidetrack this discussion. Let's get back to this child and what to do."

"You know, you don't have to worry about him," she said quickly, not at all sure what she was going to do, but words came to her in a rush. "You turned him over to me, and I'm the head of this place right now, so to speak, so you're off the hook. You can leave and know that you did a good deed."

He frowned, drawing his eyebrows together over his hazel eyes. "Whoa, hold up, how do you figure that I'm off the hook? I found him out there."

"And, as I pointed out, you brought him in here and gave him to the person in charge. Thank you, and I'll take care of it from here on out."

He stared at her hard, then leaned toward her. "Define *take care of it* for me."

She patted the little guy's back, felt him sigh and settle even more. "I'll do the right thing."

"The right thing is to call the police."

"That's your right thing, not mine. I want to give the mother a chance to come to her senses, to have a bit of quiet time and figure out what she wants to do for him and for herself."

"By giving her time, what are we talking about?"

"I don't know. An hour, or a day."

"And if she doesn't 'come to her senses,' then what?"

"Then I'll do what I need to do."

"Which is?"

She sighed. "Okay, okay, I'll call the proper authorities. Is that what you wanted to hear?"

"I wish you meant it," he murmured, sitting back a bit.

"I give you my word. If she doesn't show up soon, I'll call the authorities and he'll be fine."

"So, you're going to wait here all night?"

"No, of course not. I'll leave a note on the door, or under that rock. I'll give her my phone number, and she can call, and it'll be okay."

"And in the meantime?"

"I'll take him home with me and take care of him and wait."

He hesitated, then moved back and was on his feet, towering over her. "Just like that?"

"I'll manage," she said with a bit more bravado than she actually felt. "I could use a favor, though."

"Which would be?"

"Could you hold him and keep an eye on Taylor while I try to find a car seat, some more diapers and things that I'll need for him?"

He crouched down again, coming to eye level with her but not touching her. "I can't talk you out of this, can I?"

"No, you can't."

"I didn't think so," he murmured as Taylor came running back. Her doll was gone, but she had a stuffed elephant in her arms and she was babbling happily. "Okay, get what you need. But is there a chair in this place to sit on?"

"I've got a rocking chair in the room past my office, the Quiet Room. How about that?"

"Great, perfect," he said. "Just give me the kid and point me in the direction of the chair."

She let Quint take Travis, then led the way to the Quiet Room. Lindsey, the director and original creative force behind the center, had decided the old conference room would make a perfect room for quiet time, for naps and a place apart if a child was sick. It was a real improvement over the cramped "nap room" in the old center on the sixth floor. Soon they'd have a few changing tables, sleeping mats and cribs in here. But right now, with the rush to get in the new location, there was a rocking chair that had seen better times, and a couple of beanbag chairs set against pale-blue walls and deeper blue carpeting. It was supposed to give off an aura of peace and quietness. It did. And when it was completed, it would be wonderful.

But with Quint in there, the idea of peace was lost on Amy. She motioned to the rocking chair, and Quint sank down into it. Before Quint could settle, Taylor was by him, half climbing up his leg, the elephant now on the floor and her tiny hands crushing the material of his pant leg.

"Taylor, no. Leave Mr. Gallagher alone. Play with your elephant," she said, and reached for it, but Taylor ignored it, choosing to make a grab for Travis's pacifier. "No, no," she said.

"Let her be. I can fend her off. Just get your things," Quint said as he shifted the baby to his shoulder. "Please, just do it."

She hesitated, then said, "You aren't going to call the police, are you? I mean, you've got a cell phone, I'm sure, and if I leave, I'm not going to get some unpleasant surprise in ten minutes, am I?"

Quint stared at her long and hard, without blinking, and Amy had the thought that maybe she hadn't really said the question out loud, that she'd just stressed over the "what if's" and thought she'd said it. Or maybe he hadn't heard her, although that seemed an even more remote possibility, since they weren't more than two feet apart.

"The bottle?" he said, holding out a free hand toward her.

She'd forgotten she was even holding it. Quickly, she passed it to him, and was unnerved when their fingers brushed and she almost dropped the bottle. It was as if she'd been shocked by electricity, a spark of energy shooting through her hand and arm. Just one more thing she couldn't understand and wouldn't try to understand. He had the bottle safely, his strong hand closing around it, and he never looked away from her.

Nerves tightened in her neck and shoulders, and she finally blurted out, "Did you hear me?"

"Of course."

"And?"

He shifted, managing to hold the bottle with the same hand that was supporting Travis, then he reached inside his jacket. He took out his cell phone and held it out to her. "Here."

She didn't take it. "What are you doing?"

"Since you don't trust me, I'm making this easy for you." He paused, then asked in a low voice, "Do you trust me?"

She stared at him, at his intense hazel eyes, the set of his mouth under the mustache, and she simply turned without touching the phone. Yes, she trusted him and that shook her more than anything else that had happened with the man since they had met.

Chapter Eight

By the time Amy came back into the room, Quint had Taylor on one side and Travis on the other. Taylor was holding the baby's bottle with Quint's help while Travis drank the formula. He shifted a bit so she wouldn't see the spots of formula on his jacket lapel and said, "Just in time. I'm way too old for this."

"You look like you can handle it," she said, crossing to the three of them. She looked flushed and rushed, and beautiful. "I think I've got everything under control." She took the baby while she spoke, then, hitching the infant into the crook of one arm, she reached for Taylor with her free hand. "Come on, love, it's time to go home."

The little girl hugged her arms around Quint's arm, gluing herself to him. "No." Amy acted as if the child had said, "Isn't the weather lovely?" She smiled, reached down, and before the child knew what her mother was up to, Amy swept her up and away from Quint. The woman was amazing. Even with a newborn in one arm, she managed to tug Taylor up and onto her hip. "No," Taylor said again, pushing at Amy's shoulder.

"Oh, yes," Amy said. "It's late, and it's time to go home." Taylor looked at Quint and for a flashing second, he saw her mother in her, that stubborn lift of her little chin, the way her eyes narrowed. Then the child sagged against her mother, nestling into Amy's free shoulder.

He didn't realize that Amy was staring at him until he heard her mutter, "Oh, shoot." She was looking at his jacket, at the stains from the formula that were even more obvious now that he'd stood up. "I can't believe…" She bit her lip. "I'm sorry."

"Let's not go down that road again," Quint said. "It's not important, and I'm not going to argue about it."

She looked at him. "Easy for you to say," she said.

"No, what isn't easy is you handling the two of them. Give me the baby, and you take Taylor. I'll help you get them into the car."

He saw her hesitate, knew that she was going to argue that she could manage, but he didn't give her a chance. Instead, he took Travis, then said, "Tell me what to do, and I'll do it."

At least she was smart enough to let go, to let him do what he could for her. Without a word she turned and moved down the hall to her office. "I put everything by the back door, and all I need to get is my purse and jacket and a sweater for Taylor." She sat the little girl on her desk and tugged a pink sweater on Taylor. Then she put on a denim jacket, got her purse and was carrying Taylor again.

"I put a blanket by the door for the baby, and there's the car seat and a diaper bag I packed."

"You're like a Boy Scout, always prepared," he said.

"That's the benefit of working at a day-care center. We're ready for anything here. Thank goodness I just moved a lot of supplies down here." They got to the back security door and she pointed to the car seat. "You can put him in that, then carry the whole thing out."

Quint crouched, settled Travis in the seat, snapped the safety harness in place, then stood, holding the seat by its handle. "Okay, we'll get them out, then I'll come back for the rest."

She opened the door and they went out into the parking garage, heading toward an old blue compact car that Quint doubted would start, let alone be drive-able. There was already a car seat in the back, and Amy slipped Taylor into it, then let Quint put the infant seat in next to Taylor. "Face it backwards," she said, and he shifted it around, then fastened it with the seat belt.

"Hello there!" Quint turned to see Walt coming toward them. "I was looking all over for you, Mr. Gallagher."

Quint had the oddest feeling that he was going to give him another envelope with a check in it. But he was wrong. The man had his briefcase. "I found this out here in your car with the door wide open and grabbed it in case someone tried to steal it. I went upstairs to find you. Good thing I came back down to check out here again." He held out the briefcase to Quint.

"Thanks," Quint said as he took it.

Then the guard looked at Amy and the kids. "You got an extra one on board tonight?"

"Yes, I do," she said.

"Well, I thought you'd already gone and left the car. Maybe took a cab or something."

"Why would I take a cab?"

"This weather," he said. "There's a huge power outage in your neck of the woods, and it's raining like a—" He shrugged as he obviously rethought his expressive language. "You know, cats and dogs. If it was hurricane season, I'd think it was a hurricane for sure."

Quint had forgotten about the rain, but then again, when he'd last looked, it was just a steady rain. "It's that bad?"

"It's taken out some power grids and they won't be up until tomorrow, maybe longer. Just heard the warning on the radio. They were saying this grid's apt to be shut down so they can reroute to more important areas. Just what I need, a night in the dark with nothing working."

"You don't have emergency generators?"

"Oh, yeah, sure, but they're just for simple stuff, like security lights and one elevator. That's about it." He turned to Amy. "You drive careful out there, what with those kids and all."

With that the man nodded, then left, heading back to the security doors. As they clanged shut after him, Amy turned to Quint and said, "Well, shoot, I wish I knew if I had electricity at home."

"You've got an answering machine. Call home. If it comes on, you know you've got power."

She looked at him as if he'd just discovered the secret to life. "Fantastic idea," she said.

He took out his cell phone, and held it out to her. "Be my guest."

While she called, he looked back at her car, then saw the tires. Not exactly bald, but with little tread left. He knew that he wasn't going to let her go anywhere in bad weather with those tires. "Nothing," she said, drawing his attention back to her. "It just rings and rings."

"Chances are you're in the dark there."

"I can't take a baby and Taylor there with no electricity. And staying here…" She shrugged, a fluttery movement of her slender shoulders, and that vulnerability was exposed again. And it had the same effect on him. That need to protect and help. Damn it, he could have been a cop and been more blasé about "protecting and helping" someone, especially her. "I've got the supplies, but if the center loses electricity, too…"

"How about a family member or a friend?"

"Oh, Jenn, yeah, that's a great idea." He could get used to her approval if he let himself enjoy it for more than a fleeting moment. She dialed again, then listened, and the smile faded as she shut the phone off. "I forgot. She's gone for New Year's, with friends."

"Anyone else?"

She shook her head. "No, no one."

"Parents live out of state?"

"They're gone."

"Your husband's family?"

"Jenn's all he has…had…and she's about all we have."

He jumped in again. "Okay, no family, and you can't stay here. How about a hotel?"

She hesitated and he knew it was the money. And he knew that he couldn't offer to pay. So he compromised. "I have a huge suite, two bedrooms, lots of space, and you can bunk there with the children until the storm lets up."

Those dark eyes turned to him, but this time they looked narrowed, as if she couldn't quite look at his suggestion. "A suite? An expensive suite?"

"A very expensive suite, with balconies off both bedrooms and a terrace off the living area."

That made her shake her head sharply. "Oh, no. Thanks, but no."

"If it's the money, just—"

"No, it's not the money, but a terrace and balconies? Do you have any idea how fast a child can get loose and how deadly a balcony could be to a two-year-old?"

Of course he did, and he wished he'd thought of it first. "Okay, then if the money's not the issue, let me pay for a room for the three of you at the hotel? Just for one night?"

"I can pay," she said quickly. "And, yes, that would be doable."

He took his phone back, a bit jolted by the heat of her body caught in the plastic case when he started to dial the hotel. Even the earpiece against his ear felt warm, and he had to concentrate when the phone was answered. It took all of two minutes to find out from the desk that they were booked, what with the holiday and the weather. He hung up, told Amy and asked, "Another hotel?"

"I think they'll all be full," she murmured. "Maybe I should just stay here and take my chances, or maybe try to get home and hope it isn't so bad there."

"You aren't going anywhere in that car," he said.

"Excuse me?"

That chin was up, that subtle challenge to his statement. "Your tires, you'll hydroplane the first time you try to brake for anything. It's too dangerous."

Travis started to cry and within a second, Taylor was joining in, both of them tired and cranky now. "Okay, you've got a point. I'll stay here."

"And if the electricity goes, then what?"

She turned from him, stooped down and reached in the car to put the pacifier back in Travis's mouth. Then she reached into the front seat, found a hard pretzel and gave it to Taylor. Both kids were quiet in a matter of a minute. A miracle, and Amy acted as if it was normal. She had no idea how un-normal it was to him to be around a woman who cared about the kids and wasn't annoyed that they were interrupting her life.

"I'll deal with it," she said, and he had no doubt she would, that she'd done that very thing since her husband died. And he wasn't going to let her do it this time, not alone, not on a night like this.

"Tell you what, I know of a place that would be perfect for the kids, lots of space, food, heat and electricity. And it's empty. I can drive you there now."

"Where?"

"North of here, on higher ground, around thirty miles. And we'll have lights, heat, food. How about it?"

"I can't ask you to take me all the way out there. I can just wait here. Maybe this storm will pass soon."

"And maybe it won't, and you're taking on a newborn and trying to deal with a two-year-old? I can't go and leave you all here." He made himself smile to take any admonition out of his words. "Either I stay here with you all and rough it in there, or you agree to the smart thing and take me up on my offer. When the storm's over or your electricity is back on, we can go our separate ways."

Quint looked right at her, waiting, hoping she'd take him up on the offer, but not at all sure she'd let herself depend on anyone for anything. Her response wasn't an acceptance, rather a compromise. "Okay, I'll take the ride. I don't want to endanger the kids. But I want you to drive me to my place, and if there's electricity, we'll stay there."

"And if it's dark?"

She shrugged. "We'll go to the other place, but it isn't fancy and rich and expensive, is it? It's not a place that Taylor can take apart and I'll end up owing the owner a million or two?"

He could really laugh at that, and did. The sound echoed in the garage, and Amy was almost smiling. "God, no, it's not a palace or a mansion. Just shelter that can accommodate two kids. It's that or the No

Tell Motel and that's hardly a place for you or two kids.''

Taylor yelled and a soggy pretzel came shooting out of the open car door. Amy picked it up between her forefinger and thumb, grimaced at it and looked at Quint. She shivered slightly, and he could see that she was gradually being overwhelmed, but she'd never admit to it. "Okay, if my place is dark, I'll go with you.''

He never felt this thankful for agreement with business dealings, not even when he completed a successful assignment. The woman had him grateful for letting her use him. He didn't stop to think how out of kilter that was, and instead he found himself staying with the kids while Amy went back into the center and came out with even more things than she had stacked at the back door. "Supplies," she said and he loaded them into his car, then went back to get the kids.

Moments later, he was sitting behind the wheel of his SUV, revving the engine, with two crying kids in car seats in the back. Amy tossed the diaper bag in the passenger door, landing it on the console, but she didn't get in. "What's your cell phone number?" she asked over the cries.

He gave her the number, watched her write it on a scrap of paper, then she called over her shoulder, "Be right back," and hurried toward the door to the center.

He could see her in the side mirror stopping at the door, then crouching, doing something, before going back inside. Moments later she was running to his car. She got in, carrying Charlie in his cage.

"Couldn't leave him if things go bad," she said, twisting to put the cage on the floor in the back. She reached behind the seat to touch Taylor on the foot, smile at her, then softly pat Travis on his leg. As if her touch was magic, both children quieted and she looked at him. "Okay, we're ready."

He adjusted the heater, then started for the ramp that went to the security gates. "What was that all about with the cell phone number?" he asked as Amy twisted in the seat to rub Taylor's foot, a connection that kept the child calm.

"I left a note for Travis's mom, gave her my phone number and your cell phone number. So, if she calls you, help her get in touch with me, okay?"

Talk about optimistic, he thought, but just nodded. "Of course," he said, then looked ahead through the security gate. From this level, he could see the rain sheeting down, and water rushing down the street as if it were a roiling creek. "Whoa," he muttered.

He sensed Amy move, sitting forward to look out the windshield, then the gate went up and he pulled onto the street into a night torn by the storm. He headed toward the section of the city where Amy lived, driving at a snail's pace and uneasy about the traffic lights that had been reduced to flashing red lights only.

All of the lights around them were mere smears in the darkness, and the few cars that were on the streets were doing what he was doing—staying as close to the middle of the street as possible to avoid the mini rivers developing near the curbs. When he got to a major intersection, he realized how bad it was when he spotted two cars stalled ahead of him, water rushing up to the bottoms of the doors and submerging part of the front end of another car stalled near the curb.

He negotiated around them, thankful for the added height and surefootedness of the SUV, a car he'd leased simply because it had been available. Now he was glad that they sat higher than the other cars, and that the added weight helped to resist the driving wind to stay steady on the flooded streets.

Suddenly, lights flashed, then one side of the street went completely dark. Even the glow of the Christmas decorations had disappeared, swallowed up by the rain and darkness.

"Did you see that?" Amy asked, the sound of her voice startling him slightly. He hadn't forgotten she was there—that would have been an impossibility—but he had been so intent on what he was doing that he'd forgotten to talk. "All the lights are out. I was thinking that we should just go back to LynTech, but the building might be dark now, too. This is just like a hurricane, at least with the wind and all, even if it's the wrong time of year for it."

"You know what they say—if it walks like a duck, and quacks like a duck and looks like a duck, it's probably a duck," he muttered as he negotiated their way through another flooded intersection.

"A duck's about the only thing that belongs out on a night like this," she said. "This is just crazy."

He looked at her, a quick glance, no more than a second, but he knew right then that the crazy thing was him being in the car with two kids, in this storm, with a woman he wished he'd met years ago so he could have loved her without any barriers.

That thought jolted him, and the car lurched when he overcorrected to the left. Amy gasped, and he steadied the car and himself as he stared straight ahead. Love. He'd thought for years that it was for a select few in this world, the lucky ones who stumbled on it and kept it. The others, like him, just heard about it and never had it. He never would, but it might have been within reach with this woman if things had been different.

Even Quint's car felt flimsy to Amy as it was battered by the wind and driving rain. Thankful both kids were quiet, she glanced back to see that they were both asleep. They were so trusting, so unaware of the wildness of the world outside the car. But she was aware of that wildness, and of the man right beside her. She turned, taking a quick look at Quint. He was intent on his driving, controlling the big car with an ease that she envied, the same way she envied his ability to deal with things.

If he hadn't offered this ride, she and the kids would be sitting in an intersection, stalled, being flooded out. And she cringed to think that she would have tried to make it to her place. "You know, maybe…maybe we really should just go back to LynTech?"

He slanted her a look that was shadowed and unreadable. "Not an option," he said before glancing in the rearview mirror then ahead at the road. "It's dark back there."

She twisted and saw he was right. There was no

light at all behind them, and only a few flickering lights ahead. Colored lights, flashing. Getting closer. "What's up there?" she asked, leaning forward to try and see ahead of them.

"Police," Quint said as they got closer to the lights and saw that they belonged to two squad cars angled to block anyone going into the next intersection. A dark hulk of a man holding a flashlight came toward their car as Quint slowed to a stop, then cracked his window.

Amy leaned to look around Quint and could only see a shadow outside, but the voice was strong. "Sorry, the streets are out this way. You can't go through."

"I'm trying to get to the Bower and Sage area."

"No way, not tonight. There's no power and the streets are flooded."

"Can I get out of the city if I go north to the old highway?"

"Should be able to in this car. Just turn right here and head on out, but maybe you want to find a hotel or motel and wait this out?"

"We'll head north and see how it goes."

"Whatever you do, drive carefully," the policeman said, then backed away and motioned with his light to the right of them.

Quint raised his window, then turned right onto the side street as Amy spoke up again. "This place where we're going, what is it?"

He adjusted the heater, asking, "Warm enough?"

"Fine. We're fine. What is this place?"

He exhaled, never taking his eyes off the road.

"It's an old, rambling ranch house on a bit of property, and it can't be hurt by kids. It's got heat, or at least enough wood for a good fire."

"How do you know there's electricity?"

"It usually has it when others don't, and there is a backup generator," he said as he reached in his pocket, took out the cell phone and handed it to her. "But call and find out for yourself." Then he repeated a phone number for her.

She put in the number, but didn't press Send immediately. "So, if I call, who's going to answer?"

"If there's electricity, the answering machine will pick up. If there's no electricity, no one will answer. No one's there."

"I don't understand. Why would we go there if no one's there, even if there is electricity?"

"Because we can," he murmured, driving onto the old highway and turning north so the wind was behind them now.

"What?"

"Because we can. Because it's there. Because I have a key."

"I thought you just got here and that you were at the hotel?"

"I did and I am, but I was born and raised here, and my folks still have their place out there."

"This is your parents' place?"

"You got it," he said. "I've lived through worse than this out there, and I know it's high, dry and warm. Everything I want right now." He flashed her a look. "How about you? What do you want right now?"

She wanted just to sit back and let him take her anywhere he wanted, and she wanted not to worry about where they were going or about a need in her just to let herself sink into the safeness that this man projected. "High, dry and warm sounds good to me," she said.

"Then we're heading to the right place. If there's electricity."

She hit the Send button, and it rang twice before an answering machine clicked on. A man's voice that sounded a lot like Quint's said, "It's your dime. Leave a message if you want." Then there was a long beep.

She hung up and said, "Nice message, but there's power."

"That's his idea of making it short and sweet. Sorry."

"So, it's their place, but they don't live there?"

"Yes, and no. They're in Florida for the holidays. They've been wanting me to live out there now that I'm back, but it's not close enough for the business."

Amy was uncomfortable with this. Going to his parents' house? Just going in with them gone? "Quint, I don't know about this."

"We're in too far to turn back. We should have just gone right to the police, let them take care of the baby and then gone to my place and nailed the windows shut, or gotten a room, even if it was at the No Tell Motel."

"There isn't a place called that," she muttered, hating the talk of the police.

"Sure there is. Not here, maybe, but somewhere there is."

"You've been there?"

He chuckled, a rough, warm sound in the car. "If I have, I don't remember. But, then again, there are many things in my misspent youth that I don't remember."

"Misspent youth or not, I can hardly see you at a place with pink lights and fur bedspreads in your expensive suits."

He laughed again. "Back then not only did I not wear suits, I probably couldn't have afforded one."

She sank back in the seat. "Oh, yes. I forgot, you were poor."

She hadn't meant to sound so sarcastic, but it came out that way. And it killed his laughter completely. "I never said that. I was never poor, but we didn't have it easy. And when Mike was little, it was rough. I was working twelve hours a day, and I tried to work out of my house, so I could be with Mike."

"What about your son's mother?"

"She wasn't there for him."

"She…she died?"

That did make him laugh, a bark of a sound that had little humor in it. "No, she just left. She walked out the door and never looked back." He cast her a slanting glance. "See, mothers do just leave."

She knew that, but she couldn't quite get her mind around a woman who could walk away from a child, a child that should be that woman's whole life. It made her shiver slightly and she hugged her arms around herself. "I know that, but…"

"But you think that they just come to their senses, and turn around and come back and beg for their babies?"

He made her sound so gullible and stupid. She hated it. "They…they do, some do."

"That hasn't been my experience," he said tightly.

"Are you an expert because you found one child outside the door to a day-care center?"

"No, but I know a bit about it. Mike's mother walked out and never looked back."

She waited for anger to come into his voice, to hear some bitterness, but there was none. He simply said the words. She looked at him, and all she could think of was—how could any woman who had been loved by this man just walk away and never look back?

Chapter Nine

Amy wanted to say she was sorry, to tell him that it was the woman's loss, but she couldn't. Something in her knew that the man wasn't looking for sympathy, just showing that people without hearts lived in this world. She knew that herself.

"She just left?"

"Decided she didn't want to be a mother or wife and walked out the door. She calls Mike every now and then. It's usually on his birthday."

"So, you raised him alone?" she asked.

"I had my folks, but they were here and I was there, all over the place, and I couldn't just dump Mike and see him whenever I could make it."

"Of course not."

"Oh, it wasn't just for Mike's sake. It was for mine. He's my family. I needed him around as much as he needed me, and I lucked out being able to do a job that paid well and do it mostly out of my home." He chuckled. "The kid could do flowcharts when he was four."

"He's in college now?"

"Just graduated and got his first position out in Los Angeles."

"That's good, isn't it?" she asked, not sure.

He chuckled. "Did I sound that ambiguous?"

"A bit."

"I am. It's hard seeing him grown and out there, even though I'm damn proud of him. We had some rough times, some body piercing I didn't like much, a tattoo that he's going to regret, but he turned out good."

"Then you should be thankful."

"Years down the road when Taylor walks in and tells you that she's leaving, that she's going to get pierced ears, nose, lip, whatever, and maybe a tattoo, you let me know how easy it is to smile and say, 'Take care,' and not flinch."

She sank back in the seat, an overwhelming storm almost forgotten because of the man driving her off to God-knew-where. His voice soothed and even if the subject matter was uneasy he wasn't. "Well, we'll skip the tattoo, and pierced ears are okay, but nothing else." She sighed, unable to think of a time when Taylor wouldn't be with her. "And I think girls are different."

"Maybe. I've never had one and won't now, so why don't you get in touch with me in twenty years and let me know how she does? We'll compare notes."

"Sure," she breathed, turning from Quint to the darkness of the night and storm surrounding them. There were no lights outside, just a flash now and then from lightning way off in the distance. "Some night, huh?"

"Not what I planned," he murmured.

"Oh, shoot." She'd done it again. "You had a…an appointment, didn't you?"

"No, I didn't. I had plans for a quiet night, reading and trying to figure out what to get Terrel and Lewis's daughter for the wedding. It's expected."

She'd been shocked at the announcement from B.J., the daughter of the founder of LynTech, Robert Lewis, and the artist they'd hired to help design the new center, the day after Christmas that she and Matt were getting married on New Year's Eve. "A quiet ceremony at the loft," B.J. had said, with just her father, the boy, Anthony, and Zane and Lindsey if they could get back from Aspen for it. "Maybe they'll have to cancel if this doesn't stop. Wait for nicer weather."

"They want to be married, and I've got a feeling they'll do it, come hell or high water. And the high water is a definite possibility."

"Love isn't always willing to wait."

"They sure blame a lot of craziness on love, don't they?" he asked.

She stared determinedly ahead into the stormy night. "I guess so, but don't you think when you're in love, it's not craziness, it's that need to be with the other person no matter what?"

He was silent for a long moment, so long that she finally looked away from the stormy night ahead of them to him. Even in the dim light, she could see the muscle in his jaw working, but she wasn't sure he'd heard her or if he was so intent on his driving that the talking was going to stop. Whatever it was, there was silence in the car for some time before he spoke, but it had nothing to do with love.

"Finally," he said, and she didn't understand until she felt the car slow as they turned off the highway to the right onto a rougher road. After a short distance through the storm and night, the headlights caught a blurred image of posts of some sort that Quint drove between. "We made it," Quint said as they drove onto an even narrower road.

A canopy of huge trees overhead gave a bit of shelter, but it was unnerving to see them being whipped by the wind as if they were little more than twigs. "How can you tell where you are?" Amy asked, not able to see anything beyond where the darkness was cut by the glow of the headlights.

"I've been here often enough," he said as they broke out into an opening and the wind hit them full force, making the huge car shudder as it kept going. "I learned to drive on this road."

A flash of lightning came from nowhere, cutting through the turbulent darkness and allowing Amy to catch a flashing glimpse of some buildings, long and low, ahead of them. Quint drove toward the buildings, then circled to the left, turned right and halted the car.

He let the car idle and turned to her, touching the back of her seat with one hand. "Sit tight. I'll go in the back way and get the garage door up."

"You can't go out in that," she said.

"We don't have a choice. I don't have an opener for the garage, and you sure can't take the kids out in this.'' Then he touched her, a light, reassuring tap on her shoulder before pulling his hand back and shrugging out of his jacket. He laid the jacket over the console, then looked at her and said, ''I'll be right back,'' and he turned and opened the door.

The car was suddenly filled with a gust of damp coldness, then the door slammed shut and Quint was gone. Taylor stirred, making soft sounds, and Amy reached behind her to touch her daughter's foot. But she looked ahead to try and see where Quint was going. She caught a glimpse of him running through the night and rain, cutting through the watery beams from the headlights, then she lost him. He was gone. The night was all that was outside, and she felt a jarring sense of abandonment, that bone-deep feeling of isolation.

''Mama?'' Taylor asked in a sleepy voice, and Amy took off her seat belt so she could turn around and get up on her knees to look into the back seat. Travis was still sleeping peacefully, the pacifier bouncing in his mouth as he sucked, and Taylor was stirring, her tiny hands stretching over her head.

''Hi there, baby,'' she murmured, taking her daughter's hand and smiling at her. She could never leave her. She never would. ''It's okay, Tay-bug, we're on an adventure with Mr. Gallagher.''

Taylor yawned, then pointed to the window. ''Go bye-bye?''

''We went bye-bye and now we're…at a new place. It's Mr. Gallagher's home…at least, his home when he was a little boy.''

There was a flash of light and Amy twisted to look

back through the windshield, seeing a blur of light through the night to her right. The garage door went slowly up, then Quint was running through the beams of the headlights, and the driver's door opened.

Quint was back in the car, with the scents of rain and night clinging to him and in the flash of interior light, Amy could see him for a fleeting moment. His hair was flattened to his head, dark and slick, and his shirt was soaking wet, clinging to his shoulders and chest like a second skin. Those eyes narrowed on her, then he shook his head, sending a spray of cool moisture into the air, some of it brushing her face. "Success," he murmured as he raked his hair back from his face with his fingers, spiking it slightly.

"Wanna go bye-bye," Taylor said in a small, plaintive voice from the back seat.

Quint turned, glanced back at her and smiled. "You bet, little lady," he said as he turned and put the car in gear, swinging to the right and through the open garage door. They drove out of the fierceness of the storm.

Amy felt a sigh of relief escape her lips, and Quint turned to her. "Amen. I wasn't sure we could make it all the way."

He hadn't acted as if there was any doubt that they could get here. "You said we could do it."

He shrugged, the wet shirt tugging at his shoulders. "Should I have told you that once, when I was fourteen, my dad got caught in a flash flood so bad that he ended up ten miles away from where he should have been, with his truck on its side?"

She shivered. "I didn't need details, but I'd appreciate a fair assessment of what's happening."

That brought a smile, a jarring expression that made her heart tense. "A fair assessment? Now, that's corporate-speak, if I ever heard it. And you're not even an executive."

She turned from him, getting to her knees again to look over the seat at Taylor and start undoing the little girl's safety belt in her car seat. "I just meant, I want the truth. I can deal with it."

"The hard, cold truth, no matter what?"

She hesitated, then looked at him. "Yes, if you can manage that."

This time he didn't smile. His expression tightened perceptibly, and he got out of the car crossing to close the garage door. Then he came around to Taylor's door and opened it. "I'll take her," he said, and Amy wished that Taylor had resisted him just scooping her up out of her chair, but she didn't come close to resisting. She all but jumped into his arms, hugging her arm around his neck as he straightened. "Can you get the boy?"

"Sure," she muttered as she got out.

"I'll come back for the rest of the stuff in a bit," Quint was saying as he walked across a garage she now realized had two other vehicles in it, a beige sedan and a black pickup truck. "Come on in through this door."

She hurried around, unhooked the infant seat from the car and flipped up the handle so she could carry the whole thing into the house without waking the baby. By the time she came around the car, Quint and

Taylor were out of sight and a door just beyond a long workbench stood open.

She carried the still-sleeping baby across to the door, and stepped into a hallway that seemed overly wide, with terra-cotta tiles on the floor and old-fashioned-looking lanterns on the plastered walls. There was silence and warmth, then the silence was broken when Quint's voice came to her from a distance. "Turn left. First room."

She went past two closed doors, came to another hall and glanced right at a huge, adobe-brick-lined archway with nothing but darkness beyond it. She turned left into a short hallway with two closed doors on the right and one on the left that stood open, allowing brighter light to spill out into the hallway. Suddenly Quint was there. He reached for the infant seat, taking it from her, then he stood back and let her go past him into the room.

She found herself in a room that was blue, from the deep-blue carpet underfoot, to the pastel-blue quilt on a white iron bed, the walls an even lighter blue with white shutters on windows over the bed shutting out the night. A tulip-shaded light fixture cast a warm glow over the space. Taylor was on the floor by the foot of the bed, playing with an oversize teddy bear, and barely glanced up when Amy came in.

"My sister's old room. Mom has a way of keeping things the way they were thirty years ago."

"You've got a sister?" she asked as he went around her and set the baby carrier on the bed.

"You sound shocked that there are more like me," he said, as he straightened and started undoing the buttons on his soaked shirt. He shook the wet material away from his body.

Shocked? What truly shocked her was her instant reaction when this man did little more than move, when she saw his bare chest under the loose shirt and the dark T of hair. Shocked that she found herself wishing that the man wore an undershirt. "No...no, I didn't mean that," she said, thankful when Travis stirred.

"I've got a sister, two parents, a son and no pets." That slight grin twitched at his mustache. "How about you?"

"I've got Taylor," she said. She heard Travis whimper and crossed to the bed, carefully avoiding Quint. She reached for the infant seat, turned it toward her and said, "And Jenn."

"Not exactly a lot," he said.

She didn't look up, but concentrated on the baby, on the tiny hand that peeked out from the sleeves of the sleeper, then on his eyes fluttering for a moment before the pacifier shot out of his mouth onto the bedspread.

"When I got married, the plan was to have a lot of kids, six at least, so there would be a big family for them, and they would always have someone there." She felt the tightness in her throat and couldn't figure out why she was telling Quint this. "It didn't work out," she muttered, and reached for the baby, loosening the harness, then scooping Travis up into her arms. "But this will work out. His mother will come back and he won't be alone."

Quint looked away from Amy holding the baby,

rocking him automatically to soothe him. But it was Quint who ached at the pain in her words, for what she must have gone through. For her loss. He'd been left alone, but he hadn't been in love. He couldn't even begin to imagine a love such as she'd had—still had—for her dead husband.

He turned from her, murmuring, "I'll go and get Charlie and the rest of the things out of the car," walking out as he spoke.

He didn't stop as he went through the house, back to the garage to get the supplies, and he tried to rationalize the jealousy that was nudging at him. Jealousy for a dead man who had been loved by Amy, and for the child they'd had from that love? He'd seen it in his parents, but he'd never appreciated it until now. Odd.

"Six kids?" he muttered as he grabbed the bags and the rat in the cage, then slammed the door and headed back inside. He was in the house, going back to his sister's room, and it struck him. Some day Amy would meet a man who wanted six kids, who could love her the way she deserved to be loved, and she'd be okay. He wasn't so sure about himself. He'd keep going, hang loose, go with the flow and live. But Amy would have a life, a good life.

He got to the door to the bedroom and hesitated before going back inside. Taylor was still playing with the bear he'd given her. Amy was on the bed, sitting lotus-style with Travis in her lap. She was laughing, putting his pacifier in his mouth, letting him spit it out, then putting it back in again.

"He's got that down to a science," Quint said as

he put the bags on the floor by the bed, then placed the cage on the dresser.

"He's a smart one," she murmured, then looked up at Quint. "And he's a wet one."

"He's not alone in that," Quint admitted as he picked up the diaper bag and set it on the bed by her. "How do you want to do this tonight? There's the bed here, and I can find some pillows and linen to make a bed on the floor for Taylor so that she can be near you. But what about him?"

She laid Travis on the bed and started to take the damp sleeper off him. "He can sleep with me."

Lucky kid, Quint thought before he caught himself. "Good, fine. How about his formula?"

She motioned to the diaper bag. "I got a lot of the pre-made formula that we had at the center, enough for a couple of days and the rest of what his mother left. If you could put them all in the refrigerator and heat one up, that would be great. And after he's asleep, could you show me where the kitchen is so I can heat them up myself if he wants something during the night?"

"Sure," he said, reaching into the bag to find packages of formula. "What about Taylor? Milk, juice, something to eat?"

"I have some things for her in her bag, too."

"There's more stuffed animals in the closet, if she wants to play with them."

"Thanks," Amy said as she reached for a disposable diaper.

He headed through the house to the kitchen, heated the bottle, then went back to the bedroom. Amy was sitting on the floor holding a clean, dry baby in one arm and feeding Taylor some orange concoction out of a jar with her free hand.

She looked up at him. "Great timing. This is done. Could you wipe Taylor's face and give her a bottle out of her bag?" She dropped the spoon in the empty jar, then held it up to him and motioned with her head to the Raggedy Ann bag by the bed. "It's in there."

He took the empty jar and gave her the bottle he had just heated. Travis took to it eagerly. Quint rummaged with one hand in the bag and found a soft cloth and pink bottle. "This one?" he asked Amy.

She glanced at it, nodded and spoke to Taylor. "Mr. Gallagher has your bottle, love."

The little girl looked at him, scrambled to her feet, literally running over the bear in the process of getting to Quint. "Pink baba!"

"You bet," he said. He wiped her face then gave her the bottle. She then turned and went to Amy. She dropped down on the floor, put her head on her mother's leg and sprawled out, totally relaxed as she drank her juice. "I didn't think to ask, but is Taylor in diapers, too?"

"For now, she is. She's almost trained, but with all of this going on, I'm not pushing it."

He went closer to Amy and the babies and hunkered down to her eye level. "Okay, diapers, bottles. Is there anything else that you need for the kids?"

She shook her head. "No. They'll both be going down soon."

"And how about you? What do you need?"

She rested her head against the foot of the bed and

sighed slightly. "I've got warmth. We're dry and safe. I'd say that about covers it."

"Lady, you're far too easy," he murmured.

Her dark eyes met his. "What more could I want?"

"Food? Wine? You name it."

She smiled slightly, but there was a real shadow of weariness in the expression. "Maybe, but I'll take a good night's sleep instead." She glanced down at Travis. "Although I've got a feeling that sleeping might not be on the agenda tonight." She hesitated, then sat up straight. "Your phone?"

"You need to make a call?"

"No, your cell phone. Remember I put that number on the note?"

"Oh, sure. I'll get it and bring it in here…just in case."

"Thanks."

He glanced at Taylor; her eyes were starting to flutter shut. Travis seemed content to eat and be cuddled. "Since you've got everything under control here, I'll get the phone and see what there is to eat." He stood, backing away from a scene of such domestic peace that it literally made him uncomfortable. It was far too endearing to him at that moment. "If you need anything, there's some clothes of Meg's in the closet, not much, but maybe something you can use. Although you'll probably swim in them." The lights flickered, then steadied. "False alarm," he murmured. "And if the lights do go out, we're on propane for heat, so we'll be okay. We might be in the dark, but we'll be warm."

Amy watched Quint leave, the door closing softly

behind him, and then it was just her and the children. She was hungry, and she was tired. Thankfully she saw that Taylor was starting to settle and Travis was already sleeping again. She put the bottle down on the floor, then pushed herself to her feet and went to the bed. She tugged the quilt back and laid the sleeping baby on the bed. He sighed, wiggled, then settled with another sigh. She framed the baby with pillows, took a throw off the footboard and spread it for Taylor.

Standing back, she stretched, easing the tightness in her shoulders and arms, then stepped out of her shoes and nudged them halfway under the bed. Turning, she crossed to an archway that opened to a vanity on one side and sliding mirrored doors on the other of a pass-through to the bathroom. She slid back one door and looked into a nearly empty closet. There were clothes, but not many. A robe of white terry cloth, some folded tops on a side shelf, jeans on another shelf, a couple of sweatshirts and a jacket on hangers and one pair of well-used boots that looked sizes too big for her on the floor.

Thank goodness she'd thought to grab the extra set of clothes she kept at the center for emergencies. But she could use the robe. She reached for it, then went into the bathroom, a large room with a deep tub, a shower stall with clear glass and a vanity along one wall under high windows. She left the door open to hear the kids and turned on the water in the shower. She tugged the bands out of her hair, loosening it from the braids, then shook it out. The shower was getting warm now, and she stripped off her clothes, laid them on the vanity, then neatly folded the Super Dude T-shirt she'd worn under her clothes. She twisted a towel around her hair to keep it as dry as she could, then stepped into the stall under the gentle spray of warmth.

She stood there for a very long time, just letting the water flow over her body, taking off the chill that the storm had brought with it. This was a far cry from what she'd thought she'd be doing tonight. And she'd never dreamed that she'd be in a shower at Quint's family home.

She started singing "Rudolph the Red Nosed Reindeer" to distract her thoughts from Quint, but stopped when she stumbled over the reindeer's names. She could never get them right. "Dasher and Dancer and Prancer and...Donner." No that wasn't it, she knew, and realized it was time to get out when she couldn't even remember if there was a Blitzen in the group.

She turned off the water, stepped out onto the floor mat and tugged the towel off her hair to dry herself. She wiped at her skin with the softness of the terry cloth, and looked up to see herself in the mirrors. Behind her, she caught the reflection of the open door and Travis on the bed.

The baby was sleeping soundly and she could see that Taylor had turned on the floor, pulling the bear with her and hugging it to her in sleep. She tossed the towel on the vanity, then reached for the robe and slipped it on. At the same time she pulled it around her, she saw a flash behind her in the mirrors. She looked up, expecting to see Taylor up or Travis stirring.

Instead, she saw Quint behind her, near the doorway, a changed man in jeans, an unbuttoned chambray shirt and his hair combed straight back from his face, emphasizing the sharp angles of his features. Quint. Watching her. And she had no idea how long he'd been there.

She turned, tugging the belt of the robe around her waist and trying to tie it, but her fingers felt as awkward as her face felt hot from embarrassment. She was so used to having the door open, keeping that contact for Taylor available at all times, that she hadn't even thought to close the bathroom door. And she hadn't heard Quint come in. She prayed that he'd just walked in.

"You…you startled me," she managed to say, going toward him, making herself not cross her arms on her breasts.

"Sorry. I brought you the cell phone," he said, and held it out to her.

She looked at the phone for a long moment before she could move closer to take it from him. "Thank you," she murmured.

"The food will be ready in five minutes. Nothing fancy. Soup, bread, wine, coffee—decaffeinated, of course. Is that okay?"

"Yes, yes, sure," she said, relief flooding over her. He hadn't seen a thing. He hadn't been there watching her. She pushed the phone into the pocket of her robe. "I'll be there in a minute," she said, relaxing just a bit.

"Go through the archway and the kitchen is to your left."

Quint turned, went to the door, but instead of leaving, he turned back to her for a moment and that smile was there. "Vixen," he said.

"Pardon me?"

"You know, Dasher and Dancer and Comet and—" he paused, the smile growing just a bit "—Vixen," he said, then left.

Chapter Ten

Amy checked the kids in passing, making sure that they were still asleep, before she hurried after Quint. As she stepped out into the hallway, rolling up the robe's sleeves that fell well past her hands, she caught a glimpse of Quint disappearing to the left through the archway.

She was vaguely aware of the fragrance of fresh coffee brewing in the air, and the coolness of smooth tile under her bare feet, then she was in a kitchen, a huge room, probably as big as her entire apartment. There were stone walls, butcher-block counters and a massive table set in the middle of the space, but all she truly focused on was Quint.

He was standing to the left, in front of the stove, lifting the lid of a pot and allowing steam to escape into the air. "Excuse me," she said, breathless as she stopped a few feet from him.

He cast her a slanting glance as he reached for a large wooden spoon and started stirring the contents of the pot. "Not hungry now?" he asked.

"No...yes...I'm hungry, but that's not..." She

took a deep breath and made herself get the right words. "You were in the bedroom, weren't you?"

"I brought in the cell phone," he drawled, putting the lid back and laying the spoon on a plate on the counter.

"And I was in the shower."

He turned to her, and she knew that he knew exactly what she meant. There was something in his eyes, a look that made her want to pull the robe even closer at her throat. "Seems you were."

She bit her lip. "You...I..." She exhaled, not about to say what she wanted to ask. Not from this man. "Never mind," she muttered.

He studied her intently, then came closer to her. His still-damp hair was curling slightly, and the planes and angles of his face seemed sharper. The mustache definitely hid a lot of his expression, and she wished it didn't. "Lady," he said softly. "I told you before, I don't play games. And I'm no Peeping Tom or lascivious voyeur." His eyes flicked over her, down to her hands clutching the robe at her throat, then back to her lips, lingering there long enough to make her tremble slightly. Then he was meeting her gaze with his. "I went in, heard you singing, started to put the phone on the dresser for you, then heard the water stop, the shower open, and the next thing I knew you were in your robe, in front of the mirrors. Is that what you wanted to know?"

"More or less," she whispered.

"Less, much less," he murmured.

"Thank you."

He exhaled, rocking slightly on the balls of his feet,

bringing himself even closer to her. "You should thank me," he said, his voice touched with a subtle roughness now.

"Why?"

He was silent for a long moment, then his hand lifted and the tip of his forefinger brushed a feathery line along her jaw. "I'm going to be honest with you. Honesty is what you want, isn't it?"

She wasn't sure at all that she wanted honesty from him at that moment, because she didn't want to reciprocate. She didn't want to tell him that she could literally feel his heat around her, or that the feathery touch on her skin was as compelling as anything had been in her life. She didn't want to tell him that there was a scent about him, something beyond that freshness of soap and water, and she didn't want to tell him that he scrambled her thought processes just by being there.

She was thankful that he didn't wait for her answer. His finger traced the sweep of her jaw to her chin and stilled on her skin there. "Since I've met you, you've made me crazy, partly because you never stop, you never let me catch my breath before something else happens that literally takes away what breath I have left. You've challenged all of my rational thinking."

He could have been talking about her, about what he did to her, and she stayed very still.

"The thing is, if things were different, if I was a lot younger, if I had any desire to start all over with kids, you'd be right at the top of my list of places to start." He drew back, breaking the contact with her as he spoke. "But things are what they are. I'm going to be fifty tomorrow. I'm too old to start changing diapers and heating bottles again, and my life's been this way for far too long.'' His eyes narrowed and his voice dropped to a rough whisper. ''You don't want any sort of relationship, and, once you do, you want six kids to go with it.'' He lifted her left hand, and, never looking away from her eyes, he found her wedding ring. ''If you ever stop being married, that is.''

While he talked, something in her had been tightening. The truth. That's what he was saying. But when he touched her wedding ring, the truth turned to bewilderment. She'd forgotten the ring, for the first time in what seemed forever. And she hated herself for that. She hated him for making her forget for even a fleeting moment, and she jerked her hand back from him.

''You're crazy,'' she whispered hoarsely, but *she* felt crazy. Disturbed. Irrational. Hurting in a place that she couldn't even look at. Deep in her being.

''Crazy, maybe. But it's the truth,'' he said.

She looked away from him, but succeeded only in lowering her gaze to his bare chest, exposed by the open shirt. She thought for a minute that she saw his heart beating, but maybe it was hers. Maybe it was that thudding in her chest that she felt. She dragged her eyes away, daring to meet his gaze again, but that only made her heart bounce more. His expression was so intense that it startled her, catching her breath in her lungs. ''You…you don't know what I really want or what I…what I'm going to do with my life.''

''I can make a pretty good guess.'' He glanced

down at her hands and she realized that she was nervously twisting her wedding ring.

She made herself stop, pressing her palms together, then laced her fingers.

He shook his head. "I never had a good marriage, I told you that. When it was over, I was relieved. I was left with Mike and that was fine with me. I wish I could tell you how to get past yours and get on with your life. I wish I could do that for you."

Her eyes burned, and she was horrified that his image was blurring in front of her. "I don't need..." she started, but lost her voice as her throat tightened. She swallowed, but couldn't make anything work. No words. Nothing. Not even tears. Everything seemed gone. And it was because of this man in front of her.

"Oh yes, you do," he whispered.

She felt an explosion in her, something snapping, something she'd tried desperately to keep in check for the past two years. But it was free, and it hurt like hell, and he'd done it, and she struck out in a fury. The next thing she knew, he had her by her wrists, and she didn't have a clue what she'd done until she saw the perfect imprint of her hand on his cheek as it deepened to an ugly red. She'd struck him. She'd hurt him. But he wasn't touching his face. He held her fast.

As suddenly as the rage had come, it was gone, and she could feel herself literally collapsing. Then the tears came. A blur of life was around her, and she was in Quint's arms, holding on to him for dear life.

"Oh, God, I'm sorry," he said, his voice rumbling around her. "I'm so sorry."

She felt his heart now, really felt it, the heavy thudding, strong and sure. And she had the crazy thought that if she got close enough, his heart would beat for her, too. That she'd feel alive again. That the pain would go away. She looked up at Quint, and the feelings only grew. If she held to him tightly enough, it could work. He groaned softly and lifted his hands to frame her face. His thumbs gently brushed at her cheeks, and she trembled.

The next thing she knew, his lips found hers and the world fell away. The pain eased and dissolved, and, as his tongue teased and tasted her, she slipped into a safe place, a good place, and she eagerly went there. She went to him, holding to him, trying to be closer than was humanly possible. The connection was alive and compelling, a lifeline, a line that gave her life.

And there were tears threatening again, but this time they were tears of relief and tears of need. She felt him lifting her, raising her in his arms, never stopping the kiss, but carrying her, moving with her. And she felt as if all connections to the world were gone, leaving only the two of them, and this place that she wanted to crawl into and never leave. She felt as if she could fly, as if he held her up, and she wasn't startled when they were lying together. Softness. Coolness at her back, the heat of Quint on her front.

Shadows, heat, need, touch. She answered kiss for kiss, found the bareness of his chest with her hands, then felt skin against skin. His hands on her skin, his hands touching her bare breast, making her whole body ache and arch, yearning toward him, then his lips moved, finding the spot his hands had just discovered and she moaned, shaking from the intensity of the feelings that flowed through her and around her.

Arching back, lifting to his touch, not caring that the robe was parted, that she was naked to him. Needing his contact, feeling his touch, sensing him moving, pressing the hardness of his desire barely contained by his jeans against her thigh. Her hands skimmed lower, finding the snap at his waistband, and she tugged awkwardly, trying to take away the barrier.

But before she could manage it, there was a noise, a shattering sound that seemed to cut through the fantasy they were fashioning, a sharp, shrill noise that she couldn't place. Then she knew. The phone. Quint's cell phone. It was ringing. And reality crashed in around her. Whatever fantasy she'd willed to happen was dissolving, and she twisted, realizing she was on a couch of some sort in the shadows, and that the storm was beating on glass close by.

Quint was moving back, taking his heat, and she scrambled away, finally sitting on leather, tugging her robe around her, ignoring the ache in her that made her breasts hurt and her being throb. She fumbled in the pocket of the robe, found the phone and took it out. Her hands were shaking, but she managed to push the key to answer it, and she put it up to her ear.

"Hello?" she said, her voice almost unrecognizable in her own ears.

There was a hesitation, then it seemed as if Quint

was talking to her on the phone, "Ma'am, I'm trying to call Mr. Gallagher?"

No, not Quint, a younger-sounding version of his voice. "Excuse me?"

"This is Mike, his son. Is my dad there?"

His son. Michael. "Yes," she whispered and turned, finding Quint standing, and making no effort to hide his physical response to what had almost happened between them. She held up the phone, not caring that her hand was shaking. "It's…for you," she managed, and almost dropped the phone when he reached for it. "Your son."

She turned from him, closing her eyes for a long moment, then stood, thankful that her legs could hold her. She'd gone crazy. He wasn't crazy; she was. She couldn't even make sense out of what had happened. She barely saw the room Quint had carried her into, a den or a living area, with a series of French windows on one wall, the only barrier between them and the driving storm.

She heard Quint talking, but couldn't take in the words as she made her way through the shadows to an archway where light spilled into the room. She went through and back into the kitchen, and stopped, with no idea what to do or where to go. She could check on the babies, but she was in no condition to try and cope with them at the moment. She could barely cope with herself. She crossed the cold tiles to the far wall and the windows being assaulted by the storm.

Hugging her arms around herself, she stared out at her expression overlying the night and the fury of the storm. Her hair was tangled around her face, and her eyes were dark and fathomless. Crazy. She couldn't even think about what might have happened if Mike hadn't called. And she'd hit Quint. She couldn't remember the last time she'd struck anyone. Yes, total craziness. And it was all hers.

QUINT WISHED he could joke with Mike, but humor wasn't what he was feeling at the moment. Besides a body that couldn't forget the feeling or sight of Amy, he was filled with anger at himself. He'd never been a user of women, ever, and he wasn't going to start, no matter how much he physically wanted the woman in the next room.

"So, you took my suggestion and found a woman?" Mike was saying.

"No, we got in trouble with the storm, and that's all there is to it." He'd never lied to Mike, but, if any time was right for lies, now was the time. "We're waiting it out at Grandma and Granddad's place."

"You took her home to the ranch?"

"I didn't have a choice." He wasn't going to talk about this anymore with his son. "What's going on?"

"I know how you hate birthdays and holidays, so I figured I'd call early to wish you a happy birthday and a happy New Year."

"Thanks," Quint said, staring at the night through the windows. "How're you doing?"

"Just great. Great skiing. Lots of powder and packed snow. Wish you were here."

"Me, too," he said.

"I won't keep you from your…rescue mission any

longer. Have fun and be safe,'' his son said, then hung up.

Quint pushed the End button, then stood still for a long moment while his body began to ease. That tension had started when he'd walked into the bedroom, seen the sleeping children, heard Amy singing, stumbling over the reindeers' names, and had then moved farther into the room. He'd told her the truth, as far as it went. He'd heard the shower door open, and that moment before she'd spotted him, he'd seen her.

The high breasts, tiny waist, the swell of her hips, smooth ivory-toned skin, and his body had started to tense. Then she'd pulled the robe around herself, and looked into the mirror and spotted him. He'd tried to get out of there, and now he wished he'd never gone to give her the phone in the first place. Maybe that would have stopped him saying what he'd said and doing what he'd done when she'd started to cry. Maybe none of this would have happened.

He stepped into the kitchen and spotted her at the windows. No, that wouldn't have stopped anything. The woman literally made him stop thinking. Made him ignore reason. Everything he'd said to her was the truth. There was no way they could be together, but that didn't stop his response to her. He went toward her, and cleared his throat to let her know he was there. No more sneaking up on her.

But one glance at her reflection in the rain-streaked windows and he knew that she'd spotted him as soon as he came into the room. She watched him, then he saw her straighten and push her hands into the pockets of the robe before turning to face him.

Her expression startled him. There was a sense of distance in her. Two patches of bright color dotted her cheeks, but the rest of her skin seemed oddly pale, especially emphasized by an ebony cloud of wild curls. She was biting her bottom lip so hard that he was certain she'd make it bleed. Then she took a breath that seemed to echo in the room.

"I want you to know that I am not some sex-starved widow," she said in a tight voice.

He would have laughed at that, if there wasn't such desperate seriousness in her with each word she uttered. "Amy, don't do this."

But his words didn't stop her. "I can't believe that I let that…" She bit her lip again, then took another breath that seemed to make her whole body shake. "You had no right to say what you said, and I had no right to…to hit you. And I apologize for that. And I was so far out of line, but you were too, and we both—"

"Stop." He'd had it. He couldn't take this self-flagellation she seemed bent on dishing out. "Just stop," he said, crossing to her at the windows. "You're sorry. I'm sorry. That's it. Let it go."

Her eyes were huge, overly bright, but she didn't cry. In fact, she looked angry. Whatever was going on inside her was hurting her, and he had to kill that overwhelming need he seemed to feel to make things right for her. He couldn't. He couldn't even make them right for himself.

She exhaled and suddenly buried her head in her hands, the wedding band catching the overhead light. She took several deep breaths, then she slowly lowered her hands. "That's it," she whispered as she hugged her arms around herself.

"Yes, it is," he said, ignoring the fact that a man who told the truth to a fault was lying with every other word tonight. That *wasn't* it, and he couldn't forget what had happened, but he wouldn't repeat it. That was the bottom line. "And I'm starved. The soup is more than ready. How about some?"

She hesitated, then nodded. "Thank you," she said so softly he almost didn't hear her.

"And take this," he said, holding the phone out to her. She stared at it as if it was a snake about to bite her, then reached for it, all but snatching it out of his hand. She put it back in the pocket of her robe as he asked, "Coffee or wine?"

"Coffee," she said, moving away from him as she spoke. "I'll check on the kids and be right back," then left the room, leaving the space as achingly empty as he felt at that moment. He turned to set the table and serve up the food, but all the while that he worked, he literally had to make himself not remember. Maybe later. Maybe after she was gone. Maybe then he could let himself remember their moment of weakness. But not now.

Incredibly, the two of them ate in amiable silence as if nothing had happened. They sat at the end of the huge table, eating a hearty vegetable soup along with crusty French bread and sipping a decent red wine and strong coffee. "More?" he asked when Amy finished her bowl of soup.

"No, thanks," she said, picking up what was left of her bread and taking a nibble.

"I checked and there's plenty of canned goods, some stuff in the freezer and a well-stocked wine cellar." He glanced at the storm that wasn't letting up. "I hope you brought enough diapers."

"Plenty. We had a stock at the center, and I took all the smallest ones we had, and plenty for Taylor." That was the most she'd said since coming back from checking on the children. "We'll probably be leaving in the morning, anyway."

She sounded anxious, and he couldn't blame her. "Probably." He tore a chunk off the loaf of bread, then realized he didn't want it. Instead, he put it down, poured himself some more wine and looked at her. "Sure you won't have any wine?"

She shook her head. "I don't drink well," she said.

"It's good on a night like this," he murmured as he put the bottle down, then sipped the wine, welcoming the warmth as it spread through him. He watched her scanning the room. "What do you think?" he asked, and could see that he'd startled her slightly when she looked back at him.

"Excuse me?"

"You're looking all over the place. What are you looking for?"

He was thankful that didn't bring more tension. She didn't say an escape, any escape. Instead, she said, "I was just thinking that this room is as big as my apartment." She pointed overhead at the heavy beams crisscrossing above them. "That the ceiling took a tiny forest to make." Then she motioned to the stone walls and heavy counters. "And that you probably had plenty of money as a kid."

He sat forward, putting the glass on the table, fingering it while he debated about filling it again. "It's a ranch, and I was indeed brought up here as a kid. And we didn't have a lot of money. We had a working ranch, and this room was the center of it, sometimes feeding twenty hands at once, so it had to be big." He motioned with his head, indicating the rest of the house. "My dad built most of this out of material that was already on the land to begin with, and they've added to it, but it's basically what it always was, a sprawling ranch house."

She was breaking crumbs off the bread she was holding, but she wasn't eating it anymore. "You worked here?"

"When I was a kid. So did Meg, my sister. I went off to college and never really came back. Meg was a change of life baby, as my Mom says, or her 'oops baby.' She's only five years older than Mike. And it wasn't easy on either of my parents, but they did it. Now they're having a second childhood of their own, traveling, making up for lost time."

A cry came from down the hall, and Amy was on her feet and moving before he even realized that one of the children was awake. She was gone. He reached for the dishes, clearing the table into the dishwasher. By the time she came back into the kitchen, he was almost done. He turned and Amy was there holding Taylor on one hip and cradling Travis in the crook of her other arm. He crossed and took the baby from her, and looked at Taylor, who seemed still half-asleep.

"The baby's cries woke Taylor. I told her you

might have a cookie or something out here for her,'' Amy said, hiking Taylor higher on her hip.

''Sure, I bet we do,'' he said, taking the baby with him into the pantry, a small room off to one side of the kitchen. He found a box of graham crackers. ''We've got these,'' he said, coming back out with them. Amy was at the table, holding Taylor on her lap. ''How about graham crackers?''

''Perfect,'' she said, ''Not too much sugar.''

Quint put the box on the table, and while Amy opened it and gave one to Taylor, he sat down opposite them with the baby in his arms. Taylor ate one cracker and Amy looked across at Travis. ''He's such a good baby,'' she said. ''Taylor was fussy. She had these crying fits in the afternoon and the only way she could be comforted was by holding her like a football in your arm facedown, and walking and jiggling her at the same time.''

''He's still new. This might not last.''

He was grateful that made her smile, not a full expression, but a softening at her lips and a general lightening in her. ''True. Kids change so quickly.'' She smoothed Taylor's sleep-mussed hair. ''Taylor changes every day so much, that's why I couldn't just put her in day care and miss all of that.'' She sat back as Taylor took another cracker. ''I've got the perfect job. I'm with her and can earn a living, such as it is, and not miss her growing time.''

She genuinely loved her child, cared about her child and nurtured her child. And she was just as good with a child who had been dumped on her doorstep.

"You're remarkable," he said before he really thought and could stop the words.

"Excuse me?" she said, her expression darkening slightly.

He couldn't say what he really thought, that she was attractive on so many levels and one level was being a mother. He didn't want more lies, so he just hedged a bit, but told the truth. "You're so good at this, with the kids, as if it was the easiest, most natural thing in the world."

"It's not brain surgery." She cuddled Taylor who had had enough crackers and was snuggling back into her mother.

He smiled. "Amy, no brain surgeon could do what you're doing. Believe me."

The color dotted her cheeks again, but this time, not from anger. "I always wanted to be a mother, it just took me longer than I thought it would to get there."

"Odd," he said, honesty coming from this woman at all times. Despite the physical turmoil she caused him with her presence, there was something soothing about her. She was as soothing to him as she was to the children. "I never wanted to be a father. Then it happened. I got married and Mike came. But when he was there, I knew that he was the reason for all that had happened before that moment. And everything that would happen." He chuckled roughly. "I'm usually not good at philosophical discussions."

She shrugged. "It's not philosophy, it's life. If you hadn't met your ex-wife, you never would have had your son."

"You're right. But that doesn't change the fact that I stink at marriage. Now, as a father, I'm not bad." He tried to smile. "At least I'm passable. I got past it, and Mike's turned out just fine. Dumb luck, probably, but he's a great kid." He shook his head. "No, he's a good man. He's not a kid anymore."

She glanced at Travis in Quint's arms, and he looked down, too. The baby was sound asleep. "You haven't lost your touch."

"I guess it's like riding a bicycle," he murmured, then looked at her. God, he hated regret, but right now he totally regretted being at a different place in his life than she was at the moment. And he regretted the way he could feel himself getting more obsessed with a woman almost as young as his son, and that he couldn't stop this gradual slide into the father role he'd left behind.

He cleared his throat and glanced at his wine. He tried to stop looking at this woman who deserved more than he could ever offer her. That thought stunned. What could he offer her and what would he want to offer her? What would she take from him?

"And who'd want to ride a bike again, huh?" he heard her whisper.

He felt a sense of sadness. "Exactly."

Chapter Eleven

That night, Amy slept with Travis on one side bolstered by pillows and Taylor on the other, blocked in by the wall. The sleep was deep and easy, except for waking to feed Travis, and when he stirred around dawn, she was instantly awake. She picked him up, changed him, then managed to get dressed herself, in jeans, the Super Dude T-shirt and gray sweatshirt that she'd brought from the center.

After putting a piece of graham cracker in the rat's cage, she put the cell phone in her pocket and took Travis out into the kitchen to heat a bottle. Quint was nowhere around, and one look out the windows showed her that the storm was still going strong. After getting the bottle warmed, she carried Travis near the windows, and while he fed, she looked out at the watery world outside the ranch house. Through the blurry glass, she could see rolling green off into the distance, a dark building that looked to be two stories tall to the right, and a wing of the house jutting out to the left. The tiled roof shed the water in small rivers, and the wide overhang partially protected what looked like stone walls.

"Good morning," she heard from behind her, and turned, surprised to see Quint looking painfully fresh in clean jeans and a white shirt. What shocked her most was Taylor in his arms. He smiled as he came into the kitchen. "She found me," he said as he crossed to the pantry and disappeared inside. "And she wanted more crackers." His voice came out of the room, then he was back with the box in Taylor's hands.

He crossed and asked, "Can she use a chair or is she better on the floor?"

"She slips off chairs, but the floor's so cold," she said.

"Okay, let's go where the floor's better for her," he said, carrying Taylor across the room and through the arched doorway where he'd carried Amy last night.

She hesitated, almost afraid to go back to the scene of her insanity, then she hurried after him. She'd thought it was a den and it was, of sorts, a cozy room with the tiles partially covered by area rugs. Leather was everywhere, from the low couch, from which she quickly averted her eyes, to chairs that all but made a circle in front of a huge stone hearth. Near windows to the right stood what looked like an antique pool table, and one wall was filled with bookshelves, overflowing with books of every sort, with a television set in the middle.

Quint crossed with Taylor, sank down on the couch and put her on the carpet that ran under a massive wooden coffee table. She started on the crackers, and Quint looked up at Amy still holding Travis, only partially in the room. "If you'll watch them, I'll get something for breakfast. We can eat in here." He tapped the coffee table. "Just the right size for little people."

"Okay," she said, crossing the room, but choosing to sit on a chair that faced the couch where she could watch Taylor. She could hear Quint in the kitchen, the clatter of pots, then the aroma of fresh coffee. She burped Travis and laid him on his stomach across her thighs and slowly made circles on his back. He seemed content just to be there, and she was feeling suspiciously content at that moment, too. Taylor was happy, Travis was content, and she was…she couldn't put a word to it, so she let it go. She didn't have to understand, that was something she'd realized when Rob died. She didn't need to understand, she just needed to keep going.

"Breakfast is ready," Quint called and strode into the room with a wooden tray in his hands. He crossed to the coffee table and put the tray down—eggs, bacon, toast. Cups of coffee. A dish with scrambled eggs in it for Taylor. He sank down in the next chair, then looked at her. "Can you put him down?"

She kept stroking his back. "No, I can manage with one hand," she said, thankful that she could smile at him, and thankful that there was none of that tension that had been in the room last night. "Tay-Tay, want some eggs?" Taylor shook her head and took out another cracker. "Okay, more crackers, then the eggs," she said and started to eat her own food with an appetite she couldn't remember having for a very long time.

"Thanks, that was great," she said once she'd cleaned her plate, turning to one side to drink some coffee without having the cup over the baby on her legs. The liquid was hot and strong and good. "Just great," she said, putting the cup back on the table before sitting back.

"I thought I'd feed you before I broke the bad news."

She looked at Quint sitting forward, his coffee cup cradled in his hands, and he didn't look too happy. "What is it? I've got the phone and there haven't been any calls, but did—"

He cut her off. "No, no calls. I just listened to the news. That's what I was doing when Taylor found me. The weather's not letting up, and there's widespread flooding." He glanced at Travis. "So, we can't leave and we can't do a thing about him right now."

That uneasiness was coming back. More time here, with Quint. "Maybe we could go back to LynTech?"

He shook his head. "The main part of the city is pretty much in a blackout at the moment."

"Well, if it's that bad, maybe his mother can't get back to LynTech to find the note. We're stuck, so she probably is, too."

"That's being kind to her, but I suppose it's a possibility." He stood and picked up the dish of eggs that Taylor had been ignoring. He went around to the couch, sank down by her on the floor and said, "I've got a surprise for you."

She looked up, saw the dish and shook her head. "No. No eggs."

He looked at Amy. "She does No quite well."

"She doesn't say a lot, but she has mastered a couple of words. That's one of them."

"Okay," he said looking back at Taylor. "How about if Quint eats your eggs and makes them all gone?"

She looked at him as he pretended to eat some, then said an exaggerated, "Mmm good."

She watched him with a frown, then reached for the spoon, almost sending egg all over Quint and the couch. But he evaded the grab and offered the spoon to her. "Okay, you win, they're Taylor's eggs, all of them," and quite miraculously, she opened her mouth and let him spoon them in. "Good, huh?" he asked.

"Huh," Taylor said, nodding and opening her mouth wide again.

Within minutes, the eggs were gone, and Quint was sitting back with the empty bowl as Taylor went back to the box of graham crackers.

"Well, that's a near-miracle," she said.

"No miracle. Actually, it took me forever to figure out that if it was mine, Mike wanted it. If it was his, he didn't want it. Kids are so perverse," he said with a smile.

So are human beings, she thought as she scooped Travis up and cuddled him to her shoulder. "That's the truth," she said as she stood. "I need to get them changed."

"Okay," he said, grabbing the box of crackers and picking up Taylor almost in one fell swoop. The four of them went back through the house to Amy's bedroom, and Quint never hesitated, going to the bed with Taylor. "What's she going to wear?"

''I had some overalls at the center that I grabbed and some T-shirts, so it's not fancy, but serviceable.''

''Okay, you take care of the diapers and I'll put the clothes on.''

For the next several minutes, the two of them worked together with the children, until both were dry and clean and dressed. Amy was sitting on the floor putting on Taylor's shoes and Quint had Travis in a clean sleeper, offering him the pacifier. For a flashing moment they were like a family, a mother and father, the children, and that scared Amy. She got to her feet, then spoke without looking at Quint again. ''I'll have to figure out where to let Travis nap so I can keep an eye on him.''

''You know, there's an intercom in the house.'' She turned to see Quint cross to a box by the door and turn on a button. ''It's in what I call the 'eaves-dropping mode.' This room is strange. You can hear what goes on in here from anywhere in the house, but anyone in here can't hear what's going on out there.'' He turned to her with a boyish grin on his face. ''Something I learned about the hard way when I was a kid.'' He crossed to the bed. ''So, make a pillow barrier, and let him sleep for a while if he will.''

She went about stacking pillows, then glanced at Quint, a bit unnerved to find him watching her intently, the grin long gone. ''What?'' she asked, that uneasiness starting to rear its ugly head even more.

''I meant it before. I'm impressed.''

''You're easily impressed,'' she said, reaching for Travis and turning to lie him on the bed. The pacifier was there, Quint holding it out to her over her right shoulder. Without looking at him, she took it, gave it to the baby and was thankful when Travis seemed to sigh and his eyes fluttered shut.

"Actually, I'm not easily impressed," Quint murmured from behind her. "You can ask anyone who knows me."

"Easy to offer when I don't know anyone who knows you very well at all," she said, then looked at Taylor absorbed with the teddy bear near the bed. "So, what's the plan for today?"

"I've got some work to do. There's plenty of books in the den, a TV, a pool table if you want to play. Plenty of food." He touched her on the shoulder and she almost jumped out of her skin. She turned and was inches from Quint. "And don't worry about anything getting wrecked. This house is invincible. It can take anything Taylor can dish out."

"Okay, we'll make do," she said.

"I know you will." He went back to the door, adjusted the intercom, then turned to her. "Everything's set. You'll hear him anywhere if you're inside." That grin was there. "And it's my bet that you aren't going to be outside."

"That's an easy bet to win," she said, then Quint left the room.

Amy stared at the empty door for a long moment, then scooped up Taylor and said, "Let's go on a tour of this place, okay?" Taylor hugged the bear to her tightly. "And you can keep the bear…for now."

She started for the kitchen, wondering how one person could confuse her, calm her, upset her and heal her all at once. She couldn't begin to place the man who'd rescued her from the storm with the man from last night with the man who was so good with the kids despite his protestations of being too old for it all. And she couldn't begin to figure out why she was so relieved that he'd gone off to work for the day so she had space to think and to breathe.

That's what she needed to do, just keep her distance as much as possible until they could leave and she could put this all behind her.

"I THINK he's sick," Amy said over the yowling of the baby.

Quint was at the sink in the kitchen, running hot water over the baby's bottle to try and reheat it. "I don't think so," he said, but he was starting to worry himself. The child had been crying since before lunch, barely stopping long enough to spit up before starting up again. "Maybe it's the formula that's upsetting him."

"No, it's the same as the cans that were in his box."

He turned and saw Amy walking back and forth in front of the windows with Travis, pacing and jiggling and patting him. But nothing was helping. "It's probably colic."

He could see the distress in her face when she turned in his direction. "I think he's missing his mommy. He needs a familiar face and a familiar voice, that reassurance."

He wasn't going to get into any sort of condemnation of the woman who didn't care enough to stay with him. "I'm more inclined to think it's colic." He glanced at Taylor sitting on the floor playing with a stack of pots and pans on the tile, totally oblivious to the baby's distress, then crossed to Amy with the bottle. "Do you want me to take him for a while?"

She looked exhausted, and it was all he could do not to brush her hair back from her face. She'd pulled it into a ponytail, had no makeup on and a decided paleness to her skin. But she was lovely and delicate looking. He saw her nibbling on her bottom lip, an action he'd come to recognize as one of her signs of stress. Four hours of crying was stress enough for anyone.

"Maybe for a few minutes?" she asked.

"Sure." He shifted the bottle to his other hand, took the squalling baby from her, and tried to get him to take the bottle, but he stiffened and screamed even harder. Now Quint was walking back and forth, jiggling and patting, and wondering how Amy had done it all afternoon.

"What did you say you did when Taylor had colic?" he asked over the cries.

Amy was over by Taylor, giving her attention and she twisted to look back at him. "I would put her tummy-down on my forearm, in a sort of football hold and her legs and arms would drape over each side of my arm, then I walked and sang to her. But, I already tried that."

"What did you sing?" he asked.

"I don't know, a lullaby, something like 'Bye Baby Bunting.' Do you know that one?"

"Yes, and I don't think it's very comforting to hear

that your daddy's going out to kill a rabbit for the skin so you can wrap it around the kid.''

That brought a slight smile to Amy's face. "He won't understand. Just sing whatever you want to sing.''

He didn't sing much, never had, but he did know one song from way back, an old Beatles' tune, "Hey, Jude.'' At least he knew the tune. He could fake the words. He shifted the baby to his forearm, tummy-down, and started pacing as he sang. At first it made no impact, but gradually the crying grew lower, then, with a heavy sigh, Travis stopped crying all together.

He sensed Amy watching him, but he was almost afraid to stop. He walked across to where she was with Taylor and whispered, "What's he doing?''

"It's a miracle. He's sleeping. I tried that, and he just got worse.''

He hadn't heard that word, *miracle,* applied to any area of his life for a lot of years, but lately it had been thrown about as if people were talking about the weather. "He exhausted himself,'' he said in a low voice, thinking the only miracle would be if he could put him down without the screams starting up again. "I don't suppose putting him down is a good idea?''

"I couldn't put Taylor down. Not for a while after she quieted. If I were you, I'd keep walking,'' she said, and he had a feeling she was enjoying this just a bit.

"I was going to try and make some dinner. Maybe you could take him, and—''

"I can make dinner. You keep him,'' she said, scrambling to her feet as she brushed at her jeans.

"Just tell me what to make. I'm not a bad cook, despite the dead gingerbread family." The baby stirred slightly. "Tell me while you walk." She really was enjoying this.

He started to pace again. "Anything you want to make," he said.

"It's a deal. My New Year's Eve special, if you have the ingredients?"

"That depends what it is. There's steaks in the freezer, but nothing fresh. Mom cleaned the refrigerator out when she left."

"Chili, good old-fashioned chili, with lots of cheese. Do you have cheese?"

"I don't know, and I don't know if there's chili, either."

"I'll fake it," she said and headed for the pantry, but stopped at the entrance to the storage area to turn back to him. "Do you have popcorn?"

"That, I know we have, but why?"

"Popcorn on top of chili is fantastic," she said, just before ducking into the pantry.

"Whatever you say," he murmured as he patted the baby's back. He'd forgotten it was New Year's Eve tonight. Another year. Something he hardly ever celebrated. Now he was doing it with a woman who was making chili and popcorn, a colicky baby, a toddler who was fascinated by pots and pans, and a backlog of work that normally would have driven him crazy until he completed it. Odd, he thought. For the first time in years, he wasn't in any rush to get to work.

AMY NOT ONLY MADE chili, she found some fantastic salsa that Quint's mother must have canned. Hot and heavy with cilantro. Perfect flavor. And the popcorn. While she cooked, Quint walked with Travis and kept an eye on Taylor. A New Year's Eve unlike any she'd spent, but she found herself actually enjoying cooking and popping popcorn.

"What drink goes with chili?" Quint asked as he came over to the stove where she stood.

"Got any beer?"

"No. Is that what you drink with it?"

"Me? I…no, I…I never drink beer." She stumbled slightly as she remembered how Rob loved beer with chili. "I don't like the taste of it," she said, averting her thoughts. "Actually, milk would be good, but with no milk, I guess we're down to water."

"How about champagne?" he offered.

She looked up at Quint, Travis draped over his arm, sleeping heavily, and his eyebrow lifted slightly. "Champagne and chili?" she asked.

"Sure, why not? Start a new tradition."

She didn't want to do that, not with this man. "Whatever you want," she murmured and turned back to the stove.

She sensed him moving away from her, but she didn't look up to see where he was going. She just knew he'd left the kitchen. When he came back, Travis was not in his arms. But a bottle of champagne was in his hands. "Where's the baby?" she asked.

"Sleeping on your bed in his pillow fortress. I think I could have put him down twenty minutes ago." He lifted the champagne for her to see. "One thing my dad keeps around is a bottle of champagne for special occasions. I think your chili constitutes a special occasion.''

''Oh, I don't think so.''

''I do, but let's say it's for New Year's. Is that special enough for you?''

''Sure, of course,'' she said.

He moved past her to cupboards on the far side of the room and she heard the clink of glasses before he turned with two crystal flutes in his hand. ''And he keeps these two glasses for just such an occasion. Champagne just doesn't go in canning jars.'' He glanced at the pot of chili. ''How much longer?''

''Five minutes,'' she said, turning back to stir the pot.

''Can Taylor eat chili?''

''No. Actually, I saw some canned spaghetti in the pantry, no doubt saved for special occasions, which this is, so I guess we can break open a can of that for her?''

She thought she heard him murmur, ''Touché,'' but when she turned, he was putting the glasses on the table and holding the champagne bottle as if he was going to take the wire off to uncork it.

''I don't suppose it's tradition to drink champagne warm, is it?'' she asked.

He shook his head as he slowly rotated the bottle with his hand on the top. ''It's chilled. Dad keeps it in his office in a small refrigerator. I'll have to remember to replace it before they get back from Florida.'' There was a pop that caught Taylor's attention for half a second before she went back to playing with her doll. "Success," he said and slowly poured two glasses of the bubbly amber liquid into the flutes. "Age has its benefits, and one is practice at uncorking champagne."

He crossed with the glasses in his hands and held one out to her. "Happy New Year, Amy Blake."

She took the flute and fingered the cool glass. "Happy New Year," she echoed and took a sip of the bubbly liquid.

The phone in her pocket rang and she quickly put the flute on the counter and took the phone out. She held it, then looked at Quint and held it out to him. "You answer it."

He took it, pushed the button and pressed it to his ear. "Quint Gallagher."

She almost held her breath until he smiled and said, "I'd wondered if you'd call all the way from Florida."

His parents. She turned from him, crossed to the pantry and found the can of spaghetti. While she cooked, she half listened to Quint talking and laughing on the phone. Then, as she spooned the spaghetti into a bowl for Taylor, she heard Quint wish the caller a happy New Year and say goodbye.

She grabbed a spoon and went to where Taylor sat with the pots and pans. She didn't fight being fed, and, as Amy spooned the food into her daughter's mouth, she sensed Quint coming up behind her. "My mother," he said. "She heard about the storm and wanted to check on what was going on here."

"Does she know we invaded her house?"

"I didn't go into it, but I have a feeling that Mike called her and mentioned the situation."

Amy fed Taylor the last of the spaghetti, then stood to get something to wipe her daughter's face. Quint was there, inches from her, and, overwhelming for a moment, he took the dish from her. She ducked past him, grabbing a cloth off the counter, then went back to crouch by her daughter and wipe away the remnants of the spaghetti sauce. "You'll have to thank her for me when she gets back," she said, standing, ready to get around him quickly to get back to the stove.

But as she straightened and turned, the world seemed to explode. There was a huge roaring sound, unlike any thunder she'd ever heard, a surge of light all around them, then everything went black.

Chapter Twelve

There was silence for what seemed like forever to Quint, then noise was everywhere. Crashing thunder, Taylor yelling for her mama, Travis screaming, and Amy gasping when she ran right into him. Her hands were on his chest, then gone, and he could barely make her out as she turned from him. Gradually he could see a bit more, shadows and movement, then Taylor was quiet and in a flash of brilliance through the windows, he saw Amy with her daughter in her arms.

"What's going on?" she asked as she moved back to where he stood, Travis still screaming through the darkness.

"Probably a lightning strike on a transformer," he said. The baby's cries seemed to echo. "I'll go and get Travis. You stay here, then we'll see what we can find for light."

"Can you see to go back there?"

"No problem," he said and headed back into the deeper shadows of the house toward the bedroom. Within a minute, he had the baby and was heading back to the kitchen. There was a low glow coming through the door as he approached it, and when he stepped through, he saw that Amy had turned on all the burners of the gas stove. The flames gave enough light to make out the surroundings and played softly across her face. Haunted dark eyes, shadows at her throat, almost an ethereal image.

"Good idea," he said as he positioned the baby into the football hold again. "I'll start a fire in the den and we can eat in there." He rummaged in the drawer by the range with his free hand, and found a book of matches along with a small flashlight. He snapped on the light. It was weak, but it worked. "We can find our way, at least," he said as he flashed the light around the room. "Let me get you all in the den, get the fire going, then I can figure out what to do from there."

The plan was good, but he never got a chance to do it the way he'd laid it out. He got Amy and Taylor to the couch in the den, but when he gave Travis to Amy, the baby started to scream. Nothing she did could get him to stop, and he screamed all the while Quint rushed to get the fire started. Once he had it going and a few candles lit on the mantel, he went back to the kitchen to turn off the stove. Then he sat by Amy on the couch.

She didn't say a thing, just turned and handed the boy to him. He got Travis "in position," tummy-down, draped over his forearm, then stood, started walking with him, jiggling him softly, and the crying died off. "Well, I'll be damned," he murmured.

"Another miracle," Amy said. "And how ironic."

He jiggled the baby as he looked down at Amy,

the firelight even more enhancing to her than the gas flame in the kitchen had been. Her bottom lip was shadowed, looking full and inviting, too inviting. "How so?"

"You—the 'I'm too old for this, and I'm over kids big-time'—seem to be the only one who can stop him crying." There was a smile mingled with the shadows that played across her face. "Ironic, huh?"

"Perverse," he muttered and turned to walk around the room.

"Quint?" she called after him.

He spoke without turning on his way around the pool table. "What?"

"Your cell phone. Where did you leave it after talking to your mother?"

He glanced back at her, cursing the fact that even distance couldn't make her less desirable. He stayed where he was. "In the kitchen by the stove. I'll go and get it." He jiggled Travis who was sucking noisily on his pacifier. "I'm up anyway, and walking is what I do best."

Her soft laughter followed him from the room and was gone by the time he picked up the cell phone and slipped it in his shirt pocket. He spotted his champagne glass and refilled it. He drank half of the second glass, then headed back into the den.

Amy was cuddling with Taylor on the couch, her feet drawn up under her and her head resting on the leather back. She glanced at him, shadows hiding any expression. "You have it?"

He crossed to her and took the phone out of his pocket, holding it out to her. "It's all yours. I don't think anyone else will be calling. It's New Year's Eve and people will either be stranded or partying.''

''What about B.J. and Matt's wedding? Maybe I should call B.J. and see what's happening and if they're still able to get married.''

''Go ahead,'' he said and stood in front of her. ''Is Travis asleep?'' he asked.

She sat up a bit, looked at Travis, then up at him. ''I think so.''

He exhaled a sigh. ''Okay, I'll put him down here by you, then go and get our food.''

She tugged a throw that was over the back of the couch down to the seat and spread it out. He eased the baby off his arm onto his back on the throw, and Amy piled the excess of the throw, making a barrier between Travis and the front of the couch. His pacifier bobbed furiously, then slowed until the baby sighed softly.

''Success,'' Quint breathed and looked up at Amy close to him. ''If he starts crying—''

''He's all yours,'' she said.

''Perverse,'' he muttered again and headed to the kitchen, flashlight in hand. He needed distance from more than the possibility that Travis would start crying again. He needed to breathe without feeling as if he could inhale Amy. And he needed to remember that there was nothing that could be done about his feelings for her. It didn't matter if you loved someone or not, it didn't matter.

He stopped in his tracks just inside the heavy shadows of the kitchen. Love? He shook his head. No. It couldn't be that. Fate couldn't be so cruel as to let him finally figure out what love was, then make it impossible for him to have it, even to experience it. He pushed that idea away and crossed to the stove. Lust, need, loneliness: he could deal with all of those emotions. He could get over those emotions. But he knew that only a fool would love a woman who was half his age and still in love with her dead husband. And it would hurt like hell. He wouldn't let that happen.

AMY SANK BACK in the couch as Taylor laid her head on her lap, then dialed B.J.'s number at the loft. It took forever to connect, then it didn't even ring before a message came on that all lines were full and to try again later. She hit End and laid the phone down, then smoothed Taylor's silky hair while she listened to Quint moving around in the other room. There was the bang of pots and pans that rivaled Taylor's play earlier in the day. The clink of dishes, then a clash of metal on something hard, a muttered oath, then silence. Just as she was about to call out to make sure he was okay, he came into the room carrying a tray.

He put everything down on the coffee table the way he had at breakfast, and as he passed out the dishes of chili, he said, "A pan I didn't see that was on the floor."

"Excuse me?"

"The crash, the bang."

"It sounded bad," she said as he put a bowl of popcorn on the table by the chili bowls.

"Sorry, no cheese, but at least we have popcorn. And I brought these in, too." He set down the champagne bottle and their glasses. She eased a sleeping Taylor off her lap and onto the couch so she could eat her chili. She was starving.

When Quint sat on the floor in front of the couch and reached for his bowl, Amy did the same, slipping down off the couch onto the floor. She put a handful of warm popcorn on the chili, then reached for one of the spoons Quint had brought in with him. Before she could take her first mouthful, she sensed Quint watching her, and she looked over at him. "Was there something else?"

He stirred his chili with the spoon. "No, nothing else." He took a spoonful of chili and ate it.

Amy looked away from him, away from the face of flickering shadows and eyes that were unreadable. She ate in silence, sipped champagne and tried to avoid thinking about the man at the table with her.

"What about the wedding?" Quint asked, breaking the silence so suddenly it startled her as she sipped the last of her champagne.

"The wedding? Oh, I couldn't get through. The lines were full."

"Another product of this storm," he said, reaching for a handful of popcorn. As he let it drop on top of his chili, he looked back at her. "The lines to the house aren't working, either. I checked in the kitchen."

"What a New Year's Eve," she murmured as she set her empty dish on the table and sat back, wrapping her arms around her legs and resting her chin on her knees. "I'm sorry that your plans for tonight are gone.

I seem to have a terrible habit of interfering with your plans.''

"I didn't have any plans," he said.

She turned to him, unable to believe that he didn't have people standing in line to celebrate with him. "No date?"

"I told you, I don't date."

"You never said why."

He shrugged and his shirt parted slightly. "Until recently I would have said that I didn't have time, didn't want to, didn't believe in it and I've never been good at it."

"And now?"

"Now? It's different."

"Why? And don't say it's because you're old."

"I am."

"You're not."

"I'm going to be fifty."

"So am I," she said.

"What?"

"All things being equal, I'll be fifty in twenty years."

There was total silence for a moment, then Quint reached forward toward the table. She gasped when popcorn came raining over her. Quint had taken a whole handful of popcorn and thrown it at her. She barely managed not to scream, then she stretched to grab some for herself, but she was too slow. Quint had the bowl, and when she tried to get away, her legs tangled with the leg of the table, and she fell backward onto the carpet. The next thing she knew, the whole bowl was being poured over her.

She lay in popcorn, her hands clutched over her mouth, trying to stop the almost hysterical laughter that was all but choking her. She lay there with Quint standing over her until she could control her laughter, then pushed herself up on her elbows and managed to choke out, "You are so dead."

"You deserved it," he said, dropping to his haunches over her. Then he put the bowl down beside her. "And you can clean up the mess, too."

"Oh, I don't think so."

"Mama?"

Taylor was awake, backing down off the couch, toddling over to Amy and unceremoniously plunking down on her stomach. As if it was the most natural thing in the world to find her mommy on the floor covered in popcorn, Taylor looked around, then grabbed some kernels and stuffed them in her mouth.

Quint pushed the bowl closer to the two of them, then leaned closer and brushed at Amy's hair. She could feel kernels of popcorn trickle out of her hair. "Fifty. Not even close."

"In time."

"Yes, well, you've got twenty years and I've got a day, not even that."

"Well, old or not, you're the one cleaning up this mess," she said, pushing up until Taylor was in her lap, and the popcorn was falling off her. "You did it. You clean it." She grabbed a handful of popcorn off the floor by her and tossed it at Quint. Taylor squealed when Quint ducked the bulk of the kernels, then picked up a tiny handful and tossed it up in the air.

Quint scooped up a handful of popcorn, but stopped when the baby started crying. "Now see what you've done," he said to Amy with a grin.

"What I've done?" she said. "He's all yours."

"Oh, no, lady, I think I'll pick up popcorn. You do the walking and jiggling and pacifier retrieval."

"Chicken," she muttered as she twisted to one side to set Taylor on the floor before she stood to go to get Travis. But before she could get there, Quint passed her and scooped him up. With the ease of a pro, he had the baby on his tummy, over his forearm, nestled like a football under his arm. "No one calls me a chicken, lady," he murmured. "Not even you."

Without warning there was light, and Amy blinked at the brightness of the overhead fixture that bathed the room in a yellow glow. Taylor clapped, Travis was shocked into silence for a moment and Quint was right in front of Amy. The shadows had made things a bit easier, blurring the lines of his face, the look in his eyes. It had been easy to tease him then. Seeing that crooked grin on his face, the way his mustache twitched with humor, the crinkling of his eyes, shadows were definitely better.

"Great," she murmured. "We can finally see what we're doing."

He glanced at the floor where Taylor sat in the middle of the popcorn mess. "Yes, everything," he murmured as his gaze met hers. Then Travis started to cry again, and Quint shrugged. "I need to walk, so I'll go and put out the candles."

He walked off with Travis and the crying echoed after him. Taylor scrunched the popcorn and Amy sank down by her. "In the bowl," she said, picking up a handful of popcorn and putting it in the bowl. Taylor looked at her, reached in the bowl and took out a handful of her own which she proceeded to let trickle out of her fingers back onto the floor.

"Okay, play with it for a while," Amy said and got to her feet. She looked around, crossed to the bookshelves and flipped on the television. No matter what she did, she couldn't get anything except a blue screen. Giving up, she turned it off, then saw the radio. She turned it on, fiddled with the tuner and finally found news.

She sat back on the couch, watching Taylor and listening to the updates on the storm. Rain and more rain. Wind. Flooding. Electrical outages. And it was forecast to keep up through New Year's Day. She reached for the phone again, dialed the loft and got the same message, then hit End.

Quint came back into the room with a quiet Travis. "No luck?" he asked when he saw her with the phone in her hand.

"No, it doesn't even try to connect." He crossed with Travis on his arm, and looked down at Taylor and the mess around her. "She's having fun with it," Amy said.

"She wouldn't let you pick it up, would she?"

She shook her head. "Bingo."

"Well, it's a cheap, safe toy."

"And I'm assuming that you have a vacuum cleaner around here?"

"I'm sure we do."

"Then it's perfect."

He was trying to ease Travis off his arm and onto his chest, but it didn't work; the baby stirred, his face puckered and he started to cry again. It didn't sound as if his heart was in it, but he wasn't going to settle.

Quint stood as a song started on the radio, an old song about fate and love. "Music…maybe dancing would help?" Quint murmured.

Taylor was on her feet before he got the last word out of his mouth. "Dance! Oh, spin! Mama?" she said, coming at Amy with her arms wide open to be picked up.

Amy stood and picked up Taylor. "Sure, sweetie, spin."

Quint had the baby back in position, tummy-down on his arm. "What does she want?"

"She thinks you were serious about dancing. So she wants to spin. That's how we dance."

Amy let Taylor wrap her tiny legs around her waist, then hugged her with one hand, and held her hand with the other. Together, they twirled around the room to the music, with Taylor laughing with delight. She looked back and saw Quint dancing with Travis, but going slower, with large, lazy circles accompanied by some jiggling. The crying was gone, the music was all around and the storm outside was forgotten.

When the song finally ended, Amy all but fell back onto the couch, hugging Taylor to her, laughing. "This was like a New Year's ball." She tickled Taylor. "And you could be the princess of spinning."

Quint crossed to the radio and turned it down when the news came on, then came over to sink down on the couch. Taylor started to bounce up and down on her lap. "More spin!"

"In a minute, sweetie," she said, gasping from breathlessness and laughter.

She looked at Quint. "Spin? Peeze. Pop spin?"

Amy rested her head against the back of the couch, and shifted to look at Quint. He was grinning, easing a sound-asleep Travis onto his chest as he slid lower on the couch. "I do popcorn, not spinning," he said on a chuckle. "Popcorn's easier."

"Dumping it on me is the easy part," Amy murmured.

That brought a crinkling of his eyes. "Oh, lady, you're so right."

Taylor crawled off Amy and would have climbed into Quint's lap, so Quint twisted toward Amy, slid Travis over to her and turned to pull Taylor onto his lap.

"Nice move," Amy said.

"That's high praise, coming from the master," he said, tickling Taylor.

"The master?" She laid Travis on her chest and sank lower on the couch. "Not quite."

"Spin!" Taylor crawled higher on Quint, putting her little hands on either side of his face. "Peeze. Pop, peeze."

"Popcorn?" he asked.

She shook her head. "Spin."

"How about you spin the bear?" he suggested.

She scrambled back and off his lap, and ran to grab the bear from where she'd left it. She had it by its leg, then turned and spotted the popcorn. She crossed to the mess, plopped down in the middle of it, and picking up a handful of popcorn, she pushed it against the bear's sewn mouth.

"Nice move again," Amy murmured. "Now if you could only get her to pick up that mess."

"That's a thought," he murmured, then slipped down off the couch onto the floor. He reached for the empty popcorn bowl and picked up a handful. "Wow, look at this," he said, and Taylor turned. He let the popcorn fall one kernel at a time out of his hand and down into the bowl. "Wow, is that great?"

Taylor watched him for a moment, then came closer, dropping the bear on the floor. She picked up a single kernel, looked at Quint, then dropped it in the bowl. "Way to go, girlie," he said with a grin. "How about another one?"

Before long Quint moved back, using the couch as support while he watched the little girl plunk one kernel after the other into the bowl.

"Oh, that was a beautiful thing to behold," Amy murmured.

"I wish I could claim it as my idea, but I think it started with Tom Sawyer painting that fence. Make a kid think you're having fun, and they want to do it. Now, I can just sit back and watch."

She chuckled. "If you keep this up, I'll start thinking you've been lying."

"I don't lie," he said softly.

"Okay, what do you call that thing with the suit? 'It's off the rack,' you said. Sure."

"Okay, I readjusted the facts."

She chuckled at that. "The same way you did about

kids. You readjusted to hide the fact that you're terrific with kids and they think you're terrific.''

''Let's not get carried away,'' he muttered and got to his feet to cross to the hearth and coax the fire to new life with more wood.

Taylor lost interest in the popcorn and came over to the couch, climbing up by Amy and putting her head on her lap. Amy smoothed her hair softly, but watched Quint crouching in front of the hearth, holding his hands out to the warmth. If she closed her eyes, she could almost believe this was a real family. Her, Taylor, the baby. She closed her eyes for real, blocking out the sight of Quint. But he was in the picture. Part of it. A huge part of it.

That confusion was coming back, blotting out the soft comfort that had begun to grow in the room. She glanced down at Taylor and saw she was fast asleep. Travis was lying on her stomach sucking on his pacifier. Then she looked at Quint. The ease and peace she felt with the children dissolved, and she felt her whole being tense. She saw the way his shoulders tested the cotton of his shirt, the way he put the poker on the hearth, then raked his fingers through his hair before he stood and turned to her.

The man could tip her world with a word or a look. And that look was there now, making her tense. He studied her intently for what seemed forever before he said, ''What are you thinking about?''

She shrugged, looking away from him and down at the babies. She wasn't going to share her thoughts with him. That level of intimacy didn't belong here, not with him. That was treacherous territory, so she generalized enough to keep her real thoughts out of it. "Just how strange life can be. About the new year. Life. What about you?"

He shook his head and raked his fingers through his hair. "No quid pro quo on this," he muttered.

"That's not fair," she said.

"Life isn't fair."

She wouldn't argue with that.

He asked, "What now?"

That same question echoed in her. What now? But her thoughts had nothing to do with the next hour or even the next day. Or why she wanted to have him sit by her again and just be there. Suddenly, the life she thought she had a vision of wasn't there either. That life with her and Taylor, just the two of them, had blurred and twisted, leaving a gaping hole in it. And she knew that hole wasn't the one left by Rob's death.

She didn't understand, and she swallowed hard, trying to ease a tightness that was creeping into her throat. "I...I don't know," she said with complete honesty. She didn't have a clue what her life would be like when she walked away from here, when Travis went wherever he'd go, or when Quint was just an acquaintance at work again.

He came closer, towering over her. "Can we put the kids down now, or is it too early?"

The kids? Of course. He wasn't thinking about life and why it suddenly didn't make any sense. "No, it's not too early." She glanced at the clock on the mantel, shocked to see that it was almost ten o'clock.

"Okay," he said as he gently picked up a sleeping Taylor. "Can you get Travis?"

"Sure, I just hope he doesn't start crying again." She eased up, maneuvering the boy into her arms, and even though he started making loud sucking sounds on his pacifier, he didn't waken. She eased to her feet, then followed Quint through the house and back to her room. The light was on in there, and it was only a few minutes before Quint had Taylor settled on the bed. She placed Travis on the bed, as well, surrounded by pillows.

She tugged a receiving blanket over the baby and realized how tiny and vulnerable he looked, and how much she'd grown to care about him in the short time he'd been with her. She leaned down, brushed a kiss on his cheek, then stood back. She couldn't keep him, she knew that, but it didn't stop her from aching at the prospect of handing him over to someone else. She took an unsteady breath, startled when Quint touched her on the shoulder.

"Don't do this to yourself," he whispered near her ear.

"Do what?" she asked, not taking her eyes off the baby.

"Get so attached to him." Quint reached to touch the baby's cheek, and she trembled, feeling a sense of impending loss so oppressive she wondered how she could breathe. She turned away from the bed and walked out of the room without a clue where she was going to go.

Chapter Thirteen

Quint had decided to leave Amy alone. He'd looked at her across the room when he'd been fixing the fire, and known that he had to leave her alone. Every atom in his being responded to her. And every atom in his being knew that it was wrong.

He followed her out of the bedroom and almost bumped into her. She'd stopped in the middle of the hallway, just standing there, hugging her arms around herself and he could see her trembling. Everything in him wanted to touch her and hold her, but he kept his distance.

"You know Travis has to go...either to the police or back to his mother."

"Of course," she said, rubbing the flats of her hands on her arms as if trying to find some warmth in the world. "I don't need you to remind me of that."

He didn't know what to say. "Of course you don't."

She took a breath. "Did...did you turn on the intercom?"

"It's on."

"I need to get the phone. I left it in the den."

"I'll get it for—"

She cut him off with a vague wave of her hand as she headed back toward the kitchen. "I'll do it," she said without looking back at him.

He was going to do the smart thing and go to his room, close the door and get through the night. But he didn't. He couldn't get that sight of her trembling out of his mind, and he went after her. By the time he caught up to her, she was by the couch picking up the phone.

"Anyone you want to call is either washed out or treading water," he said.

He knew he'd startled her when the phone almost slipped out of her hand. But she caught it and pulled it to her chest, as if protecting it. "I wasn't going to call anyone," she said in a low voice. "But it needs to be charged. The battery's low. You can charge it, can't you? If she calls, she has to be able to get through."

He didn't have to ask who "she" was. "You said the lines are full, so she probably can't get through right now anyway. Meanwhile, I've got a charger for it in my room. No problem."

"Good," she said, brushing past him to go through the kitchen.

He felt as if he was playing catch-up with her, turning and heading off again, catching up to her in the hallway to the room where the kids were sleeping. She paused long enough to glance inside at the children, then continued down to his room, one more door down and on the opposite side of the hallway.

She was inside before he got there, and as he went in the door, he saw her standing in the middle of the dark room, the room he'd had since he was a boy, waiting for him. He flipped on the light, then crossed to the long, low dresser that sat under the shuttered windows on the back wall. He turned and held out his hand to Amy for the phone. She dropped it in his hand, and he put it in the desk charger.

"Safe and sound and charging just…" His voice trailed off as he turned and found her looking around the room. Her gaze skimmed over the bed his dad had made out of trees from the property, with peeled-trunk posters at all four corners, the mussed linen of sheets and the patchwork quilt his mother had made. The shelves held everything from yearbooks to model planes to comics. Not exactly a mature room, but a room that was comfortable for him when he returned home.

"I told you, my mother tends to keep rooms the way they were back in the dark ages," he said.

She glanced at him. "I'd love it if Taylor someday could go back home and find the room she grew up in."

She was twisting her wedding ring nervously and it hit him just how much she'd lost when her husband died, little things and big things. Gone. And he grieved for it for her. From the first, he'd been fighting his attraction to Amy, knowing how wrong it was, how out of time it was. He could manage dating. He could manage that just fine. But what was going on now was beyond anything that mundane and shallow.

Grief for her. Needing to ease her pain, needing to believe that someday she'd have what she wanted.

She looked past him at the phone lying on the dresser. "If it's charging can you still get calls?"

"Sure." She never stopped twisting the ring. "No problem. And I've got voice mail. We're covered."

"Good...good."

There was a faint whimper over the intercom and Amy turned immediately toward the speaker by the door. There was another soft sound, and she headed out of the room.

When she left, he felt a huge amount of tension leave with her. The room's air became more breathable, and it seemed to expand. There was another sound on the intercom, Amy's voice, a whisper that was barely audible.

"It's okay, love, it's okay," soft and gentle, and whatever relief he'd felt at her going shattered at the sounds on the intercom. "I'm here. You're okay." Words he wanted to say to her. "Shhhh, you're fine."

He stared at the intercom and could almost see Amy bending over the children, soothing and comforting them when she needed it so much herself. The lights flickered, settled into a steady glow again, then flickered and went out completely. There was total silence all around, then he turned to go to Amy. He went out the door, took two steps and ran right into softness and heat and the scent of roses. Amy.

He reached out, and his hands found her, her arms, holding her, keeping her steady, and she was holding him. Safe. And for that moment in the dark, he truly thought that he could make the world right for her.

That he could take away her pain. That he could be there for her.

In some way she was doing that for him. She was settling his world, taking away a void that seemed to surround him, and she was there.

He held her more tightly, pressed a kiss to the top of her head and felt her tremble. There were no words, no questions, just the two of them standing in the dark, holding each other. It was enough. It was total. She was an anchor for him, a solid rightness in a world that had little definition for him anymore.

And he couldn't let go. He couldn't step back and say mundane, polite words. He couldn't stop. He skimmed his hands up her back, then in the deep shadows, he framed her face with his hands. Nothing else mattered. Nothing else could. He lowered his head to find her lips.

Maybe if she hadn't responded, if she hadn't opened her lips in invitation and slipped her arms around his neck, if she hadn't arched toward him, he might have stopped at a kiss. But there was no stopping when he tasted her and his kiss was answered with an explosive passion that matched his own, a passion that had been locked deep inside him since the first time he saw her.

He lifted her higher, kissing her with the hunger of a starving man. He'd been starving all his life until her. Until this moment. He felt her presence filling him, giving a sense of completion in his soul with her in his arms, as heady as it was frightening. It was new and incredible and as fathomless as what he felt for her.

He lifted her higher and her legs circled his waist, twining around him, and he carried her back into his room, into the softness of the shadows, to the bed he'd had since he was a boy. Together they tumbled into the coolness of the mussed linens, never losing contact. As they lay side by side in the shadows, he tasted her and explored her.

The only sounds were her soft moans, their quick breathing. He felt her hands on him, working their way under his shirt, skin against skin, heat and desire mingling in a fire that threatened to consume him.

But he welcomed it. He went with it. He touched her, skimming his hand along her arm, then to her middle, finding the zipper on her sweatshirt, fumbling to undo it, as awkward as a teenage boy in the back of a car. Then the cotton of a T-shirt was pushed up and the delicate lace of her bra was too much of a barrier for him. He shifted her up, taking off her clothes, slipping them free and pushing them away until there was skin against skin. She trembled, then gasped when he cupped her breast, his thumb and forefinger finding her nipple. It immediately peaked and hardened, and her gasp turned to a deep moan, low in her throat.

He shifted, tasting her breast, skimming his hand lower, spanning her middle, then pushing the tips of his fingers under the waistband of her jeans. The fastener popped, the zipper lowered and he felt the top of her panties. He wasn't sure how he did it, but the jeans were tugged free, tossed into the shadows, then the panties were gone. He found her center and she cried out, a muffled sound of intense pleasure that sent him reeling. She arched toward him, pressing herself against his palm, and he moved slowly, the need to be in her beyond reason.

Amy was lost and found. She fell into a place with Quint where the world was kept at bay; a place where she could just be…with Quint. Guilt and reality had no standing there, just need and feeling. Everything else was on the outskirts, hovering around the fringes, but as long as Quint was there, as long as he was touching her and kissing her, nothing could hurt her.

She went to that place, she relished that place and when Quint's hands explored her and found her, she struggled to stay as close to him as she could. She would have melted into him, if she could have. She would have let him flow into her soul if it were possible. She touched him, felt the sleek heat of his skin, the brush of his mustache as he took her nipple in his mouth. She arched toward him as floods of ecstasy flowed around her and through her.

In the next heartbeat, coolness took the place of heat, and she opened her eyes, reaching out, but her hands closed on empty air. She looked up and relief left her dizzy when she saw that Quint hadn't left. He was there, near her, shadows on shadows, but she could see him moving, then he was back with her, his clothes gone, and she felt him against her. Her arms went around him, holding on to him for dear life, and that's what it was to her at that moment in time. Her life. Her breath. Her ability to live.

He shifted and was over her, his legs between hers, his strength against her, testing her, but not penetrating, and his voice, rough with need, whispered around her, "Tell me to stop if you want me to."

She touched his face, brushed the mustache with the ball of her thumb, then found his lips and she felt an unsteadiness there. "No, don't stop," she breathed, "please, please, don't stop," and she lifted her hips to him, aching to feel him inside her.

He trembled, then with exquisite slowness, he slipped into her, filling her, joining with her in a wonder that brought the burning of tears to her eyes. He was still for an eternity, and she was certain if he did anything else, she'd shatter into a million pieces. But slowly, ever so slowly, he moved, and with each stroke, she knew that there was another place to go to, a place of oneness that would blot out every pain in her life.

Her hips began to mimic his actions, lifting toward him, accepting each thrust. Feelings built in a blinding fire of sensations, higher and higher. And when she thought it was possible to die from pleasure, the world fell away and it was just her and Quint and a completeness that was indescribable. Just her and him. Two. One. She let go and soared, over and over again, until a culmination was there, perfect and awesome. Then the fall back to earth. But she wasn't alone. She was with Quint.

He didn't leave her until they shifted onto their sides, facing each other, and she snuggled into his embrace. His chin rested on her head, his heart beat against her hand, and she felt every breath he took. He shifted more toward her, one arm around her, his other hand resting on her hip. And she didn't dare breathe in case everything fell apart. She could feel it teetering, then he pressed a kiss to her hair and she closed her eyes tightly.

Later. Later she'd think, she'd feel, but for now, she had this. She knew it was a time out of time, but it was hers. And she wouldn't give it up by letting reality intrude right now.

QUINT NEVER SLEPT. He held Amy, so close to saying I love you that he quite literally thought he'd said it. She was asleep, holding to him, and he couldn't say a thing. Except he was sorry. Sorry that he was weak and so needy. That he'd thought only of himself and those needs. This was all wrong, all so selfish of him. It was his fault, so he held her and he kept his words to himself and he knew that when they got out of this bed, it was over. And he'd have to make it okay for her any way he could.

He was startled when the overhead light flashed on, flickered, then stayed on. Trying not to wake Amy, he stretched as far as he could to the right, finding the light switch on the wall with the tip of his finger and flicking it off. But the darkness hid everything, and he didn't want that now. He shifted, turned on the low light on his side of the bed, then raised himself on one elbow and looked down at Amy.

Amy in soft shadows. Amy sleeping. Amy with tangled ebony hair tumbling around her naked shoulders. He saw everything about her. The stubborn curls at her temple, the bottom lip that looked slightly swollen from their kisses, her lashes making dark arcs on her cheeks, a soft sighing breath she took every once in a while. Her hand on his stomach, her legs tangled with his and her breath brushing his skin.

His body began to respond and he shifted lower until he was by her again, but staring up at the ceiling. She was everything that wasn't his. Everything that he'd remember and regret not having again. Everything that another man would have someday when she could move on. There was no jealousy of that man now, just regret that he'd come into her life at the wrong time for both of them.

She sighed and he held her more tightly to him as a spark of foolish hope started in him. Maybe what Mike had said to him was right, that being in the world at the same time was all that mattered. He could do whatever Amy wanted. He could love Taylor…he already did. The child and the mother. So easy. So very easy. And he could protect them and care for them both and make things as right as he could for them.

He closed his eyes, letting that idea settle into him.

AMY WOKE in an instant when a noise drew her out of sleep as surely as if it had been a crashing roll of thunder. Taylor making soft noises, little sounds that she made sometimes, sounds that either meant she was waking, or that she was restless, but would settle herself.

Amy had opened her eyes to the low glow of the side lamp, and to Quint holding her. The electricity had come back on; she'd made love with Quint. She hadn't noticed the one because of being so obsessed with Quint.

She listened, waiting, and when she heard nothing else, she closed her eyes and lay very still. But she couldn't stop thinking. She couldn't stop the reality of what she'd done coming to her full force. She'd made love to Quint. She'd let him make love to her. She'd given herself in a way she'd never thought she would again to a man she loved.

The world stopped. Time didn't exist. Love? She trembled and felt Quint's hold on her tighten a bit. That didn't happen twice. It couldn't. Not that love that came from your soul and was forever. No, she closed her eyes so tightly that colors exploded behind her eyes. No. She shifted, the need to escape a living thing in her.

But as soon as she tried to move, Quint held to her, his voice near her ear saying, "I thought you were asleep," and the heat of his breath fanning her skin.

"I...I just woke up," she said, hating the unsteadiness in her voice and the fact that she didn't have the strength to just get up and leave.

"You heard Taylor?"

He'd been awake all this time, too? "I think she's settled again."

His hand moved on her, tracing the swell of her hip, moving around to circle her waist, and she trembled. "We need to talk," he murmured, his mustache brushing softly against the skin on her shoulder.

She didn't want to talk. She didn't want to feel him against her back, his body angled to fit hers. She didn't want to feel him touching her skin, or want him to keep touching her. She hated herself and she hated her weakness, and she hated it when she turned in his embrace and whispered, "Don't say anything. Please."

She hated the need in her to touch his face with the soft light behind him, to feel the bristling of a new beard, the brush of his mustache and the softness of his lips. She was thankful that his face was a blur in the shadows. Just as well, she thought, not seeing clearly, and trembled when she felt his arousal against her. She shifted her hand lower and found him, circled him and felt him gasp.

There was no more talking. Just touching and feeling and being. She wanted him so much, and she'd have him one more time. She took what he offered, kissing and touching, being filled by him, and being given pleasure that knew no bounds. Later, she thought as she went with her feelings and arched to him, giving as good as she got, and losing herself in a world of ecstasy that was its own reality.

She climaxed with Quint, the sound of mutual pleasures given and taken mingling in her ears, then the slow descent into the peace and satiation of her entire being. She lay with him, her head on his shoulder, the beating of his heart echoing around her, and she waited for the pain. She waited for the regret to drive her out of his bed. But it didn't come. It wasn't there.

She didn't move, almost not breathing, but nothing happened. Nothing took away that sense of rightness that came out of nowhere. She was doing it herself, she reasoned, making it seem right to convince herself, but amazingly, it was right. It was very right. All of the things she feared weren't there. The pain, the horror at betraying Rob, that horrible feeling of guilt at being alive and Rob not being there, too. All of them were gone.

That realization settled into her being, into her soul. All that sorrow that he would never be here again, but a joy that she was here…with Quint. And in that instant, the healing took place. Something let go inside her. A part of her let go of Rob, let him be her past, a good, wonderful past, a joy in her life for such a short time. But she could let it go and let it be her past. The stark reality that finally she could go on living was there.

Tears came, silently, making her shake, and she clung to Quint. She always cried at goodbyes, at moments when she knew that life was in front of her, and she had to put the past behind her. The past. She had loved Rob. She always would, but remarkably, she could still love now. The mourning was over, and her life stretched out in front of her. A life Quint had given back to her. And she cried.

Quint held on to Amy while she sobbed, and the faint hope that he'd held, dissolved with each sobbing breath she took. He'd been a fool in more ways than one. He wasn't the man to stop her pain, to give her any happiness. The man she was crying for was that man. And as that thought solidified, he drew back from her, easing away until the contact was broken. He had a glimpse of her looking at him, her lashes spiked from tears and her skin flushed, and he knew if he stayed in that bed, he'd do the same thing over and over again. Just love her.

He sat up, swinging his legs over the side of the

bed and just sat there for a long moment. When she touched him on the back, he jerked forward and stood, reaching for his jeans. He put them on before he turned, and he was thankful for the space he'd created between himself and Amy. Very thankful when she started to sit up and the sheets slipped, exposing her beauty to the softness of the light.

"You said we need to talk," she said in a breathy whisper that ran riot over his frayed nerves. "We... we do, we really do."

He narrowed his eyes to minimize her image, then he forced himself to do what he knew he had to do...for both their sakes. "I know, and I'm so sorry for this, for letting it happen at all." The words all but choked him. "Nothing's changed. Nothing." Lie upon lie. "I'm still who I am, and you're still...we're just in way too different places. This never should have happened."

He turned his back to her, finding it easier to talk without looking at her. Each word he said almost killed him. "Big mistake. Chalk it up to the storm, to cabin fever. Whatever." He moved to the dresser, needing more distance, and he picked up the charged phone. When he turned, he was taken aback to find Amy standing by the bed, putting on her clothes, her back to him.

In silence she put on her jeans, followed by her sweatshirt, her actions jerky and fast. She reached for the T-shirt and bra she'd been wearing under her sweatshirt and his nerves felt ready to snap. "Did you hear what I said?"

She turned, and he didn't know what he thought

would be there, but it wasn't an almost glazed look on her face. "Yes, but I was waiting for you to get to how you're too old for all of this. I bet you were just getting ready to say that, weren't you?"

"Whatever," he muttered. "Just blame me for this. I should have—"

"Blame you?" she asked flatly. "I'm not some idiot who didn't know what I was doing," she muttered, fumbling with the zipper on her shirt. "And you don't have to say anything else."

No, he didn't, but that didn't stop this need to explain and explain and explain. A man of few words, and he felt overwhelmed with words that he couldn't begin to sort out. All he could say was the truth that sat bitterly on his tongue. "You don't want this. You've made that clear before. You've got your life."

She zipped her sweatshirt and looked up at him. "And you've got yours."

He didn't even know what that life was anymore, but he'd figure that out after she was gone. "Yes," he said.

"So you've said," she murmured flatly, and he could see unsteadiness in her shoulders before she obliterated the distance between them. She came closer, looked at the phone, then took it from him. Without another word, she went to the door and left.

He stared at the spot where she'd been standing, then heard her door down the hallway close with a quiet click. He'd done the right thing. He knew that, but it was cold comfort when he went near the bed and almost tripped over the sheet Amy had wrapped around herself. It lay in a heap on the floor and when he bent to pick it up, he was certain it held a hint of Amy on it. A subtle fragrance as unique as she was herself.

He tossed the sheet onto the bed, then turned away from it, went out into the hallway and walked barefoot past the closed door to her room. He never looked back as he went through the house, toward the den to find out if a good stiff drink could help him get through the rest of the night.

Chapter Fourteen

Amy crawled out of bed while both children were still asleep, looked outside to an amazingly clear sky, then got into the shower. She stood under the hot stream of water, horribly aware of the tenderness in her breasts and the ache deep inside that had started the moment Quint had turned to her and said, *Big mistake. Chalk it up to the storm, to cabin fever. Whatever.*

Tears did no good. She had no right to them. He'd told her clearly enough what he did and didn't want, and she'd gone on ahead anyway. It was her fault, and she'd get over it. At least a numbness that had started when Quint had faced her in his room was still lingering. She'd leave as soon as she could, go back and straighten out the mess with Travis, then get on with her life. She'd figure out what that meant when she had to. Right now, leaving was all she could manage.

She turned off the water, reached for a towel and dried, then slipped on her robe and stepped back into the bedroom. Travis was waking, slowly and easily, stirring and stretching, so precious it almost took her breath away. She crossed to him, whispered, "Good morning, buddy," then looked down at Taylor.

She was stunned to find the makeshift bed empty, and it was then that she realized the bedroom door was ajar. She scooped up Travis, went to the door and stepped out into the quiet hallway. She heard a squeal, saw Quint's door was open, then Taylor came toddling out, still mussed from sleep, but wearing cowboy boots that went clean up to her thighs. She saw Amy, squealed with delight and headed for her, the boots making clunky sounds on the floor and slowing her progress.

Taylor was so serious about trying to walk in the boots that Amy smiled at her, then Quint came out of his room and her smile died. He was wearing jeans and nothing else. His hair was mussed and spiked, the beginnings of a beard darkening his jaw, and he looked as if he'd had a rough night. The sight of him brought everything back to her in a rush, and she tried desperately to hide her reaction, that instant response, the catch in her breathing and that explosive need. She wouldn't make the same mistake again.

He saw her, narrowed his eyes and grabbed the doorjamb. "I thought I was being attacked by wild animals," he muttered. "She got on the bed and used me as a trampoline."

If she hadn't been so tense, she would have laughed and felt a certain degree of satisfaction that Taylor had given him a Taylor-style wake-up call.

"Sorry," she murmured at the same time as Travis started to squirm and cry. "The storm's over. I need to leave."

He frowned, then ran a hand roughly over his face. "I don't know how the roads are."

She wasn't going to stay here any longer than she absolutely had to. "I'll find out. Maybe I can call a cab or something."

That made him start to smile, but the expression ended up being a grimace. "No cabs out here. I'll take you back if it's safe."

Well, it wasn't safe being here. "I'll get the children changed and fed, then we can go. Okay?"

"Sure, sure," he muttered and turned away from her, going back inside his room and closing the door behind him.

Taylor just barely made it to Amy before she stumbled and grabbed the hem of her robe for support. "Pop," she said looking up at her mother.

"No, no popcorn for breakfast," she said, turning and managing to get both kids back in the bedroom and the door closed before she realized she was shaking like a leaf.

IN TWO HOURS they were on their way back to Houston along roads that were still partially flooded, but Quint's car took them well. He drove Amy, the two kids and Charlie the rat to her place, helped her get them out and up to the apartment. Neither adult talked beyond what was necessary until he was putting the diaper bags on the floor by the door of the tiny apartment.

He looked up at Amy who stood in the middle of the room holding Travis while Taylor dug into a toy chest near the Christmas tree. "Do you need anything else before I go?"

"Just to say…I really appreciate all you did for us."

How could he thank her for all she'd done for him; for the glimpse he'd had into what life might have been if they'd met in another time and another place? "No problem," he murmured and he should have left, just turned and gone, but he didn't. He seldom did the smart thing where Amy was concerned. "Listen, if you need help with Travis or…anything…."

"No, I don't need help," she said, her voice painfully flat. "You can go."

"Just like that?" he heard himself ask.

She jiggled Travis as he started to fuss. "What else is there besides wishing you a happy birthday?"

He shrugged, happiness a foreign thought to him right then. "Nothing, I guess," he murmured, and would have left if Taylor hadn't come running at him, grabbing him around the legs.

He looked down into eyes the same as her mother's eyes, then hunkered down in front of her. "Hey there, you're home."

She held out her arms to him. "Pop, spin, peeze?"

Her voice was tiny, as tiny as she was, and her face sober. He took her in his arms, hugged her, then said, "No popcorn or spinning. Why don't you get Baby and spin with her?"

She was very still, then scooted out of his hold and went in search of her doll. Quint looked up at Amy, at eyes unblinking, watching him.

He'd found love, and right then he knew that love

didn't matter. It didn't fix anything. He saw by the way she held on to the love for her dead husband that it lasted, but it didn't make anything easier. It only made it more difficult for him to straighten up, turn around and walk out the door.

Two days later

"I DON'T KNOW what to do," Amy whispered, hugging the crying baby to her and trying to keep an eye on Taylor who was going through the bottom drawer of her desk at the center. "I just don't know what to do for you."

She tried to hold Travis the way Quint had. She tried to get him on her forearm, tummy-down like a football in the crook of her arm, and she tried to jiggle and get him to stop crying. But it didn't work for her. When the crying bouts came, he wouldn't be comforted. Her nerves were raw, and all she really wanted to do was go home and crawl into bed with the two kids and have all of them sleep for a week.

She'd stayed at LynTech as late as she could for the past few days, hoping against hope that a woman would show up looking for Travis. Or maybe it wasn't hoping, it was trying to tie up that loose end to figure out what to do next. But no one had shown up except the guard checking on her—and Quint checking on her, too.

She gave up walking and jiggling and sank down in her chair and started swiveling back and forth. "Shhh, shhhh," she said, frowning when Taylor tossed a package of envelopes out of the drawer, scattering them everywhere on the carpeting. "Baby, no, Taylor, no, pick them up."

Taylor looked at her, screwed up her nose and said, "No."

"Great, just great," she muttered, feeling so horribly alone at that moment that it made her eyes burn.

She hadn't felt this sort of loneliness since Rob had died, but it had nothing to do with Rob now. When Quint had been there, she hadn't felt it and that hurt her. She didn't want him to be the one to hold back loneliness, because he wasn't going to be here. Loving him had been easy, but letting go was just as hard as any goodbye she'd had to say in her life. She was still working on it, and it didn't help when he kept stopping by.

He'd been coming into the center for a few minutes in the morning, and a few minutes at night, as if he was checking on her. Or more likely wanting to know if she'd called the police about Travis. But it was wearing her out. To see him, to have him not even look directly at her, to watch him talk to Taylor, check on Travis, then leave, was more than she could stand. He hadn't been in this evening, but she was braced for the moment when he'd show up.

"Mama," Taylor said, coming over to the chair, obviously sensing her mother's distress. She laid her head on Amy's lap and looked up at her. "Mama?"

"What, love?" she asked.

"Pop?"

"Sweetheart, I don't have any popcorn. I'm sorry. I meant to get some, but I haven't." Taylor had been asking for popcorn since Quint walked out, and got increasingly upset when Amy didn't have any. If she'd had a bit of free time, she would have gone to the store for some, but she hadn't had two minutes to string together for herself since New Year's. With Jenn gone, she'd truly been on her own.

"Peeze. Pop, want pop," Taylor whined, and her voice cut across Amy's nerves.

She knew right then how foolish she was being. She wasn't some super woman who could go on with life and take care of both kids and make everything right. She wasn't even close. For the first time since Quint had appeared with Travis in his arms, she considered the fact that she might have to make that call to the police.

Tomorrow LynTech would return to normal. Lindsey and Zane would finally be home after being grounded by the storm and missing Matt and B.J.'s wedding. Matt and B.J. had taken Anthony along on their honeymoon, something that Amy hadn't even questioned. Her own life was strange enough as it was. Most importantly, she'd have to explain Travis to everyone. And she couldn't.

Not any more than she could figure out how to face Quint day in and day out the way she seemed destined to do. Maybe it was time to let go. She looked at the wall clock. Fifteen minutes to six. She looked down at her hand patting the baby's back and saw her ring. Plain. Gold. She stared at it long and hard. Yes, it was time to let go.

She slipped off her ring, held it for a long moment, then reached to put it in the top drawer of the desk.

Sliding the drawer shut, she whispered, "Goodbye," then sat back. Time to let go.

She looked at the clock again. In fifteen minutes, if a miracle didn't occur and Travis's mother didn't call or show up, she knew that she'd have to make the call. She'd have to let go.

"I DON'T APPRECIATE you doing this again, Quint. New Year's Day was bad enough, but right now I'm in the middle of something—"

Quint cut off Les Merin, his attorney from New York. "If I know you, you're spending your last day of vacation the way you spent New Year's Eve, in a hot tub with a couple of blondes."

"She's brunette and there's just one," Les muttered.

"Okay, tell her to wait ten minutes and tell me what you found out."

"Well, since you called me yesterday, and remember it's a holiday, and every sane person is having fun, I had to do some digging, but I found out what you wanted to know. I can't give you specifics, because I don't have my notes on me." He chuckled at that, but Quint didn't.

"Just give me the highlights."

"Abandoned children go into Child Protective Services, are assigned to a foster-care-type situation until the courts can hear the case and then they're put into official foster care for however long is necessary."

Quint was impatient. "Just get to the bottom line about the child and the mother."

"Okay, in a nutshell, the kid's in the system for

anywhere from three months up until he turns eighteen, and the mother, if she's found, gets arrested and depending on her age and circumstances, goes into youth authority, jail, rehab if drugs or alcohol are involved. You name it. In all probability, somewhere down the road, she gets the kid back, or she gives the kid up. She has to sign away all parental rights, and the father has to do it, too, if he's known. That can take months, and the kid stays in the system while it's done.''

Quint sank back in the chair and closed his eyes. ''So, no matter what happens, the kid's in the system for a minimum of three months? And a druggie mother could get him back if she did or said the right thing?''

''You've got it. Now, can I get back to the hot tub?''

''Okay, but could you get me the name of the best attorney out here that has full knowledge of child protection laws?''

''If you leave me alone for the rest of the night, I'll look into it as soon as I get to work tomorrow and contact you.''

''It's a deal,'' Quint murmured.

''I don't suppose you're going to tell me what you're doing out there that has to do with abandoned kids, are you?''

''Maybe later,'' Quint said and hit the Disconnect button, then stood and reached for his jacket. It was time to leave and this time he wasn't going down to check on Amy and the kids first. He knew she was still here. The guard at the front desk had said she hadn't signed out yet, but just seeing her wasn't working. He couldn't continue spending a bit of time with Taylor and Travis, and then just walk away.

He shrugged into his jacket and turned out the lights, then left his office, heading for Zane's office. Zane had come back from Aspen yesterday, gave him a call to touch base and that had been that. But he'd use Zane's elevator to go down to the parking garage. When he had the name of an attorney, he'd let that attorney contact Amy and help her with Travis. He wasn't getting into it anymore.

He went through Zane's office to the executive elevator. As he got in, he quite literally had a sensation of moving away from Amy and the kids and heading toward nothing. He pushed the button for the parking garage, and, as the elevator headed down, he realized that the craziest part of all of this was that he was doing it because he loved her.

He just wished he wasn't stumbling so badly over his own justification for what he was doing. If he was right, why was he feeling such loss? Why was he missing Amy's voice? Her presence? Why was he missing a two-year-old obsessed with popcorn and a foundling who cried most of the time? More importantly, why was Amy alone with two children and he was alone with no one?

He stepped out of the elevator, and saw that the only two cars in the garage were Amy's and his. He crossed to the SUV, gripped his briefcase, then took out his key and hit the Release button. He opened the door, tossed in his briefcase and would have gotten in, but stopped when he heard something. He looked around, certain he couldn't have heard someone crying. Seeing and hearing nothing he slipped inside his car. But just as he reached to close the door, he heard it again—a soft sobbing sound.

He got out and, looking around, he realized it came from behind a heavy support column near the center. He crossed to the column and looked around the pillar.

A girl, a teenager, was sitting on the cold concrete, her head in her hands, crying softly. He hesitated, then went closer and tried not to startle her too much. "Excuse me?"

Her head jerked up, and she scrambled to her feet. Medium height, with long blond hair tangled around her face, she looked miserable. Her blue eyes were swollen from crying and her skin was blotched with spots of bright color. Green overalls worn with a yellow sweater made her look sallow, but as she pressed back against the pillar, Quint didn't have to ask who she was. She'd come back for Travis.

"Sir, I'm real sorry," she said in a soft Texas twang, and scrubbed her eyes. "I'm leavin'. I'm sorry." And she would have taken off if he hadn't stopped her.

"Don't go." She stopped. "He's your baby, isn't he?"

She paled at his words, to the point that he thought she might pass out. "I don't know what you're talkin' about," she muttered.

Amy had been right. The mother cared. She really cared, but she was a scared teenager who obviously hadn't known what to do. "It's okay," he said. "I'm not going to get you in trouble. In fact, maybe I can help you.''

She looked uncertain. ''I don't see how you can help me.''

''Trust me, I can.''

She seemed to collapse a bit, leaning back against the pillar and hugging her arms around herself. ''I'm goin' to go to jail.''

''No, you aren't. I promise you that.''

''You sure?''

''I'm sure. You've got my word on it.''

She sighed. ''I knew when you got him, you were a nice man,'' she said in a low voice. ''And I knew that lady in there would be good to him. I watched her and she's so kind. She's like, real good with kids.''

She'd checked out Amy before leaving the baby. That meant a lot to Quint and to what he was thinking of doing. ''What's your name?''

She hesitated. ''Shannon.''

''Shannon, just answer me one thing?''

''What?''

''Do you want the best for Travis?''

''Oh, yes, I do, but I can't keep him. I can't do it. I mean, I want to, but it's…'' She bit her lip. ''I want him to be happy and safe, but I'm so afraid. I don't know what to do. I can't keep him, but I couldn't stand it if he was hurt or somethin'. I'm so afraid of doing the wrong thing.''

At that moment, Quint understood something about himself, something basic and startling. He knew exactly why he was trying to walk away from everything he loved, Amy and Taylor and Travis, and what there could be with the three of them. It wasn't his age. It wasn't him not wanting to do ''the kid thing'' again. It was fear. Plain and simple. Fear of loving them like a part of his own soul and knowing that he could lose them, of knowing that if he told Amy how he felt, it might not mean a thing to her.

Just watching the fear in Shannon's face was like looking into his own soul. But he had choices and the power to make them work for everyone in a way that she didn't. And his choice at that moment wasn't just to walk away. His choice was to fight. Amy and the kids were worth a fight to the death.

''I need you to come with me,'' he said.

''You promised I wouldn't get arrested,'' Shannon said, moving back a bit.

''You won't. I want you to come in and talk with the lady who has Travis. She needs to meet you.''

She shook her head. ''No, no, I can't.''

''If you love Travis and want the best there is for him, you will.''

She looked at him, and he could almost see her thoughts, wondering if she could trust him, what she should do. Finally, she simply nodded. ''Okay.''

He motioned to the back door to the center. ''Let's go.''

She went with him and he opened the unlocked door, letting her go inside first. He heard the crying as soon as the door opened, and he led the way toward the sound. Amy's office.

Shannon was holding back, and he smiled at her. ''Let's go inside together.''

She could have bolted, but she didn't. Instead, she went into the room. He took it all in, Amy trying to keep a crying Travis on her shoulder while she reached for the telephone. Then Taylor turned, saw him and came running for him, passing Shannon without a glance, launching herself into his arms. He lifted her, hugging her to him, and looked over his head at Amy as she drew her hand back from the phone. Slowly she stood, the crying Travis in her arms.

Everything made perfect sense to him. Life fitted into a sanity that wrapped him with the hope that he might not be too late, that maybe Amy could do what she said she couldn't do. Maybe she could care enough for him to let him be with her. Maybe his love would be enough for all of them. Or maybe it wouldn't be. But he wasn't leaving until he knew for sure, one way or the other.

Chapter Fifteen

Amy was reaching to make the call when she heard something and looked up to find Quint coming into the office. Her hand froze in midmotion. Taylor was throwing herself at him, being scooped up and hugged, talking in babble that had "Pop" and "Spin" liberally scattered through it. And to his right was the miracle she'd wanted to happen. A young girl in green and yellow, with a pale face and eyes of deep blue, stood very still, never looking away from Travis.

She didn't have to ask to know that the baby's mother had come back. And she'd come back with Quint. Amy stood slowly, trying to comfort Travis, and the girl came toward them. She stared at the baby, but didn't offer to take him. "He…he cried for me, too, sometimes. Like, I couldn't stop him," she said in a low voice that was almost blotted out by the baby's wails. "He was real good most of the time, but that crying just made my mama real mad." Her hands stayed in the pockets of her overalls and she finally looked up at Amy. "He's a good baby though, you know?"

"Yes, I know," she said. "I'm Amy Blake."

"I'm Shannon Douglas."

The girl couldn't have been more than seventeen or eighteen years old, and she was so far out of her depth with the baby that it broke Amy's heart. "Honey, why did you feel you had to leave him like that?"

Shannon shrugged, her eyes welling up with the brightness of tears. "I couldn't do it no more."

"You don't have any family?"

"My mama and me live in an apartment and it's small and she works a lot, and she…she never wanted me to have him at all. But I couldn't just…" She bit her lip. "I didn't know what to do, and I was over near here with her trying to get the bus and I saw you and your little girl, and you were so nice." She shrugged sharply. "The guy at the door said you ran this place, and you had one kid and you were a great mom, and I watched you a couple of times, and you stayed late. I didn't just leave him, you know. I waited to make sure he was okay."

Amy cringed when Travis let out a heartfelt cry, then Quint was there, silently taking him from her and she let him. He turned the baby over, got him in "the hold" and started pacing with him, jiggling him up and down. Almost immediately Travis quieted. There was a heavy sigh, then silence.

Amy looked back at Shannon who was staring at Quint with total disbelief. "How'd he do that?" she asked in a hushed tone.

"I don't know," Amy said. "He just does it. He's a natural with kids. A real miracle worker."

Quint glanced at her, then crossed to Taylor who'd

started kicking the scattered envelopes on the floor. Quint crouched with Travis in his hold and picked up an envelope with his free hand. He dropped it in the empty box with a flourish and said, "Oh, look at that. A perfect basket."

Taylor looked at him, watched him drop a couple more in the box, then started doing it herself. Amy would have laughed if there was any humor left in her. Then Quint was standing by her, looking at Shannon. "The father's not involved in any of this?" he asked her.

She looked sort of uneasy, then said, "I'm not real sure who his daddy is. And no matter who it is, they wouldn't want nothing to do with him...or me."

"Your mother won't keep Travis for you?"

"Oh, no sir. She won't do that. She's got this boyfriend who can't stand babies, and she—"

He cut her off. "You can't keep him on your own?"

"No, sir. No way."

"If I found someone wonderful to take the boy, would you be willing to have him adopted?"

Shannon hesitated, but finally said, "Yes, sir. That would be good, as long as he was taken real good care of."

"You like Amy don't you?"

"Oh, yes, sir."

"What if she adopted Travis?"

Amy was horrified at his words. She'd take Travis home in a heartbeat, but she'd just admitted that she could barely take care of Taylor and herself. The past few days had clearly proven that she was in over her head. She spoke quickly. "Listen, Shannon, I'll go with you to people who can help you, who can make sure Travis gets the home he deserves."

He stopped her without touching her, just by speaking. "I thought you loved him?" he said, looking right at her.

She could barely meet his look. "Of course I do. You know that. I want him to be safe and happy."

"If it was possible for you to adopt him, would you?"

"That's not even—"

"Would you?" he asked in a low, intent voice.

She looked into his hazel eyes and exhaled. "Yes, yes, yes, but I can't. I can't do it. I can't make it work. I've tried and tried, but I finally realized that I can't do it."

"But you love him?"

She bit her lip. "Yes."

"Answer me one more thing. Do you think you could ever care about another man?"

She stared at him, the words there between them, but they made no sense. "What?"

"I don't mean love, I just mean caring, being okay with another man. Is that possible for you?" She could have sworn that he looked afraid for a moment, a pure fear in his eyes, then it was gone and he repeated, "Is it possible?"

"Quint, stop it. Don't do this."

He didn't move. "Listen to me, very carefully. What if I'm in love for the very first time in my life? What if I totally loved you and Taylor and Travis?"

She barely believed her ears. She wouldn't believe

them. She couldn't go through that pain again, of hoping, then knowing that it was all wrong. "You...you have to..."

"No, let me finish," he said, his voice lower and slightly unsteady. "You don't have to love me. I'll make this very easy for you. All you have to do is let me take care of the three of you. I came back to Houston thinking I might stay. And now I know for sure. I'm selling the place in New York and, if you'll let me, I'll be here for all of you. Just be with me and let me share your life. Amy, I want you to take away this loneliness and let me live."

She let his words settle in her heart and soul and tears came, silently slipping down her cheeks. Taylor was there, pushing between her and Quint, and Shannon was saying, "What's goin' on here?"

But all she saw was Quint, blurred and so incredibly dear to her. She tried to speak, but nothing would come. Then his free hand touched her cheek, the ball of his thumb brushing at her tears. "Oh, I'm sorry," he breathed unsteadily. "I'm rushing this. I'm no good at this, I told you that before. And as old as I am, I don't think I'll ever get good at it. The truth is, I thought I knew what I wanted, I really did. But I was dead wrong."

She covered his hand with hers, and could feel herself shaking all over. "Oh, Quint."

"Lady, if you'll just take me on, I'll love you enough for both of us. That's a promise. And the kids...I love them. You're the mother Mike should have had, the woman I should have fallen in love with back then and had children with. But we're here and now, and alive at the same time. And that's all that matters to me. Just let me love you.''

She tried to speak and had to clear her throat before she could make the words come. ''You...you could love the three of us?''

''I do love the three of you. I'm not sure I can do six or seven more kids, but one more wouldn't be all bad.''

Amy felt something in her, that life that had begun for her when she and Quint had made love, filling her with hope and joy, something that felt almost alien to her.

He was very still, and she realized he was looking at her hand. ''The ring?'' he breathed.

''I put it away to keep it safe, but I'm not wearing it anymore.''

''Are you sure?'' he asked, his voice low and unsteady.

''I'm sure,'' she said. ''Just as sure as I am of the fact that I'll let you take care of the three of us, but only if you'll let me love you for the rest of my life.''

''Oh, lady,'' he breathed, then leaned toward her, Travis and Taylor between them, but he managed to kiss her quickly and fiercely before Taylor pushed hard on both of them. ''No. Pop!'' she said.

Quint looked down at Taylor. ''I don't have any popcorn,'' he said.

''Pop,'' she said, lifting her arms to be picked up.

Quint shifted a finally sleeping Travis to Amy, then picked Taylor up in his arms. ''Okay, as soon as I can find some, it's yours,'' he said.

Shannon was looking from adult to adult. "I don't get all of this," she said.

Quint looked at Amy, smiled, then turned to Shannon. "We want to adopt Travis. We'll love him and care for him, and you'll know that he's safe. Will you let us do that?"

"Are you her husband or somethin'?"

Amy felt a twinge at the wording, but one look at Quint and she was okay. Everything was okay with Quint by her side. "I will be soon, very soon," he said.

"You two..."

"We're getting married," Quint said, glancing at Amy long enough for her to nod, then he looked back at Shannon. "I'll get a good attorney and we'll do this right. And I want you to be okay, too, Shannon. We'll try to help you as much as we can."

Taylor touched Quint on the cheek, making him look at her. "Pop?"

"I don't have any popcorn," he said.

"I think she's calling *you* Pop," Shannon said.

Amy looked at Quint and Taylor, then realized that Shannon was right. She'd been crying for Quint for two days, not for popcorn. "Shannon's right," she said.

Quint looked at Amy, his expression touched with shock, then pleasure. "Pop?"

"Huh," Taylor said, poking him in the chest. "Pop."

He moved closer to Amy, putting his arm around her and pulling her tightly to him. "Pop it is," he murmured.

Amy looked at her daughter, then down at Travis and finally she looked at Quint. She saw her future, a wonderful future. And she knew the miracle that it had taken to fashion it for all of them. "Yes, Pop it is," she said, leaning against him, letting him support her and loving him with all of her heart.

Valentine's Day

THE DAY-CARE CENTER was filled with people, adults and children, and the grand opening was a complete success. Heart-shaped balloons, pink streamers and paper hearts on the walls completed the festive feeling in the main room of the center. Just for Kids was officially in its new location, with more room, more supplies and more children than it had ever had before.

"It's a success," Quint said, coming up behind Amy who was standing to one side watching the scene with great pleasure. Her black cocktail dress with a cowled neckline had been a gift from Jenn, a "dress-up" outfit that seemed right for this occasion. Quint slipped his arms around Amy's waist and kissed the side of her neck, the distraction immediate and wonderful.

She closed her eyes. "I was just starting to wonder where you went."

"Did you miss me?" he whispered by her ear.

She could barely explain to him even now that when he wasn't close, she felt as if she was lost. "Of course," she said, covering his hands on her waist with hers. Her solitaire he'd given her sparkled in the overhead lights.

"I see Charlie came to the party."

She opened her eyes and looked over at the tree, to Taylor and Walker, Zane and Lindsey's son, on the floor with the rat's cage between them, trying to push popcorn through the mesh sides. "Taylor insisted. And Jenn thought the rat would add to the atmosphere."

She looked over at Jenn, dressed all in pink, holding Travis and talking to Jackson Ford, a man Amy hardly knew. He had the title of Executive Senior Vice President at LynTech, but he'd been in Europe working for the company since she'd been here. Jenn was talking intently to him, leaning toward the dark-haired man in a double-breasted gray suit. "Does Jenn ever dress in plain clothes?" Quint asked, following her line of sight.

She laughed. "Sure, but when there's a special occasion, she dresses for it. 'Theme dressing,' I think she calls it. It comes from her love of fabric and design, I suppose."

Right then, Quint's parents approached Jenn. His mother, a slender gray-haired woman who had passed on her smile to her son, put her arms out for Travis. The baby went to her without a murmur, and snuggled in. Quint's dad, John Gallagher, an older version of Quint with snow-white hair and tanned, weathered skin, smiled at his wife and their newest grandchild, then turned and went over to Taylor.

He crouched by her, much the same way his son did, getting to her level and the next thing Amy knew,

Taylor was in his arms and, in one movement, up on his shoulders. She laughed and squealed, thrilled to have a "horsey" ride. Walker watched Taylor, then ran to Zane, arms out, saying, "Horsey, horsey," and was on his daddy's shoulders right by John and Taylor. Lindsey was watching the two of them, and Amy knew a simple truth—pregnant women glowed, even when they were only six weeks along like Lindsey. The woman who thought she'd never have her own kids had taken Walker as her own, and now she had one on the way.

Life had its little twists and turns. Amy was an example of that. She'd thought she'd never have love again, but now she was surrounded by it. She'd never thought she'd be here with Quint, feeling a happiness that knew no bounds. Never suspected that they would have had a wedding that was more a barbecue than a grand affair, at the ranch they were making their home. Or that she'd have a stepson who was seven years younger than her. Or be so complete with a man who had become her life despite the fact that both had fought it right from the start.

A real miracle on all counts.

"Come and get it!"

She looked up at B.J. coming out of the kitchen with Matt, the two of them holding huge trays with hot dogs and chips and juice. Matt didn't look like one half of the CEOs at LynTech, any more than his wife looked like a spoiled rich girl. B.J. set the tray on the side table and started helping the kids get their food, explaining half were meat hot dogs and half were tofu dogs. "Just wonderful things," she promised each child.

Matt poured the punch, but looked up at his wife. "I'll take one," he said, and B.J. glanced at him. They didn't touch, but the look was a connection that was so evident between them. Even Robert Lewis saw it, smiling at his daughter before he got back to work with Anthony on putting together the train set he'd donated to the center. The older man and the nine-year-old boy had bonded completely, and couldn't have been more of a grandfather and grandson than if they'd been blood relatives.

Miracles on miracles.

"So," Quint said. "Are you ready?"

She looked around the room. "For what, a hot dog?"

His hold on her tightened slightly. "No, for my present for you." His voice had an edge of roughness to it, and she turned in his hold, and didn't think she'd ever get used to the way she felt just looking at him, that instant need to be closer, never to let go.

There was no suit tonight, just a collarless black silk shirt and snug dark slacks, setting off his graying hair and tanned skin. She felt her heart skip slightly. "Present?" she breathed, feeling her face heat just at the look in his narrowed hazel eyes. "Mister, this isn't exactly the ranch, you know. There are tons of people all over the place, and Travis is due for another crying spell any minute now and we cannot go into the Quiet Room and—"

He touched her lips with his forefinger, hushing her. "Jenn's agreed to watch out for Travis and Taylor for an hour and she's got plenty of help from Mom and Dad. So, we have one hour, okay?''

''Are we going to bake a gingerbread family?'' she asked, smiling at him, the expression getting just a bit unsteady when she felt him pull her even closer. His heart beat against hers, and she had the certain knowledge that she was one with him, completely joined, forever.

''Lady, we aren't going to burn this place down,'' he said on a rough chuckle that seemed to rumble against her where they touched.

Then he took her hand and led her away from the party, past her office, and out the back door to the parking garage, across to the executive elevator where he pushed a card in the slot. The doors opened and he stepped in, taking her with him, then hit the button to go up to the twentieth level.

Amy held his hand, staring at the two of them in the muted reflection in the doors, neither one talking. The car stopped and they got out, going through Zane's darkened office and the reception area. Quint led the way down the hall past the secretary's desk and back to his private office.

She stepped into his office ahead of him. It was a sprawling space dominated by the huge desk by the windows, a wall of bookcases and filing cabinets and a conversation area to the left with a long couch and two chairs in a semicircle. The only light came from the lamp on his desk. She turned to Quint as he clicked the lock on the door, then came across to her. ''Oh, that's your present,'' she murmured, putting her arms out to reach for him.

He stepped into her embrace, and just held her for a long moment, then moved back slightly. "Hold that thought." He eased her back against the desk and reached around her. "Here's your present," he said, holding out a folded piece of paper.

She looked at him, then took the paper and opened it. She read the single-page fax, then looked at Quint. "Is this true?" she asked.

"Les just faxed it. It's true. He found the father in Arizona and the guy's more than happy to sign away his parental rights." Amy couldn't stop the tears, and Quint touched her cheek. "I know, you can't conceive of someone walking away from a baby like that, but we have him. Travis is fine. We're fine." He took the paper from her hands, then was holding her again. "Hell, lady, we're better than fine, as long as you keep your end of this deal."

"Deal? What deal?"

"To love me for the rest of your life," he said, his voice vaguely unsteady.

"Oh, Quint," she said, tears there again. She swiped at her eyes, and sniffed. "No problem," she whispered, and she circled his neck with her arms. As she reached up, he lifted her off her feet until she was at eye level. "Is the door locked?" she asked.

"Absolutely."

"And we have an hour?"

"Fifty-five minutes, or thereabout."

"Let's not waste any of it," she breathed and found his lips with hers. That brush of his mustache, his heat, her completeness.

He carried her over to the couch, then lowered her

to stand in front of him. "I know Jenn was thinking of you when she got you this dress, but she wasn't thinking of me." He turned her around. Buttons ran down the back of it. "A thousand buttons," he said, starting to undo them.

She helped, slipping the top down, then finally wiggling out of it, and while he stripped, she took off the rest of her clothes. They faced each other for only a moment before coming together. They tumbled into the softness of the couch cushions, and Quint braced over her, his body along hers and his desire instantly there. "Oh, lady," he whispered, touching her, moving against her, and she marveled at the instant passion that exploded between them. White-hot, fire, consuming, and all-encompassing.

She lifted her hips to him, willing him to take her, and slowly, he entered her. There was no hesitation, just a total surrender, that moment when she felt part of him, when their souls met. And she went with him, higher and higher, gladly letting go of everything except him, and the culmination was a splendor that defined all rules and reality. One. Together. That melting of two spirits into one. It excited and completed her, and she tumbled with him back to earth.

Quint rolled to one side, holding her close, and pressed a kiss to the top of her head, then moved from her, standing by the couch. She looked up at him, marveling at the sight of him. "What are you doing?" She glanced past him at the wall clock. "We've got more time." She grinned and held her hand out to him. "Lots more time."

He crossed naked to his desk, opened a drawer,

then came back to hand her a small jewelry box. "Just a little something extra."

She sat up, took the velvet box and looked up at her husband. "This is too much. You got Travis's adoption on track, and..." She could feel the heat in her face, blushing, even though he was hers now. "...everything."

He crouched by her. "Just look."

She flipped up the lid and found a brooch, a gold rat with diamond eyes. She laughed, touching the smooth gold body. "Oh, goodness, Charlie never looked so good."

"You like it?"

"Oh, yes. And I love you," she said, reaching up and pulling him back down to the couch with her. "You're a lifetime project, but I'm up for the job."

"So am I," he chuckled and went back to her.

WITH TWO MINUTES to spare, they got to the back door of the center. Amy pushed back the barrier, and instead of the noise of partying, there were shrieks, kids squealing, then one voice raised above the others, "It's a rat. Get him!"

Quint reached for her hand, tugged the door shut, closing out the noise and he caught her in his arms. "Let them catch Charlie."

"Well, that should take a miracle," she said, putting her arms around his neck.

"Well, I believe in miracles."

"That makes two of us," Amy whispered and kissed her husband again.

COWBOY SANTA
Judy Christenberry

Dear Reader,

Christmas is a family time—an important theme for my stories. Nothing catches my heart more than new families forming—or old families renewing their love and commitment. When you throw in snow, mistletoe and a handsome cowboy, what could be more perfect? Here's wishing you and your family a glorious Christmas holiday with lots of love and kisses—just like Joni, Sam and Brady.

Judy Christenberry

Chapter One

"Ho, ho, ho, little boy, what's your name?"

Sam Crawford eased the little guy onto his lap, smiling beneath his white beard. The kid didn't look at all nervous.

"Brady," the child said in a sturdy voice.

"Brady. That's a fine name. What's your last name?"

Sam, aka Santa, had never seen the child before, and he had to get all the information so the child's list could be sent to his parents. After all, each family was donating five dollars to charity for that very reason.

The little boy stared at Sam. "I thought Santa knew everything."

Sam shifted in his thronelike chair. "I know most things, but there are so many children to keep up with. It helps if you remind me."

"Oh. So you don't get me mixed up with other kids?"

"That's right."

"Brady Evans."

"Aha. Brady Evans. Good. Tell me, Brady, what do you want Santa to bring you for Christmas." While he was asking the standard question, he checked out the clock on the wall. Five more minutes and Kevin would be relieving him, taking his turn in the big red suit.

"A train," the little voice said determinedly, as if sure of his list.

He scanned the crowd, wondering which set of parents had produced this little guy. He was great.

"A train? Well, I'll see what I can do. Is there anything else you want?"

Sam noticed one woman watching the little boy closely. Ah, had to be his mother. And a very good-looking mother she was, too. Lucky daddy.

"A horse."

"A rocking horse?"

"No, a real one."

Sam raised his eyebrows. A horse was a little larger than a train, and more difficult to deliver. But in Wyoming, it wasn't unusual for a child to have his own horse. Though maybe not at four years of age, which was what he guessed his latest customer to be.

"Well, now, Brady, a horse is kind of big. Do you have room for one?"

"He can sleep with me." The little guy beamed up at him, as if he'd promised to deliver the animal.

"Uh, no, Brady, horses can't sleep with people. They need a stable, and a big pasture." Did his mother know what her son was asking for? Sam looked for the strawberry blonde he'd earlier spotted, but he couldn't find her.

"We have a big backyard," Brady assured him solemnly.

"Um, it might be better to start with a smaller animal, like a puppy. Have you talked to your parents about a puppy?"

"I want a horse," Brady said stubbornly, his little jaw clenched. Man, his parents were going to have a tough time when he got old enough to enforce that hardheadedness. Sam grinned. His own mother had complained often enough about him for the same reason.

"We'll see. I can't make any promises about a horse. They're kind of big to carry in my sleigh."

He couldn't keep from giving the child a hug, sort of a consolation for not promising him his Christmas wish.

"Well, now, you be a good little boy, and I'll see if I can find a few other—"

He stopped because Brady was tugging on his whiskers. He feared the child would soon expose him as a fraud. "Don't pull my beard, Brady. It hurts Santa."

"I'm not through."

"How old are you?" Sam demanded, checking the child out a little more closely. He seemed pretty self-possessed for such a little guy.

"Four," the boy said, holding up that many fingers.

"Okay. What else?"

"I want a daddy. He's not as big as a horse, is he?"

JONI EVANS held her hand out to Brady, a big smile on her face.

Yes, she'd made the right decision. One day in town, and already things were better.

"Did you talk to Santa?" she asked her beloved child.

Brady nodded. "He said a horse can't sleep with me."

Joni's eyes rounded. "Wise Santa. Did you ask for a horse?"

"'Course I did, Mom. How can I be a cowboy without a horse?"

"You have a point, Brady, but I think we may have to wait a little while before we get a horse. You know, settle in, get to know our neighbors." Maybe even unpack first. They'd arrived in Saddle that morning, having had time only to drop their belongings at the house the school district had located for her.

"But, Mom, all the other kids will have horses," Brady complained, using the standard argument children employed anytime they wanted something.

"Uh, Mrs. Evans?"

Both Joni and Brady turned around, surprised. They'd only met the school superintendent, Mr. Brownlee, that morning. No one else in town knew them.

"Hi, Santa," Brady said, more enthusiastically

than when he'd first approached the man in the red
suit. "Did I forget something?"

Joni tried to hide her smile when Santa appeared
surprised by Brady's question. Before he could discover an answer, Brady had another question.

"Look! There's another Santa! How many Santas
are there in Wyoming?"

Santa appeared even more panicked. "Uh, I'm supposed to— I have to— Mrs. Evans, I need to talk to
you."

Had Brady said something wrong? Joni eyed her
son even as she considered the Santa's words. "I'm
going to show Brady some of the decorations. Why
don't you look for us after you, um, change?"

Relief filled his gaze. "Right. I'll just be a few
minutes."

He hurried away. She watched him leave, then
turned to look at the new Santa. Not as big. Santa
number one must tower over the elves. The new
Santa's padding looked more believable, too.

"Do I need to talk to the other Santa, too?" Brady
asked. "I want to be sure he knows what I want."

Joni had an answer at once. She didn't want to
stand in line another half hour. "No. Remember, in
Chicago, I told you all those Santas were the real
Santa's helpers. It's the same way here. The first
Santa will report what you wanted. Come over here.
I think I see some gingerbread houses."

Brady scampered ahead of her in the direction
she'd indicated. Joni took a deep breath. She'd worried she'd moved too fast for her four-year-old, taking

this job suddenly, moving almost overnight, right before Christmas.

But it was as if a fresh breeze had blown through their lives. They'd shed the angst of Brady's grandparents and discovered a real Christmas spirit.

Thanksgiving at the Evanses had been tense and sad. Joni and Brady had left the next morning for Wyoming. They arrived this morning, Saturday, and discovered the town of Saddle had a Christmas party, with Santa, for the entire town.

They even had a spare Santa or two.

Joni smiled as she watched Brady exchange a rapid-fire conversation with the lady guarding the gingerbread houses from hungry fingers. What a relief to see him discard his silence.

Maybe she'd regret that later, she thought with a chuckle.

"Mrs. Evans?"

It was the same deep voice that had accosted her before. She turned with a smile in place. Then almost swallowed her tongue.

This was Santa? This big hunk? He wasn't much older than her, early thirties, probably. Not an ounce of fat on his muscular body, now encased in boots, jeans, a sheepskin-lined jacket and a cowboy hat.

"Santa?" she asked, her voice rising in disbelief.

When he grinned, she almost fainted, though she'd never done so in her life. If the women in Chicago knew what they were missing, they'd move en masse.

"Yes, ma'am. Temporary Santa." His blue eyes sparkled with the humor of his smile.

"Well," she said with a sigh, "I think you've ruined his image for me. I'll never be able to think of him as a round, jolly little man after this."

He seemed to enjoy her teasing. "I'll try to eat more."

"You do that," she said with a chuckle, figuring he ate a lot as it was to fill up his tall frame.

"Where's Brady?"

"Over there, looking at the gingerbread houses. Did he do something wrong?" She had visions of her son using an inappropriate word he'd heard at day care. Surely Santa had heard them before.

"No, he's a neat kid. And you'll get your letter. At least, that's why I want to talk to you."

"Oh, you need our new address? We just got here today, so I guess you wouldn't know it. We've moved into Mrs. Lindstrom's house on Sombrero Road. The number is—"

"You filled out the form before, remember?"

She laughed. So much had happened so quickly, it wasn't a surprise that she'd forgotten. "Oh, of course. Then—"

"Mom?" Brady interrupted. "If I can have a dollar, I can win a neat gingerbread house. Can I? Can I?"

"Yes, of course, sweetie. Excuse me a moment, Mr.—uh, I don't know your name." She dug into her purse and pulled out a dollar for her child.

"Hi," Brady said with a smile, showing no shyness.

"Hi, yourself. My name's Sam Crawford."

Brady stuck out his hand, man-style, which brought another smile to Joni's lips. "I'm Brady."

The man took his little hand and shook it with serious intent, as if Brady were as tall as him. "Glad to meet you. Welcome to Saddle."

Brady beamed at him, then said, "I'll be back in a minute."

After he dashed away, Joni looked at the handsome man. "You're great with kids. No wonder they let you be Santa."

"Let me? Lady, I was drafted," he protested, but he kept smiling.

"Now, what's the problem with Brady."

"Uh, I assume you're single?" he asked.

She stiffened. What did her marital status have to do with Brady's visit with Santa? Or was the man asking for personal reasons? That thought had her cheeks heating up. "Why do you want to know?"

He must have read her mind because he snapped, "Not for why you think! I mean, your son asked for a daddy for Christmas."

SAM COULD BELIEVE that a lot of men hit on Ms. Evans. She was a beauty, no doubt about that. But he wasn't one of them. 'Cause he'd just signed his final divorce papers last week. It wasn't like he was out looking.

No, *sirree*. He wasn't ready for that kind of mess again, if ever.

He took a step back as she drew a deep breath, pulling his gaze from an inappropriate part of her well-shaped anatomy. "Look, lady, I just thought you should know."

That defensiveness disappeared and she smiled at him, a real winner of a smile. "I'm so sorry. I didn't mean to be— I mean, we're new to town and— Anyway, no, I'm not married. Brady's daddy was a policeman in Chicago. He was killed a year ago last summer."

"I'm sorry," Sam said, his brows snapping together. She was altogether too young and beautiful to have such a tragic history.

"Thanks," she said, her smile still in place. "And thanks for the warning about Brady's request. I guess I'll have to—to head him off at the pass." Her smile widened and just the hint of a dimple appeared in her left cheek. "I'm trying to work on my Western vocabulary so I'll fit in."

The urge to place a kiss just where the dimple appeared surprised him. What was wrong with him? He'd sworn off women. Taking another step backward, he said, "I'm sure you'll fit in just fine, Mrs. Evans."

Tipping his hat to her, he turned away, only to be stopped by Brady's return.

"Mr. Crawford?"

"Yeah, Brady?"

"Do you got horses?"

He could feel her brown-eyed gaze on him, drawing him, filling him with a fierce need to escape. But he wasn't going to be rude to the little boy. "Yeah, Brady, I do. I live on a ranch."

Brady's eyes widened. "Wow! Could I see your horses?"

"Brady!" his mother said. "It's impolite to ask for an invitation."

Sam knelt down. He was a soft touch with children. He'd always wanted—expected—to have some of his own. Too bad that having children meant having a wife, too. "Tell you what, after you and your mom get settled in, maybe you can come out to the ranch and meet my nephew. He's four, too."

Brady was practically bouncing up and down. "Really? 'Cause I don't know any boys here. Thank you."

To Sam's surprise, he threw his arms around Sam's neck and squeezed tightly.

"Brady! You should thank Mr. Crawford, not attack him."

"I did, Mom!" Brady protested. "Didn't I?"

"You certainly did," Sam agreed with another smile. "Say, did you see the reindeer outside? When you leave, get your mom to take you by the corral."

"Okay. Come on, Mom," Brady insisted, taking her hand and tugging her toward the door.

The lady paused before following her son. "Thank you again, Mr. Crawford. You've been very gracious to a couple of strangers."

Sam nodded. The lady wouldn't be a stranger long in their little town. The bachelors would swarm around her like bees to honey. Brady would probably have his Christmas wish filled in no time.

But not by Sam.

"GOOD NIGHT, SWEETIE," Joni whispered, kissing her child just as he was nodding off. Sometimes it seemed that was the only time he stayed in one place long enough for her to hug him.

When she reached the hallway, she debated which chore to do next, now that Brady was down for the night. Their furniture was in place, thanks to the movers, but she had a lot of boxes to unpack.

With a sigh, she turned to the kitchen. Organizing the kitchen was the most important of their needs. She'd bought shelving paper that afternoon, before she'd called a halt to her work to take Brady to the Christmas party.

Again, she told herself she'd made the right decision. Last Christmas had been difficult. Her husband Derek's parents hadn't recovered from his loss. Brady deserved more than the misery they'd shared last year.

She'd expected Mr. and Mrs. Evans to gradually recover, but instead, Mrs. Evans seemed to grow worse. She was trying to make Brady into Derek.

Joni hadn't known what to do. Then, as if it were meant to be, she'd seen an ad asking for a teacher immediately…in Saddle, Wyoming.

In the middle of the semester?

She'd waited until her conference period the next day and called the number given. After that, a roller coaster of events brought her to this snug little house in a small town nestled at the foot of a mountain range. The town was named for the shape of a nearby peak in the Rocky Mountains, said to resemble a saddle.

What a change from Chicago.

But a good change. Brady had immediately taken to his new home. She laughed softly to herself as she remembered his asking her if he really could go outside whenever he wanted. Probably the freedom of having a yard had inspired the horse request.

And the daddy request?

She didn't think Brady remembered Derek. He'd been two when his daddy died. And Derek hadn't been much for babies. She'd loved her husband, but after Brady was born, they'd had a difficult time of it.

Maybe she wasn't cut out to be a wife. Just a mother. And she'd gotten lucky because her child was wonderful. And she'd do anything for him.

So here she was, feeling as if she'd taken a role in a Western movie, with every man wearing a cowboy hat and boots and drawling his words. And some of them, like Sam Crawford, looking like cowboy heroes come to life.

Enough of that! she told herself. She needed to get them settled in and make plans for Monday. Brady would go to a sitter that she planned to interview tomorrow, and she would start teaching a class of second-graders who had lost their teacher when her husband had taken a new job in California.

She didn't need to be thinking about a long, lean cowboy with a smile that could rev any woman's engine.

Even Mrs. Claus's.

SAM TUGGED AT HIS TIE before he'd even gotten out the door of the church the next morning. A lot of men in Saddle didn't bother with the blasted thing, but his mother would be horrified.

"Hey, Sam!" his friend Dustin called.

He turned around. The two of them had grown up in Saddle, attended school together, played sports and now worked their fathers' ranches. "Hey, Dusty, how's it going?"

"Great. Did you see the new lady in town?"

"You mean Mrs. Evans?" Who else could Dusty mean? They didn't have people moving to town all that often. And he'd seen her several rows away. Her hair was like a golden halo. Besides, Brady had waved to him.

"Don't know her name, but she's a beautiful blonde. Great curves, if you know what I mean. And a smile that lights up a room, with a little—"

"All right, already. I've seen her. What about it?" He didn't need all that detail thrown in his face again.

"Just thought you might be interested. I mean, after all, you're through with Linda, aren't you?"

"Off with the old, on with the new? You're moving a little fast for me, buddy."

"You can't waste time. You know she'll have her opportunities around here. Why, I heard three guys have already asked her out."

Sam let out a sigh of relief. She'd be hitched up with someone in no time. And he didn't prey on other people's property. "Good."

Dusty shrugged his shoulders. "Yeah, but how did you know she turned them all down?"

They had continued walking out to the parking lot, but now Sam came to an abrupt halt. "What?"

"You didn't know?"

"How do you know? What are you, the new gossip in town?" The woman had only been here two days. How could three men be after her already and already been rejected?

"She was at the town party last night. Mick Bowman cozied up to her right away. Everyone saw that. Except you 'cause you were playing Santa. She sent him away with his tail between his legs. Then Larry Cranston told me himself he asked her out to Sunday dinner today, but she said no. Didn't even say she'd take a rain check."

"Hell, she just moved in. They should give her time to breathe."

Dusty grinned. "We're starving for beautiful single women out here. If you wait too long, you won't even have a bone to gnaw on."

"If Lisa hears you talking like that, she's going to wonder if you still love her."

"Nope. She knows," Dusty assured him, a satisfied look on his face that brought pain to Sam. He'd thought, when he asked Linda to marry him, that he'd be satisfied, too.

"Well, I'm sure she'll settle into a social life soon."

Dusty wasn't about to be put off. "Don't you want to know who else she turned down?"

"There's more?"

Dusty held up three fingers and ticked off the two names he'd mentioned. Then he said, "The other one was the pastor."

Sam stared at his friend. The minister had moved there about six months ago. Everyone understood that he had a lady waiting for him in Kansas City. "I thought he was engaged?"

"Me, too, but if he is, he's not following his own advice. You know, about honesty and all."

"Yeah, I know." He looked back at the congregation standing in groups, chatting, even though the weather was cold. At least there wasn't a fierce wind. Unusual for the end of November.

"So, don't you think you should ask her?" Dusty said, nudging him with an elbow.

Had he missed some of Dusty's conversation? "Ask her what?"

"Man, is your brain frozen today? Ask her out on a date."

He wished other parts of him were frozen, because he didn't like the way his body responded to the sight of Joni Evans in a powder blue suit, the skirt short enough to show a great pair of legs.

"Nope. I don't think so."

But if she kept turning the men of Saddle down, he'd have to do something. To make sure he didn't let temptation overpower him.

He started mentally composing a list of men who could fulfill Brady's request for Christmas.

But he wouldn't put his own name on the list. Oh, no, not him.

Chapter Two

"You're not going to leave, too, are you?" one of her new students asked Joni as she accepted a hug goodbye at the end of her first week.

"No, of course not, Allison. I'll see you on Monday."

As if she hadn't answered, the little girl said, "'Cause Mrs. Miller told us goodbye on Friday and she didn't come back."

"I promise I'll be back on Monday. I like it here." And that was the truth. She hugged several other children and waved goodbye as they left her classroom.

Her first week had been remarkable. No hint of the violence that had seemed to surround her children in Chicago. No parents storming through her door with complaints.

The faculty was friendly, the parents grateful, and the children an absolute delight. The superintendent had told her that her class size would be small and supplies were no problem. She hadn't quite believed him. But the oil and coal-rich area had plenty of funds.

She sank back into her chair with a satisfied sigh. Brady was happy, too. He loved his day care, which was fortunate since it was about the only one in town. Every morning this week he'd been eager to leave the house.

"Ahem."

Joni spun around at the sound.

Standing in her doorway was Sam Crawford, the handsome Santa. He was holding a beautiful little girl about two years old. Beside him were two little boys.

One of them hers.

"Brady! What are you doing here? Is something wrong?" she demanded as she sprang from her chair to clutch her son to her breast.

"Nothing's wrong, Mrs. Evans," the man assured her calmly.

"Then why did Mrs. Barker let you take my son?" she demanded, shoving Brady behind her, as if to shield him.

He stared at her as if she'd lost her mind. "Because I told her I'd bring him to you. What's wrong with that?"

"Brady knows not to go with anyone but me," she said. Her voice was strong but it faltered as she reached the end of her words.

This wasn't Chicago.

"Do you—do you know Mrs. Barker?"

He nodded. "I guess so. She was my Sunday school teacher when I was five. My Cub Scout leader when I was seven. A chaperone on my senior trip. My—"

"All right." Joni interrupted, holding up a hand, feeling ridiculous. "I get the picture. I'm sorry, but in Chicago—"

"This isn't Chicago."

Well, she'd already told herself that. She couldn't blame him for saying the same thing.

"Of course." With a bright smile that covered her unease, she hoped, she nodded. "Thanks for bringing Brady."

"But, Mom," Brady protested. He'd at least realized she was dismissing the cowboy, even if Sam Crawford hadn't moved. "He asked me!"

She looked down at her child. "What, Brady?"

"He asked me to come play with Peter."

Peter. Her son had talked about Peter all week. A little boy who came every morning to Mrs. Barker's day care for half a day of classes. He and Brady had become friends, making Joni's life easier.

"How do you know—" she started asking Sam, but her gaze fell to the little boy standing beside him. "Is this Peter?"

"You haven't met him? He's at Mrs. Barker's every day."

"But only in the morning. I've been in a hurry this week in the mornings. I didn't go in and visit." She chewed on her bottom lip before she asked her next question. "Is—is Peter your son?"

"No. He and Katie here are my nephew and niece."

Drat! She hadn't wanted any connection with the

tall, handsome cowboy. He was too tempting for words, and she didn't want to be tempted.

"I'm glad to meet you, Peter. Brady really likes playing with you." She smiled at the little boy and he shyly smiled back.

"My sister's quite pleased, too. Peter is, uh, not outgoing, and she put him in child care so he could learn to socialize."

"I'm sure he's doing well," Joni said with an encouraging smile for the little boy. "Brady, why don't you and Peter go draw me a picture on the blackboard?"

Brady hadn't been in this schoolroom before, but he'd visited his mother's work in Chicago. He had no hesitation in leading the way. Peter followed in his footsteps.

Once the two boys were busy, she said softly to her guest, "Mr. Crawford, it's best not to talk about a child in front of him, as if he were invisible."

"I didn't mean—hell, I—" He came to an abrupt halt as he realized he'd committed another faux pas in front of children. Very carefully, he began again, "I just wanted you to know that my sister is pleased Brady is Peter's friend."

She ducked her head to hide her grin. Macho man didn't like her pointing out his error. But he'd handled it nicely. "Then it's mutual. I look forward to meeting her."

"Hey, Mom, look. Me and Peter drew some horses," Brady called.

Joni thought the horses in Wyoming must be quite

different from any she'd ever seen, or the two boys were not destined to be artists. "Terrific. Those are amazing horses. Can you erase them now? We need to go home, and the boards have to be clean before we go."

Instead of doing as she asked, Brady put down his chalk and raced back to her side. "No, Mom, I told you. He asked me."

"What are you talking about?"

"Uh, Mrs. Evans, the reason I picked up Brady, too, is that I thought he might spend the evening out at the ranch."

She stared at him, unprepared for the invitation.

"With Peter and Katie," he hurriedly added. "And me," he added again, when she still stared at him. "I usually baby-sit the pair of them on Friday nights so my sister and her husband have a little free time."

"That's very kind of you, Mr. Crawford," Joni began, "but I don't think—"

"Mommy, please!" Brady asked, an anxious look on his face.

She knew how much he wanted it because he called her Mommy. Normally she was Mom. But she was going to have to disappoint him. And things had been going so well. "Sweetie, we have a lot to do, and we're just getting to know everyone. I think it might be best if we put off your visit for a week or two."

Peter had returned to Sam Crawford's side, slipping his hand into his uncle's larger one. "Is she saying no?" he whispered, but everyone could hear his question. "I'll be really good," he added, staring at Joni anxiously.

Joni knelt down to his level. "Of course you would be," she assured him. "But," she began as Brady slid an arm around her neck, "we're new to town, and it makes me nervous for Brady to go off without me."

"Aw, Mom," Brady complained, but he leaned his head against hers.

"You could come play, too," Peter said, his gaze flying up to his uncle. "Couldn't she, Uncle Sam?"

Joni stood, swinging Brady to her hip, embarrassed by the turn of the conversation.

"Of course, you're welcome to come along, Mrs. Evans. But I should tell you that I live with my parents. My mother is quite good with children." Sam Crawford sounded as if the last thing in the world he wanted was for her to tag along.

"Perhaps another time," she told the two boys.

"We was going to have so much fun," Brady said, his mouth drooping. "Sam said we could have a wiener roast."

"You should call him Mr. Crawford, sweetie. And it's too cold outside for a wiener roast."

"I asked him to call me Sam, and we were going to have a wiener roast in the house," the cowboy said, correcting her, his voice stern, as if she'd offended him.

"And marshmallows," Peter added, a hopeful look in his gaze.

The little girl, silent until now, clapped her hands and repeated, "Marshmallows."

"I don't—"

"Mrs. Evans," Sam interrupted. "Come along with Brady, so the kids can have their fun. You can meet my mother and father, who, I promise, are upstanding members of our community. You don't have to let Brady out of your sight the entire time, and I'll bring the two of you back whenever you say."

"Please, Mommy, please?" Brady appealed one more time.

Joni didn't want to say yes. She didn't want to spend an entire evening anywhere near the handsome cowboy. Especially not date night in the U.S.A. But it meant a lot to Brady.

"I suppose we could put off our chores until tomorrow, if Mr. Crawford is sure I won't be a bother by inviting myself." She challenged him with a cool stare.

"Not at all. I think we have plenty of wieners. Shall we go?"

Both boys cheered and Brady wriggled to be put down. When Joni did so, he and Peter raced for the door.

"Brady?" she called.

"Yes, Mom?"

"You forgot to erase the blackboard."

The look of apprehension disappeared from his face, replaced by a big smile. He raced back to the blackboard, Peter right on his heels.

"It's not necessary for you to drive us," she said quietly. "Just give me directions, Mr. Crawford, and we'll stop by the house, so I can change, and then—"

"There aren't a lot of street signs out in the country, Mrs. Evans. I'd better drive you the first time. And I think you can quit being so formal. My name's Sam."

"Ah. I should be informal with you while you call me Mrs. Evans?" She'd noticed that he never relaxed around her.

"I don't know your first name," he replied.

Her cheeks rosied. "Sorry. I'm Joni," she said, wondering if she should offer her hand.

"We're through," Brady announced as he and Peter arrived at their sides unnoticed.

"Oh, good, sweetie. You and Peter did a good job." She looked back at Sam to find him watching her. "Do you mind following me to my house so I can change?" She didn't think her skirt and blouse were appropriate for a wiener roast.

Sam indicated his jeans. "We're definitely casual."

Great. All she needed was an invitation to stare at his strong, muscular legs. She snapped her gaze back to his face. "I promise it won't take me long to change."

"No problem. Ready, guys?"

The two little boys followed him out of the room, and Joni quickly gathered her things to join them. Brady asked to ride with Sam when they reached her car. She understood why when she saw his big truck. Brady loved trucks.

"Yes, but wear a seat belt."

She expected Sam to remind her that they weren't

in Chicago again, but he said nothing. At least some things were the same in Wyoming.

SAM ENTERTAINED HIS NIECE with a doll and the boys with questions about their day, until Joni Evans re-emerged from her house.

As she opened the door, he sucked in his breath.

"What's wrong, Sam? Did you hurt yourself?" Brady asked.

He reluctantly drew his gaze from Brady's mother and swallowed. "Uh, no, I just banged my knee on the door, that's all."

Sam's gaze returned to Joni. She was shrugging into a coat as she walked toward them, and Sam was glad. Anything to cover those delicious curves that could inspire a lot of fantasies.

She'd released her long blond hair from its earlier bondage, letting it fall on her shoulders. And the tight jeans and waist-length lilac sweater that clung to her curves, now covered by her coat, didn't remind Sam of any schoolteacher he ever had.

"Yea! Mom brought some cookies. She makes good cookies," Brady assured his friend as Joni opened the door.

"What kind of cookies?" Peter asked.

Joni smiled at him as she slid into the front seat next to Katie's car seat. "Oatmeal raisin. Do you like them?"

While Peter was giving her enthusiastic approval, she looked at Sam. "I thought they would be a good snack for the children."

"That's thoughtful of you, but not necessary. We do have food at our house." He was being difficult, he knew, but somehow she rubbed him the wrong way. Wrong verb! he quickly cautioned himself. He was going to avoid touching her in any fashion.

She stiffened beside him.

"Sorry, I didn't mean to sound— The cookies are fine. In fact, I'd like one right now." He couldn't think of any other way to apologize.

Her eyebrows shot up. "You don't mind the children eating one now, too?"

"Of course not."

She unwrapped the plate of cookies and offered him one. "Sorry. My husband never wanted Brady to eat anything in the car."

She served the boys each a cookie, then asked about Katie.

"If you don't give her one, you'll hear her scream from here to Casper," he assured her. "Katie is no shrinking violet."

"Good," Joni said with a smile as she held out a cookie for the little girl.

"Cookie!" Katie crowed with excitement, holding it up to Sam. He pretended to bite her cookie and she jerked it back to her chest, squealing.

Everyone laughed at Katie's antics, and some of the tension left the cab of the truck. As he took a bite of his cookie, Sam put the truck into gear and backed out of their driveway. "Hey, these are good."

"I told you," Brady said from the jump seat.

Sam grinned at Joni, then turned his attention to the driving. It was safer.

"How far do you live from town?"

"Not that far. About ten miles. My great-grandfather built the house on the corner of our property closest to town."

"So your family has been here a long time."

"Yeah. Is your family still in Chicago?"

"I don't have any family. My husband's parents are there, along with his two brothers and their families."

He frowned. It must be tough to be alone, but she didn't show any stress about it. "Will you go visit them for Christmas?"

He noted that Joni checked to see if Brady was listening before she answered. The two boys were whispering and giggling. "No, I don't think so. We've just gotten settled in here. Maybe we'll visit them next summer."

"So you're planning to stay?"

"Oh, yes. So far it's been great."

"Cold weather doesn't bother you?"

She chuckled, a husky sound that made him think of warm, thick honey. "I'm from Chicago, Sam, not Florida. It's not exactly balmy. We're known as the Windy City, remember?"

"Then you'll fit right in here. Most of our snow comes sideways because of the wind." When she returned his smile, he hurriedly looked away.

"Cookie!" Katie squealed.

They both laughed as the little girl beamed at them, cookie crumbs and drool all over her face.

Joni pulled a tissue from her purse and twisted around to clean her face.

"Cookie!" Katie demanded again.

"Me, too," the boys called.

"Sorry," Joni said. "They're for dessert, after dinner."

Though the boys grumbled, they agreed to wait. Sam liked the way she handled the four-year-olds. Katie, of course, was another matter.

"Cookie!" she continued to shriek.

"Oh, sweetie, your tummy is so little, I'm afraid your mommy would be unhappy if I gave you another one. How old are you? Are you two?" She held up two fingers.

Distracted, Katie reached for the fingers.

"She's two. Marty calls them the terrible twos."

"I remember them," Joni agreed with a smile, but Sam thought her gaze held a hint of sadness.

"Was Brady a handful?"

Her smile broadened again. "Always."

He could believe it. Her son was the opposite of shy Peter. Although his nephew had been more exuberant today, in Brady's company, than he could remember.

They turned onto the gravel road that would carry them to the ranch, making the ride a little rougher. "Glad you didn't bring your car?" he asked.

"Frankly, yes, but I hate for you to drive us back later."

"No problem. Peter and Katie will spend the night, but once they're in bed, it won't take long to bring you back."

"Your mother will watch them while you're gone?"

"Of course," he answered indignantly. "I know better than to leave two little ones alone. I'm a good sitter, aren't I, Peter?"

"Yeah, Uncle Sam. You're the best."

Sam grinned triumphantly at Joni, as if he'd proved his worthiness.

"All you'd have to do to get a four-year-old boy's approval is feed him cookies," she suggested, teasing him.

He stared at those warm brown eyes, the elusive dimple that appeared, and he couldn't help smiling back. Then he caught himself as he almost drove off the road.

Man! The woman was dangerous. Or it had been too long since he'd been with a woman. Hell, he knew that was true. He and Linda had been separated the past six months prior to the divorce, and things hadn't been too good before that.

He cleared his throat. "Uh, there's the ranch house."

Pride filled him as he stared at the house he'd been born and raised in. Last New Year's, he'd promised Linda he'd build her her own house. He'd started it once the snow had melted, not far from his parents' house, but it stood half-finished. He'd lost heart when it became clear Linda wasn't staying.

His parents' house was a sprawling two-story, with lots of room for a big family. His father had wanted lots of kids, but his mother had miscarried her third child and the doctor had warned them not to try again.

When his sister Martha, or Marty as they called her, had married Paul Kessler, she'd moved into town. Paul was the only lawyer in Saddle and kept offices in the downstairs of their house.

Then Sam had proposed to Linda. He hadn't seen the need to build a separate house a few feet from his parents'. There was plenty of room for four people. But Linda hadn't seen it that way.

"Are they building a new house?" Joni asked.

He should have known she'd ask. "No."

She looked at him when he offered no other explanation, but he wasn't going to say anything else.

When he pulled the truck to a stop, the two boys jumped out, Peter anxious to introduce his friend to his grandparents.

For the first time, Joni seemed nervous. "Are you sure your mother won't mind that I came with you?"

"Nope. She likes to have company. You two will get on like a house afire." Strange. He didn't know why he was so sure of that fact. Linda and his mother had had little in common.

He took Katie out of the car seat. "Come on in. And don't forget those cookies, or the boys will revolt."

She sent him a grateful smile that had his pulse racing again. He'd better start concentrating on the kids.

"Mom? You home?" he called as he pulled open the back door and motioned for Joni to precede him.

"Of course I am. I've just met— Well, hello," his mother, Loretta, said with a smile when her gaze fell on Joni. "I didn't know we were having company."

Sam hastily made the introductions.

"I hope you don't mind. It's just that we only moved in last weekend and—and I don't know Sam that well, so I was nervous about letting Brady—"

"Land's sake, child, you don't have to explain to me. Better safe than sorry. Come right in. You're welcome here anytime."

"Thank you so much, Mrs. Crawford," Joni said, and Sam could see the earlier tension fading. "Everyone here has been so friendly."

"Yeah, I heard the men are after you already," his mother returned with a chuckle. "You should know that we have a great gossip chain around here. It's our entertainment, and you certainly have kept us entertained."

Joni's cheeks turned bright pink, which only made her more attractive.

Sam interrupted. "I told Joni she could join us for hot dogs tonight. We have plenty, don't we?"

"Sure. I bought everything you asked for," Loretta assured him.

"And I brought cookies for dessert," Joni said, holding out the plate.

"Cookie!" Katie squealed, once more reminded of what she wanted.

"Oops, sorry," Joni apologized to Sam.

"No problem. Come on, Katie, let's go find Grandpa."

As he started out the door, his mother called, "He's upstairs in the shower."

Sam paused, turning to stare at his mother. "Why?"

"We're going out this evening. You don't need us to help you with the kids, and Mabel and Ed asked us over to play forty-two. That's okay, isn't it?"

Sam stared at Joni, his mind awhirl. He was going to be left alone with Joni? But he'd planned on his parents being there, to chaperone.

Joni, as well as his mother, was staring at him. When she licked her lips, he almost groaned.

"If it's not, perhaps your parents could give us a lift back into town."

"Nonsense," Loretta said, a mischievous grin on her face. "Sam will be glad of the company. He's been alone too much lately."

Uh-oh. His mother was matchmaking.

Just what he didn't need.

Chapter Three

Joni noticed the sudden tension between mother and son. "Please, if it's any trouble, we—" She didn't know what. After all, she didn't have a car.

"Don't be silly. Let me show you where everything is for the hot dogs while Sam entertains Katie," Loretta said, still staring down her son.

"Be careful, Mom," he said, warning his mother of something, but Joni wasn't sure what.

Once the door had closed behind him, Loretta showed Joni all the fixings she'd prepared. "I hear you're a widow," she chatted. "So young. What a shame. How did your husband die?"

"He was killed on duty as a Chicago cop."

Loretta straightened, her gaze filled with sympathy. "How sad."

Joni wasn't still mourning her husband. Nor her marriage, except as it had been that first year. She'd thought they would always be that happy. She smiled at Loretta. "It's been a while."

"Good. You're getting rave reviews from the parents already. They say you're very gentle with the little ones."

"They're all adorable."

"Even Jeremy Leghorn?" Loretta asked with a knowing look.

Jeremy was a second-grader but he was built like a boy years older, already towering over everyone. And he was a firm believer in "might is right."

"Jeremy keeps life from getting boring," Joni assured her hostess with a laugh.

"My, what a pretty smile," Loretta said, surprising Joni.

"Thank you. What will Katie eat?"

Thankfully her question sidetracked Loretta from any more personal comments for several minutes. Then she invited Joni to sit at the kitchen table and enjoy a cup of tea while they waited for the others' return.

"I just want to tell you I'm grateful you came along tonight."

Joni raised her eyebrows. "You don't trust Sam with the children?"

"Oh, it's not that. He's a great baby-sitter. But I worry about leaving him alone right now."

Joni didn't waste breath replying. She knew Loretta would tell her.

"You see, he signed his divorce papers last week and, well, I worry about him. You know how mothers are."

"Last week? He seems quite composed for— I

mean, he doesn't seem to be—'' Joni wished she'd said nothing.

"Oh, he hides his emotions well. And the marriage was truly over much sooner. But it's hard, even so."

"Yes, I'm sure. Well, I'll help with the children."

"Just protect my kitchen. That boy is helpless in here. I guess I've spoilt him. As capable as he is—he's wonderful running the ranch—he can't seem to keep a kitchen clean."

"I'll do my best," Joni assured her just as the door opened and all three kids, Sam and a man she assumed was his father came through the door.

The older man spoke first. "Howdy, Brady's mom. Your son is sure a talker," the man, a handsome older version of his son, said.

"I'm afraid so, Mr. Crawford. You'll have to tell him when you need some peace." She stood as she spoke and extended her hand. "I'm Joni Evans."

"Well, no wonder my son brought you home," the man said as he shook her hand, a smile on his weathered face.

"Dad!" Sam protested.

"Actually I invited myself because I'm an overprotective mom. You can't blame Sam for that, Mr. Crawford."

"Uh-uh," he said with a grin directed toward Sam. "And make it Tom."

"I will, Tom. You and Loretta are being so friendly. I really appreciate that."

"We're glad to see a new face. You ready, Mother? Are we still going?"

"Of course we are. You know how Mabel loves her forty-two. Besides, now that Joni is here, we don't have to worry about Sam."

"Mother, she is not baby-sitting me!"

"Of course not, dear," Loretta said blandly and kissed both her grandchildren and added a kiss for Brady.

The lady won Joni's heart in that instant, making Brady feel a part of the family. Tom followed suit with hugs all around.

When the door closed behind them, Sam was still glowering.

Joni tried to hide her smile. "Do we eat now, or is there something else on the agenda?"

"I was going to play Candyland with the boys, but I don't know if we can keep Katie from eating the cards. We're already missing two."

"Let me play with Katie while you entertain the boys. I've missed having a baby around since Brady has grown so much." She reached out her arms and hugged the little girl as she came to her. "Ooh, you smell so good, Katie. Your mommy must've given you a bath just before your uncle came to get you."

"Yeah," Sam said with a nod. "That's where I draw the line. It's bad enough with Pete, here. He splashes me, but she's a maniac in the bathtub."

They all trooped into the family room and Joni fell in love with it at once. It was huge but cozy. A massive rock fireplace dominated the room, with plump sofas around it. In another area, a game table, with a lamp over it, invited one to indulge in games and puzzles. There were several other easy chairs with reading lamps, and a big-screen television.

Best of all, one wall was a huge picture window that looked out on the snowcapped Rockies. She would never tire of that scene.

"How beautiful," she murmured, her gaze traveling around the room.

"Yeah. Mom's doing."

"Is this where we're going to roast the wieners?" Brady asked, standing in front of the fireplace.

"Oh, no, dear," Joni said at once, sure that such a messy undertaking would be banished to the kitchen.

"Of course it is," Sam contradicted. He looked at Joni. "Don't worry. Mom says everything in here is washable."

Joni hoped so.

Sam led the two boys to the game table where Candyland awaited them.

Joni stared after him. He was every woman's dream—strong, intelligent, sexy and he was going to spend Friday night with three children, none of them his own.

"How long have you been doing this?" she asked before she thought about what his mother had told her.

"Doing what? Playing Candyland?" he asked, looking over his shoulder.

"No, of course not. Taking care of Peter and Katie."

"Off and on since Peter was born. I like kids."

She wondered if that had been the reason for his marriage breakup. But it was none of her business.

"Does Katie have some toys?" she asked, hoping to distract herself from such thoughts.

"Ask her," he suggested with a wry grin.

Katie was delighted to show Joni her box in one corner, crammed with toys. She introduced Joni to every item in the box, stopping to play with her favorites and inviting Joni to do the same.

An hour later, Sam suggested they have dinner.

"Bored to tears yet?" he asked under his breath as everyone headed for the kitchen.

She stared at him, surprised. "Of course not. I was thinking I wish I had a little girl, too. Boys are fun, but they don't want to play with dolls."

"Eeew! Yuck!" Brady said as he passed by her. "I would never play with dolls."

"Me, neither!" Peter seconded, but Joni noticed he gave his uncle a quick look, as if to be sure he didn't rat on him.

"Who's hungry?" Joni asked to change the subject. She didn't want Peter embarrassed. "How many hot dogs will we need?"

"Better bring the whole package," Sam suggested. "Here's a tray. If you'll gather all the ingredients, we'll spread out an old blanket in front of the fire and put on some more wood." Sam led the two boys out to the porch.

"Well, as usual, Katie, it looks like the women get to do the cooking."

"Me help," Katie assured her. Joni gave her some spoons to carry to the table.

When Sam came back in with the boys, he wore a frown.

"Everything okay?" she asked.

"Yeah, sure."

She didn't think so, but he obviously didn't want to say anything in front of the children. She grabbed the loaded tray, called to Katie and went into the den.

They settled on the blanket on the floor in front of the fireplace, and she helped the boys put their wieners on roasting forks and kept Katie out of everything until Sam could fix her a plate. She almost forgot Sam's preoccupation.

Once the children were eating, the two adults cooked their own wieners. In a low voice, she asked again, "What's wrong?"

He seemed surprised by her question. "Nothing, really. I mean, I knew we were supposed to get a snowstorm in a day or two, but it looks like it got here early."

"It's snowing? We'd better eat in a hurry so you can take us home right away," she said, pulling her wiener from the fire.

"Joni, I can't leave the kids here with my parents gone. And I don't like to take them out in bad weather unless I have to." He shrugged his shoulders. "It's not like you're in any danger here."

"You mean we have to spend the night?" she asked, her voice rising.

"Shh! No, of course not. As soon as my parents

get back, I'll take you home. They don't stay out late, especially if the weather gets bad.''

She fixed her plate, but she was still uneasy about their situation. When the wind rattled the window-panes with a particularly gusty blow, she jumped.

Katie whimpered and the two boys looked alarmed, but Sam assured them it was a snowstorm. Instead of being concerned, like all little boys, they cheered and raced to the window. Katie crawled over into her uncle's lap and snuggled against him.

Joni found herself almost envious of the child before she realized what she was thinking. But it had been so long since strong arms had held and comforted her. And Sam Crawford's arms appeared particularly inviting.

She looked up to discover him staring at her. With an awkward grin, she got to her feet. ''I'd better start putting everything away. I promised your mother I'd leave her kitchen clean.''

''I'll help,'' he said, starting to get up.

''No, keep an eye on the kids. I'll take care of the dishes.'' It would give her time to escape the powerful pull she felt toward the man. He had to have some flaws. No one could be as perfect as he appeared to be.

Half an hour later he came into the kitchen. ''How's it going in here? Are you about finished?''

''Yes, actually. How are the kids?'' They'd been amazingly quiet the past few minutes.

''All tucked up, waiting for a good-night kiss.''

She stared at him. ''Where's Brady?''

"I just told you, all tucked up—"

"Wait a minute. Brady's not sleeping here," she protested.

"Maybe not, but what's the point in keeping him awake until we leave? He might as well—"

"Don't you think you should've asked me before you made that decision for my child?" Maybe she was overreacting. But her husband had been a dictator when he was around, which, fortunately after Brady was born, wasn't often. But her in-laws had also wanted to make all her decisions.

She wouldn't tolerate it from them, so she sure wouldn't tolerate it from a relative stranger.

"Hey, settle down, Joni. You want him out of bed, march right up those stairs and ruin the best fun he and Peter have had in a while. Play the role of the wicked witch. I don't mind."

She couldn't believe he would blame the situation on her. "It wouldn't be my fault if they got upset. It would be yours for making a decision you had no right to make!"

The arrogant man just cocked his hands on his hips and raised one eyebrow. She drove past him, so angry she felt like taking a bite out of him.

By the time she reached the top of the stairs, she'd calmed down somewhat. "Brady?" she called softly.

"In here, Mom. Isn't this neat? Peter and I are having a sleep-over. I've never had one before."

By the time she reached the door of the bedroom, she knew she wasn't going to take her son back downstairs. But she had to warn him that he'd probably be in his bed in the morning. "Hi, sweetie, Peter. Are you both comfortable?"

The two boys giggled and assured her they were "snug as two bugs in a rug." "That's what Uncle Sam says," Peter added.

"I see." She tried to smile at the mention of the irritating man downstairs. She really did.

So neither of them would be upset if they each awoke alone, she said, "If Brady is gone when you wake in the morning, Peter, it will be because your uncle Sam took us home. We need to leave when your grandparents get back. But we'll plan a sleep-over at our house real soon, if this one gets cut short. Okay, guys?"

"Sam said it's okay, Mom. I don't take up much space," Brady assured her with a confident smile. It seemed Sam had taken on hero status sometime during the evening.

"Well, we'll see. At least you're all warm and comfy for now. And I've come to collect two good-night kisses," she said, stooping over each little boy.

After she stepped out into the hallway, pulling the door closed behind her, she heard the soft music of a child's toy and opened the door across the hall to discover Katie already asleep in a white crib.

She might be angry with Sam Crawford, but she'd have to admit he was efficient. She hadn't gotten Brady to bed that fast in a long time.

Sam was standing at the bottom of the stairs, waiting for her. "What, no Brady kicking and screaming at being dragged out of bed?"

She marched stiffly past him into the den. "I had no intention of being cruel. But I don't like other people making decisions about my child."

He followed her. "I don't think putting a child to bed is something that needs a lot of discussion. He was as tired as Peter. They'd had a busy day."

She ignored him and ostentatiously checked her watch. "How long do you think your parents will be?"

"They should be back by ten."

An hour and a half alone with him? She nibbled on her bottom lip, as she did whenever she was thinking. Suddenly he was beside her and his thumb brushed across her mouth.

"Don't do that."

She jerked her head back. "What are you doing?"

"You don't understand how tempting it is for me to do the same thing."

When she stared at him, not understanding what he meant, he added, "Nibble on your lips."

She gasped and backed up.

He turned away, as if everything were normal, but Joni's heart was beating a rapid tattoo in her chest.

"Want to watch some television? We have a satellite dish, though we may not get good reception in the snowstorm."

"Is it getting worse?" she asked, moving to the windows and pulling the curtain aside. "Oh, my."

There was an outside light on the porch, but it was barely visible. The snow was blowing, as Sam had predicted, but it was thick and heavy.

"Yeah. I hope my parents get back okay."

"Will they even try?" she asked, her stomach sinking.

"Yeah. It's not as bad as it looks, if you know the roads. And Mabel and Ed are our closest neighbors." He stepped back from the window, giving her a little more room to breathe.

Then he added, "So, are you up to TV?"

A picture of the two of them on one of the sofas, snuggled together watching a movie, was completely unacceptable. She shook her head.

"I don't suppose you play chess?" Before she could even answer, he continued, "Most women don't, though I don't know why. It's a wonderful—"

"I'd love to play chess," she said, interrupting him. At least, that way she knew there would be a table between them.

AN HOUR LATER, when they barely heard the sound of a car over the noise of the wind, Joni was much happier. Concentrating on the chess game had helped her ignore the potent attraction of the man across from her.

Besides, though she'd lost the first game, it had been a close match. She'd seen a measure of respect appear in Sam's eyes that she'd enjoyed.

"Must be my parents," he said as he moved one of his pawns, then stood. "I'll go see if they need any help."

"I'll come with you."

She followed him into the kitchen, thinking about

their time together and almost regretting its end. She hadn't had much adult company in a while. By her choice, of course. Several of her husband's colleagues had invited her out, but she wanted nothing to do with another policeman.

Tonight, she and Sam had started out as adversaries, wary of each other, but their chess game had lessened their antagonism, somewhat.

When Sam swung open the door, a blast of cold wind and driven snow came inside with two bundled figures. Joni wrapped her arms around herself and shivered.

"My, my, my," Loretta said as she pushed the hood of her coat back. "That is some storm. We just barely made it. Everything all right here?"

"Yes, of course," Sam said.

"Shall I put on some water to heat? To make a cup of tea or coffee?" Joni suggested.

"Good idea, Joni," Tom agreed. "I feel half frozen. The truck didn't heat up much before we got here."

She filled the teakettle and got out two mugs.

"I'll take one, too, Joni, and you might as well join us," Sam suggested.

Joni couldn't expect Sam to go out in the storm without fortifying himself, and she wouldn't mind a cup of hot tea as well. She did as he asked, even if his words had sounded more like an order than a suggestion.

"I thought maybe you'd start home a little earlier," Sam said.

"Would've been back sooner if we'd realized how bad the storm was. But you know your mother and Mabel. They were whooping and hollering so loud 'cause they were beating us men that we couldn't even hear the storm."

Loretta grinned as she settled in at the kitchen table. "Your father hates losing," she said primly. "He always exaggerates because of that."

Joni enjoyed her hostess's smugness. "Do you two ever play as partners?"

Tom's only response was "Ha!"

"We have a few times, but he doesn't like the way I play, and I don't like him telling me how to play. We find it works much better if we play against each other," Loretta said with pleasure.

The water started boiling and Joni waved Loretta back into her seat. "I'll bring it all to the table."

"Thanks." Loretta settled back down. "I'm still half-frozen."

Joni loaded the tray she'd used earlier, adding what was left of the oatmeal raisin cookies.

"Cookies? I didn't know you had time to bake, 'Retta," Tom said.

"I didn't. Joni made them."

He bit into one, then smiled at Joni. "You're welcome here anytime, young lady, as long as you come with a plateful of cookies."

While Sam and Loretta protested his saying Joni wouldn't be welcome without cookies, Joni smiled at his teasing. "Thank you, Tom. I'll remember that."

They chatted a little longer, but Joni was becoming

anxious for them to be on their way. "I don't want to rush you, Sam, but shouldn't we get started before the storm gets too much worse?"

The other three stared at her. Finally Loretta said, "Oh, dear, Joni, the storm was bad enough just coming from Ed and Mabel's. Sam would never make it all the way to town and back. You'll have to spend the night."

Chapter Four

Sam watched Joni as she took in his mother's words.

"But I can't—we can't—spend the night. I don't have any clothes or— Your truck is very big," she added, turning to Sam.

Tom spoke before Sam could. "I almost went off the road several times. And the storm seems to be getting worse."

"I'll find some things for you to wear," Loretta said. "And there's plenty of food. We'll be fine."

"I—thank you. I'm sorry to be such a burden," Joni returned, then glared at Sam.

What had he done?

He'd kept his damn hands off her all evening. That in itself qualified him as a saint. Because she was mighty tempting.

"Oh! I just remembered!" Loretta said with a laugh.

Sam looked at his mother warily. She was enjoying their predicament just a little too much.

"Remember that white elephant Christmas party last year?" She beamed at all of them. "My present was those red bikini panties. I bet they'll fit you just perfect.''

With a suppressed groan, Sam leaped up from the table. He could remember those panties just fine. And now he'd picture them on Joni all night. Fat chance he was going to get any sleep. ''I'll head on up to bed,'' he muttered.

''Before you do, son, dig out that terry-cloth robe Marty and Paul gave you last year. And a T-shirt for Joni, along with a pair of socks.''

''Oh, no, I couldn't—'' Joni protested.

''Won't hurt nothin','' Tom assured her. ''That boy hasn't never worn a robe. It's been hanging in his closet since the day he got it.''

Sam looked at his parents and shook his head. They were working this storm thing too hard. Yep, they were definitely matchmaking. What was wrong with them? He'd just gotten out of a disastrous marriage a week ago. They were already pushing him down the aisle again?

Well, they could forget it.

He stood. ''Come on, I'll find those things for you.''

With an uncertain look at his parents, Joni rose and followed him from the room.

Neither spoke on the way upstairs. When they reached his room, however, he closed the door behind them.

''I just want to make something clear,'' he growled, not bothering with the niceties.

''Yes?''

"I'm not looking."

She stared at him, blinking several times. Then, with a frown, she said, "I beg your pardon?"

Was she dense? Anyone could see what his parents were doing. "No matter what my parents tell you, I'm not looking for a wife." He glared at her to emphasize his words. Some women were hard to discourage.

He saw realization dawn in her eyes. Then anger. "Thanks for the warning. Maybe now I won't go into a decline when you ignore me." The saccharine sweetness of her words had him arching one brow.

"Just wanted you to know."

"Do you give every woman this warning, or am I special?"

She was still angry. Good. "Aren't that many women around here. And my divorce was recent. No way am I going to fall into that trap again."

"Trap? And you think only men feel trapped in marriage?" She put her hands on her hips and glared back.

His gaze traveled up and down her taut body, from her breasts, covered in a lilac sweater, to her hips, outlined faithfully in tight jeans. "It's the woman who always wants a ring. If you're interested in something else, just say so. I don't object to you sharing my bed...but not my life."

"No, thank you!"

She turned to leave.

"Wait. I've got to give you those things, or my

mother will be wanting to know why. I don't want to explain. Do you?''

She shook her head and stood stiffly at attention.

He shouldn't ever have mentioned her sleeping in his bed. Between that thought and the bikini panties, he might not sleep for a year or two.

He dug through the hangers until he found the white robe in the back. Of course, it would be white. He tossed it to Joni as he strode over to his chest of drawers. Whipping out a neatly folded T-shirt and a thick pair of white socks, he carried them to her. ''That's everything.''

With a nod, she turned and opened the door.

Unfortunately his mother was standing there.

''Oh, I thought maybe Sam had already shown you the guest room.'' She eyed the two of them speculatively, and Joni's cheeks burned.

''It took a while to find the robe,'' he muttered.

''Of course. Which proves he never wears it,'' Loretta said with a smile directed at Joni. ''Your room is right next door to Sam's. And you'll share this bath, across the hall.''

''Thank you,'' Joni said softly, ignoring Sam completely.

''There's plenty of towels if you want a shower tonight. Sam will be a gentleman and let you go first, won't you, son?''

''Yeah.'' Visions of sharing a shower with Joni came unbidden to his mind. Great. He was going to lose his mind.

''Then, if Sam doesn't mind, I think I will go first.

Thank you again for all your hospitality, Loretta,'' Joni said as she edged toward the bathroom.

''Wait, don't forget these,'' Loretta laughed as she dangled the red bikini panties in front of both of them.

Sam closed his eyes, wishing he could blot out his mind as easily. He didn't open them until he heard the bathroom door close.

''Mom,'' he muttered softly. ''I'm not interested.''

With a saucy smile, she whispered, ''Doesn't look that way to me.''

''She's a beautiful woman, and I am alive, but I'm not going to marry again. So forget whatever plans you've made.''

His father hit the top of the stairs in time to hear his words. He held up one hand, as if warding off evil. ''I didn't hear a thing.''

''Dad, tell her to butt out.''

''Not me. This is between you and your mother. Besides, I like Joni.''

Sam wanted to explode. ''That's not the problem!''

''Shh!'' Loretta warned. ''She'll hear you. And so will the babies.''

He couldn't take any more. He spun on his heel and went into his bedroom, closing the door behind him. Now he had to wait for Joni to finish taking a shower in his bathroom, and put on his T-shirt, his socks and those blasted red bikini panties.

It was going to be a long night.

WHEN JONI WOKE the next morning, she stretched under the covers, feeling reluctant to get out of bed.

Today was Saturday. She had a lot of chores to— She wasn't at home!

With a flash, last night's events came to mind. She'd spent the night at the Crawford ranch.

That thought had her rushing to the window. The storm had ended, but everything was white. Thankfully the snow didn't appear too deep, but a fierce wind kept blowing it across the land.

She spun around and reached for the terry-cloth robe Sam had loaned her. As she shrugged it on, she discovered a pile of clothing in the chair by the door.

A quick check confirmed what she'd suspected. Those were the clothes she'd worn yesterday—now freshly laundered and neatly folded. Loretta must have been up early. Joni checked her watch, only to discover it was already 9:40.

She stared at it. She couldn't possibly have slept that late. Always, she was up by seven.

But then she didn't usually lie awake half the night thinking about a man. An irritating, arrogant, handsome man. Sam Crawford had probably fueled many a woman's dreams.

But she wasn't going to let him fill hers, ever again. After all, he was bossy, and he wasn't interested. Two definite strikes against him.

She slipped into her sweater and jeans before carefully making her bed. Then she gathered the T-shirt, socks and underwear to take to Loretta's laundry room. The robe she left hanging across the back of a chair.

Downstairs, she found Loretta in the kitchen.

"Loretta, thanks so much for washing my clothes. I didn't even need to borrow the robe since I slept so late."

"I'm glad you slept well. And there was nothing to get up early for," the older woman said with a smile. "Sam won't be back to take you home until lunchtime. He and Tom went out to check on the stock."

"Oh. Well, I'm glad I didn't keep anyone waiting. Where are the kids?"

"In the den drawing. We've already made a snowman. Even Katie helped."

"My goodness, you've been busy. Can I do anything to help?" She felt like such a slacker.

"Well, you might check on the kids. I'm putting together a stew for lunch," Loretta explained with a smile.

Joni headed to the den. The boys were industriously drawing pictures at the game table, while Katie was once again going through her toy box.

"Good morning, guys," she said, greeting each with a kiss. "How are you this morning?"

Both boys showed her their numerous drawings, and Katie brought over a baby doll. She spent the rest of the morning with the children, though her gaze strayed occasionally to the window as she worried about a certain stubborn man out in the cold.

LORETTA WAS IN THE BARN doing some of their chores when Tom and Sam got back in.

"What are you doing out here?" Tom roared. "You'll freeze to death."

"Nonsense. It's not that cold in the barn," she said calmly, cleaning out a stall where they were keeping watch on a sick mare.

"But what about the kids?" Sam demanded.

"They're doing just fine. Joni is keeping an eye on them. She's so wonderful with children. And such a pleasure to be around," she added with a smile.

"Mom, don't start."

"I can't say nice things about someone without you thinking I'm trying to marry you off to her?"

"Nope, 'cause we both know you are. Here, let me finish that," Sam suggested, abandoning the argument.

"Both of you go on to the house and thaw out. I'll be up in a minute," Loretta ordered.

"You go on up, son," Tom said. "I'll stay with this stubborn woman until she's through." He dropped his left eye in a wink to Sam, then grabbed a pitchfork to help Loretta.

Sam shrugged and did as ordered. He really was cold, but he would have stayed in the barn if it would have done any good.

When he opened the kitchen door, he knew he should have stayed in the barn anyway. There was Joni, bent over from the waist to check the rolls in the oven, giving him a perfect view of her perfect derriere. Perfect.

"Ahem," he said, to alert her to his presence.

She stood and whirled in one move, a breathless

look on her face that he found even more stirring than the earlier view. "You're back!"

"Yep. Half-frozen, but we're back."

"Where's your dad? Loretta's in the barn and—"

"I know. They'll both be here in a minute. I'm going to wash up."

"I'll pour you a cup of coffee."

He stalked out of the kitchen. Did she have to fit in so perfectly? Linda hadn't wanted to lift a finger around the house, much less greet him when he came in.

The thought of Joni flying into his arms, warming his cold lips with her own, making him feel as if he was the most important man in her world, was enough to make him ignore his frozen toes. "Forget it," he warned himself, as he turned on the hot water in the downstairs bathroom and grabbed a bar of soap.

He could make it without a female cheerleader to encourage him. He was more mature than most men. He was...damn lonely.

The sad thing was, he'd been lonely married to Linda. Somehow, he'd thought his marriage would be like his parents'. They shared the ups and downs of life, laughing along the way, best friends and lovers.

He dried himself off to a stiff lecture from his conscience about remaining alone. When he reentered the kitchen, he was prepared to ignore the sexy Joni Evans.

"Coffee's on the table," she said as a greeting.

"Where are the kids?"

"We've already fed them. They're watching television. Your mother thought you might be too tired to mess with the children at lunch.''

He sighed. Too tired, yes, but they would have been a distraction. ''Sleep well?''

She looked at him warily, then nodded. ''Yes, thank you. And you?''

''Sure.'' So what was another lie? He'd tossed and turned all night, thinking about Joni, dreaming about Joni, cursing Joni.

''Were the cattle all right?''

''Fine.''

Fortunately they both heard the voices of Tom and Loretta as they trudged through the snow. Since their conversation was going nowhere, maybe his parents could enliven it.

Joni poured two more cups of coffee and set them on the table. Then she took down bowls and scooped hot, savory stew into them.

''Lunch is ready,'' she called out as the other two came in. ''I'll put the rolls on the table while you two wash up.''

''We'll be right there,'' Tom assured her, and the two passed through the kitchen holding hands.

''That's so sweet,'' she murmured, staring after them.

''What?''

''Your parents. You'd think they were newly-weds.''

He lowered his brows and trained his gaze on his cup of coffee. Especially since Joni had bent over to the oven again. This time she brought out the cookie sheet with the rolls on it and scooped them onto a plate.

When his parents came back, lunch was on the table and waiting.

"What a treat, having such service," Loretta said with a big smile.

"I didn't do much. You'd already fixed the stew, and it smells terrific. Since my taster gave it his seal of approval, I can't wait," Joni returned. "Oh, and I found the ingredients for banana pudding, so I made some. I hope that's all right."

Both older Crawfords praised her efforts.

Sam ignored her.

What else could he do? Any compliment would be interpreted as interest, for sure by his parents, maybe by Joni.

So should he refuse dessert? Naw, he wasn't that much of a masochist.

"Did you feed the kids some pudding?" Tom asked.

"Yes. Katie certainly likes it."

"Yeah, I figured. She takes after her grandpa," he agreed with a grin.

By the time they'd finished their hot stew followed by delicious banana pudding, Sam would have succumbed to a nap, preferably with Joni, if he'd had the choice. Instead he was going to drive her and Brady to their house.

"The snowplow came by about ten this morning," Loretta reported as she and Joni stacked the bowls. "And Henry did our driveway earlier."

"Then we'll be on our way as soon as you're ready, Joni," Sam said. "Shall I tell the kids?"

"Yes, please. As soon as we finish the dishes, I'll be ready."

She didn't bother to look at him, which meant he could look his fill. Until his father caught him.

"Never you mind about the dishes," Loretta said. "I'll have all afternoon to tidy up this little mess. Especially if Peter rides with y'all. Katie should be ready for her nap."

Sam shrugged. Lucky Katie.

WITH THE ROAD PLOWED, driving wasn't too bad, even if the truck did slip a little.

"I haven't done much driving on roads like this," she said finally, after a long silence between her and the driver. "In Chicago, I usually took the El."

"You'd better be sure you have snow tires on your car," he said, staring straight ahead.

Another pause.

"It was kind of your parents to make me feel so welcome."

"Folks are neighborly in Wyoming."

Dead silence, except for the boys' whisperings in the back seat.

Okay, fine. She could take a hint. Folding her arms across her chest, she stared straight ahead until he pulled to a stop in front of her house.

"Can Peter come in and see my room, Mom?" Brady asked.

"I don't know if Sam can spare the time," she

replied, putting the decision on the silent man beside her. She wasn't about to let him think she wanted him in her house.

"Sure, I can spare five minutes, Brady. But not much longer. I need to get back and help my dad."

The boys tumbled out of the truck to plow through the snow to the front porch.

"You need to hire someone to clear your sidewalk," he said as he opened his door.

She glared at him. "I'll manage."

"Do you even have a snow shovel?" he asked as he came around the front of the truck.

"Of course I do. I told you it snows a lot in Chicago." She just wasn't sure where she'd stored the shovel. Surely it was in the garage somewhere.

"Bring me the shovel and I'll get you started while I wait on Peter."

Orders, orders and more orders.

"That's all right." As if she wanted to be indebted to him. Or wanted to see his broad shoulders, strong arms, flexing in front of her. Wanted—

"Come on, Joni, you're wasting time."

She stiffened. "But it's my time, isn't it? So I can waste it if I want to."

He shot her a disgusted look. What for? Not bowing down and following his every command? Then he strode through the snow to the garage, pulled up the door and disappeared inside, leaving her standing in the snow, dumbfounded.

"What are you doing?" she demanded, hurrying after him.

He reappeared, snow shovel in hand, before she could reach him. Then, without any comment to her, he crossed to her sidewalk and began shoveling.

She debated her options. She could try to arm-wrestle the shovel away from him, but she had as much chance of success of that plan as she did of the snow melting away before bedtime.

Her second option seemed the better one. She'd go inside and hurry the boys along. And she wouldn't thank him for his efforts, either. After all, she hadn't asked for his assistance.

The boys were exploring all Brady's toys, the posters she'd put up on his wall, and the books that filled an entire shelf.

"Peter, I'm sorry, but your uncle is waiting. Why don't I call your mother and see if you can come over to play next Saturday? Then you can look at everything."

"Okay! You'll call her?" Peter asked eagerly.

"I'll call her. This afternoon, in fact. Now, put your coat back on. Your uncle's waiting."

She reminded Brady to put his coat on to accompany Peter to the truck. She didn't want any colds in their house. The three of them came to the door.

Sam, his muscles indeed flexing beneath his sheepskin coat, had almost half the sidewalk cleared.

"Peter's ready," Joni announced with determination.

Sam looked up. "Good. You two boys have a snowball fight while I finish this walk, okay?"

The boys had no difficulty following his orders, but Joni protested. "No! I mean—it's too cold."

He gave her a cool stare. Or maybe even an icy one, considering the weather. "It'll only take a couple of minutes." Then he went back to work.

Frustrated, Joni turned back into the house. She was not going to stand there and admire him. She wouldn't give him that much satisfaction!

"Mom, Sam's through!" Brady called.

If she didn't reappear, her son would think she was angry with him, not Sam.

She walked to the door. The three males were standing on the now scraped sidewalk, admiring Sam's work. She opened the door and moved to the porch. But no farther.

"Thanks, Sam."

"No problem. If you ask around, you'll find several people with snowblowers willing to clear your driveway for a couple of extra bucks."

"Thanks for the suggestion," she returned. Her words may have been gracious, but her tone wasn't. And she knew it.

His chin rose. "I'm getting a lot of thanks."

"Yes."

He took several steps closer to her, and the boys wandered toward the truck, not interested in adult matters.

"But somehow they don't sound sincere," he said softly, watching her.

"I didn't ask you to clear my walk," she said pointedly, her shoulders stiffening.

"Maybe not, but I did the job. I think I deserve a real thank-you." He came up the steps.

"I gave you a real thank-you."

"Not the kind I want."

Before she realized his intent, he pulled her against his hard chest, wrapped his arms around her and took her mouth with his.

Suddenly, instead of winter, it felt like the Fourth of July, with fireworks going off all over. His hands slid inside her jacket, under her sweater, flesh to her flesh. Hot. Wanting.

And she wanted back. Mindless, impulsive, out-of-her-head wanting.

He lifted his lips, but before she could regain her breath to protest, if that had been her intent, he settled them on hers again, at a different angle, to tease her, to lure her to greater depths.

Who knows what would have happened next, if another truck hadn't come along the almost deserted road.

"Hey, Sam!" a male voice roared. "Way to go, buddy!"

Chapter Five

"Mom, hurry! We don't want to be late," Brady called from the door to the garage.

Joni slid her feet into black pumps, grabbed her black wool coat and joined Brady. "I'm glad you want to go to Sunday School, Brady, but we have plenty of time."

"Peter will be waiting for me."

Joni rolled her eyes as her son pulled her toward their car. He climbed in and fastened his seat belt while she lifted the garage door. The driveway cleared of snow reminded her of yesterday's disaster.

Like she'd forgotten Sam's kiss.

With a weary sigh, she got into the car. If she didn't remove Sam from her life, she was never again going to get a decent night's sleep.

But she had made arrangements to have her driveway blown free of snow all winter. So Sam had actually helped her in spite of his causing her lack of sleep. She'd considered sleeping in this morning, but Brady had been eager to go to church.

Last week, their first Sunday in Saddle, they'd only

gone to the church service, not the Bible Study held beforehand. Since becoming friends with Peter, Brady was determined to attend both.

After finding the proper room for Brady and watching him reunite with Peter, Joni looked at the elderly lady who had guided them upon their arrival.

"Let's see now, dear, you'll go to the singles group. Come this way."

"You have a singles group?" Saddle was small. She'd thought the adults would be all together.

"Yes, right here."

Joni looked in the door and wanted to turn around and run. Because, of course, the singles group included Sam Crawford.

"Thank you," she murmured and slipped through the door. At the moment, Sam had his back to her, talking to some other men. If she could make it to the back row, perhaps she could avoid him altogether.

An older man, probably the teacher, saw her, however, and crossed the room to introduce himself. "Hello, I'm Jerry Williams. You must be Sam's friend."

Joni froze. The rest of the room all turned to stare at her. Sam included. Finally she said, "His family has been very friendly. Everyone in Saddle has been wonderful."

"Good, glad to hear it. Come right in. There's a seat here by Sam."

Without waiting for her to accept the invitation, he led her to a seat on the front row and called everyone to order. Sam sat down beside her.

When the class finally dismissed, Sam and Joni had not said a word to each other. But she'd been aware of his presence the entire time.

"I have to go find Brady," she said to no one in particular and almost ran from the room.

Brady was waiting impatiently. Beside him was Peter and an attractive young woman with dark hair like Peter's.

"Are you Joni?" she asked, stepping forward.

"Yes. You must be Marty."

"Yes, I'm so glad to meet you. Peter talks about Brady nonstop."

"Brady talks about Peter, too."

"Are you staying for the service?"

Joni knew what was coming. She just didn't know what to do about it.

"'Course we are," Brady said with a broad smile.

"Then why don't you join us? The boys will enjoy being together." Marty smiled warmly, and Joni couldn't say no.

She nodded and followed Sam's sister into the auditorium. After Marty introduced her husband, she let him sit by the boys. She followed him into the pew and motioned for Joni to sit beside her. When Loretta and Tom joined them, Joni breathed a sigh of relief.

Until Sam appeared at the end of the row. He tried to sit beside his father, but Loretta insisted Tom scoot to the end of the row. Then she shifted, leaving the only vacant spot beside Joni.

That's when she knew Sam was right. His mother was matchmaking.

"HAVE YOU GOTTEN your Christmas tree yet?" Marty asked after the service.

Glad to have a normal, impersonal topic, Joni smiled. "No, not yet. I'm still unpacking boxes. But we'll get one soon."

"Come with us, then. We're going to cut one down on the ranch. We do it every year and we can just as easily cut two as one."

Joni's eyes widened in horror. She had fallen into another trap. Particularly since Brady had heard the invitation.

"Yeah!" He immediately ran to Peter and informed him of the treat in store for the two of them.

"Brady!" she protested, but she knew it was already too late.

Before she could talk to her son, Loretta agreed with Marty. "Tom and I will follow you to your house so you can change."

"No. No, I need to drive so you won't have to bring me back home." She was sure of that.

"Oh, no, Joni. Tree hunting takes a long time. We don't want you driving back after dark by yourself." Without waiting for Joni to agree, she went off to find Tom.

Joni gave it one last effort. "Marty, Sam is going to be furious."

"Why?"

"Because he thinks your mother is matchmaking. I think so, too."

"It gives Mom something to do. Besides, if you don't cut down your tree, you'll have to drive to the next town to buy one. Saddle never has any trees for sale because they're all over the place.''

Tom and Loretta appeared beside her, ready to head for her house. She called to Brady, giving up the fight. At least Sam wasn't around anywhere. Maybe he didn't participate in the tree hunt.

Of course, he did.

When she and Brady arrived at the ranch, along with Tom and Loretta, Sam was waiting in the kitchen, having already been informed by Peter, she was sure.

The greeting she received could have been described as surly, if one wanted to be generous. She didn't. Crossing the room to stand beside him, she whispered fiercely, ''I couldn't get out of it. This isn't my fault.''

He stared at her in disbelief, only making her temper grow hotter.

''Hey, no whispering, you two,'' Paul called from across the room. ''I certainly wasn't allowed to when I was dating Marty.''

''We're not dating!'' Joni and Sam said in unison.

''Well, maybe you should,'' Loretta said as she tied an apron around her waist.

Sam and Joni shot off in opposite directions, trying to put as much distance between them as they could. At least, Joni assumed that was Sam's intention. It certainly was hers.

During Sunday dinner, she sat between Tom and Brady and pretended Sam didn't exist. With all the conversation, it wasn't too difficult.

When she tried to help with the dishes, Loretta shooed her out of the kitchen. "Katie and I are going to stay here while the rest of you hunt for all the trees."

"All? How many are we cutting down?" Joni asked.

"One for us, one for the bunkhouse, and for you and Marty. Four in all. You'll take Tom's truck and Sam's."

Joni felt panic build in her. She turned to hurry out the door, grabbing her coat and gloves on the way. She wanted to make sure she got a seat in Tom's truck.

Too late. It was already bouncing its way across the pasture. Sam was standing beside his truck, his arms folded.

"Where are the boys?" Surely Brady and Peter would be riding with them.

"They didn't want to wait." He gave her a killer look that told her everything was her fault.

"They're all in Tom's truck?"

"Yep. Dad seemed to think it was a good idea." His words dripped with sarcasm.

"Sam, I told you, I didn't plan on coming. Marty asked me about a tree and—never mind. But it wasn't my idea."

"Doesn't matter. They're determined."

"But what can we do? Did you tell them you weren't interested?"

He uncrossed his arms and put his hands on his

hips. "Lady, I have told everyone in Saddle. But it doesn't seem to make any difference."

"Well, don't blame me. I'm not the one who grabbed someone and kissed them in front of the entire town!" She was not going to be blamed for his difficulties.

He didn't pretend to be innocent. "I know. That was a big mistake."

"It certainly was!"

"'Cause I want to do the same thing again."

She couldn't believe he'd said that. And she took a step back just to be cautious.

"Don't worry. I know better. Mom's watching out the kitchen window. So get in the truck and let's go find those stupid trees." He strode around the truck, got in and slammed the door. Waiting for her.

Joni finally opened the passenger door, got in and closed it. Then she clung to it as if it were a lifeline.

"What are we going to do?" she finally asked as they followed in Tom's path.

"I'll take care of it. I've got a plan."

She shot him a curious stare. "Do you want to tell me about it?"

"Nope."

She glared at him. "Then how can I help?"

"I'm not sure your help would be all that beneficial. After all, you're here, aren't you?" He stared straight ahead.

Heat surged through her. If he wasn't driving, she'd slap his face. She'd already told him it wasn't her fault. Clearly he didn't believe her.

SAM WATCHED JONI as she picked the first tree they came to. He'd made her mad and she wasn't going to prolong her visit.

Good. He had enough to deal with without the temptation of kissing her.

"No, Mom," Brady protested. "It's too little."

"And has a big hole in the back," Marty added. "Let's look at that one on the hill." She led the charge up the snow-covered hill.

Paul looked at Joni. "I should've warned you. They seek perfection. At least we're not out in a driving snowstorm like last year."

"A snowstorm? And they still were picky?" she asked in disbelief.

Though his eyes were twinkling, Paul nodded solemnly. "Great family. But they're nuts about their Christmas trees." Then he followed his wife up the hill.

Janie looked around in exasperation until she seemed to realize she and Sam were the only ones left standing near the trucks. Without a word, she ran after the others.

"Like I was a grizzly bear, threatening her," Sam muttered to himself. Okay, so he hadn't been exactly nice in the truck. But after that kiss yesterday, he was on guard. The lady packed a real punch, and half the town considered them a couple already.

He'd thought about finding her a man before. But it had been a halfhearted idea. Now he had no choice. He really was going to matchmake. Because if he didn't find Brady a daddy for Christmas, he was going to be in big trouble.

When he reached the top of the hill, he discovered an argument in progress.

"No, Brady. It is definitely too big."

"Mom, it won't touch the ceiling." Suddenly spying Sam, he asked him to verify his words.

"Probably not. Looks to be about seven feet. Right, Dad?"

"Right, son. Don't you like it, Joni?"

"It's beautiful, Tom, but I'd have a hard time getting it in the Christmas tree stand. Something smaller would be better."

"I'll put it in the stand for you." Sam couldn't blame Joni for the incredulous look she shot him after their conversation in the truck. But it was a Christmas tree. And it was Brady's choice.

"Good enough," Tom said. "Who's going to chop it down?"

"I will," Sam said. "Go look for three more so we can get home before our toes freeze."

The others, minus Joni and Brady, tromped farther up the hill.

"What are you doing?" Joni demanded in a low voice.

"Chopping down your tree, hurrying up the process. I'm cold." But he was getting warmer the closer she came.

"Can I help?" Brady demanded, interrupting their whispering.

"Maybe in a couple of years, son," Sam said with

a smile. "Axes are kind of dangerous. Move over there with your mom while I cut the tree down."

His ax was sharp and it only took five or six swings to fell the tree. "Okay, Brady, now you can help. We'll drag the tree to my truck."

The boy was delighted to be included, and Sam sensed some of the anger leaving Joni. He gave her a sideways grin. She was such a good mother, he knew she could always be charmed by kindnesses to her son.

But that wasn't why he let Brady help. It was Brady's Christmas tree. He should get to help. His father should be letting him help. But until he got a father, Sam would share Christmas with him.

THREE MORE TREES were quickly found, a record Paul assured everyone. As soon as they reached the ranch house, Joni insisted Sam take her and Brady, and their tree, home. She resisted Loretta's persistent arguments that they stay and decorate the family tree.

Sam wasn't going to be able to accuse her of trying to stay close to him.

She even silenced Brady with a sharp command when he began to whine. With a sigh, she ruffled his head, offering a silent apology. But when he appeared ready to argue again, she gave him her sternest look.

At the house, she dragged out the tree stand, packed away in the garage, and took it outside to Sam.

"You go on inside," Sam ordered. "Brady and I will have the tree ready in a few minutes."

More orders. That's all the man did, give her orders.

"I'm perfectly able to help."

"I have Brady to help. I don't need anyone else," Sam said evenly, staring at her.

She looked down at her son and read the pride in his eyes. "Okay, since you have such good help," she said, smiling at her son.

Once inside, she put on a pot of hot chocolate. It was the least she could do. But she'd offer to make Sam's to go. He deserved that, even if he was being sweet to Brady.

When they brought the tree inside, Joni showed him where to put it.

"Will you help us decorate it?" Brady asked, hopping up and down in excitement.

Both adults answered together. "No."

Joni quickly added, "I made hot chocolate. If you don't have time to stay and drink it, I have a foam cup."

The difficult man refused to escape. "I have time to drink some."

She left him standing in the living room. "Fine."

"Hey, Mom!" Brady called after her. "Bring marshmallows, too. Sam loves marshmallows."

She plunked down a bowl and filled it with marshmallows. She hoped they all went to fat at once on the lean cowboy. It would serve him right.

When she carried the tray into the living room, Brady and Sam were staring at the tree.

"What's wrong?"

"Nothing," Sam drawled. "We were just trying to decide if this is the tree's best side. What do you think?"

"I think it looks perfect. Here's the chocolate."

"And marshmallows, Sam," Brady added, pushing the bowl closer to his guest.

"Thanks, son," Sam replied with a smile.

"Stop calling him that!" she ordered, unable to hold back her irritation.

Sam stared at her, as if she'd lost her mind.

"I like it, Mom," Brady protested.

She wished she'd never spoken. "Is your chocolate too hot, Brady? I brought some extra milk to cool it down."

"Yes, please," he said, but she could tell he hadn't forgiven her comment.

"Thank you for your help today, Sam. We're pretty well set now. I shouldn't have to bother you for anything in the future." That should tell him she wasn't going to cling.

"It was no bother. Brady's a good helper, so it went fast."

Brady puffed out his narrow chest and flexed one arm. "I'm really strong, aren't I?" He looked at Sam. "This is how you show your muscle. Show me yours, Sam."

Joni tried not to look as Sam, having shed his coat, flexed his muscle for Brady. The seam on his shirt-sleeve strained as he did so.

"Mom doesn't have much muscle. Show him, Mom," Brady ordered, scorn in his voice.

"No, sweetie, I don't think so."

"You afraid to be called a weakling?" Sam asked, a smile on his firm lips.

Unfair. She didn't like to resist a challenge. Without too much thought, she flexed her muscle.

"I reckon I'll have to feel it since you're wearing that thick sweater," Sam said.

Before she could pull her arm away, he settled his warm hand around it and gently squeezed.

"Hey, Brady, she does have some muscle. Kind of puny, but at least it's there."

Brady giggled. "Mine's bigger."

The phone rang and Brady set down his chocolate and dashed into the kitchen, calling, "I'll get it," over his shoulder.

Joni's eyes widened in alarm. She jerked her arm from Sam's hold. "I—I think you should leave before—"

"Mom, it's Peter. I'm going to talk, okay?" Brady called from the kitchen.

"Yes, okay," she called back. Then she started again. "I think you should leave before Brady comes back."

"Yeah, you're right," Sam said, taking one more sip of his chocolate and then standing.

"Thank you for your help, but we won't be needing anything else. We won't bother you." Her voice was breathless as she also stood. Too close to Sam. She took a step back.

To her surprise, he took hold of both her arms and tugged her forward.

"Sam! What are you—"

Doing? What was he doing? He was kissing her, as he had yesterday on her porch. All thoughts disappeared as sensations took over.

Then he released her and stepped back.

"I thought I deserved one more kiss before I put my plan into action." Then he turned around and walked out, leaving a stunned Joni staring after him.

What plan?

It couldn't be any more devastating than his kiss.

Chapter Six

Wednesday, Sam was ready to put his plan into action.

He figured by midnight tonight, his problems would be over. Joni would have a man in her life. Brady would have a potential father.

Sam would be left alone.

He stepped into the classroom after a lot of children ran past him. Expecting to find Joni alone, as he had before, he was surprised to discover another woman sitting beside her desk.

"Oh, uh, excuse me," he muttered as both women looked up.

"Why, Sam Crawford," the woman said, and he recognized Elsie Perkins, an old school chum. "I heard you were sniffing around Mrs. Evans, but I didn't know anything would get you off the ranch during the week."

Damn! It was a good thing he had a plan.

Joni tried to help out. "I'm sure he's here about his nephew, Mrs. Perkins. Peter and my son are great friends."

"Yeah, right," the woman replied, laughing. "Well, thanks for your help, Mrs. Evans. I'll try your suggestion tonight. So long, Sam."

Sam stayed by the door until he could see Elsie leave the building. Then he faced Joni's glare.

"Sorry. I thought you'd be alone."

"What do you want?"

She didn't sound welcoming. He understood why, but contrarily, it irritated him. "I'm trying to fix things, but you don't seem too appreciative."

"I wonder why."

Time to cut to the chase. Before her big brown eyes lured him closer. "I'm going to take you and Brady out for pizza tonight."

"Thanks for the gracious invitation," she said, arching her brows, "but no thanks."

"This is part of my plan," he emphasized, stepping closer.

"Being seen together will make people stop talking about us? I don't think much of your logic. If we just ignore each other, the talk will die down, Sam. That's the best way." She started organizing papers on her desk.

Like she could just ignore him.

"No, it's not. My way is best." He was sure of that. After all, Brady wanted a father, deserved a father. He was a great kid.

And Sam had to have a good reason not to sleep with Joni.

She gave him a sugary smile. "I wouldn't know,

since you haven't bothered to share your plan with me." Then she went back to shuffling her papers.

"Can't you just trust me?" he asked, moving closer to her desk.

"You didn't trust me when I told you my being there Sunday wasn't my fault."

He leaned over and put his hands on top of her papers, stopping her movement and forcing her to look at him. "Yes, I did. I apologize. I was frustrated and took my anger out on you. That was wrong."

He didn't like to apologize, but if he was going to, he wanted to do it right. Her brown eyes softened, and her full lips gentled.

"That was a nice apology. Thank you."

"It's the truth," he added with a smile. "So, will you trust me tonight? Will you and Brady come with me for pizza?"

"Why?"

"I think things will go better if you don't ask. You'll get a free meal."

He lost some of the ground he'd gained as she glared at him. "Brady and I are not charity cases! I can pay for our meals. In fact, I'll go, but only if we go dutch."

He leaned a little closer, his gaze on those soft lips. "Sweetheart, the cost of the pizza isn't a big deal. But we've got to get our lives straightened out before someone gets hurt."

He was thinking of Brady, of course, but Joni's cheeks flushed with color.

She looked away. "Okay. What time shall we

come to the pizza parlor?'' There was only one in Saddle.

"I'll pick you up at six-thirty. And wear something pretty.'' Unable to resist, he leaned over and gave her a quick kiss. Then he hightailed it out of there before he gave in to temptation and hauled her out of the chair into his arms.

JONI WAS SURE she'd made a mistake.

If she'd read Sam's request about her attire correctly, she was to dress as if they were on a date. And she didn't see how the evening would solve their problem.

Even so, she chose a soft blue wool dress with long sleeves and a scooped neck, one of her favorites. She curled her hair and pulled it back on the sides with combs.

When she felt she was looking her best, she went searching for Brady. She hadn't yet told him of the treat in store for him.

"Wow, Mom, you look pretty," he exclaimed when she came to the door of his room.

"Thank you, son. Um, are you hungry?"

"Sure. Is dinner ready?"

"We're going out for dinner. Go wash your hands and comb your hair."

"Are we going to the ranch?" he asked, excitement building in his voice.

"No."

"Oh. I haven't seen Sam since we put up the tree.

And he hasn't seen it since we decorated it. He'll really like it, Mom. Maybe if you called him he'd—''

She couldn't take any more, so she interrupted him. ''Sam will be here in ten minutes.''

''Wow!'' Brady exclaimed and leaped to his feet. ''I'll go turn on the Christmas lights!''

''Brady, I'll turn on the lights. You go wash up.''

With a sigh, she went to the living room and plugged in the lights she'd strung on the tree Monday night.

Almost before she'd finished, Brady came barreling down the hall. ''Mom, you know what Peter said today?''

Since most of Brady's conversation was full of reference to Peter, she wasn't surprised. ''No. What did Peter say?''

''If you and Sam got married, we'd be brothers!''

Joni froze, alarm spreading through her. ''Brady— Brady, Sam and I aren't going to get married. And you and Peter wouldn't be brothers even if we did.''

''But Peter said—''

''If Sam and I married, the two of you would be cousins. But that's not going to happen. So you get to be best friends. Isn't that just as good?''

''Why can't you marry Sam?''

Her child was nothing if not stubborn. ''People marry because they love each other. And Sam and I don't love each other.'' She didn't even want to think of the man in terms of love.

''Can't you try?'' Brady pleaded.

She bent down and kissed her son's cheek. Sadly

she said, "No, baby, you can't try to love someone. It just happens." But you could try not to love someone. That was a definite possibility.

A knock on the door stopped the conversation.

Before she went to open the door, however, she cautioned her son. "Don't say anything to Sam about what we just talked about. Okay?"

Brady nodded.

She swung open the door, the sight of the handsome cowboy making her catch her breath.

He nodded to her and stepped into their living room. His attention moved to Brady after his gaze covered her from top to toe. "Nice looking Christmas tree, Brady. I could see the lights from the street."

Brady beamed. "Thanks. I wanted Mom to put lights up outside, but she said she couldn't."

"You should've called me," Sam said, turning to Joni. "I would—"

"I'm sure you were busy," she said firmly. "Besides, I think our tree will provide us with plenty of Christmas spirit."

"Yes, of course," Sam said, nodding in agreement. "Well, are you ready for pizza, Brady?"

"Sure. I love pizza. Is Peter coming?"

"No, I'm afraid it'll just be the three of us. Unless we run into someone we know."

Joni noticed that Sam didn't look at either of them as he added that last sentence. What was going on?

He led the way out to his truck, after they unplugged the Christmas lights, much to Brady's disappointment. "It wouldn't be safe, son," Sam said, his hand on Brady's shoulder.

Joni sighed. She'd already voiced her displeasure that he called her child son. She figured his careless term of affection only added to Brady's dreams.

When they reached the pizza parlor, Sam, after asking Joni about her preferences, told her he and Brady would go place their order. She could choose a table.

More orders. The man assumed she would go along with whatever he said. And she did, she had to admit. Granted, he had to reason with her for their outing tonight. But he'd won.

She chose a table against the wall, out of the traffic pattern of people arriving and ordering. In spite of Sam's assurance that he had a plan, she wasn't anxious to be spotted by the gossips of Saddle.

He and Brady found her. He set their drinks on the table, then looked around. "It's kind of dark at this table. Don't you want to sit closer to the center of the—I mean, where there's more light?"

Yes, there was definitely something going on.

"I like it here," she said calmly, not moving.

"Okay," he agreed, drawing out the word as he settled into a chair across from her, with Brady between them.

"Sam ordered two big pizzas," Brady said, seemingly impressed with that much pizza.

"Two large pizzas? You must be starving," she said to Sam.

"Uh, yeah, well, I wanted to have plenty of pizza

in case Brady here needs more. He's a growing boy, you know.''

With those heavy hints, Joni wasn't surprised when Sam hailed another man as if he were a savior just after their pizza was delivered to their table.

''Billy! I haven't seen you in weeks. What are you doing here?''

Since the man was standing in the center of the room, looking as if he was searching for someone and stopped looking as soon as Sam hailed him, her suspicions were confirmed.

''Joni, let me introduce you to Billy Hawkins. He has a spread about thirty miles outside town. Join us, Billy. I ordered too much pizza and we need help eating it.''

''Don't mind if I do,'' the man replied with a big grin and plopped down in the empty chair.

The next half hour was trying for Joni. Though she wasn't sure why. The man was muscular, almost as tall as Sam, friendly, intelligent. She had nothing against him. Except she was being pitched to him as if she was the snake oil those traveling salesmen used to sell as cure-alls.

As soon as Brady finished his pizza, Sam invited him to play a video game with him on the other side of the restaurant. Brady, of course, didn't hesitate.

Once they were alone, silence fell between Joni and Billy. Finally the man leaned forward. ''I, uh, wondered if you'd like to go into Lander to see a movie this Friday. They've got a real nice theater and it's only about a forty-five-minute drive…unless it snows, of course.''

Joni was prepared. ''That's very kind of you, Billy, but since we just moved here and Christmas is around the corner, I really don't have any extra time for socializing. Besides, I'm not interested in dating.''

''But Sam said—'' he began, then stopped.

''I know. But Sam didn't understand the situation. His parents are matchmaking and he's afraid I'll cooperate.'' Her voice hardened. ''But he has nothing to worry about.''

Billy stared at his plate of half-eaten pizza before he raised his gaze to her face again. ''You know, I came tonight because of Sam. But I asked you out because I want to get to know you better.'' He stood to leave. ''After you get settled in, let me know if you change your mind.''

SAM ONLY KEPT HALF of his attention on the video game. The other half was on Joni and Billy across the restaurant. He frowned when Billy reached across the table to touch Joni. His friend was moving a little fast.

He'd have a talk with him.

Then he realized Billy was saying goodbye.

''Sam?'' Brady said.

''Uh, yeah, son?''

''Why is that man staying with Mom?''

''He wanted to get to know her,'' he said, staring at Joni as she now sat alone. Maybe he should've explained his plan, but he was afraid she'd feel awkward. Instead he had a sinking feeling she hadn't co-operated.

"Your mom's alone now. We need to go back to the table."

Brady asked to finish his game, and Sam couldn't think of a reason not to.

Until a man sat down at the table next to Joni and struck up a conversation. Damn, it wasn't safe to leave her alone.

He hurried Brady back to the table.

"I'm still hungry," he announced loudly, staring at the stranger.

"There's plenty of pizza left." Joni didn't crack a smile.

The stranger nodded to Sam. "Sorry to interrupt. Your wife was giving me directions."

"She's not—" Brady began, but Sam covered his mouth with a big hand.

"He was going to say his mom's not good with directions, but that wasn't tactful, Brady." He smiled at Joni, but she didn't respond. "She has other talents."

Those words got a response. Her cheeks reddened and her gaze sparkled with anger. But maybe the stranger would think it was affection. Yeah, maybe.

"Ready to go, honey?" he asked, figuring he'd better get her out of there before she exploded.

"I thought you wanted to eat more pizza?" she asked, staring at him.

"Brady, go get one of those boxes. We'll take it home with us." As the boy ran to do his bidding, he took one of Joni's hands and pulled her to her feet. "Come on, sweetheart, it's time to go home."

She wasn't happy with him. "Your home or mine?" she muttered, but he didn't think the man heard her. Brady returned with the box and he slid in the slices of pizza. "Well, let's go," he said, slipping his free hand around Joni's shoulder.

Startled, she stared at him, but he ignored her response. Until they started toward the door and ran into one of his mother's friends, Mrs. Elkins.

"Why, Sam, I haven't seen you in ages. And who is your ladyfriend? I hadn't heard you were on the prowl again."

Joni looked at him as if she thought he deserved exactly what he'd gotten. Maybe she was right.

"IT'S YOUR FAULT for turning down Billy. I was going to excuse myself and let him take you home."

She couldn't believe the gall of the man. "My fault? I didn't even know what was going on, because you hadn't told me. If you had, I could've explained that I wouldn't accept a date from Billy."

"What's wrong with Billy?" Sam demanded in a loud roar.

Joni closed her eyes briefly. Then she stared at Sam. "There's nothing wrong with Billy. But you'll be explaining that to Brady if you don't lower your voice."

Sam had brought them home, come in and visited with Brady until his bedtime. Now that Brady was safely tucked away, Joni was trying to work out their difficulties.

Without much success.

He did as she asked, responding with a low growl. "But you've messed things up. If we don't hook you up with someone else, we're going to end up together."

She tried to ignore the pain his words dealt her. After all, she wasn't looking for a husband. But being rejected wasn't pleasant. "Your mistake, Sam, was assuming I would cooperate with your parents. That I wanted a husband."

"Don't you?"

"No."

"Why not? Brady is a great kid and deserves a father."

"Of course he deserves a father, a good, loving father, but I can't marry the first man off the street for Brady's sake. That wouldn't work."

"Why? Billy's a good guy."

Frustrated, she abandoned her calm reasoning. "Fine! You marry him!"

He grabbed her arms and pulled her closer. "You're being ridiculous!"

"Yes, I am, because I can't get you to understand. You can't go around ordering other people's lives. I'm not going to marry, and I don't want to date anyone. I'll leave you alone, and everyone will catch on eventually that we're not a couple."

"How long will it take Brady to catch on?"

That was hitting below the belt. She bent her head

and it rested on Sam's chest. "I don't know. I told him not to say anything to you."

"He didn't. But Peter thought his idea was worth sharing."

Wearily she lifted her head. "I'll talk to him again."

"But he wants a daddy, sweetheart. If you'd try dating, just a little, he'd realize I'm not the only prospect. And you might find someone you like."

She already had. That idea flashed through her mind before she could shut it down. It was the truth. She liked Sam. With any encouragement, she'd love Sam. But Sam was going to great effort to tell her he wasn't interested.

Maybe she should do as he asked.

"Fine. I'll look for someone to—to date."

"I'll take care of it," he assured her.

"I can find my own dates, Sam. I'm sure that man tonight would've asked me out if you hadn't shown up at the table when you did."

"Yeah," he agreed, irritation in his voice. "I'm sure he would've, too, but it wouldn't be safe."

"Fine. I'll be careful, take my time and choose someone nice."

"We don't have much time. Christmas is two and a half weeks away," he insisted, squeezing her shoulders.

"Sam, I don't have to be dating someone by Christmas. Brady isn't going to get a daddy for Christmas. He'll have to understand that."

"But you could at least start seeing someone. Fri-

day night—no, I know. Saturday night, we'll double-
date. Mom will keep Brady for you. When he sees
me with another woman and you with another man,
he'll understand.''

He had a point. Until Brady saw Sam with another
woman, he'd probably think his mother was just being uncooperative. "Fine. If you can set that up, I'll
go along. But not Billy. He's too nice to play games
with.''

"Right. I'll take care of it. Saturday night we'll
have everything taken care of. Do you have a preference as to what kind of man—I mean, mostly we
have cowboys and ranchers. There's a mechanic or
two and—I know. The vet. He'll be perfect.''

"A veterinarian? He's not married?''

"Nope. You'll like him. His name is Donald.''

She hated the name Donald. But she wasn't going
to say so. After all, what she liked wasn't the point.

"Okay. That will be fine.''

She must not have shown enough enthusiasm in her
response. He squeezed her shoulders again, pulling
her just that much closer. "It'll be all right, Joni. He's
a nice man.''

"I'm sure he is.''

"He's a friend,'' he added, but Joni didn't understand his point.

Sam spoke again. "I would never betray a friend.''

She stared up at him, puzzled.

"That's why I'm going to kiss you now. Because,
after Saturday, when you're Donald's girl, I can't ever
kiss you again.''

Chapter Seven

"Merry Christmas, Mrs. Evans," the children shouted as the bell rang on Friday. Christmas vacation was only one week away, and they were all excited about the coming holiday.

"Not yet, class. I'll see you on Monday," she returned as they left the classroom.

When all the children had disappeared, she slumped back in her chair. She'd been on the job two weeks, and she felt quite settled in. However, she, too, was looking forward to Christmas vacation. Since she'd started work as soon as they arrived in Saddle, she'd had little time to spare. Another week, and she could organize her house, do a little shopping.

Prepare for a new year.

Without Sam.

How could the man have become so important to her in such a short time? Maybe it had something to do with those incredible kisses. When he'd grabbed her Wednesday night, she'd told herself to resist. Until their lips met, his warm hands caressed her, his body pressed against hers.

"Joni?"

She started and turned toward the door.

Mary Bledsoe, the other second-grade teacher, was staring at her. "Are you all right? Your face is flushed."

"I'm fine." She hurriedly changed the subject. "Are you ready for Christmas?"

Mary was a quiet, shy woman about Joni's age. Unmarried. Joni hoped they would become friends as the year progressed.

"I thought I was, but…last night, Sam Crawford called me."

Uh-oh. Joni braced herself. "Really? Are the two of you friends?"

"Not exactly. I mean, we know each other, of course, since we both grew up here, but…anyway, he asked me to help him out by going into Lander to dinner and the movies Saturday night." She stared at Joni, a question in her look. "He said you and Donald Steel would be going with us."

"Um, yes," Joni said, rearranging things on her desk. "Sam mentioned an outing like that. It'll be fun, won't it?"

"I guess. But since I don't go out much, I thought I should see what you're wearing."

Joni hadn't given her wardrobe any thought. She'd been doing too much thinking about Sam's kisses. "I'll probably wear a sweater and a skirt, not too dressy, not too casual. Does that sound all right to you?"

"Oh, you'd know better than me. I don't have much of a social life." Mary sounded apologetic.

"I think most people just pretend to have a big social life, Mary. I haven't dated since my husband died."

"Except for Sam."

Joni choked. "Uh, I'm not dating Sam. He's just been helpful since we moved here."

"Oh."

Joni was feeling more and more confused. Why had Mary accepted a date with Sam if she thought he was interested in someone else? But she didn't know Mary well enough to ask that question.

"Did Sam mention what movie we're going to see?" Joni couldn't think of anything else to ask.

"No."

"Well, I'm sure it will be fun." She smiled, then thought of something else. "Do you know Donald?"

"Not really. I've seen him. But I'm sure I'll like him. It will be so nice to have something to do. I have to go, but I'll see you tomorrow night."

Joni stared at the place Mary had been. She was sure she'd like Donald? What had Sam done?

SAM HAD EVERYTHING arranged.

He'd picked up Donald Steel first. He thought he should tell the other man about some of Joni's likes and dislikes. Donald had listened intently. That was a good sign.

Of course, when they picked up Mary, she'd insisted on getting in the back seat, saying the leg room was better for the men up front. He'd borrowed his mother's car, a Lincoln Town Car, so they'd have plenty of room. But Mary was still sitting primly in the back seat.

Probably they'd all trade places when Joni joined them.

He pulled up in front of Joni's little house and looked at Donald. When the man didn't move, he said, "You want to go see if Joni's ready?"

"Oh, yeah, sure."

He and Mary sat there in silence. He didn't know what to say to her. He'd already told her she looked nice.

Fortunately the door opened almost immediately and Brady raced down the sidewalk. "Hey, Sam!"

He waved to the boy and watched as Donald held open the back door of the car. Brady slid in, followed by Joni. Okay, so they'd start out with the ladies in the back seat. They still had to drop off Brady at his mother's.

He'd intentionally planned it that way so Brady would see him with another woman. His mother had asked Brady to spend the night, telling Joni she'd bring him to church in the morning. This was the only way Brady would know that Sam was on a date with Mary.

Except now he didn't know.

Because Donald was sitting in the front seat.

Sam frowned. But he couldn't think of anything else to do.

"Where's your truck, Sam?" Brady asked. He was holding his overnight bag on his lap.

"It's at home. I thought we'd use the car for the ladies. They'd be cramped in the back seat of the truck."

"Girls, yuck!" Brady said.

"Young man, you'd better remember who cooks your meals and washes your clothes," Joni warned, but she was smiling.

Sam kept trying to think of ways to show Brady that Mary was his date as he drove to the ranch, but nothing came to mind. Mary wasn't a flirt, so she didn't help the situation any.

Joni got out with Brady and walked to the door, knocking on it. Loretta opened it and spoke briefly, then sent Joni back to the car. Brady didn't show any hesitation at staying with Sam's mom.

"It's so nice that Brady gets along with your parents," Mary said.

"Uh, yeah," Sam agreed, but his mind was spinning. Why would Mary say that?

"Ready," Joni said as she got back into the car. "What movie are we going to see?"

Her question distracted him and he explained their choices. Both women voted for the latest romantic comedy. He'd expected as much. Besides, he hoped it would give Donald some ideas.

The restaurant he'd chosen had several cozy booths, but Donald asked for a table for four, explaining that he always felt claustrophobic in a booth. Mary surprisingly agreed with him.

During dinner, Sam noticed that Mary and Donald seemed to have a lot in common. He'd always thought Mary a shy woman, quiet, but tonight she chatted with Donald about his customers and their pets, particularly when some of them were the parents of her students.

Sam took another bite of his steak, watching the two of them. Finally he turned to Joni, sitting on his right. He noticed a smile playing around the edges of her lips. Lips that were eminently kissable.

"What's going on here?" he whispered.

"I think you didn't make things clear," she returned, her breath teasing his ear.

Frowning, he said, "Of course I did. I told them the four of us would go out."

"That's what I thought." Joni straightened in her chair and smiled at the other two, who were watching them. "Do you like the actor in the movie we're going to see, Mary?"

"Oh, yes, he's so romantic. And handsome. I like men with blond hair, don't you?"

Sam frowned again. That wasn't a good sign. Donald had blond hair, not him. Not that he wanted Mary to fall for him, but in terms of the evening... No, it wasn't a good sign.

"Actually I prefer dark-haired men," Joni said with a smile. "Not that you're not attractive, Donald."

"Everyone has their preference. I happen to like brunettes," he said, ducking his head.

Mary's cheeks reddened, but she smiled, one hand going to her brunette curls.

Donald leaned across the table. "How about you, Sam?"

Lost in his worries, Sam stared at Donald blankly. "How about me what?"

"Do you prefer blondes or brunettes?"

He stared at Joni's blond curls before turning back to Donald. "I prefer redheads," he snapped.

Joni took a sip of her tea. "Good. A hot-tempered redhead is what you deserve." She pushed back her chair. "Excuse me."

"Oh," Mary said, as if Joni had startled her. "I'll go with you."

JONI WONDERED if Sam would try to explain Donald's role to him while the women were absent from the table. But when she and Mary came back, both men were talking to a third she didn't know.

Sam and Donald stood and pulled out their chairs before Sam introduced Joni to the visitor, a rancher from the area.

"Jed came by just after you ladies excused yourselves," Sam said, giving Joni a speaking look.

"Right," the man said with a hearty laugh. "I guess I'd better make myself scarce now that you pretty ladies are back. Nice to see you, Sam. You, too, Donald." With a wave, he strolled away.

Joni hid her smile. Sam sounded frustrated. She'd considered trying to hint to Mary, but then she'd thought better of it. This plan was Sam's, not hers.

When they reached the theater, they discovered a long line at the ticket booth.

Sam pulled out his wallet. "You ladies go on in and get in line for popcorn and drinks, and we'll get the tickets." He handed Joni, who was standing closest to him, some money.

"No popcorn for me," Donald said. "I have to watch my cholesterol."

"Me, neither," Mary said when they went inside. "Just get some for you and Sam."

Joni wasn't about to pass up popcorn. That was part of going to a movie. She got one large popcorn and four drinks, and waited for the men.

"Let's go," Sam said, taking his drink. "I think the movie's crowded."

They all stepped into the semidarkness. The theater was almost full.

"I think we'll have to split up," Donald whispered.

"But—but I only got one popcorn," Joni protested.

"That's okay. Mary said she didn't want any, either," Donald said. Then he took Mary's arm and headed down the aisle.

Joni stared at them. She shouldn't have been surprised, but she was. She looked at Sam.

"Do you think they didn't understand? Or was it the popcorn?" Sam asked wryly. "I assume you like popcorn?"

"I can't stand to watch a movie without it."

"Neither can I. Come on, let's find a couple of seats."

They squeezed into two seats in the middle of a row only three back from Donald and Mary.

"There they are," Joni whispered after they were seated.

Sam put the popcorn between them and then took a handful. "I don't think it matters anymore."

"Why?" Joni asked.

"Because they're obviously interested in each other. Neither of us could get a word in edgewise at the restaurant. I bet he rides in the back seat going home."

"Maybe if you explained—"

"Nope. It's too late. I'll think of someone else, but for tonight, we might as well relax and enjoy ourselves."

Since the previews began at that moment, Joni decided Sam was right. They shared the popcorn and whispered comments about the future movies. Then, when the main feature began, Sam slid his arm around her shoulders and pulled her against him.

Oh, yes, she was enjoying herself.

WHEN THE MOVIE ENDED, Sam reluctantly moved away from Joni. The movie had been good. Holding her against him had been better. They waited in the lobby for Donald and Mary.

The couple came out with their arms wrapped around each other. Even when they saw Joni and Sam waiting, they didn't pull apart.

Nope, they definitely hadn't understood.

"Ready?" Sam asked. When Donald nodded, Sam

took Joni's hand and led the way. They shrugged into their coats and headed for the car.

Just as Sam had predicted, Donald and Mary got into the back seat. Five minutes into the ride home, Donald and Mary were getting very friendly in the back seat.

Joni turned around once to initiate some conversation, but she quickly faced front again, her cheeks red. Sam reached out and touched her.

"Come over here. I'm lonely."

She hesitated, but then she undid her seat belt and slid over next to him, fastening the center belt. "Aren't you worried about giving them the wrong impression?" she whispered.

"Sweetheart, I'm not sure they even remember we're in the car. And if I don't get us home soon, I'm afraid we're both going to be embarrassed."

They didn't talk much more, but Sam wrapped his arm around her shoulders, as he'd done in the theater. She fit against him perfectly, as if she'd always belonged there.

Without any discussion, he dropped Mary and Donald off first. Then he drove much more slowly to Joni's house.

Her head was resting on his shoulder when he stopped the car. Had she gone to sleep? "Joni, we're home."

Abruptly she straightened. "Oh, thanks. It was a lovely evening. I'm sorry things didn't—"

"I'll take you in, make sure everything's all right," he said and opened his car door.

"That's really not necessary," Joni called as he circled the car.

By the time he reached her side she had her door open and was getting out. "Really, Sam, I'll be fine. You don't need to come in."

He ignored her, catching her hand in his, as he had at the movie theater, and pulled her up the walk behind him, then waited quietly while she dug out her keys.

Once they were inside, he walked through the house, making sure no one was there. It wasn't that they had a lot of crime in Saddle. He didn't want to leave.

She remained in the living room. Pausing at the door, he stared at her. She was studying the Christmas tree, with its lights unplugged, but he found Joni more interesting.

Quietly he stepped behind her and wrapped his arms around her. He felt her jump in surprise.

"Shh," he whispered, ducking his head so they stood with their cheeks pressed together.

Joni leaned back against him, but she said, "Sam, we shouldn't do this."

"I'm only holding you. I've tried to give you away, but you keep coming back to me."

She stiffened. "I'm not a book, or a—a coin. You don't have the right to give me away because you've never had me!"

He groaned. "Don't I know it. But I'm willing to have you, sweetheart, for a night. And we'd both wake up a lot more satisfied than we are right now."

She broke free from his hold. "I'm not interested."

"Do you intend to remain celibate the rest of your life?" he asked, watching her, wanting her.

"I don't know." She moved farther away. "But I think making love should mean more than—than lust."

The problem was, he did, too. And it would, if he and Joni made love. Which meant it was a good thing she resisted. "You're right. I'll go now."

She turned and stared at him and he wasn't sure if she was happy or sad about his agreement.

"Thank you," she said softly and opened the door for him.

Okay, so he was going. But he ought to have at least a kiss. He dipped his head and brushed her lips with his. Nothing deep, but it stirred more hunger. He exited in a hurry, before that hunger could make him change his mind.

He hurried down the sidewalk and got into the car. Slipping the key into the ignition, he turned it, already reaching for his seat belt as he did.

Nothing.

He frowned, then turned it again.

Still nothing.

He checked all the dials, but he couldn't see a problem. When he turned on the radio, however, he discovered the battery must be dead. He didn't know why the battery should choose now to die.

He just knew it was really bad timing.

He got out and opened the trunk. If his mother had jumper cables, he could get Joni to give him a boost.

No jumper cables.

With a sigh, he trudged back up the sidewalk and knocked on the door.

Joni opened it after a couple of minutes. "What's wrong?"

"The battery is dead. Do you have jumper cables?"

She stared at him, her eyes wide. Then she shook her head. "No."

"Damn."

"What do we do now?" she asked.

"I could call Dad, but it's almost one o'clock." He waited, but she said nothing. "Look, if I promise to keep my distance, could I stay here until morning?"

"Sam, you'll never convince anyone, especially your parents, that we're not dating if you stay here. Everyone will see that car and—"

"Damn it! I know that. You want me to stay in the car all night? I'll be a Popsicle in the morning if I do."

"No, of course not, but—" She sighed and shrugged her shoulders. "Of course you can spend the night."

She swung the door wider for him to enter.

He did so before she could change her mind.

"I'll put clean sheets on my bed," she said and walked out of the living room.

Sam stared after her. Had she changed her mind about sleeping with him? He hurried after her.

"Joni, I didn't mean—you don't have to share your

bed. I'll sleep on the couch." He'd prefer to share with her, but not if that wasn't what she wanted.

"Share with you? I'm not going to share with you!" she said, astonishment in her gaze. "I'm going to sleep in Brady's bed. It's too small for you."

"Oh. Of course. I didn't realize—I can sleep on the couch. I don't want to put you out."

"I'll be comfortable in Brady's bed." She continued to strip the sheets off her bed. Then she walked past him to put them in the clothes hamper. When she returned with clean sheets, he shook himself from his stupor and took one corner of the bottom sheet to help her.

His mind kept picturing the two of them on the pristine white sheets, making him incredibly clumsy. As soon as they finished, she moved to the door, then stopped.

"I don't have anything for you to wear to bed."

He gave her an uneasy smile. "I don't need anything."

"One of my bulky sweaters might—"

"Joni, I don't wear anything to bed."

"Oh!"

"I'll call Dad first thing in the morning. He's always up about six."

"Good. Maybe he can get here before the rest of the town sees your car."

"Right." And maybe he could get here before Sam broke his promise and carried Joni to bed. Maybe.

Chapter Eight

Joni just barely heard her alarm the next morning, but
she automatically thrust out her hand to shut it off.

And found nothing.

Frowning, she struggled to sit up and open her
eyes. Not an easy task since she couldn't get to sleep
last night. Not with Sam in her bed.

That thought set off an even louder alarm.

Sam in her bed.

Her eyes, seemingly stuck closed a second ago,
popped open. She breathed a sigh of relief when she
realized she was in Brady's bed, not her own. Where
Sam was sleeping.

Her location also explained why she couldn't shut
off the alarm. It was in the room next door.

She grabbed her robe at the foot of Brady's bed,
pulling it on as she hurried to the kitchen. She sighed
as she paused on the threshold. Sam was standing
there, his shirttail hanging out, stubble on his face,
talking on the phone, and he still looked good.

"What? I can't believe it. How is she?"

Joni's eyes opened even wider and she hurried to Sam's side. "What's wrong?"

He held up his hand to stop her. "Yeah. We'll work out something. Can you come give me a jump, or do I need to call Dusty?"

After a pause, Sam said, "Okay. I'll see you in a few minutes."

"He's coming? Has something happened? Is Brady okay?" Joni asked, bubbling with questions.

"He's coming. Brady's okay," Sam said, answering two of her three questions. Then with a sigh, he added, "A lot has happened."

"What?"

"After we left, Marty called. They'd just gotten word that Paul's father had a heart attack. Mom offered to keep the kids so Marty could go to Denver with Paul. After they dropped the kids off, Mom fell and broke her wrist."

"Oh, no!" Joni said with a gasp. "How is she?"

"She's taking pain pills. Dad said he had to take her to the emergency room last night. He got one of the cowboys to come over and stay until they got back." Sam rubbed a hand over his face.

Joni didn't know what else to say, so she acted instead, making a pot of coffee. She didn't think Sam got much more sleep than she did last night.

Then she took a box of muffin mix and quickly had a filled muffin tin in the oven. Tom wouldn't have had breakfast, either.

Sam had been standing there, watching her, but saying nothing. As she took bacon out of the refrigerator, he finally spoke. "You don't have to do all this, Joni. Go on back to sleep."

"Don't be silly, Sam. You need breakfast, and your dad will, too. Then I'll follow both of you back to the ranch and get Brady. Your mother doesn't need that added complication."

He gave her a wry grin. "You want three for the price of one?"

"You mean Peter and Katie? How long will Marty be gone?"

Sam shrugged his shoulders. "I don't know. She hasn't called yet." With a sigh, he added, "I'd better finish getting dressed before Dad gets here."

Ten minutes later, both men were sitting at her breakfast table.

"This was real thoughtful of you, Joni," Tom said. "I left 'Retta sleeping. I reckon either me or Sam will be doing our cooking for a couple of weeks."

She gave him a sympathetic smile but said nothing.

"You know what was bothering that crazy woman the most?" Tom asked them both.

Sam tried guessing. "Not being able to take a shower?"

"Nope. She hasn't finished wrapping Christmas presents. Now she can't. I told her we'd like the presents whether they were wrapped or not, but she's fretting about that."

"I can understand," Joni said. "Christmas is a big deal, and especially her grandchildren won't understand when things aren't like they expected." She slanted a hesitant glance at Sam, then added, "I can do the wrapping for her."

"That's mighty kind of you, Joni. Maybe that will stop her from worrying so."

Joni doubted it. Loretta played an integral part in the ranch life, she thought. There was a lot to do. But she wasn't going to upset Tom.

She cleaned up after breakfast as the men went out to jump-start the car. Then she dressed, grabbed her hat, gloves and coat and went to the garage, opening the door and starting her car.

Leaving her car running, she walked out to the two men, standing watching the Lincoln's engine run. "Is it all right?"

"Yeah," Sam said. "But it'll need a new battery. We're going to drop it off at Ronnie's shop in town."

"Shall I go on out to the ranch?" If she could find her way.

"Would you mind following Sam and bringing him to the ranch?" Tom asked. "I'd like to get back to 'Retta as soon as I can."

"Of course I will, Tom."

He surprised her by giving her a hug. Then, after disconnecting the cables, he said goodbye and jumped into his truck.

In seconds, Joni and Sam were standing there alone.

"Guess we'd better get started," he said. "Are you ready?"

"Yes." She nodded. "But I'll have to follow you because I'm not sure where the garage is located."

"Okay, but stay in your car. They won't be open, and I'm just going to park the car. I'll bring the keys in to them tomorrow."

"Oh. Okay." Again she was reminded that she wasn't in Chicago anymore.

It only took a few minutes to do as he asked. Then, they were on their way to the ranch.

They found Tom in the kitchen, attempting to prepare breakfast for both Loretta and the three children. Joni immediately offered to help.

Tom gratefully accepted. "I guess me and Sam here are spoiled. 'Retta's always taken care of us."

"I'm sure you'll manage," she said.

"I'm going to go check on 'Retta again. Sam, you help Joni, okay?"

Sam stared after his father. "He's still upset."

"I know. Isn't it sweet?" she asked as she finished mixing the biscuits Tom had started.

"Sweet?" Sam asked with a frown.

She couldn't hide the longing in her gaze. But she hoped he wouldn't realize what it was. "The love they share is—is breathtaking. And restores my faith."

Sam stepped closer to her. "You didn't believe in love? But you were married."

"So were you."

"Yeah, but my marriage ended in divorce. I'm supposed to be cynical." He slipped a finger under her chin, forcing her gaze back to him.

"How a marriage ends doesn't necessarily agree with—with what was going on in the marriage." She twisted from his hold and took a cookie sheet out for the biscuits.

He followed her to the counter and leaned his back against it so he could see her face. "Am I to take it from that strange remark that your marriage was unhappy?"

Joni concentrated on rolling out the biscuit dough and cutting perfect circles from it, then placing them on the cookie sheet.

"Joni?"

With a sigh, she stopped and stared at him. "My marriage was—was happy until I got pregnant."

Sam stared at Joni. She was a beautiful woman, with a warm heart. If he loved her—*if*, he reminded himself—and she was carrying his child, he would hold her even closer. Why would her husband react any differently?

"Why?"

She had finished cutting out the biscuits. Setting them aside, she took down a bowl and began breaking eggs for scrambling. "He didn't like not being the center of attention."

He couldn't believe her words. "What are you saying?"

She shrugged one shoulder but said nothing else.

"What did he do? He wasn't abusive, was he?"

"No, other than ignoring me. And ignoring Brady."

He reached out and traced her hair behind one ear, then caressed her cheek. "He must've been crazy," he whispered.

Joni stared at him, tears filling her eyes and her lips, those soft lips, trembling.

Just then the room exploded with the sound of two little boys running into the kitchen.

"Mom!" Brady exclaimed. "What are you doing here?"

"Hi," Peter added. "Where's Grandma?"

Sam replied, "Up to the table, you two, and we'll explain everything."

Joni hugged her son. "Sam, would you pour them both a glass of orange juice? Maybe that will keep them from starving until I've scrambled the eggs."

He poured the juice, then sat down with the boys. "Grandma hurt her arm last night."

"Is she gonna die?" Peter asked, his lip trembling, like Joni's only a moment ago.

"Of course not. But she'll have to wear a cast for a few weeks. And she won't be able to do much cooking."

"Are we going to starve?" Peter asked again, his eyes even wider.

Joni laughed, which did Sam's heart good. She stepped over to the table. "Of course not. Uncle Sam can cook."

"I can?"

"If you get hungry enough," she assured him.

"Eeew," Peter said, frowning. "I want Mama."

Sam and Joni exchanged smiles before they reassured Peter that he was in no danger.

"Oh, I hear Katie," Joni said suddenly. "Breakfast or baby?" she asked Sam.

With a waggle of his eyebrows toward the boys, he said, "Baby."

"Okay, but that means changing her diaper, too," she reminded him.

"No problem," he assured her. As he stood, he couldn't resist kissing her cheek. "Just save me some eggs."

"You want a second breakfast?"

"Yep. Seconds are good." Then he headed for the screaming Katie.

SHE NEEDED TO GO BACK to her little house. To go back to reality. Sam was too much for her to deal with.

Sensitive, caring, supportive. All the things she'd dreamed of in a husband. And hadn't found in her own. She'd adored Derek as a young girl, growing up next to his family. She'd been a foster child. Her foster parents were kind, but she never felt as if she was part of a family.

Next door had been the Evanses. Mrs. Evans opened her home to Joni, talking about always wanting a daughter. Instead she'd had three big, handsome boys. And Joni had fallen for the most handsome, the strongest, the brightest.

She'd thought him perfect.

And he was as long as she believed that, as long as she did whatever he wanted and never complained.

The first morning she'd woken up to morning sickness, unable to cater to her husband's whims, their marriage had begun to fall apart. Gradually he built a life away from home, that didn't include her.

After Brady was born, Joni was glad her husband left them alone. He showed no interest in his son, and Joni refused to abandon Brady to party with Derek.

No, her marriage had not been ideal.

Now she was falling in love with a man who never intended to marry again. So she needed to get away. As soon as possible.

"Mom? Can I have more juice?" Brady asked.

"No, sweetie. I want you to drink milk with your breakfast. I'll pour you both some. Peter, what does Katie usually eat for breakfast? Will scrambled eggs do?"

"Yes, she likes them. Mama feeds her cereal, too. I think Grandma has some in the pantry."

"We'll stick to eggs this morning since they're ready." She poured the milk and put bacon and eggs on the table, along with the biscuits. Sam appeared in the doorway, holding Katie.

He looked like a perfect daddy.

"Um, here, I'll feed Katie," she said, taking the little girl out of his arms. "You sit down and eat."

"I won't argue with those orders," Sam agreed with a grin.

Only seconds later, Tom and Loretta came in, his arm around her in support.

"Loretta! You should've stayed in bed. I was going to fix a tray for you," Joni said.

"Oh, no, you've done so much already, Joni. And

Tom told me about your offer to wrap presents. That is so sweet of you.''

''It's nothing. Just helping out like you did when it snowed. Sit down and I'll get you some coffee.''

Once they were all settled around the table, silence fell as attention turned to food.

When the boys finished and asked to be excused, Loretta nodded. They scooted from their chairs and raced up the stairs.

''I wish I felt as good as those two,'' Loretta said with a sigh. ''What are we going to do?'' she asked her husband.

''About this morning? We're going to stay home,'' Tom said firmly. ''The church won't close its doors because we miss a Sunday.''

''I know. But the children—Marty—''

''We'll have to wait until we hear from her. Could be Paul's father is doing great.''

''I'll be glad to do anything I can to help,'' Joni said, unable to resist offering. They were such nice people.

''But you have to work,'' Loretta said pointedly.

''Yes, but Peter and Katie could go to Mrs. Barker's all day, like Brady. Then I could take them home with me.''

''Oh, dear, that would be too much for you to do after teaching all day. I couldn't ask that of you.''

''It would only be for a few days, Loretta.''

The phone rang, and Tom got up to answer.

Everyone gathered at once that Marty was the

caller, but it was hard to figure out what was going on by Tom's responses.

But Joni noticed that Tom didn't tell his daughter about her mother's accident.

He hung up the phone and returned to the table.

"Well?" Loretta demanded.

"Paul's father is having surgery in the morning, a triple bypass." Tom sighed. "I couldn't tell her about your accident, honey, 'cause she said Paul's mother was falling apart and clinging to her. You know Paul's an only child."

"No, of course you couldn't tell her," Loretta agreed, but Joni could hear the worry in her voice.

"I'll be able to take care of the kids until they get back, really, Loretta." She couldn't stand not offering to help.

"I don't know—could you stay here? I mean, it would be better. We have more room, and I can help some. I just can't do everything. Would you do that for me, Joni?"

Joni heard Sam draw a deep breath. She knew exactly how he felt. Last night they'd spent a miserable time only a few feet from each other. She'd gotten through it by telling herself it was only for one night. Now she was supposed to move into his house and stay for a week?

But she couldn't turn Loretta down.

"I—I suppose we could try it, Loretta. But maybe it would be better if I went home each night and came back early in the morning."

Even Sam joined in protest against that idea. "You'd wear yourself out, Joni."

She stared into his blue eyes. Then sighed and looked away. "You're right. I just hate to impose—"

"Don't you even think of saying that!" Loretta protested. "You're doing us a huge favor. I'll never be able to pay you back."

"She's right, little lady," Tom said even as Joni started to protest. "Me and Sam will help you all we can, but you're saving us."

Sam shoved back his chair. "Why don't I ride with you over to your house to pack. I think Katie will be all right for an hour or two, and the boys are playing. Dad, you help Mom back to bed. Then you can read to Katie or something."

Everyone seemed satisfied with his organization except for Joni. "I want to clean the kitchen first, before I leave."

To her surprise, he accepted her alteration of his plan. Not only accepted, but began helping her, too.

Yep, he was definitely too perfect.

THEY HAD TO CLEAN a second kitchen when they got to Joni's house. The two of them worked in silence. Sam didn't know about Joni, but he was worrying about having her next door to him every night for a week.

He hadn't slept too well last night.

Finally he said, "Are you sure you're all right with this?"

"By 'this' do you mean staying at your parents' house?"

He nodded.

"It won't be—be convenient for the two of us, but I had to offer to help. Your parents are such nice people. And Marty shouldn't have to leave her husband at a time like this when I can help out."

"Hey, I'm grateful you offered. I'm not complaining," he assured her. Only a jerk would think of himself in a situation like this.

"I'll try to keep out of your way."

"Joni, stop. You're going to have me down on my knees begging for forgiveness. You're doing a wonderful thing."

"Thank you."

He remembered what she'd revealed earlier in his kitchen about her marriage. Her husband had been a jerk. Sam wasn't going to make the same mistake.

"You go pack and I'll finish up here," he suggested.

She gave him an uncertain look, then nodded and left the kitchen.

He sighed deeply after she was gone. He was going to have to keep control of his senses this week. Maybe he could convince his dad to spend more time at home while he put in longer hours in the saddle.

That way he'd come in tired, too tired to have any racy thoughts about Joni. He was tired today, too. Real tired. That's probably why he hadn't protested her staying at the house. That and the fact that he hadn't had another solution.

Joni stuck her head in the kitchen. "Are you doing all right? Any questions?"

Her cheeks were flushed and her hair mussed. And he was tired. And he wanted to carry her to that bedroom of hers and make love to her. Man, he was in trouble.

"Fine. I'm almost finished."

"Okay." She disappeared.

He hurried with the cleaning. The sooner they got out of Joni's house, the better off he'd be. At least at home they wouldn't be alone.

When he finished, he called to Joni.

She came down the hall with two suitcases in hand. "I'm ready," she said, her voice breathless.

"Here, I'll take those out to the car, while you check my handiwork and turn off the lights."

He took her keys and opened the trunk. As he was lifting the larger suitcase, Joni locked the front door and came out to the car.

A truck came down the road and braked to a halt beside them, and his friend Dusty rolled down the window.

"Hey, Sam, you two eloping already? Wow, I wasn't even close in the pool. I put my money on Valentine's Day."

Chapter Nine

Though Sam gave an elaborate explanation to his friend, it didn't appear to Joni that he convinced him that they weren't even dating, much less getting married.

She drove without commenting while Sam sat hunched over, resting his head in his hands.

Finally she said, "Surely, when everyone knows about your mother's accident, they'll understand why I'm at your house."

"Of course they will. But that won't eliminate those romance rumors."

"But when we don't marry, they'll die down," she suggested, as she had before.

"But what about Brady?"

"Sam, you're taking your role as Santa Claus too seriously. You can't supply a child with a father just because he wants one."

"What is Santa bringing him? Did you get him a train?"

She rolled her eyes. He wasn't listening to her. She

was the one who would play Santa for Brady. "Yes, I bought him a train. Before we left Chicago."

"The other thing he wanted was a horse." Sam scratched his jaw and stared into the distance.

"No."

"No? He wants a daddy, and you say no. He should have a pony if he's not going to get a daddy."

"Sam! You're being ridiculous. We don't have room for a horse. Not only that, I don't know anything about taking care of one. Do you think Brady does?"

"I could teach him."

Joni gave a gusty sigh and turned into the driveway for the ranch. "He's four, Sam, not fourteen. If I decide we're going to stay here, maybe I'll be able to find a house on a little bit of land. Then we can think about animals."

"I thought you said you liked it here."

It felt as if his blue eyes were drilling holes into her. "I've only been here two weeks, Sam. Everything is going well, but reasons might develop that would make it difficult to stay." Like falling in love with a determined bachelor.

"What reasons?"

"I might develop an allergy to stubborn cowboys!" she snapped, frustrated with him.

His gaze narrowed. "Are you talking about me?"

"If the shoe fits..." She parked the car beside the house. "We'd better get in the house and make sure your parents survived."

"Would you go back to Chicago?"

She stared at the mountains in the distance, the big, blue sky, now that there was no storm. "No."

Her one-word answer seemed to satisfy him. He got out of the car and stood waiting for her to join him.

"I'll check on the kids. You might want to start thinking about what we'll have for lunch," he said with a grin as she came around the car.

"Lunch? It's only nine o'clock. You can't be hungry already."

"I thought we could have lunch at eleven since we won't be in church. Breakfast was early this morning."

"Which one?" she asked, raising an eyebrow.

"The second one was just a snack, to keep everyone company. You're not going to hold that one against me, are you?" he asked with a grin as he took her car keys and opened the trunk.

She shook her head. She couldn't hold anything against him when he smiled that way. It was a good thing she liked to cook, though. She had a sneaky suspicion that would be her main job at the Crawford ranch.

BRADY WAS THRILLED that they were going to spend the week at the ranch, with Peter and Katie.

"You know, Mom, it's like we're a great big family. Isn't it great?"

Tears crowded her eyes and she blinked fiercely. It seemed her craving for a family had been passed on to her son. She wanted to warn him not to lose his heart to the Crawfords, but she couldn't. Why spoil his fun now? It would still hurt if they had to leave.

"Yes, sweetie, it's great. But it'll only last a week."

He beamed at her, but he didn't acknowledge her gentle warning.

"Now, I need some help from you and Peter. I want you both to unpack your clothes, dividing up the drawers. Then figure out what you're wearing to school tomorrow, and lay them out. I'll check your choices later. It's going to be hectic with all three of you going with me. And I can't afford to be late."

With a nod, he raced up the stairs to relay the orders to Peter. Joni sat down with a sheet of paper at the kitchen table and began making a list of what she had to do.

Sam found her there. "You're a list-maker?"

"Not usually, but I think life may be a little complicated this week. If I'm going to be temporary mom, housekeeper and teacher, I'm going to have to be very organized."

"I'm going to try to get Dad to stay here with Mom most of the time. He's not much of a cook, but he can handle the laundry and dusting, waiting on Mom. Things like that."

"I don't think that will be necessary after a day or two. Your mother has to get over the shock, but after that she can take care of herself."

Sam seemed irritated with her response. "We'll see."

"Can you transfer Katie's car seat to my car?"

"Yeah. But you could take one of the trucks."

"I'll be more comfortable in my car."

He studied her, and she wondered what he was thinking. "Okay, but if it snows, or there's even the hint of a storm, you'll take a truck."

"You love to give orders, don't you?" she replied, her chin going up.

Instead of answering, he bent down and kissed her. Then he straightened, just before she reached out to embrace him. "Yeah, especially if it's for your safety."

The difference between this man and her husband suddenly struck Joni. She could trust Sam to make his orders based on what would be best for her and the children. Her husband's orders had only concerned his wants or preferences.

She leaped to her feet. "I need to go make up my bed."

"I'll help."

"No! No, you transfer the car seat."

As she hurried away, he called, "Have you thought about lunch?"

"Pot roast" was her succinct answer. It must have pleased him because she didn't hear any complaints.

THE NOON MEAL was the first time the boys really focused on Loretta's cast. They examined it from every angle and discussed writing their names on it.

"Mrs. Crawford, I saw one with pictures on it, even," Brady explained.

"Dear, you mustn't call me Mrs. Crawford. Why don't you just call me Grandma, like Peter."

Joni shared a stricken gaze with Sam before she tried to intervene. "Oh, I don't think—"

"Okay, Grandma," Brady agreed. Then he looked at Tom. "Can I call you Grandpa?"

"A'course you can, Brady."

"Tom, don't you think other people might think—"

"That we feel like you're family? Probably, but it's the truth, so what's the problem with that?" Tom asked with a warm smile.

Joni couldn't argue with such nice sentiments. She looked to Sam for help. He shrugged his shoulders and said nothing.

"By the way, Joni, this dinner is excellent," Loretta said. "And we can have sandwiches tonight from the leftovers. I don't want you wearing yourself out making meals."

"I enjoy cooking."

"You hear that, Sam? Not like Linda, is she?"

Joni wanted to hide her face under the table.

"No, not at all."

"Who is Linda?" Brady asked.

Peter leaned over. "She was Uncle Sam's mommy, only they didn't have no kids."

"She was my wife," Sam said, correcting him.

"What happened to her?" Brady asked.

Joni sat there, helpless to stop the interrogation, because she didn't know what to say.

"We got divorced," Sam said briefly.

"Oh. That happened a lot in Chicago."

"But you're not in Chicago anymore," Loretta said. "It doesn't happen very often in Saddle. But Linda didn't like it here."

Joni couldn't hold back her question. "But didn't she know Sam would live here? That he worked here?" Her logical mind couldn't accept such delusion.

Tom looked at his son. "Didn't we say she's not like Linda?"

"I got the point, Dad," Sam said sternly.

It was Loretta who answered the question. "She thought she could force Sam to leave. She withheld—"

"Mom!" Sam yelled, getting everyone's attention.

Loretta stopped but she wasn't happy. "Well, she didn't leave any of us in any doubt about what she was doing."

Joni stared at Sam. How awful for him. To have his life's work discarded as if it meant nothing. And to have his wife use sex as a barter for his obedience.

She wanted to reach out and tell him how sorry she was for him, but she couldn't do that. Instead she sent him a warm smile. And said, "Sometimes divorce is the only answer."

Sam looked away and spoke to Brady. "After we clean up the kitchen, how about your mom and I take you boys to the barn. We can pet the horses and I can show you how to take care of them."

"Sam!" Joni protested. The man never gave up.

"Mom, don't you want to see the horses?" Brady asked incredulously.

"Yes, of course, but we'll have to put Katie to bed for her nap, first."

Katie whacked her spoon down on her high chair tray. "No! Me go, too!"

Brady wiped a lump of mashed potato from his forehead. "Girls," he said with a sigh. "They can be such a problem."

The adults laughed, but Joni heard Sam mumble, "I know what you mean."

"Wow," BRADY SAID SOFTLY, standing in front of a large box stall. Inside was a mare and her foal, born only three days before.

"I think he's real beautiful," Peter said, expressing what Brady couldn't seem to say. "Almost as beautiful as my horse."

Brady turned to stare at his friend with even greater awe. "You have a horse? Your very own?"

"Yeah. Santa brought him last Christmas."

All three males turned to stare at Joni, as if Brady's lack of a horse was her fault.

She turned to Peter. "And where do you keep your horse, Peter? In town at your house?"

"No. Grandpa keeps him here for me."

She looked at her son and forced herself to make her point even though it would make him sad. "Too bad we don't have a family member with a ranch, Brady, but we don't."

Her heart swelled with pride when her son accepted

the truth. "I know, Mom. But one day I'll have a horse."

"Maybe Grandpa—" Peter began.

"No, Peter. That's too much to ask. If we stay in Saddle, maybe we'll find a place with a little land," she said, repeating what she'd said to Sam earlier. "And you'll be older, sweetie, and will know how to take care of a horse."

"I have an idea," Sam said quietly, putting a hand on Brady's shoulder.

"What?" Brady and Peter spoke at once.

"We haven't named this little guy," Sam said, gesturing to the colt. "Why don't you help me do that?"

"You mean it?" Brady said, his voice breathless. "You really mean it?"

"I really mean it."

Joni stared at the man, wondering how she could not love him. He was so caring of her little boy, so much more than Brady's daddy had ever been.

"Got any ideas?" Sam asked as he helped Brady climb the rail of the stall so he could see the colt clearly.

"I don't know," Brady said, still awed with the honor. "What do you think, Mom?"

"Well," Joni said, giving the decision all the importance she knew it held in Brady's heart. "He was born at Christmas, so a Christmas name would be nice. How about Noel?"

"That sounds like a girl," Brady said, frowning.

"You could call him Christmas tree," Peter suggested with a giggle.

The two boys began naming everything they could think of connected with Christmas.

When Brady said Christmas cookie, everyone laughed. But he studied the colt, a buckskin like his mother. "That's it!" Brady shouted. "I'll name him Christmas Cookie, and we'll call him Cookie for short. His skin looks just like cookie dough."

"Good enough," Sam agreed with a grin.

"Let's go tell Grandpa and Grandma," Peter suggested, as excited as Brady.

Almost before Joni realized what was happening, the two boys barreled out of the barn, racing across the snow-covered lot to the house—leaving her alone in the barn with Sam.

She cleared her throat. "That was a nice thing you did, Sam. Thank you." She laughed nervously. "And I hope you don't regret your generosity. Christmas Cookie isn't a very elegant name."

He stepped closer. He was wearing his sheepskin coat, hat and boots and looked every inch the rough, tough cowboy.

But Joni knew he had a soft heart.

"Naw, we don't go for the elegant out here. Just whatever fits."

"Well, Cookie is a sweetheart."

"Yeah. So is Brady. And his mom's not too bad, either."

She felt her cheeks redden and took a step back. "Uh, I think I should return to the house. Your mother—"

He took her arm. "Is being well taken care of by

my father. You just cooked a huge meal and cleaned up after it. You deserve a little leisure time.''

''I had a lot of help. You and the boys cleared the table.''

Sam grinned. ''I may be a lot of things, Joni, but adept in the kitchen isn't one of them.''

She couldn't hold back a return smile. ''But that doesn't stop you from pitching in. I like that.''

''Good. And I like this.'' And he kissed her.

Oh, she liked it, too. His firm lips took control of the kiss. They urged, even pleaded, for her cooperation, and she was quick to give it. Then he lifted his mouth and angled for a deeper kiss, one that sent all thought flying from her mind.

At some point, he must have shucked his gloves because his fingers worked their way beneath her coat and sweater to her skin beneath. ''Sam—''

His lips, having inched their way to her neck, flew back to her lips to stop whatever she was going to say. She couldn't remember.

She was filled with a delicious enjoyment of his touch, but it wasn't his touch alone that thrilled her. It was the man himself. His caring ways with her son. His love for his parents. His blue eyes.

She trembled as she realized what she'd refused to admit the past few days. She loved Sam Crawford. She loved the man who had already warned her he never intended to marry. She loved the man who was going to break her heart.

What was she going to do? How could she protect herself?

She grew even more alarmed when he swung her up into his arms, however. "Sam, what are you doing?" she asked, almost groggily, her senses overwhelmed.

"Getting more comfortable."

She understood his meaning when he laid her in some hay, then followed her down. Suddenly her entire body was enveloped in Sam's warmth, his sexiness.

Even as he pushed her sweater up and his lips traced her bra, sending shudders through her, her mind was trying to warn her. But it was a struggle.

And she wanted to kiss his chest.

"Sam, we can't—"

"Yes, we can. Who would come out here on a Sunday afternoon? We're—"

The sound of the barn door opening proved him wrong.

"Sam? Mom?" Brady's voice rang out in the barn.

Sam sprang to his feet, then extended his hand to Joni. She yanked down her sweater, then accepted his assistance to get up. As she hurried by him, she felt his hand in her hair.

"Hay," he muttered.

"Hi, Brady," Joni began, trying to sound nonchalant. "Did you tell— Oh, hi, Tom. I guess you came out to see Cookie." Her cheeks were flaming, but she didn't know anything to do but try to be brazen about it.

"Yeah. 'Retta is sleeping, like Katie, and I thought it wouldn't hurt to step out to the barn." He was grinning like a Cheshire cat at the two of them, as if he had a pretty good idea what they were doing.

Peter stared at them, frowning. "What were you doing in that stall?"

Joni certainly had no explanation.

Sam was silent beside her.

"Oh, I asked Sam to check out the hay. Sometimes it gets old. I imagine Joni was helping him," Tom said glibly enough.

"I guess that's why you have hay on your jeans, Mom," Brady agreed and turned his attention to Cookie.

"Thanks," Sam muttered to his dad, and Joni wanted to add her gratitude, too, but she remained silent. It was too embarrassing, to be caught making out like a couple of teenagers.

Especially with a man who'd already told you he didn't want you.

But he did. She now had no doubt that he wanted her, wanted to make love to her. She'd felt his arousal against her body. And she wanted him.

But their wants were different.

She was stuck here until Marty returned. She'd have to be on her guard every minute, because once he kissed her she was lost.

THE CRAWFORDS HAD A PARTY.

They'd all gotten back to the house a half hour later, after admiring the colt a little longer, when trucks and cars began arriving.

Joni was stunned by the number of people, all bearing food, arriving at the Crawford ranch. Loretta, refreshed from her nap, invited them all in, of course, and immediately asked everyone to dinner.

"Do all these people live nearby?" Joni asked Tom.

"Most. We're not that large a community, but we're all real close. When something happens to someone, we all pitch in. Loretta has been a Trojan about that. She's always taking baby presents, or meals, or running errands for someone."

Joni blinked several times to hold back the moisture that filled her eyes. "That's wonderful."

Tom gave her a quick hug. "You're a country girl at heart, even if you did come from Chicago. Linda, Sam's wife, well, she wouldn't lift a hand for anyone."

"Maybe she didn't understand," Joni suggested, trying to be generous.

"Ha! She understood."

Several more people came in, and Tom moved to greet them, taking Joni with him.

"Howdy, Brad, Steve. Now don't tell me you cooked something," he said, teasing the two men who had entered.

"You're lucky we didn't," the first one said. "But we thought we could offer to help out for a day or two if you need it."

"Thanks, guys. Joni, this is Brad Stover and Steve Bigelow, from the next ranch to the east. This is Joni Evans, a new schoolteacher. She's going to help out with the little ones."

They both greeted her. Then Steve leaned closer. "Your husband here?"

Joni gave a brief smile. "I'm a widow."

Steve's smile widened even as he expressed his regrets. Then he frowned. "You dating Sam?"

"No! Not at all." Her heart hurt with those words, but that was what Sam wanted.

"Glad to hear it. Come on over here and let's get acquainted." He put his arm around her and began urging her toward a sofa.

Sam came back into the room from running an errand for his mother and caught sight of them. Joni expected him to be pleased. After all, she was allowing the cowboy to commandeer her time to satisfy Sam's quest to dispel all the rumors. Her flirting with Steve should take care of that. Of course, she wasn't having to make much effort. Steve was taking care of that aspect.

Whatever she expected, it wasn't the roar that filled the room.

"Get your hands off that woman!"

Chapter Ten

Sam knew he'd made a mistake.

The roomful of people stopped dead in their tracks and stared at him.

Joni's cheeks grew pale, and he was afraid she was going to faint. He took a step toward her and then stopped. What was he going to do? Especially in front of the entire community.

"Uh, sorry, folks. Steve is such a flirt, I thought I should warn Joni," he said with an uneasy smile.

The rest of the audience may have laughed at his words and begun their conversations again, but Steve wasn't buying his little joke. In fact, the cowboy still had his arm around Joni's shoulders and was staring at Sam.

Sam tried to cross the room casually, as if he had no particular destination in mind. But he ended up beside the couple as Steve turned to Joni.

"Well, now, darlin', I thought you said Sam had no claim on you."

"We're friends," Joni said. "I guess he's a little

protective when it comes to cowboy flirts.'' She made an effort to smile.

''That's right,'' Sam agreed. ''I know how you are with the ladies, Steve. Joni's too innocent to be left alone with you.''

''Hell, she's a widow, not some teenager!'' Steve protested. ''Besides, before you married that—uh, your wife, you had a reputation, too. And soon will again, I suspect.''

Sam almost groaned aloud as Joni asked, ''What was Sam's reputation?''

''Darlin', there was no one better at mowing down the ladies than Sam here.'' Steve was quite emphatic.

Joni stared at Sam, as if seeing him for the first time. ''Yes, I can imagine.''

''Hey,'' Sam protested. ''That was in my younger days.''

''Yes, you're so ancient now,'' Joni agreed softly.

Steve laughed.

''You've still got your arm around her,'' Sam reminded. ''I told you to take it off.''

''The lady hasn't asked me to remove it,'' Steve said with a smirk. ''Until she does, what you say doesn't matter.''

Sam felt betrayed. He glared at both Steve and Joni.

Joni at least recognized the anger building in him. ''Maybe it would be best if you unhand me, Steve. I don't want to cause any problems.''

''It won't be a problem, darlin'. If me and Sam

come to blows, we'll take it out behind the barn so it won't break up the party,'' Steve assured her.

Sam was ready to head for the barn. He had so much steam rising in him that a release would be welcome.

''No!'' Joni protested. ''No, that would be absurd. Please release me, Steve. I won't have the two of you fighting, ruining Loretta's party.''

Steve, instead of doing as she asked, leaned over and whispered something in Joni's ear. Sam's hands curled into fists.

But Joni eliminated the need for action. She pushed herself away from the cowboy. ''You're moving a little too fast for me, Steve. I have a child to raise and—''

''You have a kid?'' Steve demanded, his brows suddenly lowered.

''Yes. Brady. He's four years old.''

Steve backed away. ''Nothing against you, darlin', but I don't mess with ladies with children. I don't want to build a nest. I'm still circling the sky.''

Then he disappeared into the kitchen.

Joni laughed awkwardly. ''I hadn't realized Brady was a date repellent. I'll have to remember that.''

''Only for jerks. Steve's a flirt.''

''But he would've served your purpose well. Only you yelled across a crowded room for him to take his hands off me. It was the perfect remedy for your problem. Why did you do that?''

Sam couldn't...or didn't want to explain his actions. But he did want to hold her close, to wipe away that momentary hurt when Steve rejected her because of Brady. And he couldn't do that in front of their company, who, he noted, were still watching them out of the corners of their eyes.

"He's not one to play around with. You'd find yourself in his bed in nothing flat," he muttered, hoping no one would overhear him.

"Do you think I would allow that? I don't fall into just anyone's—" She halted abruptly and her cheeks flamed.

Sam hoped she was remembering how little resistance—none, in fact—she'd given in the barn. He certainly liked remembering it, feeling her soft, warm body beneath his, her arms around his neck, stroking, caressing—

"Hey, Sam!" someone called from the door.

He spun around, prepared to protect Joni again, only to discover his friend Dusty at the door with his fiancée, Lisa.

"Come on, you might as well meet Dusty and Lisa," he said to Joni as he took her hand and tugged her behind him.

After they were introduced, Sam found four chairs together and they all sat down.

"So when are you getting married?" Joni asked.

Lisa eyed her fiancé. "Soon, or the engagement's off."

"Lisa!" Dusty protested.

Lisa smiled at Joni. "Sorry. We've been having this argument all day long."

Joni appeared alarmed, so Sam thought he'd help out. "He told me he was anxious to marry you."

"He was. Until I made a big mistake."

"What are you talking about?" Sam asked.

"Something about giving away the milk before the cow is bought," Lisa said, her voice charged with feeling.

Sam got the inference at once, but it took Joni a minute. "What— Oh." She glared at Dusty, as did Lisa, then, standing, she abruptly said, "Let's go to the kitchen, Lisa."

And the two women disappeared.

"Damn, I didn't expect a public discussion," Dusty complained.

"You idiot," Sam returned. "I thought you loved her."

"I did. I mean, I do. But, well, I need to save money and—"

"And as long as you're getting sex, what's the hurry?"

"I knew you'd understand," Dusty said, relieved.

"Understand, hell! I'm with the ladies. You're being a jerk. She trusted you and now you're betraying her trust." Maybe Sam wouldn't have been so sure about this topic if he hadn't almost made love to Joni. But he knew if Joni trusted him to that point, and he'd promised to marry her, he wouldn't renege on his promise. The pleasure that rose in him at the thought of bedding Joni frightened him, however.

"No!" he burst out.

"No, what? I'm gettin' real confused. Are you telling me I should marry Lisa, or not?"

Sam wiped a hand over his face. He wasn't ready for this—for committing to another woman. For trusting his heart. The timing was wrong.

That was it. Joni was sweet, wonderful—but the timing was wrong.

"Well?" Dusty prodded, drawing Sam back to reality.

"If you love her, and you've already taken her, I think you should marry as soon as possible. What are you waiting for?"

"I told you. I need to save money."

"You've already bought her a ring."

"And that's why I have to save money. I want to take her on a nice honeymoon."

"Did you tell her that's your reason?"

"Of course not. You think I want to admit how little money I have?"

"From what she said, you're going to lose her if you don't explain." He watched his friend. If Dusty loved Lisa, he'd find a way to keep her. If Joni had committed herself to him, he'd do the same.

But she hadn't, of course. The timing was bad.

Dusty leaped up. "I've got to find Lisa."

"Yeah, and I'd hurry, if I were you. Steve Bigelow is here."

Sam followed Dusty into the kitchen. He figured Dusty would drag Lisa off somewhere private, leaving him alone with Joni. He just wanted to protect her from Steve's advances, of course. That was all.

Dusty, however, was too upset. He found Lisa and Joni in the corner of the kitchen, talking. Without any greeting or an attempt to take Lisa somewhere private, he said, "Lisa, sweetheart, the only reason I wanted to postpone the wedding is because I spent most of my money on your ring and I can't afford a honeymoon. But I'll marry you whenever or wherever you say, if you don't mind not having one."

Sam didn't think his friend had drawn breath through his entire speech. That was too bad, because he sure didn't get a chance to breathe with the kiss Lisa planted on him.

Sam decided he and Joni should be the ones to leave, but there was nowhere to go. The kitchen was almost full.

"Oh, Dusty," Lisa said as she broke the kiss. "I just want us to be married. I don't care about any silly old honeymoon." She kissed him again.

Sam discovered Joni had tears in her eyes. His arm slipped around her shoulders and he cuddled her against him. "Hey, don't cry. They're happy."

"I know," she whispered and hurriedly wiped her eyes.

Lisa turned to Sam. "I don't know what you said, but thank you."

"I didn't do anything," Sam quickly assured her.

"I'm glad you're going to be his best man," Lisa said, ignoring Sam's words. "Better get your suit ready."

"Say," Dusty said, beaming with happiness.

"Let's get married on Valentine's Day. Then Sam and Joni could join us and I'd win the pool!"

"The pool?" Joni said, her voice rising. "You mean people are still betting on whether or not—" She broke off to glare at Sam.

"Hey! I haven't bet anything. Don't get mad at me," he protested.

She didn't smile, either. "I thought you would have stopped it by now." Then, she ran out of the kitchen.

"Thanks, Dusty," Sam said in disgust.

"Sorry, buddy. I didn't mean to cause you problems. Especially after you just helped me."

"I'll go talk to her," Lisa said and followed Joni.

"Maybe Lisa can bring her around," Dusty suggested.

"Around to what?" Sam exploded. "I told you there's nothing going on!"

People were staring at him again.

Dusty lowered his voice. "Well, for nothing going on, there's a whole lot of something going on."

Sam sighed. That muddled statement just about summed up his state of mind since Joni's arrival on the scene.

THE CLEANUP wasn't too bad from the party, since some of the guests had brought paper plates and cups. After putting the children to bed, Joni returned to the kitchen.

Even better, as a result of the food gifts, she wouldn't have to cook most of the week. The ladies had brought lasagna, pot roast, chicken salad and more. All kinds of cakes and cookies, too.

She set about making lunches for her and the two boys with the chicken salad. Katie would have jars of baby food. Then she sliced the roast beef and put it in a plastic bag. In another she put sliced tomatoes and shredded lettuce.

That way the men would have no problem making themselves and Loretta a sandwich.

When Tom came into the kitchen, she explained what she had prepared.

"Thanks, Joni. That will make it easy. Of course, we could eat with the hands, but I'd still have to fix something for Loretta."

"Has she gone to bed? Should I bring her some coffee?"

"No need. I'm her personal servant tonight," he assured her with a laugh and a hug.

Sam walked in.

"Uh-oh, I'd better take my hands off you," Tom joked, "or that cowboy is gonna slug me."

Joni blushed bright red and turned away.

"Dad!" Sam protested. "I was—Steve's a flirt."

"He sure is," Tom agreed, still grinning. "But I don't see a brand on Joni, saying she belongs to anyone."

Before Sam could answer, and Joni wasn't sure he intended to, the phone rang.

Tom picked it up. "Marty!"

For the next few minutes, Sam and Joni listened in

to Tom's side of the conversation. It didn't sound as though things were going well.

When Tom hung up the phone, Sam asked, "How is he?"

"He's had some complications. And his wife isn't holding up well at all," Tom admitted. He looked at Joni. "You know, I'm not a women's libber, but I think women should be a little stronger. Marty's having a hard time with her mother-in-law."

Joni smiled at him. "I'm not sure women's lib had all that much to do with it, but I agree. I think every person should be able to take care of him or herself."

"That's right," Tom agreed. "They should all be as strong as you."

Joni blushed. "Well, it may be that she'll grow stronger with time. She's probably in shock."

"Yeah, well, I'll take this coffee upstairs and tell 'Retta about Marty's call." Tom fixed a mug of instant coffee and then headed for the stairs.

Joni began putting everything she'd prepared for tomorrow back into the refrigerator.

"Making lunches?" Sam asked.

"Yes. It's much easier if everything is ready in the morning."

"Were you in shock?"

She looked up, surprised, to find Sam's blue eyes trained on her. "You mean when my husband was shot?"

"Yeah."

She let out a slow sigh. "Yes, of course. You never

expect someone that young to die. And a violent death is always shocking.''

''Did you have someone to help you, support you?''

She didn't want to talk about that time. But Sam stood waiting. ''My foster mother came over. I still talked to her occasionally, and she stayed with me for a couple of hours.''

''What about your husband's parents?''

''His mother didn't handle it well. She sounds like Marty's mother-in-law. I was better off without her around.''

''Your sisters-in-law?''

''They were with Mrs. Evans. It doesn't matter, Sam. I got through it, Brady and I. We're fine.'' She put the last of the food away and faced him. ''I guess I'd better head for bed, so I'll be prepared for the morning.''

''It's not even ten, yet, Joni. Tell me about your foster mother. What happened to your real parents?''

''They were killed in a car accident when I was ten. Too old to be adopted.''

''No family?''

She shook her head. ''Well, there was an elderly aunt, but she wasn't prepared to take on a child.''

''But you weren't abused or anything, were you?''

She fought for a smile, difficult when she thought about those years. ''No, no abuse. But no—never mind.'' She moved toward the door, anxious to end their conversation. He caught her by the arm.

''No what?''

She shook her head, but he didn't let her go. Finally she gave him the answer he wanted. "No love. My foster parents were kind, but I didn't belong to them. I wanted so badly to belong."

She kept her head down, not wanting to see pity in his eyes. That's why he surprised her with an embrace that took the chill out of her body. That lonely little girl in her past absorbed his warmth and felt cared for. Which only made her love him more.

Then the warmth began to sizzle as her body responded to his closeness. Danger.

Apparently Sam recognized the danger, too. He released her and said, "Let's go watch the news. I need to hear a weather report before you start out in the morning."

"Surely we wouldn't have another snowstorm so soon? I mean, don't they—"

"There's no rhyme nor reason to weather, especially in Wyoming. Come on." He grabbed her hand, something that was becoming a habit, and led the way into the den.

Joni wasn't sure that sitting on a couch alone with Sam, even with the weather for company, was a good idea.

"Don't you think you should tell your dad the weather is coming on? He might want to watch it."

"They've got a television in their bedroom."

"Oh."

"Nervous?"

"No, of course not," she lied, tugging her hand from his so she could cross her arms over her chest.

The news portion of the program was just starting when Sam turned on the television. Joni sat as far away as she could without appearing rude and trained her eyes on the screen.

"How do you like our Christmas tree?"

She jumped, shifted her gaze to Sam and then quickly on to the tree. "It's beautiful...and huge. Much larger than the one you cut for us."

"Yeah. We always get a big one. It's a family tradition. Did you have a big one in Chicago?"

"No. Brady didn't know the difference, and it was much easier to get a small one."

"Your husband didn't help with it, did he?" he asked with a frown, as if that fact offended him.

Joni smiled wryly. "No."

"Did he work long hours?"

"Sometimes."

"And the rest of the time?"

"Sam, why are we talking about him? I don't want to."

"I'm trying to understand what kind of a marriage you had, that's all."

"A lousy one. Now, do you want to talk about your marriage?"

"I already told you mine was bad. That's what divorce means."

"Not necessarily. Some people get divorced and remain friends." She was just as curious as he was, but she shouldn't ask questions. The less she knew about Sam Crawford, the less she'd have to remember if she had to go away.

"We didn't. I can't figure out why she married me in the first place. She didn't like anything about me or my life."

"I'm sure she was attracted to you. You're a handsome man."

"Yeah, but not one she wanted to live with. I guess that sounds conceited but—"

"No, I think you'd sound silly denying that you're attractive to women."

"You didn't exactly repel Steve today, either."

"Oh, yes, I did. As soon as I mentioned Brady."

"That's different."

She suddenly realized he'd shifted on the couch, their bodies now almost touching. "Sam, about what occurred in the barn today. It shouldn't have happened. I'd appreciate it if you'd not kiss me anymore."

He reacted as if she'd struck him. "Why?"

"Because I don't indulge in—in making out. I'm an adult, not a teenager with raging hormones." How she hoped he couldn't read her mind, or he'd know she still had raging hormones.

"I don't think a little kissing is making out."

"That's where we were headed, and you know it. I don't want to have to explain myself to Brady."

"Kids see their parents kissing all the time," Sam protested.

"Exactly my point. You are not my husband, or Brady's daddy, and have informed me that you have no intention of being either one."

"Hell," Sam protested, leaping from the couch.

"You're as bad as my parents! Trying to force me into marriage. It's too soon. I don't know that I'll ever want to tie myself down again."

"You think I'm forcing you into marriage?" Outraged, Joni jumped to her feet. "Listen to me, Sam Crawford! I haven't tried to force you into anything except to quit touching me! You don't have the right to maul me whenever you get the urge."

"Maul you? You almost strangled me with your hold around my neck!"

"Well, I can assure you that won't happen again." With that icy return, undermined by her shaking voice, she stomped from the room.

SAM STOOD THERE, wondering when he'd turned into a blithering idiot. He'd just alienated Joni.

Maybe it was for the best. He'd told himself the timing was bad. That he wasn't ready to trust his heart.

But his body wasn't listening.

The urge to touch her whenever she was within sight was leading to some complications. Like the time in the barn. He knew if the boys and his father hadn't come in, he would have had Joni naked beneath him. And loved every minute of it.

Until their lovemaking ended.

Because of the timing.

The time was wrong for commitment, but it sure as hell was right for sex.

Which would put him in the same category as

Dusty when he and Lisa had arrived at the party. Taking his pleasure without paying the price.

He despised men who did that.

So maybe it was a good thing that Joni wouldn't let him near her.

Because he sure as hell couldn't trust his body to back away.

Chapter Eleven

Monday was a long day for Joni.

It shouldn't have been. After all, she had to go to the sitter anyway, but getting all three children in the car, properly dressed, was a challenge. Especially when Katie decided she didn't want to get dressed. Then they'd forgotten their lunches until she had them in the car.

She'd had to leave them alone, with a stern warning about staying in their places, retrieved the lunches and raced back to the car.

At school, the children were all hyper, since this was the last week of school. She'd planned a cutting and pasting activity where the students used tiny squares of colored paper to create a picture of Santa.

As simple as it sounded, the activity turned messy when several little boys glued paper to the nearest girls, and there was a spate of tears as the girls worried about their clothing. When she punished the boys, there were more tears and pleas that she not inform their parents, or even more importantly, Santa.

As a trade-off, Joni made the boys clean the tables

and let the victims be first in line for lunch. After all, it was almost Christmas.

In her spare time, Joni tried to get started on the paperwork necessary for the end of school, since the semester ended before Christmas.

When she got back to Mrs. Barker's, the children were ready to go home. Peter and Katie, in particular, were tired, since they weren't used to day care all day. Katie came running to Joni, whimpering.

"Oh, poor baby, did you have a long day?" Joni asked as she snuggled Katie to her, giving her soft kisses.

"She did fine," Mrs. Barker assured her. "It's just when you came in that she got fussy."

She thanked Mrs. Barker and herded her crowd out to the car. She'd always wanted more children, not wanting Brady to be an only child, but she could see that it would take more energy, or a very supportive husband, to manage a larger family.

Sam would be supportive.

She immediately rejected that ridiculous thought. Sam wasn't even going to marry again, much less help his wife with the children.

When they arrived at the ranch, the boys, after taking their backpacks to their bedroom, as Joni requested, asked to go to the barn, where Loretta had said Tom was working. Making sure they were bundled up well, Joni gave them permission.

"Did everything go well here?" she asked, settling Katie in the den where Loretta was sitting.

"Just fine, except that I didn't get the wash done.

I thought I could manage, but I'm not very good with my left hand. And I don't have much energy. I watched those danged silly soap operas today. Do you know what goes on on those shows?''

Joni grinned at her. "Yes. Fascinating, aren't they?''

Loretta laughed. "Yes. I can see how they might be addictive. Do you watch them?''

"No. Actually I prefer books. But during the school year I don't have much time for reading.'' Since she noted Katie was happy with her toys, she asked Loretta to keep an eye on her while Joni put in a load of wash.

When she had dinner almost ready, she walked to the barn to round up the boys and Tom. Her heart was beating overtime in the hope that Sam would be there, too. She'd heard nothing from him since breakfast early that morning.

But he wasn't there.

"Is he still out on the range?'' she asked.

"He said he was going to try to cover the entire fence line on the east meadow,'' Tom said. "I tried to get him to take one of the hands with him, but he refused. Fixed himself a lunch and hasn't been seen since.''

Joni stared out the barn door at the snow-covered land. "Aren't you worried?''

Tom shrugged his shoulders. "Well, maybe. But we'll go to the house and call him.''

"Call him?''

"Yeah, we use cell phones these days. We're 'high-tech,'" Tom said with pride.

Joni was glad, because it meant she'd know Sam was okay in a couple of minutes. She urged everyone to the house, and the phone.

After washing up, Tom called Sam. No answer.

"What does that mean?" Joni asked, sure that some disaster had occurred.

"Probably that he's down in a swallow. A low place," Tom explained. "I'll try again in a minute."

Joni bit her bottom lip and poured milk for the boys. They came running down the stairs, after being sent to wash up, and the three children kept her busy for several minutes.

But she still worried about Sam.

Just before Tom sat down at the table, he went to the phone again. Joni held her breath.

"He'll be all right, honey," Loretta said, patting Joni's hand.

"Oh. Of course. I—I couldn't help worrying—"

"Hey, there. Where are you?" Tom's voice cut through Joni's explanation, grabbing her attention. "Okay. Well, we'll save you some dinner."

"Is he okay?" she asked as soon as Tom hung up the phone.

"Yeah. He said he'd be home in about an hour. That'll be about dark. Dang fool boy tried to do too much. He's a worker, Sam is," Tom said with obvious pride.

"I'm going to be a cowboy when I grow up," Brady informed everyone. "Just like Sam."

Loretta beamed at him. "Good for you. Sam will teach you everything he knows."

Joni bit her lip to keep from saying that they might not be around that long. She'd been worrying all day about staying in Saddle and resisting Sam. Somehow, those two things didn't work well together.

She cleaned up after dinner, but Sam still didn't arrive. Tom offered to help with the dishes, but she asked him to read to the children instead.

When she went into the den, Tom held a sleeping Katie in his lap, with a boy on each side of him. Loretta was dozing in a nearby recliner.

"I'll take Katie up to bed," Joni whispered.

When she came back down, it was time for the boys to be tucked in.

They resisted. "But we haven't seen Sam yet," Brady said pointedly.

"Ranchers work long hours, sweetie. Sam can't always be here, you know. He has things to do."

But Joni knew how Brady felt. She wanted to see Sam, too.

It was more like two hours after dinner when she saw a lonesome cowboy silhouetted against the snow, dragging into the barn. She dropped the curtain and hurried to the kitchen to heat up the lasagna and make a fresh pot of coffee.

SAM SMELLED THE HOT FOOD as soon as he opened the door. How had Joni known he was here? he wondered.

"Wash up. Dinner's ready," Joni said softly as he entered the kitchen.

Since he was hungry down to his frozen toes, he didn't waste time talking. In two minutes he was back at the table, his hat hung on the rack near the door.

Wolfing down the food, he didn't pause until he'd finished and Joni filled his coffee a second time.

"I sure hope this is decaf, 'cause I want to sleep good tonight."

"It is. How about some of Mrs. McGilvey's coconut pie?"

"There's some left over? I won't turn that down. She makes the best coconut pie in the county."

Joni sniffed. "You haven't tasted mine."

Surprised, he stared at her. "You make pies?"

"Of course."

"What kind?"

"Coconut, pecan, all kinds of fruit pies, chocolate."

"Man, whoever marries you will think he's died and gone to heaven," Sam said with a big smile. It slowly faded as he realized he'd offended Joni. Her smiled disappeared and she walked out of the kitchen without a word.

"Damn!" he muttered under his breath.

"You find a rock in that pie?" Tom asked as he came through the door.

"Uh, no. How'd everything go today?"

"Fine. I had an easy day…as you planned."

Sam jerked his gaze to his father. "What?"

"You intended to double your work and halve

mine, but I'd like to remind you that it's your mother who got hurt, not me.''

"I know, but I figured she'd like you close to home until she gets feeling better.'' Sam turned his attention back to the pie.

"Some little boys I know would like to have you come home before their bedtime, too.''

Sam wiped his mouth with a napkin. "I'll go see if they're asleep.''

He slipped past the den without seeing Joni. When he reached the boys' room, he opened the door slowly and tiptoed over to the twin beds. Brady was in the first one, and he stirred.

"Sam,'' he mumbled, "you're home.''

"Yeah, little guy, I'm here. Did you have a good day?''

"Yeah. Grandpa let me pet Cookie and feed him a little hay. It was fun.''

"Good.'' He leaned over and kissed Brady's forehead. "I'll see you in the morning. Good night.''

"G'night.'' Brady shifted, snuggled under the cover, and went back to sleep.

Sam stood there in the shadows, relishing how good it felt to pretend Brady was his. His own son, eager for his daddy to come home.

It was a dangerous delusion.

He backed out of the room, closing the door.

"Were either of them awake?''

He spun around to find Joni staring at him. And this time he saw the weariness in her face. He'd been so hungry earlier, he hadn't noticed.

"Brady kind of woke up. Listen, I didn't thank you for having my food ready so fast. I was starving."

She nodded and turned away.

"Where are you going?"

"To my room. I'm tired. I'm going to read a little and then go to sleep. Six o'clock comes early."

He couldn't think of a reason to stop her. Except that he longed to hold her against him. There was a part of him that was still frozen—and would be until he held her again.

WHILE SAM DID THE READING duties Tuesday night, Joni began organizing the gift-wrapping. Loretta told her where the wrapping paper, scissors and tape were located, and she brought them to the den along with some of the gifts.

"Joni, where did you learn to make bows like that?" Loretta asked after Joni had completed the first present.

Joni smiled. "My foster mother taught me."

"Once I'm able-bodied again, would you teach me?"

"Of course, Loretta."

Joni continued to work, but Sam had stopped reading. Brady elbowed him. "Come on, Sam. Read."

She looked up in time to catch his stare before he turned his attention back to the story.

Even though they'd hardly exchanged a word, Joni was much happier that Sam had made it to dinner. It was alarming how much she depended on seeing him to complete her day.

When Marty returned, Joni would go back to her house, and Sam wouldn't be a part of her day. He might not be a part of her life, if she and Brady left. She'd been giving their departure a lot of thought. She didn't have to get a job right away, since she'd saved almost all the insurance money that came to her with her husband's death. And she received a benefit check every month.

She and Brady could find another small town in Wyoming, with nice people, like those in Saddle. Surely there would be a teaching position open in the fall.

Maybe she would get that land she was talking about, and Brady could have his horse.

A poor substitute for Sam, but the best she could do.

It was a good plan. A workable plan.

But she didn't like it.

Her gaze drifted back to Sam. No, she didn't like the thought of being far from him. Of not seeing him. Not even being able to anticipate seeing him.

He looked up, and she quickly stared at the package again.

When he finished, Brady and Peter spread kisses around the room, then went upstairs with Sam. He came down a few minutes later, reporting that the boys were in bed.

"You're getting good at tucking them in, son," Loretta said with a smile.

"It's easier when there are two of them."

Joni didn't look up. But she grew alarmed as long,

jean-clad legs came to a halt nearby, then folded up as Sam sat down on the floor beside her.

"What can I do to help?"

"Oh, nothing. I'm doing fine."

"Mom, are there other presents to bring down?"

"Yes, but Joni can't wrap all of them tonight. Why don't you go to my closet and get one more stack of boxes. But don't peek in any of them," his mother warned.

After fetching the boxes, Sam gathered up the ones Joni had wrapped and put them under the tree. "I always think a tree looks kind of lonesome without presents under it," he said, staring at the brightly colored packages.

His thought echoed Joni's. "Yes. Though Santa's gifts aren't wrapped, I always pick out a couple of things to put in boxes. But I'm afraid our tree never gets very filled, with just the two of us."

"You'll have more packages under your tree this year, I'm sure," Loretta said with an arch look at her son.

Joni's breath caught at Loretta's inference, that Sam would be buying her a gift. "No, I mean, I don't think—"

Sam helped her out. "I know Peter is already thinking about a gift for his best friend."

She smiled her thanks. "Yes, we've been shopping for Peter and Katie, too."

Tom spoke up. "Sweetheart, I think it's time for you to turn in. You still need to get extra rest." He helped his wife up and led her up the stairs.

Joni, trapped with a pile of gifts still to be wrapped, found herself left alone with Sam.

"I was thinking about a gift for Brady," he said as he passed her the tape she needed.

"You don't need to buy him anything," she hurriedly said.

"Brady and I are friends. I reckon buying him a gift is something I can do if I want."

She gave him a sharp look. "As long as it isn't a horse. We don't have room for a horse."

"Hmm. And what do you want Santa to bring you, Joni? I don't believe you sat on Santa's knee."

That image, her sitting in Sam's lap, took her breath away. After coughing several times, she said, "Nothing. I mean, I want Brady to be happy. That's all."

"Everyone ought to get something for Christmas. Maybe we need to arrange for a private session with Santa."

Joni hoped not. What she wanted Santa couldn't deliver, just as she'd told Brady about his wish for a daddy. And private time with Santa would only make life more difficult.

JONI WENT TO BED before the weather that night. When Sam reached the kitchen the next morning, he said, "You need to take a truck today. They think a cold front might hit us late this afternoon, with snow in it."

Joni didn't want to drive one of the big trucks with

stick shift. She looked out the window. "There's not a cloud in the sky, Sam. I think you're overreacting."

"These fronts can move in fast out here. It'd be safer—"

"If it gets dangerous, I'll take the kids to my house. I need to stop by there anyway."

"Why?" Panic filled him, as if she were planning to leave. That was ridiculous, of course. But he liked having her close.

"I need to check on my plants. Be sure nothing's frozen. Water the Christmas tree."

"Keep a close watch out, okay?"

She nodded and put breakfast on the table.

All day Sam watched the sky. When the clouds, pushed by the Wyoming wind, topped the mountains to the west at about lunchtime, he hurried in and ate his food in front of the television.

The forecaster warned that the storm was building up to be a big one, but he said it wouldn't hit until that evening. Joni and the kids would be back long before that.

He and his dad returned to work, but Sam felt uneasy all afternoon. He told himself it was his food that didn't sit well, but his gaze kept watching the mass of clouds building up. They were about half an hour west of the house when the snow started falling.

Almost at once, his dad's phone rang.

"Okay. We'll be right there."

"What? What's wrong?" Sam demanded.

"Weather forecaster has changed his mind. The full storm will be here in a couple of hours. We've got to get back home.'' He turned and shouted to his men. Fortunately they were all working together today.

''I'm going to get Joni,'' Sam yelled, not waiting on the others. He flicked his horse with the reins and rode as fast as he dared on the snow already on the ground. At the house he traded his horse for a truck.

When he reached town, he picked up the kids first.

''What are you doing here, Sam?'' Brady asked.

''There's a snowstorm coming, so I thought we should get you home early.''

The three kids cheered. Even Sam smiled. He could remember those days. If he was any judge, there wouldn't be any school tomorrow, and they would cheer again.

When he got to the school, he hated to take the three kids out in the snow, but he didn't feel comfortable leaving them in the truck alone.

There were several children still in Joni's room, and she frowned at Sam. ''We heard about the storm,'' she said softly.

''Didn't they let school out early?'' he asked.

''Yes, but these two haven't been picked up yet. I can't leave until I'm sure their parents get them.'' She smiled and shrugged her shoulders.

Sam wanted to sweep her into his arms and ignore her sense of duty. But he couldn't do that. ''Mom gave me a list of things to buy at the grocery. Can I leave these three here while I shop?''

''Of course. If my charges leave, I'll load them into my car and—''

"No! Your car is going to stay here. Or at your house if the storm's not too bad. But you're not driving that little car out to the house. It's too dangerous."

"Fine," she said, her voice soothing. "Go do the shopping. Come here, Katie," she said, extending her arms to the little girl.

Sam stared at her, suddenly wishing those arms were extended for him. When she stared at him questioningly, he shook his head and stepped back out into the storm. The coldness, and distance from Joni, helped him think more clearly.

Half an hour later, he returned to find Joni free to go. Together they loaded the children into his truck.

"I'm going to drive my car to the house."

"I'll follow you," Sam replied. "But if you start sliding, we'll park it wherever it lands. I'm not taking chances."

She nodded and hurried to her car. The snow was so thick, he could barely make out the outline, and he wasn't parked far away.

"I can't see Mom," Brady complained as they made their way to Sam's truck. There was a hint of fear in his voice.

"She's getting in her car. We're going to follow right behind her."

"Why can't she ride with us?"

"She wants to leave her car in the garage so it won't freeze up. She'll ride with us to the ranch."

Brady seemed satisfied.

It seemed like hours until they reached Joni's

house. Her car had slid all over the local streets. The plows were out in full force, trying to keep ahead of the storm, but losing the race. The snow was getting deeper and blowing fiercer. Sam realized it was foolish to chance the drive to the ranch—not with the kids in the car. He pulled into the driveway behind Joni. Cutting the engine, he took Katie out of her car seat.

"Are we going in?" Brady asked. The children had been unnaturally quiet on the drive.

"Yeah, buddy, we are. The snow's too thick to make it to the ranch. But we'll all be safe here." And hopefully they would manage to call the ranch before the telephone lines were knocked out.

"Gather up your stuff and be careful. Hold on to each other, boys, because it's deep. We don't want any more broken bones like Grandma."

With Katie tucked inside his jacket, they made their way to the front porch and he banged on the door.

Joni opened it almost immediately and helped them inside, taking Katie from Sam. "What's the matter. Do we need a bathroom break?" she asked, her voice anxious.

"Nope. We have to take a storm break. We can't make it to the ranch. If you don't mind, we'll be spending the night here."

Her eyes widened. "Of course. That's fine. Uh, boys, take your things to Brady's room." She watched them leave the room. Then she turned to face Sam again. "There's only one problem. We only have two beds for five people."

Chapter Twelve

"We'll manage," Sam assured her. "I can sleep on the floor, if need be. Right now I need to call Mom and let her know we're safe."

"Oh. Of course. The phone's in the kitchen."

The two boys came running back down the hall.

"Mom," Brady called. "Me and Peter can't fit in my bed. We're too big."

Joni wasn't surprised. Brady's bed was not even twin size. He'd had it since he moved out of the crib. "Um, I guess the two of you had better take my bed, and we'll put Katie in yours."

"But where will you and Sam sleep?"

Good question. She stared at the small sofa in the living room. She could fit on it, but Sam was much too big. But he was her guest. She couldn't put him on the floor while she took the sofa.

"I got through to Mom," Sam announced as he came back into the living room.

"Oh, good. Are they all right?"

"Yeah. Do you have any wood for the fireplace?"

Joni hadn't had a fire in the fireplace since they arrived. "I haven't used it. Are you cold?"

"No, but if the electricity goes, it will get very cold. I'll see if there's any wood in the garage or on the back porch." He walked out before Joni could get out any words.

Shock held her silent. Electricity goes? Did he mean they would be without heat? She stared out the front window at the white rage that was coating the world in snow.

"Mom, are we going to freeze to death?" Brady asked, his eyes wide.

She shook her head. "No, of course not. We'll be just fine. We, um, need to get organized. You can share a pair of your pajamas with Peter. Katie can wear one of your long-sleeved shirts and a pair of socks."

"What's Sam going to wear?"

Brady's question almost distracted her from their situation. The thought of the long, lean cowboy in white cotton briefs, assuming he wore that much, made her mouth go dry.

Sam's arrival rescued her from her paralysis. He was covered with snow, clutching a load of wood to his chest. "I think there's enough wood on the back porch."

"Hey, Sam, you're a snowman!" Brady exclaimed, chuckling.

"That's right and you'd better keep your distance or I'll melt on you," he returned with a smile.

"Boys, take Katie to Brady's room and play with her while I help Sam," Joni ordered.

"I can bring in the wood," he protested.

"I thought I'd bring in the things you bought at the store," she said. As the children left the room, she added, "And I'm praying diapers were on the list."

Sam grinned. "Your prayers were answered."

"Thank you," she muttered with a relieved sigh.

"But I'll get the groceries after I bring in the rest of the wood," he assured her.

"Don't go all macho on me, Sam. It's already getting dark." She was pulling on her coat even as she spoke. When she turned toward the front door, he grabbed her arm. Irritated that he would try to stop her, she spun around, ready to tell him what she thought of macho men who counted women helpless.

Instead of protesting, Sam kissed her. As he lifted his lips from hers, leaving her reeling, he murmured, "Be careful." Then he turned and headed for the back porch.

She stared after him, stunned by his kiss, until the children's laughter awakened her. "Oh, yeah," she responded when he couldn't hear her. She'd be careful.

The force of the storm struck her as soon as she stepped out the front door. By the time she'd made two trips to get all the groceries, she was frozen and exhausted.

Sam met her at the door on her second trip, taking the packages from her at once. "Any more?"

"No, that's the last of them."

"Go sit down by the fire and I'll put these things away," he ordered.

For once she didn't protest. It was nice to have someone want to take care of her. Even temporarily.

When Sam came back to the living room, he carried a cup of hot tea for her.

"How thoughtful of you, Sam. Thanks." She sipped the hot liquid, feeling it seep through her frozen body. "Oh, that tastes good." She studied the pile of wood Sam had put on the hearth. "Do we have enough wood? Should we be using it already, while the electricity is still on?"

"I think we have enough. And I've only made a small fire so we'll be ready. Do you have any candles?"

She set down her cup and headed for the kitchen. Once she'd rounded up what candles she had, she decided to start dinner. "I don't want to cook over an open fire. I've never done that before."

"I have. I'll become cook if the electricity goes," Sam assured her.

"Gee, it might be worth doing without electricity to see you cook over the fireplace," she teased with a grin.

"Yeah, and I could wear one of those aprons that say 'Kiss the Cook.' Or you could," Sam said softly and came closer.

"I've got to make dinner," she said breathlessly. "Go check on the children." After a look that seared her insides, he walked out of the room.

She leaned against the kitchen counter, waving her hand in front of her face. She thought there had been a sudden heat wave named Sam. Who needed a fire-place?

WITH EXQUISITE TIMING, the electricity went out just as they finished dinner. Sam took the children upstairs to dress for bed while Joni did a quick cleanup in the kitchen by candlelight.

When she went hunting for the rest of them, she discovered them all in the living room, with a few adjustments. The mattresses from both beds were on the floor in front of the Christmas tree.

"Look, Mom. We're going to have a slumber party," Brady announced as she entered.

"Yes, I see." She looked at Sam. "We're all going to sleep in here?"

"Yeah. By keeping the doors closed and the fire going, we'll be pretty warm."

"Unless we have to go to the bathroom," Brady whispered.

"Yeah," Peter added, "and the water's real cold."

"Ah. Thanks for the warning."

"You'd better go change while the bedrooms have a little warmth left," Sam suggested. "The kids have changed."

Yes, she could see that. Katie was wearing a pair of Brady's thick socks that came all the way to her diaper, topped by a long-sleeve knit shirt. The boys both wore flannel pajamas and thick socks.

"I don't have anything for you to wear, Sam," Joni said, frowning.

"I'll sleep in what I've got on. Don't worry about it."

A few minutes later, she returned to the living room, dressed in an old pair of sweats and thick socks, carrying all the bedding she had. Sam had all the kids sitting in front of the fire, leaning against him, telling them a story. Katie, snuggled in her uncle's arms, was already drifting off.

When she reached for the little girl, Sam said, "Put her on the sofa."

"She'll fall off," Joni warned.

"Use a chair to block the edges."

She did as he asked, but where they would all sleep occupied her mind while Sam finished the story. They sat quietly, seemingly mesmerized by the snapping, crackling fire.

Then Peter tugged on his uncle's sleeve. "Uncle Sam, are my mommy and daddy all right?"

"Sure they are, Pete. They're down in Denver. It's probably not even snowing there. Besides, you know your daddy will take care of your mommy. That's what daddies do."

"My daddy didn't," Brady said abruptly.

"Brady!" Joni exclaimed with a gasp, stunned by her son's words.

"He didn't, Mom. I remember he made you cry."

Joni wanted to crawl under something to hide her embarrassment. To her surprise, it was Sam, with his arm around her son, who came to her rescue.

"Well, Brady, all we men mess up sometimes and make our ladies cry. But we try to make up for it. Your daddy may not have had time to do that before he was shot. That means you've got to remember to apologize if you do something wrong."

"I will, Sam," Brady promised solemnly.

Joni stared at the fire, barely able to deal with the emotions that flooded her. For the first time since her son was born, someone else dealt with a problem.

Sam's words hadn't taken long. But they'd been a tremendous help to Joni. He'd given respect back to Brady for his father. Whether her husband deserved it or not wasn't important. Brady needed it.

She turned her head to discover Sam watching her. Though her lips trembled, she gave him a grateful smile.

"Time for bed, boys," Sam said, giving each of them a hug.

"But where are we going to sleep? My bed is too small for both of us," Brady assured Sam.

"Naw, it's not. The closer you are to each other, the warmer you'll be."

"Are you and Mom going to sleep on the other mattress?" Brady asked even as he and Peter jumped onto his mattress.

"Yeah. We're going to keep each other warm, too," Sam said casually, not even looking at Joni.

She couldn't breathe.

Was the man crazy?

She stared at him until he asked her if she intended to kiss the boys good-night. "Oh! Yes, of course."

She scooted over to the mattress and hugged each boy, warning them to be quiet in the morning if Katie was still sleeping.

Then she returned to sit in front of the fire, her back to Sam.

Maybe she'd stay there all night.

WHEN SAM CAME BACK into the living room after his turn in the bathroom, he discovered Joni still staring at the fire burning brightly, her back rigid.

He picked up several more logs to add to the fire before sitting beside her. "You all right?"

"No, I'm not." Her voice was more frozen than the world outside.

"Did I overstep my bounds, talking to Brady about his daddy?"

She faced him, her cheeks red, all stiffness gone. "No! Not at all. In fact, I appreciate what you said. I—I didn't know what to tell him."

Sam grinned back, glad she'd forgotten to be angry. "No problem. From what I've heard about your husband, he wasn't worth much, but Brady doesn't have to know that."

They sat silently, watching the fire. Then Sam added, "Whatever I think about your husband, I have to give him partial credit for a great kid." He noted moisture in Joni's eyes and decided it was time to tease her again. "And fine taste in women."

She immediately fired up, as he'd known she would. "Sam Crawford! You are an awful flirt!"

"Can't help myself, Joni," he assured her. "You're too much for a man to resist."

"Well, you'll just have to work harder at it. And for your information, we're not going to share that mattress."

"We have to, Joni. In spite of what I said earlier, I'm too old to sleep on the floor, and we need each other to keep warm. I promise to behave."

"You?" she questioned, clearly doubting his promise.

"Hey, I keep my word. Besides, we have too many chaperones for me to try anything," he admitted ruefully.

She sighed, then nodded. "Will Katie be all right sleeping by herself?"

"Yeah, she's snoozing just like the boys. Come on. Let's get tucked in." In spite of himself, his pulses began racing at the thought of holding Joni in his arms.

"What if the fire dies out?"

"It won't. I'm going to sleep on the side by the fireplace so I can replenish it during the night." He sat on that side of the mattress and removed his boots.

"Are you going to be comfortable in your jeans?"

"Are you asking me to take 'em off?" He cocked one eyebrow at her.

"No!" Her cheeks were bright red and he wanted to warm his hands there. "I—I was worried about—never mind!" She slid under the covers and turned her back to him.

He blew out the candles and joined her in the bed.

As soon as he stretched, he reached for her, pulling her back against his chest.

"What are you doing?" she gasped.

"We're not going to keep warm if we cling to the edges, Joni. Just relax and get some sleep. I bet the kids will be up early."

She held herself taut for several minutes before she capitulated, her body sinking against his.

Heaven.

And hell.

"SAM?"

The whisper barely penetrated Sam's head as he snuggled against Joni. When it was repeated, he struggled to open his eyes.

"Hi, Brady," he muttered. "What's up?"

"The fire's almost out. Should I put some more wood on it?"

Reluctantly Sam withdrew from Joni and slid from under the covers, the difference in temperature considerable. Last night he'd lectured the boys about not touching the fire. He didn't want to go back on that order.

"I'll do it. Thanks for wakening me."

Brady hovered nearby while Sam built up the fire.

"Get on this end of the couch and I'll put a blanket over you."

Brady did as he ordered but the boy kept his eyes on him. "Are you leaving?"

"Nope. I'm going to the bathroom, then I'll see what I can find for breakfast."

When he returned a few minutes later, Sam had a pan with water in it that he sat on coals, some granola bars and two cups, one with instant cocoa, the other instant coffee.

As soon as their drinks were ready, he scooted under the cover with Brady.

"Why did you wake up so early?" he whispered to Brady.

"Peter kicked me in the stomach. He rolls around a lot while he sleeps."

Sam smiled. "Yeah, I forgot about that. He's kicked me before, too."

"Does Mom kick?"

Sam's gaze strayed to Joni, curled up under the cover. She hadn't kept him awake by kicking. But her sexy body had done a number on his attempts to sleep. "Uh, no. I didn't sleep because—because I was worried about Dad doing the chores by himself this morning."

"It's still snowing."

"I know."

"If we were at the ranch, I'd help you with the chores. Will Grandpa be able to feed Cookie?"

"You bet."

They sat in silence for several minutes, and Sam drank the coffee, hoping the caffeine kicked in soon.

"Sam?"

"Yeah, Brady?"

"I wish you were my daddy instead of my real daddy."

His arm tightened around the little boy.

"Is that bad?" Brady asked anxiously.

"Not bad, no. If I had a little boy, I'd want him to be just like you. But—but I'm not ready—I can't get married right now." He must have built up the fire too much. He was sweating.

"Why not?"

He looked down into Brady's anxious eyes, warm brown just like his mother's, and tried to come up with an answer the boy would understand. "Marriage is serious business. I've already messed up once. I can't marry again until I'm sure it's forever."

Brady tucked his chin into his chest. "Oh."

"Your mom's a pretty lady. She'll find lots of guys who would like—I mean, you'll have a family again. Just be patient."

"But not you," Brady said sadly.

"Brady—"

"You're up early, son," Joni said, sitting up suddenly in bed. "Couldn't you sleep?"

"No, Peter kicks," Brady said succinctly.

Joni looked at Sam, her gaze cold, before she turned back to Brady. "Sorry, sweetie. Sometimes life is like that."

Sam didn't think she was talking about sleeping with Peter.

"Why don't you come help me check the kitchen? There might be something there for breakfast," she said as she rolled out of bed, stretching out her hand for Brady.

"We've already found some granola bars," Sam protested even as Brady left him.

She shot him another cold look and led Brady out of the room without speaking.

Sam had the feeling she'd overheard all their conversation.

"ARE YOU MAD AT ME for getting up early?" Brady asked as Joni stared at the pantry shelves.

"Of course not," she assured him, stooping down to give him a hug. "How about oatmeal? It's nice and warm, and I have some raisins to go in it."

"I like oatmeal."

"Why don't you go get the pan from the fire and bring it to me? And don't burn yourself."

He ran out of the kitchen and she leaned against the doorjamb, letting out a long breath. She'd heard Brady when he first whispered to Sam, so she'd been privy to all their conversation. She'd wanted to cry at Brady's sad response.

Instead she'd vowed that she would take her son away from Saddle, away from the man he wanted as a daddy. Away from heartbreak.

She couldn't do anything about it until the snowstorm disappeared, but she would as soon as she could. She'd been holding out against a move, hoping things would work out.

But she couldn't do that any longer. Brady was already too fond of Sam.

The door swung open and she straightened. But it wasn't Brady carrying the pan. It was Sam.

"I told Brady to—"

"I was afraid he'd burn himself."

She couldn't argue because he protected her son. She reached out for the pan.

"I'll take care of it. You want more water heated?" Sam asked, watching her.

"Yes, please. We're going to make oatmeal." She turned her back on him to take the oatmeal from the pantry.

"How much did you hear?"

She turned to face him even as he filled the pan. "Everything."

"I tried to be honest," he said defensively.

"Oh, you were brilliantly honest." She gave the package of oatmeal a savage rip, trying to release her anger.

"I didn't want to hurt him."

It wasn't easy to hide the heartbreak. But she did. After all, it wasn't Sam's fault that both of them fell in love with him.

"What are you going to do?"

She wouldn't tell him she was leaving. Not yet. "I'm going to do what I should've done in the first place. I'm going to keep my distance from now on. No more of your misguided attempts to fool everyone. We're going cold turkey, Sam Crawford. Turkey as cold as a Wyoming blizzard."

Chapter Thirteen

It was hard to be aloof when you were trapped in one room with the object of your aloofness.

That was a truth Joni discovered as the day progressed. She tried to avoid conversation with Sam, but with three children under their care, even talking couldn't be avoided.

But her quietness didn't disturb Brady. In fact, he seemed in agreement with her. Frequently, while Sam played with his nephew and niece, Brady sat quietly by his mother, watching.

"Don't you want to play with us, Brady?" Sam asked, frowning. He'd been on all fours chasing Katie and fighting off Peter who pretended Sam was a bucking bronc.

"No, thanks. I'm helping Mom," the boy said. In actuality, he was holding the mending basket with thread and extra needles while Joni repaired some of his clothes.

"And I appreciate it," she said with a hug.

Sam eyed the two of them, as if they were keeping a secret from him. "Well, I was kind of hoping you'd pick out your favorite storybook, so I can rest while I read it to the three of you.''

Brady couldn't resist that lure. He slid from the sofa and made a mad dash to his bedroom, hurrying back before he got cold. "This is it," he said, handing a much read *Peter Pan* to Sam.

"Aha!" Sam said with a grin. "Are you never going to grow up, like Peter Pan?"

"Yeah!" Peter yelled.

Brady, who in the past had expressed such feelings, looked first at Sam and then his mother. "I don't know."

Joni smiled at her little boy, knowing he was growing up before her very eyes. She wished it wasn't so painful.

Sam, too, seemed to realize Brady was having difficulties. Scooping him up in his arms, Sam sat on the sofa. "Don't worry. You've got time." Then he motioned to Katie, toddling toward them. "Come on, baby. You, too, Peter. We're going to read."

About one o'clock, the phone rang. When Joni answered, she discovered Loretta on the line. "Loretta! How's everything out at the ranch?"

"Fine. Marty called. They're in Cheyenne tonight and will be home tomorrow."

"That's wonderful. How's Paul's dad?"

"Doing much better. How are my grandkids?"

"Fine. I'll let you talk to Sam."

She called Sam to the telephone and went back into the warm living room to tell Peter and Katie that their parents would be home tomorrow.

When Sam came in a few minutes later it was to announce that the snowplows were out again. They could go back to the ranch within the hour.

Peter cheered and Katie followed suit, though Joni doubted that she knew why she was cheering. Brady looked at his mother.

"No, sweetie, we won't be going with them," she said softly.

He didn't say anything, as if resigned.

"What are you talking about?" Sam demanded.

"I was explaining to Brady that we won't be going back to the ranch with you. Since Marty and Paul will be back tomorrow, I'm sure your mother can manage until they arrive."

"They have a generator at the ranch. You can't stay here without electricity." He sounded in charge, as always.

Joni ignored him. "I think we have enough time for cookies and milk. Anyone interested?"

Katie's favorite word, cookie, always got a reaction from her. Brady and Peter also accepted the offer, though not as enthusiastically. They were whispering between them.

When Sam tried to follow her to the kitchen, she reminded him he had to keep an eye on Katie around the fire.

But he hadn't gone away when she returned with a tray of milk and cookies. Taking it from her, he poured Katie her roly-poly glass of milk, and glasses for the boys. Then he faced Joni, his hands on his hips.

"I'm not leaving you and Brady here without electricity. And I don't want any argument."

He was a formidable foe, his aggressive stance emphasizing his muscle and determination. But Joni wasn't going to back down. "Brady and I are staying here."

"Why?"

"Because Brady has been hurt enough."

He opened his mouth, then closed it again. He reached out and held her arms. "I'll go stay in the bunkhouse, but—"

"And how would you explain that to your folks? We'll be fine and you know it. There's still plenty of wood left. We'll be at school again tomorrow, I'm sure. We'll be fine."

"Joni, I don't think—"

"Aren't you gonna have cookies and milk, Uncle Sam?" Peter asked, interrupting them.

Joni sagged in relief when, after staring at her, Sam turned to Peter and joined the tea party.

JONI AND BRADY stood on the front porch and watched as Sam's big truck drove slowly away, following the tracks of the snowplow.

"Will they make it all right?" Brady asked in a small voice.

"Yes, sweetie. You know Sam's a good driver."

He looked up at her. "He's good at everything."

Her smile wobbled a little but she held on to it. "I'm sure there's something that Sam's not good at, but I can't think of what it is right now." She squeezed Brady's shoulder. "Let's go inside and figure out what we're having for supper."

After they'd eaten, the two of them sat on the end of Joni's mattress and watched the fire burning.

"I like having a fire," Brady said.

"Yes, it's good company, isn't it?"

"Yeah. Are we going to stay here, Mom?"

Trust her son to cut straight to the important stuff. She didn't know what to say. "I'm not sure. Why don't we wait until after Christmas. We'll talk about what we'll do then. I think we ought to enjoy Christmas first."

"Yeah," he agreed with a sigh, and laid his head on her shoulder.

IT WAS A RELIEF to return to the normalcy of school, even if the day wasn't normal. The children were so excited, she could scarcely keep them in the room. There wasn't much work done, but at least they had no more gluing incidents.

In fact, each child had made a gift for Joni, making her feel so welcome, tears filled her eyes. When the bell rang, instead of their wild rush from the room, each child gave her a hug, thanking her for coming to teach them.

When the last child left the room, she slumped in her chair, glad she would have two weeks to recover. And decide what she intended to do. Could she and Brady be happy in Saddle without Sam in their lives?

Mary stepped to her door. "All gone? Were they as wild as mine?"

"I suspect so."

"Are you going to the church party this evening?"

They'd announced the event when she'd visited the singles class, but she hadn't thought of it again. "I had forgotten all about it. Besides, I'm not a member of the church yet."

"That doesn't matter. You're still invited. Besides, I was hoping you would go."

Joni stared at Mary's disappointed face. "Why? Are you going?"

"Usually I don't, but I thought—well, I wanted to go to see Donald again."

"Hasn't he asked you out?" From their enjoyment of each other last Saturday night, Joni assumed they were now a couple.

"We went out for pizza on Monday night, but he's been so busy with the storm, animals getting hurt and all, that I haven't even heard from him. I thought I might see him at the party tonight. Every single in town usually goes."

"And you wanted us to go together?" Joni asked.

"Well, I figured you might be going with Sam, but just in case you weren't—" Mary broke off, her cheeks flushed.

Joni hadn't planned to go, but if Mary was right, her not going with Sam would make an impression. And she wanted Mary's romance to succeed, even if hers didn't.

"If I can find someone to keep an eye on Brady, I'll go with you, Mary. But I won't know until later. I'll have to call you."

"Okay," Mary agreed eagerly.

"Um, what do I wear? I mean, what kind of party is it?"

"Oh, it's wonderful. We all pile on a bed of hay, pulled by Mr. Wilks's big horses, and we go to several nearby ranches to carol. Then we come back to the church and have hot chocolate and visit. So dress warmly."

"Okay. I'll call you."

After Mary left, Joni leaned back in her chair and sighed. She hadn't wanted to go out this evening. But if she had any hope of staying here, and she wasn't sure she did, she had to find a life without Sam.

And she had to convince the town there was no connection between the two of them.

When she reached Mrs. Barker's, she asked the lady about keeping Brady that night, but the woman already had plans. She gave Joni the names of some possible sitters, but she also passed on a message from Marty, Peter's mother, asking Joni to call.

At home, it seemed strange to be there without Sam and the other two children, but Joni reminded herself that they had only moved in three weeks ago. It would take a while to feel at home. And at least the electricity was back on.

Brady moped into his room, and Joni picked up the phone to call Marty. When she answered, Joni asked about her in-laws and the drive back. Then Marty thanked her for all the help she'd given the Crawford family.

"I also wanted to ask if Brady could come spend

the night. You deserve some time off, and Peter missed Brady all day long.''

"Oh, Marty, you don't want an extra after all you've been through.''

"Peter is so much happier when Brady is here. It will be easier on me, Joni, I swear.''

"Are you doing this because Sam asked you to? Because of the church party?'' she asked.

"Oh, no, I forgot all about the singles party. Everyone in town goes. But no, I haven't even seen Sam today. Are you going?''

"Well, Mary wanted me to go with her, but I didn't have a sitter.''

"Don't give it another thought. Bring Brady over right now, so you'll have plenty of time to get ready. But why aren't you going with Sam?''

"Sam and I aren't dating, Marty. He's just been a friend,'' Joni hurriedly explained.

"Well, whoever you're going with, bring Brady over. Peter will be leaping for joy when I tell him.''

"Thanks, Marty. I will.'' She took down directions and, after hanging up, walked to her son's bedroom door. He was slumped on his bed, staring at the ceiling.

"Feeling kind of down?'' she asked.

"Yeah. I miss Peter and Katie, and Grandma and Grandpa. And most of all I miss Sam. And Cookie.''

Joni knew just what he meant. Their house seemed small and empty. "Well, I can't take care of all those problems, but Peter's mother called and asked if you could come spend the night. Would that make up for some of them?''

Brady shot off his bed as if fired from a cannon. "Yeah! Can I, Mom? Can I?''

Joni smiled at the change in her little boy. "I suppose so, if you promise to mind your manners.''

"I gotta pack a bag,'' Brady announced, diving into his closet for the overnight bag he used to visit the ranch. "Peter wants to play my new video game. And I should take my G.I. Joe. He has one, too. And—''

"How about some pajamas and clean clothes for tomorrow? I think they should go in there, too.''

With Brady's suddenly energetic assistance, Joni had him ready to go in about ten minutes. She drove him to Peter's house, chatted with Marty a few minutes, then returned home.

After calling Mary, who insisted she would pick Joni up, Joni indulged in a hot bubble bath. Normally she didn't even try since her son found several emergencies that needed her personal attention anytime she did.

As she lay in the hot water, surrounded by sweet-smelling bubbles, she considered her situation. She'd already admitted to herself that she'd fallen in love with Sam. Not only was he handsome, sexy, intelligent and charming, but he was also sweet to Brady. Caring, fatherly. But the timing was wrong. She knew he wasn't interested in forming a family.

So, she had to establish a separate identity from the sexy Santa she'd met on that first day. Tonight was the first step. She would make friends with the other singles in town. Already she was becoming friends with Mary.

Maybe she'd even flirt a little. Just a little. Sam's idea of her dating someone else was a good one. As long as she didn't let anyone get serious about her. Because, if there was no pressure on Sam, he might one day realize how perfect they would be, the three of them.

She swirled her hand through the evaporating bubbles. Was she misleading herself? Was there no hope? She didn't think so. She knew Sam was attracted to her. And she knew he cared about Brady.

All she needed was patience.

And distance.

Okay, so she had a plan of action.

Tonight she would socialize.

SAM GOT BACK TO THE HOUSE after dark. He'd planned to come in early, but he'd found several head of cattle trapped in a deep snowdrift and had worked for the last three hours to free them. He was frozen and exhausted.

The electricity had been restored that afternoon, his mother told him as he came in.

"Then I'm heading for a hot shower. It's the only way I'll get warm."

Tom, already in the kitchen, said, "Your mother and I will have you some hot food ready when you get out."

Sam had just walked back into the kitchen when

the phone rang. Tom answered, then held out the receiver to Sam.

"Hello?"

"Sam? This is Donald. Are you picking up Mary as well as Joni for the party?"

The party. Sam had forgotten all about the church party while he worked that day. "Damn! I forgot all about it. We haven't made plans. Why?"

"Well, I got back late and—well, I'd forgotten to say anything to Mary about it and when I called, there was no one home."

"Just a minute." He covered the receiver with his hand. "Have you talked to Joni today?" he asked his mother.

"No. Marty did."

"Did she say anything about going to the party?"

"The singles party?" Loretta asked. Sam thought she was pretending innocence and nodded impatiently. "Why yes, she did. Marty is baby-sitting Brady so Joni can go."

"Alone?" Sam demanded.

"I think she's going with Mary."

He turned back to the phone. "Mom says Joni and Mary are going together."

"They won't be alone for long, with all the guys. You know they always outnumber the women. I've got to hurry."

"I'll swing by and pick you up. No sense in having too many cars there."

"Good thinking. When will you be here?"

Sam eyed the food on the table hungrily. "In about fifteen minutes."

Loretta began making him a roast beef sandwich before he'd even hung up the phone. He raced back upstairs to put on a warmer shirt and came back down. "Thanks, Mom," he said as he grabbed the sandwich, stuck a soda into his coat pocket, put his hat on his head and ran for his truck.

"Good thing that boy has no interest in Joni," Tom said with a big grin. "Otherwise he might've had to forgo his dinner to get there in time."

"I know," Loretta said with a smile. "Isn't it wonderful?"

EVERYONE ARRIVING for the party met in the room they used on Sunday morning. When Mary and Joni walked in, there were already more than a dozen people present. Though normally shy, Mary felt an obligation to introduce Joni, and they both found themselves talking to several of the men.

However, neither Donald nor Sam was present.

That was a good thing, Joni hurriedly assured herself. Of course, not for Mary. Mary seemed to have fallen for Donald and wanted to see him again.

At least Donald seemed open to the idea of dating. Mary was lucky.

Billy, the man she'd met at the pizza parlor, walked in. When he saw Joni, he came over at once.

"Hey, Joni, how are you?" he greeted her, a smile on his face. "Where's Sam?"

Joni seized the opportunity to demonstrate her singleness. "Sam? I wouldn't know."

Brad, a well-built cowboy who had a cocky grin, moved a little closer. "I heard you and Sam were an item."

Joni smiled. She wasn't impressed with him. He would be terrible father material. But as a way to establish her availability, he was perfect. "No, not at all. Actually I'm friends with his sister. So he's helped me out occasionally."

Brad wasn't buying her story yet. "Sam's not one to pass up a pretty face."

"Thank you for the compliment. But I think you've forgotten that Sam just got divorced. Sometimes it takes a man a while to be interested again."

Several people nodded agreement, and Brad stepped a little closer. "How about I help you stay warm while we're riding in the hay?" he offered.

Joni wasn't ready to move quite that fast. "I brought a blanket to keep me warm. But I wouldn't mind the company."

Brad grinned and offered her his arm. "My pleasure. Have you ever been on a hayride before?"

Joni laid her hand on his arm, but she didn't feel anything. Why should she? Only Sam seemed to evoke that response from her.

"Why, no, they don't have a lot of hayrides in Chicago. Will you show me what I'm supposed to do?" She batted her lashes as she smiled.

"Oh, darlin', before we get back tonight, you're

going to learn a lot,'' he assured her amid the laughter of those around him.

"Don't forget, Brad,'' one man called out, "this is a *church* social. You gotta behave yourself.''

Brad smirked at his friend and said nothing, but Joni knew the man had no intention of behaving.

But she was a big girl. She could take care of herself.

When they reached the parking lot, she saw the large flatbed trailer covered with a mound of fresh hay. The horses attached to it were Clydesdales. "Oh, I want to look at the horses. They're magnificent,'' she exclaimed.

"Sure thing,'' Brad agreed, leading her to them. "They're friendly. Go ahead, pet them.''

She rubbed the velvety nose of the closest one, telling him how pretty he was. Before she moved to the others, Mary called out to her.

"Come on, Joni. They're going to help us up.''

She returned to her friend's side, closely followed by Brad. One of the men was already up on the trailer, and they had placed a small stepladder next to it. Mary climbed to its top step and took the man's hand. Joni followed her as Mary settled in the hay on the blanket she'd brought.

Brad put an arm around Joni. "You don't need to let someone else help you up. I'll do it.''

She didn't want to be too encouraging. "That's all right.'' She stepped to the ladder. The man beside it took her arm as she climbed to the top step. Then the man on top reached down for her hand. As he pulled her, and her blanket, to the top of the trailer, a truck screeched to a halt in the parking lot.

Chapter Fourteen

"Isn't that Joni?" Donald said, peering through the windshield as Sam brought his truck to a stop.

He threw the truck into Park and scrambled out. "Come on, before they leave us behind."

In all, almost twenty-five people were gathered for the caroling, and Sam and Donald were the last ones to climb aboard. They discovered their quarries surrounded by a number of men known to be unattached.

"Make room," Sam calmly ordered. "I need to share Joni's blanket because I forgot my own."

Brad didn't move. "Sorry. Joni offered to share with me."

Sam glared at Joni, sitting next to Brad.

While she didn't welcome him with a big smile, she did lift a corner of the blanket. "I think there's enough for three of us."

Sam insinuated himself in a space on the other side of her, unhappy that Brad was there. But at least he was next to her, too.

"I didn't know you'd decided to come," he whispered in her ear as the horses started their stately gait. The trailer creaked along behind them.

"Mary wanted me to come with her," she returned before answering a question Brad had asked.

Before there was more conversation, the leader of the group began passing out music for their caroling.

"Did everyone bring a flashlight? I have a couple of spares available if you didn't."

Joni pulled a flashlight out of her purse. Mary had warned her to bring one. "Did either of you bring—" Joni began, then stopped. The two men were busy glaring at each other and didn't seem to care about the music.

"What are you doing here, Sam?" Brad demanded in a low growl. "I heard you were too heartbroken about your divorce to be interested in the social scene."

"Who told you that?" Sam growled back.

Brad nodded his head in Joni's direction and she chewed her bottom lip at Sam's angry stare.

"Brad asked if you and I were dating. I thought I should explain why we weren't."

"After all, you don't usually pass up a pretty lady," Brad added.

"Just because I'm not ready for—for a commitment doesn't mean I don't enjoy a lady's company."

"Most ladies like to know there's a future in a relationship," Brad said.

"Then why would they ever go out with you?" Sam demanded.

Feeling she was sitting in the center of a war zone,

Joni wrapped her blanket around her and scooted several feet away, bumping into Donald.

"Hey!" Sam protested.

"Where are you going?" Brad demanded.

"Away from you two. I don't sense a lot of Christmas spirit between you." She smiled at Donald. "Hi. How are you? Mary said you've been busy with a lot of customers."

"Mary said that? Is she angry with me?"

"Why don't you go ask her?" Sam suggested, shifting closer to Joni again.

"Sam!" Joni protested.

What was wrong with her? She wasn't interested in Donald, was she? She hadn't acted upset last Saturday when Donald had devoted himself to Mary.

Donald looked longingly at Mary but made no move to get closer.

"You know," Joni said softly, "Mary came with me. Not any of those men. And she was hoping to see you."

"But there's no room over there."

Sam gave a disgusted sigh.

Joni patted the vet's arm. "After we stop to carol at the first house, maybe you'll have a chance to sit beside her when we get back on the trailer."

Since Brad had followed Joni to sit beside her too, the three men surrounded her. Sam hoped she was happy. But she'd encouraged Brad, so it was her fault he was there. And she's the one who moved to Donald's side.

So their unmatched foursome was her fault.

After all, he was only there to protect her.

JONI DECIDED MEN were crazy.

When they reached the first ranch house near town, they all climbed down from the truck and formed a loose semicircle in the front yard. Sam and Brad each maintained their positions, beside her.

Donald, however, seemed to recognize his opportunity. He moved through the crowd until he reached Mary's side. Her welcoming smile must have convinced him she was glad to see him. His arm went around her and they stared into each other's eyes.

Joni was happy for them. She was glad that at least one romance was going well. Because hers certainly wasn't.

She glared over her shoulder at Sam. What was the man trying to do? It had been his idea that she show interest in another man. He wanted off the hook. He'd told her time and time again that he wasn't interested in a future with her. So why was he clinging to her now?

They began to sing "Joy to the World." Joni joined in the singing, trying to remember why she was here tonight, in addition to making people believe she and Sam weren't dating. She was here to celebrate Christmas with her neighbors, to sing Christmas carols as a gift to others.

"Think they've got the hang of it?" Sam asked, a half smile on his lips, nodding in Donald and Mary's direction.

She looked at him, then away. "Yes, I think so. At least Donald knows what he wants."

"Do you?"

His whispered question shook her. Of course she did. But she also knew it was impossible. She turned to Brad, determined to shut Sam out of her life. "You have a beautiful voice."

"Thank you. I'll serenade you anytime you want."

She smiled but said nothing. The man responded to mild encouragement like a love-starved old maid. When they finished the song, the leader announced their next song would be "Silent Night," Joni's favorite Christmas carol.

It was easy to believe in a silent night, long ago, especially away from the busy, noisy city streets of Chicago.

Wrapped up in the music, she scarcely noticed when Sam's arm went around her shoulders. His baritone voice joined with hers and, for Joni, the choir became one of two people, her and Sam.

"Look up at the stars," he whispered in her ear.

She did as he said, stunned by the beauty of the night. It was hard to believe that twenty-four hours ago, they'd been trapped by a blizzard. Now, shiny stars numbered in the millions, it seemed, twinkling in the crisp, cold air.

Sam chuckled. "Mom used to tell us those were God's Christmas tree lights."

"And you believed her?" Joni asked, her voice husky.

"Yeah, until I noticed they were still there a month later." He tightened his arm around her.

The carolers began "O Holy Night" and they joined in.

As she lifted her voice in song, Joni didn't think she'd ever experienced such a wonderful celebration of Christmas. She wished Brady were here to experience it.

As if he read her mind, Sam said, "Too bad Brady isn't here to see it. Kids need to know there's more to Christmas than Santa Claus."

A round of applause interrupted them, letting them know the caroling was over for this house, and the other singers were moving back to the wagon.

Joni told herself she was glad they were interrupted. It was too easy to fall under Sam's spell.

She hurried over to the driver of the large horses. "May I share the seat with you so I can see how you drive the horses?"

He stared at her. "Well, I reckon, if you're sure you want to. Seems to me there's lots of fellows who would be more interesting company."

She beamed at him. "Not at all. I can't wait."

He led her to the trailer and showed her how to reach the driver's seat. By the time Sam reached the wagon, she was already in place.

Sam, however, wasn't so easily dismissed. "Hey, Bill, would you let me drive the team for a while?"

"Ain't you got better things to do?" Bill asked, but there was a smile on his face.

"Nope."

"Well, come on. You can drive to the next stop."

Before Joni could protest, Bill climbed onto the hay, leaving his seat for Sam.

When he settled down beside her, she protested. "What are you doing? How are you going to convince everyone that we're not dating if you stay at my side?"

"I thought you rejected that plan," he said mildly, gathering the reins.

"Not exactly," she said with a shake of her head. "But it wasn't working. I thought if I came to the party without you, people would realize—and it would've worked, too, if you hadn't acted like Brad was trespassing!" she snapped.

"He's a dangerous flirt."

"Another one?" she asked incredulously. "This county must be full of them."

"Just Steve and Brad. You seem to attract them."

"I must, since you're included in that group."

"Hey! I'm not a flirt."

"Ready to start!" someone shouted and Sam gathered the reins, slapping the horses on their backs.

Joni actually did enjoy watching Sam handle the reins. As with his truck, he seemed in complete control of the majestic animals. And the jingle bells attached to the harnesses rang through the night air, reminding her of childhood dreams of Santa.

"Brady would love the bells."

"Yeah, he would. He'd probably want to decorate Cookie with bells."

They drove in silence, and Joni felt isolated with

the man she loved. In the darkness of the cold night, lit by a full moon and the twinkling stars, she could almost pretend her problems were solved. That Sam loved her as she loved him, and that he wanted to be a family with her and Brady.

Almost.

Desperate for something to distract her from her dangerous thoughts, she studied his large hands as they managed the reins.

"Is it difficult?" she asked.

"Managing the horses? Not these. They're well trained." He looked at her. "Want to try?"

"Would it be all right?" she asked, thrilled at the idea.

"Sure. Here, hold them like this," he said, offering the reins to her. As she tried to imitate his grasp, he looped his arm around her, pulling her against him.

"What are you doing?"

"Helping you, that's all." Since his right hand, the one that had snaked around her, grasped her hand and helped her hold the reins, she couldn't dispute his claim.

"You can feel them pulling the load," she exclaimed, beaming at Sam.

He dropped a kiss on her lips.

"Hey, no kissing while you're driving," someone called amid a burst of laughter.

Joni was horrified. "Sam, my plan is never going to work if you keep doing things like that."

"And your plan is what?"

"The same as yours. To show people we're not a

couple. You're the one who thought it was so important."

"I know. But I've been thinking."

She held her breath. Had he decided he was interested in a future with her and Brady?

"What?"

"You're widowed. I'm divorced. We're both used
to, uh, certain things. I'm not ready for a commitment
yet, but I think we should, uh, explore the possibili-
ties. I mean, who knows what the future will bring?"

Joni's heart ached and she slapped the reins back
into his hands, inadvertently signaling the horses to
go faster.

"Oh!" she gasped, grabbing the seat as the horses
picked up their pace.

Sam, with his arm still around her, eased back on
the reins, settling the horses into their steady gait.

As soon as he'd done so, Joni tried to duck beneath
his arm, so she wasn't in his embrace any longer.

He lifted his arm, making her escape easier.

"Hey, what's going on up there?" someone called.

"Amateur driver," Sam shouted back. He drove
silently for several minutes before he looked at her
again.

Joni stared straight ahead.

"Did I upset you?"

"Yes."

"I'm trying to be honest, Joni. You know I'm attracted to you. Physically we're well suited. I'm just
suggesting we let our relationship follow its natural

path. Who knows, we may not be physically compatible.''

She almost burst into laughter. And would have if her heart hadn't hurt so much. ''I don't think there's much hope of that.''

''Maybe not. But it wouldn't hurt anything. We'd be taking our relationship to the next level. It happens every day.''

''We're not even dating, Sam,'' Joni said pointedly. ''That's what I was trying to prove tonight.''

''But we both know that's not true, Joni. We're connected, even if we're not following the normal pattern of two people who are interested in each other. You just agreed that we share an attraction.''

''You're right, I can't deny that,'' she agreed in a low voice.

Sam pulled the horses to a stop, and she panicked, afraid of what he might do. Her control was fragile.

''Easy. We're at the next house,'' he said in a low voice.

He swung down from the seat on the opposite side of the trailer from where the others were unloading and held up his arms to Joni. After hesitating, she climbed down. Halfway, he pulled her into his arms. Before she could protest, his mouth covered hers, and she experienced the blankness she had before as her senses went into overdrive.

Her arms circled his neck, and the cold night air heated up. His hands slid beneath her coat, stroking her back. One hand sank to cup her bottom, pulling her tighter against him. She was left in no doubt that he was aroused.

Which only increased her need.

He lifted his lips and reslanted them to go deeper, to bring them closer. She did her best to accommodate him.

"Hey!" Brad shouted.

She and Sam broke apart to discover the cowboy staring at them.

"Sorry," Joni began.

Sam was less diplomatic. "Mind your own business, Brad. Joni and I had some private discussion to take care of."

"Yeah, I saw what kind of discussing you were doing. What about your ex-wife?"

"What about her?" Sam challenged, taking a step forward.

Joni took the opportunity to slip around him and head for the group getting ready to sing. She only hoped the two men would be sensible.

Because she couldn't make sense out of anything right now.

SAM REMAINED BY HER SIDE the rest of the evening. As their voices blended in Christmas carols, his warmth wrapped her in a fantasy that promised as much hope and love as the holiday itself.

On the hay wagon, he held her close, stealing the occasional kiss. There was no conversation. Sam seemed to realize she needed time to think.

And the evening was as convincing as he was. In

the pure night air, it was easy to believe that tomorrow would be as magical, as wonderful as being held in Sam's arms.

Even the hay beneath them reminded her of that moment in the barn, with Sam beside her, his hands caressing her, driving her to heights she'd never reached before. She didn't think she'd ever smell the scent of hay without thinking of Sam.

Sam leaned even closer. "You thinking?"

She nodded but didn't speak. His words, however, pushed her to consider the most serious part of his plan.

Brady.

As much as she loved Sam, and that love appeared to be growing every day, she loved her son more. And Brady was her responsibility. She had to think how her and Sam's relationship would affect her little boy.

If Sam were committed to family, to the three of them, she'd have no hesitation at all. He'd be the perfect father for Brady. And Brady would be ecstatic.

But his offer to date, to explore their attraction, to make love wasn't the same thing. And it could lead Brady to believe that it was.

And break his heart.

SAM HELD JONI against him in the dark, loving the warmth of her that spread through him. He wanted to try to persuade her to let them grow closer. But he wanted her to come to him willingly, not because he'd overwhelmed her.

He still had difficulty with the thought of remarrying, but he also had difficulty with the thought of walking away. He needed time, but he also needed Joni.

He figured in six months he would have worked out his problems. By then, he and Joni would have shared a lot of intimacy, an idea that made his heart beat faster. And he and Brady would be even better friends.

A lot of couples anticipated their wedding vows. Dusty and Lisa had. Of course they were engaged, but that didn't make that much difference, did it?

An uneasiness filled him. Maybe he was lying to himself, being unfair to Joni. He'd told Dusty he should go ahead and marry Lisa. Sam snuggled a little closer to Joni, as if afraid she'd be torn from his arms. Damn it, he needed her!

But he'd have to wait for her to decide. He wasn't going to force her into a corner. He couldn't when he—he closed his eyes. He panicked as he realized he'd been about to admit to loving her. No. He cared about her. That was it. He cared about her.

And that was the first step to loving her, of course. Which made him feel good. When he was ready for commitment again, it would be to Joni. But the timing was wrong.

Damn it, the timing was wrong.

When the hayride ended, Sam led Joni to his truck, still holding her close, wrapped in the magic of their warmth. Neither spoke on the short drive to her house.

Sam eyed its silent emptiness with appreciation. He loved Brady, but he didn't need the boy here tonight.

By the time he'd gotten out of the truck and reached Joni's side, she was already standing in the snow. He took her arm and hurried her up the sidewalk.

Tonight he was going to satisfy the hunger that filled him whenever he touched this woman.

As they reached the porch, he couldn't wait. Pulling her into his arms, he kissed her with all the desire that filled him.

And she responded.

Anticipation built and he took the keys from her hand. "Come on, sweetheart, let's go inside," he suggested, longing for the comfort of bed...and a naked Joni.

She pulled away from him and took her keys back into her grasp. Then she looked up at him.

"No."

Chapter Fifteen

"No?" Sam replied, pain filling the one word.

Joni stood rigid, avoiding his stare. "No," she repeated. "I'm—I'm not ready."

Sam eased his hold on her, and tilted up her chin. "Damn, sweetheart, if either of us were any more ready, we'd be naked in the snow."

She bowed her head, resting her forehead against his broad chest. "I have to think, Sam. And I can't do that around you."

"It doesn't require any thought, sweetheart. Just let your body do the talking. I'll take care of you."

"There's too much involved. I—I have to think of Brady. I want to be sure I'm doing the right thing." She pulled away from him. "I have to go in."

He was frustrated. She didn't have to look at him to know that fact. She recognized it in herself. But she had to be sure.

As she walked to the door, he finally spoke. "Fine. You know where to find me if you change your mind."

She slipped inside before she could change her

mind right then. And leaned against the door until she heard the roar of his big truck disappearing down the road.

Then she quickly undressed and got into bed, curling into a little ball of indecision. What was she going to do? She wanted to make love with Sam. But she wanted their union, their loving, to be something to celebrate, something on which to build a future.

She had a lot of thinking to do.

The next several days, she could scarcely function. Brady frequently complained about his mom's distraction.

"Mom, are you listening?"

"Yes, dear," she muttered, cleaning the kitchen after breakfast on Tuesday.

"What are we gonna get Sam for Christmas?"

Her cheeks flamed. She knew what Sam wanted.

"We're going to get him a present, aren't we?"

Yesterday, they had shopped for presents for Peter and Katie. And in the afternoon, they'd baked cookies to fix a plate for Marty and Paul. Tomorrow, she intended to bake a special Christmas cake for Tom and Loretta.

But Sam?

"I—I don't know. I guess we can go shopping. Or we could give him a plate of cookies." Her fingers were shaking. The man was driving her crazy.

"I don't want to give him cookies. I want to buy him something," Brady said, his brow furrowed in thought.

"How about a nice pair of leather gloves. He has

a pair to work in, but I don't think he has a pair to wear to church.''

That was the least personal gift she could think of that Sam might use.

''How do we know if they'll fit?''

''We'll call Loretta and ask her. She'll keep the secret,'' Joni assured her son.

''Okay. But tell her not to tell Sam.''

Relieved that they'd settled on something so easily, Joni reached for the phone.

Once she'd explained her reason for calling, Loretta not only told her what size but where she should shop for the gloves.

''Thanks, Loretta.''

''We've missed the two of you,'' Loretta said as Joni prepared to hang up.

Joni cleared her throat, trying to ease the tightness she felt there. ''Um, we enjoyed staying with you. How are you managing?''

''Okay, though cooking is definitely difficult.''

''May Brady and I come see you tomorrow afternoon? We're going to make a special cake for you, so you won't have to worry about having something for Christmas.''

''Joni, you are the sweetest person. Plan on staying for dinner.''

''No, we can't, Loretta, but thanks for asking. We'll come about two o'clock. Have to go, thanks for the advice,'' she added before hanging up the receiver.

"You didn't tell her not to tell Sam," Brady said urgently, his gaze full of concern.

"Sweetie, Loretta knows it's a gift. She won't tell Sam." Joni hoped she wouldn't mention their going to the ranch, either. She needed to avoid Sam.

LATER THAT AFTERNOON Joni and Brady bundled up and headed for the store Loretta had recommended. Joni hadn't visited it before, because she hadn't had all that much time for shopping.

Brady had no interest in looking around. He immediately went to the gloves section.

"Well, howdy, young man. Can I help you?" an old man asked.

"Yes, I need to buy gloves."

"These are men's gloves. The ones for you—"

"No, it's a gift. For a man."

"Ah, buying your daddy a Christmas present?" the man asked with a smile.

Joni cringed.

"No, he's not my daddy. But I wish he was." Brady turned heart-filled eyes to Joni.

She ignored his blatant hint. "Choose which gloves you think he'll like, Brady."

Brady began looking at the several styles and colors, but he seemed unable to make a decision.

"Maybe if you tell me something about him, I can help you," the man said.

Joni sucked in a deep breath.

"Sam's a cowboy," Brady began, "but we're buying gloves for him to wear to church."

"Sam? Sam Crawford?"

"Yeah. Do you know him?"

"I sure do. And I know just what he'd like." The man handed a pair of black leather gloves to Brady, then smiled at Joni. "Sam's a good man."

She didn't need to be told that. She needed to avoid adding to the rumors. "We're friends. He's—he's been very helpful."

"I heard. You must be Joni Evans."

The man extended his hand, and Joni shook it, but she wished she'd never entered the store.

"I like these, Mom. Can we buy them for Sam?"

"Yes, of course, you can give them to Sam." She looked at the man who had introduced himself as the owner of the store when they shook hands. "Brady wanted to buy Sam a present because he considers him a friend."

"He let me name one of his horses," Brady said, his little chest puffed out with pride.

"And what name did you give it?" the man asked as he wrapped the gloves in tissue and put them in a box.

"Christmas Cookie, 'cause he's the color of cookie dough."

The man chuckled. "Good choice." He told Joni the amount she owed and rang up the sale after she'd paid him.

"If these don't fit Sam, you tell him to bring them back to me and I'll fix him up," he said as Joni took Brady's hand and headed for the door.

It was a nice store, but she wouldn't be back anytime soon.

JONI STARED AT HER IMAGE in the bathroom mirror. She was going to have to make a decision. Otherwise she'd look like an old hag and Sam wouldn't be interested.

The dark circles under her eyes were the result of not sleeping again last night. Because she wanted Sam. How could she not want him? She loved him with all her heart. She ached for him.

But she feared putting Brady's heart at risk.

Her only hope was that Sam would come to need her as much as she needed him. Did men grow dependent when they were intimate with someone, like women did?

She didn't have the answer to that question, but she did know that she couldn't continue as she had.

With Brady's help, she carefully made the cake for Loretta and Tom. It was in the shape of a Christmas tree, and they spread green icing on it, adding M&M's for Christmas ornaments.

"Grandpa and Grandma are going to love this cake!" Brady exclaimed.

"I'm sure they will," Joni said. She'd bought a pretty Christmas platter as part of the gift.

"When are we going?"

"I told Loretta we'd be there about two."

"Then are we going to Peter's house to deliver his and Katie's presents?"

"I suppose we might as well. But, Brady, they may

not have presents for you, so don't get your feelings hurt, or expect anything.''

Brady grinned at his mother but said nothing. She suspected he and Peter had already discussed the present situation, but she couldn't be sure.

The doorbell rang and Joni's heart double-clutched. Then she calmed herself. It wouldn't be Sam. After all, it was the middle of the day and he'd be working outdoors.

But she didn't realize how much she'd hoped it was him until she opened the door and said hello to the postman. Depression filled her.

''Got a big package for Joni and Brady Evans,'' the man announced cheerfully. ''Here, let me set it inside for you. It's kind of heavy.''

''Thank you,'' Joni said, then asked him to wait. She returned with a plastic bag of Christmas cookies.

''Why, thank you. Those are my favorites. Merry Christmas.''

After the door closed, she turned to her son. ''Look, Brady, a package from Grandma and Grandpa Evans. Let's open it.''

''Okay,'' Brady said, no excitement in his voice, ''but we have to hurry 'cause we're going out to the ranch.''

The boxes inside the large one were individually wrapped. She let Brady choose one to open early. He picked the largest, discovering a toy gas station with cars.

He frowned. ''Cowboys don't work at gas stations.''

"Yes, but cowboys drive cars and trucks and go to gas stations."

"That's true. Me and Peter can pretend we're hauling hay, or picking up a new horse, and we have to stop and buy gas."

"Right." In Brady's head, everything centered around cowboys now. And she knew whom to thank for that fascination.

"Is it time to go to the ranch? I want to tell Sam about my gas station."

"We have to eat lunch first."

"Grandma will have something to eat. She won't mind."

Joni sighed. "Brady, she might, but it's impolite to invite yourself to a meal. And you must remember she's not your grandmother."

Brady scowled and kicked the big box.

"Put the rest of the presents under the tree while I fix us some lunch."

She escaped to the kitchen, but she couldn't escape her thoughts. Their lives seemed to revolve around Sam Crawford, like a moon circling a planet. She stared into space, thinking of Sam, until Brady came to the kitchen.

"Where's lunch?"

SAM CAME IN TO LUNCH a frustrated man. He couldn't forget Friday night and the feel of Joni in his arms. He couldn't forget her answer.

She'd ask for time.

Hell, how much time did she need?

She'd had five days. He'd counted every one. Every lonely one.

He missed touching her, talking to her, seeing her.

Damn it, he missed Brady, too.

"Hurry and get washed up, Sam," Loretta called. "I'm going to need some help."

His mother was doing fairly well. She'd gone back to the doctor Monday and had her wrist X-rayed. He'd put on a small cast, that left her fingers free. But some things were still difficult for her.

When he came into the kitchen, his father was helping her put food on the table.

"Looks good," he remembered to say, for his mother's sake.

"*Humph!* The way you've been eating, you'd think I've forgotten how to cook," Loretta complained.

Sam felt his cheeks redden. Okay, so he'd been off his feed a little. There was no need to make a big deal about it.

"Hasn't been sleeping well, either," Tom added.

"How do you know?" Sam demanded. "I haven't bothered you."

"Nope. But you've got such big bags beneath your eyes, I thought maybe you'd packed all your belongings and was leaving." Tom grinned, daring his son to contradict him.

"Cute, Dad, real cute," he returned in disgust. It wasn't nice to make fun of his discomfort.

He only hoped they didn't know what was going on. Because if they heard what he had in mind, he figured they'd be angry with him. They treated Joni as if she were a daughter.

He filled his plate, then pushed the food around with his fork, his mind turning back to Joni and whether or not she'd ever speak to him again.

"Sam! Eat! With everyone coming this afternoon, I want you to help me clean the kitchen before you go back to work."

He frowned. "Everyone? What are you talking about?"

"Marty and the children are coming out this afternoon to bring some presents. And Joni and Brady are bringing us a Christmas cake."

"Joni and Bra—Joni's coming here?" he asked, leaping to his feet.

"Yes, at two," Loretta said calmly, staring at her son. "Sit down and eat your lunch."

Sam sat down, his mind racing. Joni was coming to the ranch. She must have made a decision. She wouldn't come if she didn't want to see him, would she?

"Did she ask about me?"

"No, dear, she didn't. Well, I take that back. There was one question but—"

"What? What did she ask?"

"Brady had a question about your Christmas present."

His eyebrows almost met in the center of his face, he frowned so fiercely. That wasn't the answer he wanted. He wanted Joni to ask about him. To—

"You do have a present for Brady, don't you?"

Tom asked. "Your mother and I found a sheepskin coat just like yours. We thought that would make him happy."

"Yeah." In fact, he had two presents for Brady. A plastic horse with all the gear he could put on and take off. Sam figured Brady could learn about horses with it. And a cowboy hat, a real Stetson. Just like his.

They were going to look like twins.

Or father and son.

Not what he'd offered Joni. Not yet.

"Do you have a present for Joni?" Loretta asked.

He nodded and said nothing else. He'd visited the only jewelry store in town on Monday and bought a diamond-and-ruby drop necklace for her.

He hoped she didn't throw it back in his face.

"Well, eat up. We need to get the kitchen straightened."

Sam followed his mother's orders. When they finished cleaning the kitchen, it was only one-thirty.

His father kissed his mother's cheek, picked up his hat and headed for the door.

"You coming, son?"

"Uh, I need to, uh, there's something, uh, I think I'll wait to say hello to Brady."

Tom grinned and nodded. "Good idea. Say hello for me, too."

MARTY AND THE KIDS arrived first. "Sam, what are you doing in the house? I thought you'd be working."

"Uh, I wanted to see you and the kids," he muttered, bending to kiss her cheek.

"How sweet of you," she said in disbelieving tones and then looked at her mother.

Sam saw Loretta's quick shake of the head, indicating Marty shouldn't ask any more questions. That was okay with him, as long as his mother didn't say anything.

"Hi, Uncle Sam," Peter said, catching his hand. "We've got presents in the car."

"Terrific. Want me to carry them in?"

"Yeah, and I'll help. I'll show you which ones 'cause we have things for Brady and his mom, too."

Sam looked at his mother. "You haven't told them?"

"Why, no, I forgot to mention that Brady and Joni are coming by this afternoon."

Marty smiled. "Oh, that explains—"

"She's bringing us a Christmas cake," Loretta hurriedly added, interrupting Marty's words.

Marty continued to grin, but she didn't say anything embarrassing. "Then, Peter, you and Uncle Sam can bring in all the presents. You can give Brady his present when he and his mom arrive."

Sam grabbed his nephew's hand and headed outside, leaving the two women whispering.

"I've missed Brady. We're like brothers," Peter said.

"Yeah, he's a great friend."

"Mommy said even if you and Joni got married,

he wouldn't be my brother. But wouldn't he, kind of?''

''He—he'd be your cousin. That's almost a brother.''

''Great!'' Peter exclaimed as Sam opened the door to the car.

''Peter, Joni and I aren't— I mean, she's a friend.''

''Oh.''

They heard the sound of an engine coming closer.

''I bet that's Brady!'' Peter shouted.

Sam saw the car in the distance. Yeah, that would be Joni. His ''friend'' was certainly making his heart race almost as fast as her car. After five days, he was finally going to see Joni Evans, his friend.

And he hoped she'd changed her answer to yes.

JONI KNEW she was in trouble the moment she saw Sam standing beside Marty's car.

''Look, Mom, Peter's here. He's with Sam!'' Brady exclaimed, stretching as far as his seat belt would allow to see the ranch house.

Joni wanted to bury her head in the snow, close her eyes to avoid looking at him, or at least turn the car around.

She couldn't do any of those things.

''How nice,'' she said, trying to keep her voice from trembling.

She must not have been successful.

''Are you gonna cry?'' Brady asked in concern.

''Of course not. Why would I cry?''

"I don't know, but you've been acting kind of funny lately."

How sad when she can't even hide her worries from her four-year-old. She pressed her lips firmly together, determined not to let Sam know how his intentions affected her.

She stopped the car beside Marty's and shut off the engine. Brady immediately undid his seat belt and jumped out of the car, shouting Peter's name.

While Brady moved toward Peter, Sam was coming in the opposite direction. Toward her.

She got out of the car, her knees knocking. Hunger consumed her. She'd missed him so much. Just to see him brought more joy than she'd experienced in a while.

Sam had no intention of settling for a look.

Without a word, he pulled her into his embrace, his lips covering hers, his hands pressing her against him.

Oh, boy, she was in trouble.

Chapter Sixteen

Somewhere during that kiss, that devastating, mind-blowing kiss, Joni gave up the fight.

When Sam finally lifted his mouth from hers, he growled, "The answer had better be yes."

All she could do was nod.

His lips joined hers again.

"You two ever coming in?" Loretta called from the door.

"That wouldn't be my first choice," Sam whispered in Joni's ear after he released her lips.

She closed her eyes and leaned against him. "We have to go in. They're watching us."

He lifted her face and touched foreheads with her. "Okay, but don't move more than a foot from me. I've missed you."

Without waiting for her agreement, he took her hand and led her to the house.

Loretta and Marty hugged her, but Sam didn't move away. He stood patiently, waiting for her to turn her attention back to him. She was afraid to do so.

She wasn't sure she could keep from touching him, kissing him, asking him to hold her.

"Mom, where's the cake? Didn't you bring it in?" Brady asked anxiously.

"Oh, sorry, I forgot," she replied, turning back toward the door.

"She was distracted," Marty said with a grin.

Sam glared at his sister, then turned to Joni. "I'll get it. You stay here where it's warm."

Joni watched him leave until the door closed behind him. Then, when she faced the other two women, she found them watching her with smiles on their faces. "I'm—I'm afraid he might drop it. The snow is icy today."

"He'll be careful," Loretta assured her. "It's so good to see the two of you. Did you find Sam's present at the store I suggested?"

"Yes. Uh, Brady, you and Peter should go help Sam. You can bring in all the presents we brought." She shrugged her shoulders. "I don't know why I didn't think of that."

"Like I said, you were distracted," Marty repeated, this time with a laugh.

Joni's cheeks flamed. Even if his family didn't know that Sam wasn't ready to consider marriage, she did.

When Sam and the two boys came back in, Joni rushed to take the platter of cookies from Brady. He was holding it at a precarious angle and she feared the carefully decorated cookies would splatter all over the kitchen floor.

"Look at this, Mom," Sam said, holding the Christmas cake out for his mother to see. "Joni did a great job, didn't she?"

"And Brady," Joni hurriedly added. "He did more of the decorating."

Loretta exclaimed over the cake, setting it in the center of the table. "I'm putting it here so Tom can see it before we cut it. This will be the perfect touch to Christmas dinner. You and Brady will come, won't you?"

"Oh, no, I—"

Before Joni could complete her refusal, Sam's arm went around her shoulder and he said, "They'll be here."

Brady and Peter whooped and hollered until Marty suggested they go play in the den. "Shall we make them save their presents to each other until then?"

Joni was uncomfortable. Marty and Loretta acted as if she and her son were about to become family members. But they were wrong. "I— Whatever you think."

"Sit down," Loretta urged. "I'll make us some tea. Sam, are you going to help your father work?"

Indecision, surprising in Sam, was on his face. Before he could answer, however, the boys came rushing back into the kitchen.

"Mama, can Brady come to my house? And spend the night?"

Joni started to protest, but Sam grabbed her hand and squeezed.

"I think that's a lovely idea," Marty replied with

a smile. "Would you mind, Joni? Maybe it would give you a chance to do some last-minute things, and the boys would have such fun."

"But, Marty, tomorrow is Christmas Eve. I'm sure you have lots to do."

"Not at all. Besides, I have Paul to help me. Please?"

Brady, of course, stared at his mother, on tenterhooks for permission.

Feeling the inevitability, Joni nodded. "Of course he can, if you're sure."

"I'm sure. We'll follow you back to your house and he can pack an overnight bag."

"Well, I'm going back to work. Uh, Joni, will you walk me outside?" Sam said.

His mother and sister pretended his request was normal, but Joni knew better. She didn't turn him down, however. She knew it was an excuse for him to kiss her.

As soon as they were on the porch, and the door closed, he pulled her into his arms and kissed her, his lips conveying his desires quite clearly.

When he lifted his mouth, he muttered, "I'll be there as soon as I can get away."

Then he strode off toward the barn, his hat pulled low on his forehead, determination in his every step.

JONI WAS A NERVOUS WRECK.

Brady had left with Marty and her children several hours ago. Joni had tidied the house, as if Sam would notice, and then tried to relax in a hot bubble bath.

But she couldn't.

She'd fixed a light supper, in case Sam was hungry.

She'd turned on the Christmas tree lights so the house would look festive.

She'd put on a red dress.

There was nothing left to do but pace the floor and worry. What if their lovemaking fell short of expectations? She wanted Sam so badly, yet it had been a long time since she was with a man. In fact, she'd never been with a man she wanted as much as Sam.

The sound of his truck sent panic shooting through her. What if *he* didn't want her after tonight?

He banged on the door, impatience in every knock.

Joni froze, feeling as if she were poised on a cliff, about to jump off without a parachute.

"Joni?" he called.

If she didn't answer the door, he'd alert the entire neighborhood. She crossed the room and opened it.

As if he were a whirlwind, Sam blew into the house and scooped her up into his arms. His lips settled on hers, tasting and teasing, as if he were as starved as she. She struggled to be let down, not because she wanted to escape, but because she wanted to feel him with every inch of her body.

When he finally let her breathe again, his chest heaved with his own breathing. But he didn't let her walk away. His arms held her against him.

"I—I turned on the Christmas lights," she finally whispered, unable to think of anything to say. Her gaze remained fastened on his incredible lips, longing for more kisses.

"Very festive," he agreed. Then his lips took hers once more. As if she were coming home, she fit perfectly against him, willing him to come closer with every breath. All her nervous fears had disappeared. She was where she wanted, needed to be.

He broke off the kiss and leaned his forehead against hers. "These past few days have been awful. I missed you more than I thought possible."

"Me, too." She wasn't sure of the proper etiquette in this situation. "Have you eaten? I fixed a meal."

He blinked several times, then smiled. "That would be great. I didn't take time to eat at home."

She led the way into the kitchen and quickly set the supper on the table. When she would have sat down, however, she found Sam had a different idea of dinner. He pulled her into his lap. "What are you doing?" she shrieked, taken by surprise.

"Preparing to enjoy my meal. I don't want you too far away, so we'll share a chair." He picked up a fork and speared a piece of chicken, lifting it to her mouth.

After chewing, she said, "I cooked for you, not me." She took the fork away from him and fed him a bite.

"Mmm, good. But not as tasty as this." Then he kissed her.

He was right.

They continued to feed each other occasional bites, interspersed with heated kisses. After shoving off his coat, something they'd both forgotten, Joni began unbuttoning his shirt, delighting in touching his chest.

The heated flesh and rough hairs thrilled her as she rubbed her hand across it.

"Joni," he protested.

"You don't want me to touch you?" she asked, concerned.

"Baby, I love for you to touch me, but I can't hold out much longer. And I want to do a lot of touching, too, before I lose control," he finished with a groan as she ran her fingertips over one of his nipples.

He abruptly stood, with her in his arms, and headed for the bedroom.

After several long, deep kisses when he reached her bed, he whispered, "This is a beautiful dress, Joni, but I've dreamed of seeing you without anything. Mind if we get a little more comfortable?"

Her answer was to push his shirt off his shoulders. She wanted to see him, too. She stroked his muscular chest, then slid her arms around his neck as he stood her on the floor.

"Hey, no fair," he protested, but he was grinning. He lowered the zipper on her dress and it pooled on the floor with his help.

The sudden urge to cover herself was chased away by the excitement in Sam's eyes. "Nice underwear," he teased. She'd chosen red lace to match her dress. "I like my Christmas present."

"I'm glad," she whispered. "But you're overdressed."

He pulled his boots off. As soon as he stood, Joni reached for his belt. Between the two of them, they were naked on the bed in seconds. Joni went into Sam's arms without hesitation.

She loved this man, more than she'd ever loved anyone. She wanted nothing more than to be with him. His hands touched every part of her, memorizing her, teasing her...loving her.

And she returned the favor. His strength, his passion, his gentleness, gave her incredible pleasure. She tried to give as much back. She'd never felt so safe, so loved...or so excited in her life. His broad shoulders were her anchor and she clung to them, dropped kisses on them, as Sam loved every inch of her.

"I'm crazy about this little freckle," Sam whispered, his lips touching her just above her left breast.

"I've—I've always thought it was ugly."

He reached up to kiss her lips again. "There's nothing ugly about you, sweetheart, inside or out."

Her heart swelled. Knowing she pleased this man filled her with incredible joy. And even greater anticipation. "Sam, I can't wait any longer. Please," she urged, pulling him closer.

"Me, neither," he whispered, positioning his large body over hers.

She arched up to meet him, eager for his total possession. "Yes, Sam," she intoned. Her hands trailed down his back to his buttocks, urging him even closer.

When he entered her, it was greater than anything Joni had even imagined, much less experienced. All her earlier doubts were swept away in a flood of intense feeling. Sam's body seemed made for hers, and his every move brought her closer to fulfillment. As she stepped over the brink he joined her, and together they found the ecstasy they'd sought.

Long afterward, she held him against her, reveling in the feel of his weight atop her.

"Joni," he finally whispered, "I'm afraid I'm crushing you. Did I hurt you? Are you all right?" He slid to one side, his arms drawing her with him.

Burying her face in his neck, afraid he'd see how much she loved him, she said, "I'm fine. Better than fine. I'm— It was— I can't—"

"Me, too," he said, then kissed her again. And again.

"Oh, Sam," she moaned, stunned by her hunger for him.

"Yeah." He chuckled, she supposed at her incoherent response. Then he pulled her into his arms and began to love her again.

THE ALARM WENT OFF at four-thirty. Joni struggled to awaken, wondering why she'd wanted to get up so early. Especially when she was so snug and warm.

"I have to go, sweetheart," Sam whispered in her ear.

Reminded of the events of the night, Joni's eyes popped open. Dawn hadn't even begun, but their night of lovemaking had ended.

Sam kissed her, then shoved back the cover and got up. She stared at his hard, muscular body in the shadowy room, remembering how she'd claimed it as hers during the night. Her cheeks flushed.

He slid on his underwear and jeans, then his shirt. Sitting down on the bed, he pulled on his boots. With every article of clothing he put on, depression filled Joni.

Turning around, he leaned across the bed for one more kiss. Her arms went around his neck, wanting to hold him there, to keep reality from intruding.

But she couldn't.

"Say hello to Brady for me," he said, smiling.

She stared at him, her heart aching. She couldn't tell Brady about their night. That had been her compromise. She'd promised herself she could explore her relationship with Sam if she could keep it from hurting Brady.

"Are you all right?" he whispered, frowning at her.

"Yes, I'm fine," she assured him. She even tried to give him a smile. It wasn't a great success.

"I'll call you," he said, then added a kiss before she heard his whispered goodbye.

She lay still and silent in the bed, listening to his booted footsteps, the shutting of the front door, the sound of his truck driving away.

She hadn't even realized silent tears were coursing down her face until she lay alone in the silent house.

In the last two minutes she realized she wasn't going to be able to juggle her emotions, to stop hungering for Sam until they could steal time alone. She wasn't going to be able to hide this part of her life from her son.

She was an all-or-nothing girl.

And she'd just made the biggest mistake of her life.

SAM TUGGED on the barbed wire fence, scowling at it. He'd just spent the entire night making love to a wonderful woman. He'd never imagined sex could be so fulfilling, so exciting. Even now, he wanted her.

But something was wrong.

It wasn't the sex.

It wasn't Joni.

He yanked on the reel of barbed wire, sending it rolling until it hit a fence post. Henry looked at him questioningly, but Sam said nothing to the ranch hand. How could he explain when he didn't understand himself what was wrong.

What was wrong?

He hadn't promised her anything. She knew that. It wasn't like Dusty when he'd promised to marry Lisa.

Sam had explained to Joni that he wasn't ready to commit to anything. Not yet. But he wanted to explore their relationship. To explore Joni, he added, a smile appearing from nowhere as he remembered their night together.

Maybe after a few months…one or two…he'd be ready to make a commitment. He should at least take a little time after his divorce to be sure. He didn't want to make a mistake again.

After Henry nailed the wire to the fence post and they moved to the next one, he said, "Heard you got yourself a new lady. A real looker."

Sam's chest ached. "She's a friend."

Henry laughed. "Yeah, I heard."

Sam started to protest again, but he didn't have the stomach for it.

"Got a little boy?"

"Yeah. You've probably seen Brady around the ranch. He's a great kid."

"It's tough being a stepfather."

"Yeah." And there was part of the problem. He wanted to be Brady's stepfather, his "daddy" for Christmas. He loved the little guy.

He tried to shut out the thought that came barreling after that one. But he couldn't.

He loved Joni.

Loved her to distraction. Wanted her in his arms constantly. Wanted to show her off, brag on his lady. Instead he'd made love to her all night and snuck away before dawn.

Like a thief.

He threw himself into his work, trying to avoid his thoughts, but he couldn't. He'd said he should wait to make a new commitment. He'd said he didn't know if he'd ever want to marry again.

He was wrong.

The picture of Joni coming down the aisle toward him had his heart racing, his libido working overtime. He already knew they were perfect in bed together. Perfect? Even that word didn't come close to describing the heaven he found in her arms.

How could he deny they were perfect for each other in every other way? She was a loving, generous woman. And he wanted to claim her as his own.

"Henry, I lied."

Nailing wire to the next post, Henry looked up, surprised. "About what?"

"About Joni. I'm going to marry her."

"Congratulations. Now pull that wire a little tighter." And he went on with his work as if Sam had said the weather was good.

Sam laughed out loud, joy filling him.

ALL DAY, Joni did what she had to do, but her heart wasn't in it. She was facing a difficult decision.

She couldn't stay here in Saddle. She couldn't carry on with Sam without others finding out. And then Brady would know. She wasn't even sure why she'd thought she could.

Though she'd enjoyed every minute of their love-making, wanted it to last forever, it hadn't. It wouldn't. Sam would come to her in the dark of the night and leave as he had this morning. Hiding what they shared.

As much as she loved him, she couldn't remain in Saddle.

How she hated the thought of telling Brady.

She decided Brady deserved Christmas without that pain. But could she face going out to the ranch and looking at Sam? And did he intend to see her before Christmas Day? She had her excuses ready. Brady would be with her.

And he'd stay with her until they left the town. There would be no more long nights of loving with Sam Crawford.

She wept.

That night, she and Brady sat beside the Christmas tree, admiring the bright lights, the ornaments they'd placed on it, even the candy canes.

They were drinking hot chocolate before she tucked Brady in.

"I wish Sam were here," he said with a sigh, snuggling against his mother.

"I thought you would want Peter."

"No, I want Sam. Peter's my friend. But Sam's— Sam's like a daddy."

She hugged her son tightly against her. "We're okay, just the two of us. Don't you think?"

"Sure, Mom, but it would be nice if Sam was here."

After a painful silence, Joni said, "Sometimes we can't have what we want. I didn't want your real daddy to die, but things happen."

"Were you sad?"

"Of course I was, Brady. Your daddy and I didn't have a good marriage, but we might have worked something out. And I wouldn't wish harm to him."

"I know. I don't really remember him much, but I remember you being sad."

"You always made me feel better. You're the best son a mother could have," she told him with a smile.

He hugged her neck. "You're the best mommy, too."

He leaned against her, seemingly content. Until he asked his next question. "Does Sam make you cry?"

"Why do you ask that?"

"Today you seem sad."

"With Christmas coming?" She forced a chuckle. "I'm looking forward to opening my presents."

Her son stared at her.

And that was why she couldn't hide anything from her son. He seemed to sense her mood.

Hugging him close, she said, "Everyone in your life can do things that make you happy or sad. But it's up to you to deal with it. We're all responsible for our own happiness."

"If you tell Sam what's wrong, he'll take care of it, Mom. I know he will."

His faith in Sam was endearing, even if he was wrong.

"Sweetie, things don't always work out the way we want."

Before he could ask any more questions, questions that she couldn't answer, she said, "Time for bed, young man." She shifted him off her lap and stood up. "Santa has to come visit you."

"Mom, can Santa really bring what I asked for?"

"A train? I imagine so."

"No, not the train." He turned a troubled face to her, and she went down on her knees beside him.

"I don't know, sweetie," she whispered as she hugged him. "Just remember, Santa will do his best. If he doesn't bring you everything you asked for, it's not because he doesn't want to. Some things aren't possible."

He pulled back from her embrace. "But it's okay to hope, isn't it?"

Praying the tears in her eyes wouldn't fall, she hugged him again. "Of course, Brady. We can always hope."

SAM AND HENRY had repaired the fence line on the east end of the ranch, working in amiable silence for the last few hours. For the first time in his life Sam felt the work couldn't go fast enough. All he could think about was rushing to be with Joni, to tell her of his feelings. He closed his eyes and saw her incredible smile. Just then the wire whipped out of Sam's gloved hands and buried itself in his cheek and hand. At his outcry, Henry rushed over, pulling out his wire cutters and releasing Sam. Blood flowed from the nasty cuts.

Henry helped Sam to his horse, and they rode hard toward the ranch house. On the cell phone Henry called Tom to meet them with the truck. Sam needed medical attention.

When he balked at going to the see the doc, Tom insisted. On the ride to the clinic all Sam could think of was seeing Joni. It was as if thoughts of her shut out the pain of the cuts. He felt nothing but elation. He loved Joni Evans, and her little boy. And as soon as he could get fixed up, he was going to tell her.

It was already late afternoon. Sam had intended to go see Joni tonight, but he couldn't do anything until the doctor finished with him, particularly since his father was standing guard.

"Dad, I told Joni I'd call her. Can I at least use a phone?"

The doctor entered the cubicle at that moment, and

Tom didn't bother to answer. They gave him local anesthesia and sewed up the damage. But the pain-killers they gave him afterward knocked him for a loop. He barely remembered returning to his father's truck and starting the drive home.

"We Crawfords aren't having much luck with our hands lately," Tom complained, obviously thinking of Loretta.

The word hand reminded Sam. "Dad, we gotta go by the jewelry store."

Tom stared at him. "What are you talking about? It's Christmas Eve. I'm sure the store closed hours ago."

"Call Cy and get him to open up." His words were slightly slurred, but he was determined. "He'll do it for you."

Tom slowed to a stop. "Are you sure, son?"

"Damn sure."

An hour later, with his father's help, Sam staggered from the store, satisfied with his transaction. As he sat in the truck, his purchase safe and snug in his jacket pocket, he lay his head back and relaxed for the first time all day.

And promptly passed out.

"Mom, Santa's here! Santa's here!" As Brady burst into the living room, his screams woke Joni with a start. At some point during the long, difficult night, she'd stumbled out to the couch. She couldn't lie in her bed without remembering the time spent there with Sam.

Now, with her son shaking her and pulling her arm, she slowly pushed herself up from the pillow, her head feeling groggy.

"You mean he's been here," she stated. She was glad her son was so ecstatic over his train and the other things she'd spread out beneath the tree.

"No, he's here!" Brady assured her with a giggle. "Come look."

Dread filled her stomach. She grabbed her robe, shrugged it on and followed Brady to the front door he now had standing open.

A familiar truck was parked in front of her house, with a horse trailer connected. And a tall, handsome cowboy emerged from the horse trailer, leading a buckskin colt.

"See, he's wearing a Santa coat," Brady said pointedly, giggling again.

Sure enough, Sam sported the Santa coat he'd worn their first day in Saddle. There was no padding this time, just a lean muscular body underneath. He wore his cowboy hat, not a Santa cap, and jeans and cowboy boots. But the boots were black.

And he was leading the colt up to the front door.

Great. He'd not only broken her heart, but he was also determined to break Brady's, too.

Anger surged through her.

"Brady, go get dressed, and don't come outside until I say you can."

"But, Mom—" her son protested.

"Do as I say, Brady," she said sternly, fighting back the tears.

"Okay, Mom," Brady whispered. Gone was the happy little boy who had awakened.

She felt like a monster.

And someone was going to pay.

As soon as Brady headed to his room, she stepped out on the front porch, pulling the door behind her.

"What do you think you're doing?" she asked in an angry voice.

"Playing Santa," Sam said, a big smile on his face.

"Take that animal and get out of here."

"But, Joni—"

"I told you you couldn't give that horse to Brady," she suddenly wailed, losing her self-control. "You've ruined Christmas for him!"

Sam stared at her, as if she'd lost her mind. Maybe she had. She'd certainly lost her heart.

"You said only a parent could give a present like Cookie."

"So?" What was wrong with the man? If he didn't leave soon, she was going to embarrass herself.

"Well, I figure I've got the right, then."

Joni didn't know what to say. She was afraid to hope, even though she'd told Brady last night it was okay.

Sam tied the colt to the porch railing, then stepped up to Joni's level. "I want to be Brady's daddy for Christmas."

Joni stared at him, unable to speak.

"And most of all, I want to love his mommy—for the rest of our lives. I don't intend to sneak out before dawn ever again. I want to tell everyone you're mine." He cupped her face with his hands. "Joni, will you marry me?"

"But—but you said you weren't ready."

"I was wrong. I can't wait. I don't want to lose you."

"But I didn't tell anyone we were leaving," she said, unable to think.

"You were leaving?" Sam didn't wait any longer for her answer. He swept her into his arms and kissed the breath out of her.

When he let her go, she asked the question she'd gotten sidetracked from earlier. "Sam, what happened to your face?"

He grinned. "That's why we have to get married. You distract me too much."

"You hurt yourself because of me?" she demanded, anguish in her voice.

"Hey, sweetheart, I'm okay. I got careless with some barbed wire. But I'm patched up. I couldn't come last night so I wanted to get here before Brady woke up this morning."

"Too late. He's already up."

"You are going to marry me, aren't you?"

She loved the worry in his voice. She wanted to marry him with all her heart, but only if that's what he wanted. "Are you sure?"

"So sure I got this last night." He pulled a box from his pocket and popped open the lid. Joni stared at a perfect diamond ring. He took it out of the box and put it on her finger. "If you don't like it, we can exchange it. But not till tomorrow. I already bothered Cyrus enough last night.''

She threw her arms around his neck. "Oh, Sam, it's beautiful. I love it." She didn't bother to wipe the tears that welled in her eyes and spilled down her cheeks.

Sam did, and then he kissed her.

"Can I come out now, Mom?" Brady whispered from the door.

Sam released Joni and looked over her shoulder. "Sure you can, Brady. Come see what Santa brought you."

Joni nodded to her son, reinforcing Sam's invitation.

"Do you mean it, Sam? Do I get to have Cookie?"

"You do, son. He's your very own horse."

Brady flew down the steps, his arms encircling the colt's neck. "Wow! I never thought—I mean, Santa brought me almost everything I asked for."

"I think Santa can do better than that. He's a pretty special guy, you know. What else did you want?" Sam squatted down to Brady's level.

After shifting his gaze from Sam to his mother and then back again, Brady ducked his head. "I—I wanted a daddy."

"Will I do?" Sam asked softly.

Again, Brady looked at his mother. When he saw her nod, he leaped toward Sam, his arms going around the cowboy's neck. "Really? Really? Are you sure? You mean I could be your real little boy?"

"My real little boy," Sam agreed, hugging him

back. With a silent prayer of thanks and with Brady in his arms, he reached out for Joni. "My real family. My real love."

He was grateful he'd been given a second chance for love, for family. He couldn't ask for a better son than Brady. And a better wife than Joni.

Playing Santa was the smartest thing he'd ever done.

Epilogue

Christmas Eve.

Sam leaned against his pitchfork, grinning. It had been a year since Joni and Brady had come into his life. They had a lot to celebrate.

"Dad?"

He turned to the sturdy five-year-old who had just walked into the barn. "Yeah, son? Everything okay at the house?"

"Sure."

Sam studied the boy. Lately, it seemed something had been bothering Brady, but he hadn't said anything.

"You sure?"

Brady dragged his booted toe in the straw. Then he said, "What if I changed my mind?"

"About what?"

"About the baby. I don't want it anymore."

Sam drew a deep breath. He and Joni—and Brady—were expecting a new addition to their family any day. It was a little late to have a change of heart. "Why is that, son?" he asked.

Brady climbed on the railing and stared at the mare in the stall. "'Cause Mom is tired all the time. And she didn't even go cut down the Christmas tree with us."

"She will next year. All that bouncing in the truck wouldn't be good for her right now."

"What if—what if you love this baby more than me?" Brady finally asked in a low voice.

"Whatever gave you that idea?"

"Peter said this baby would be part you," Brady said, still staring at the horse. "I'm not."

Sam put aside his pitchfork and plucked the child off the railing into his arms. "Yes, you are."

"Peter said—"

"Peter doesn't know. You see, you're part of my heart, like your mom. You believe I love your mom, don't you?"

Brady nodded.

"I got to choose you and your mom, and I love you both with all my heart. Love isn't limited, son. The more you give, the more there is to give. And you know what?"

Brady, his gaze more hopeful, slung his arm around Sam's neck. "What?"

"This baby will be my second son. You'll always be my first son."

"We're having a boy?" Brady asked, excitement in his voice.

Sam and Joni had known the sex of their baby, but they'd kept it secret from the rest of the family. "Yes, we are," Sam told him, hoping Joni would forgive him for breaking his word.

"Wow! I thought it would be an old girl."

"We'll try for a girl next time." Sam assured him with a chuckle. "But this little boy is going to need his big brother to show him everything. Think you'll be up to the job?"

"Yeah, sure. I'll even let him ride Cookie. When he's older. Just for a little while till he gets his own horse."

"So you don't want to take back your request to Santa?"

"Naw. Besides, Santa does a pretty good job. I got you, didn't I?" Brady said with a laugh.

"You sure did. And that same Santa is going to give you a little brother."

The cell phone he carried with him at all times now, even to the barn, rang. Sam's eyes widened. Lowering Brady to the barn floor, he grabbed the phone.

"Yeah?"

"Sam, I think it's time."

"Santa's on his way," Sam assured Joni and scooped up Brady, then raced to the house.

It was time for another Santa delivery.

Escape into

Just a few pages
into any Silhouette®
novel and you'll find
yourself escaping
into a world of
desire and intrigue,
sensation and
passion.

Silhouette

Escape into...
INTRIGUE™

Danger, deception and suspense.

Romantic suspense with a well-developed mystery.
The couple always get their happy ending, and the
mystery is resolved, thanks to the central couple.

Four new titles are available every month on
subscription from the

READER SERVICE™

Escape into...
DESIRE™

Intense, sensual love stories.

Desire are short, fast and sexy romances featuring alpha males and beautiful women. They can be intense and they can be fun, but they always feature a happy ending.

Six new titles are available every month on subscription from the

READER SERVICE™

Escape into...
SPECIAL EDITION™

*Vivid, satisfying romances, full of family,
life and love.*

Special Edition are romances between attractive
men and women. Family is central to the plot. The
novels are warm upbeat dramas grounded in reality
with a guaranteed happy ending.

Six new titles are available every month on
subscription from the

READER SERVICE™

EN/23/RS2 V2

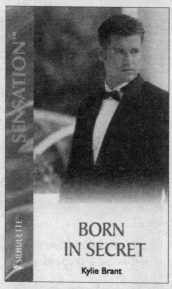